DESOLATION STATION

A Jimmy Blue Novel

IAN W. SAINSBURY

Chapter One

EAGLE SPRINGS, **New Mexico**

WHEN THE DOORBELL RANG, Lydia Garcia had been asleep for less than an hour, dreaming about Snuffy and a talking dolphin. For a few seconds she stared at the ceiling in confusion, half of her still exploring the underground city where the dolphin lived. Snuffy turned out to be an excellent swimmer, which was surprising, as she didn't have any legs.

Where was Snuffy, anyway?

Lydia's flutter of panic receded when she felt the lump under her back. She shifted to one side and scooped up the tatty, faded, soft toy.

"Sorry, Snuffy. Did I squash you?"

Snuffy said nothing. Her fabric face stared back in the half-dark. When Dad said the toy rabbit looked complicated, Mom laughed. Lydia hadn't understood what was so funny about being complicated, even when Mom said the word was constipated. Lydia didn't know what that meant.

1

It didn't matter, anyway. Dad was wrong. Snuffy wasn't complicated or constipated.

Lydia kissed the rabbit's nose, listening. Dad was talking to someone at the front door, his voice louder than usual. Lydia slept at the rear of the bungalow. A central corridor led from her room to the front door. She slept with the door open. Snuffy didn't like to be shut in. So Mom and Dad kept their voices low when they were in the hall. But Dad spoke loud and clear tonight.

"Honey? We have visitors."

Lydia's body went cold. She clutched Snuffy. A long time ago, Dad had been a police officer. And he had been hurt. When Lydia asked, he explained most people were good, kind, and honest, but not everyone. Some people were bad. The bad people hurt other grown-ups, children, and even animals. Dad told Lydia she might live her whole life and never meet one of these bad people. But she should be prepared, just in case. He told her if any bad people ever came to hurt him, Mom, or Lydia, he would say a word that sounded normal to everyone else, but not to the family.

Mateo Garcia never used pet names for his loved ones. He called Lydia Lydia, never sweet pea, or pumpkin. He called Mom Angélica, or Mom. Never dear or darling. Dad insisted their names were beautiful, which is why he loved saying them. But he had just called Mom *honey*. Lydia understood what that meant. It meant the bad people were here.

Lydia had practised what she needed to do now. Dad had made a game of it, but Mom had called him something strange. Something to do with birds. That was it. She said Dad was being parrot annoyed. Adults said some pretty odd things.

She got out of bed. Her hands were shaking, and she

was breathing faster than normal. She took a quick glance down the hall before pulling her head back. No one there, just muffled voices from the kitchen. She wanted to go to them, but she remembered her promise. A promise made to Dad. She must keep that promise. Dad had been right to make her practice, and he was right about the bad men coming. Mom shouldn't have called him an annoyed parrot.

Lydia's legs seemed locked in place, bare feet stuck to wooden floorboards. She willed them to move, but nothing happened. Her breathing quickened. She remembered Snuffy and looked down into that needy face. She would do it for Snuffy.

After the first step, it got easier. Right foot forward, left foot forward, right foot forward, left foot forward. The muffled voices got closer, but she couldn't make out any words. She didn't want to think about the bad men, so she tried remembering her dream. The dolphin, the wide underwater streets. But the pictures in her mind disappeared the moment she made them, bringing her back to her bare feet on the floor, pyjamas damp with sweat, arm muscles aching with the effort of holding Snuffy so close.

She padded along the hall to the closet and pulled the door open without thinking. A coat fell from its hook. The sound wasn't loud, but to Lydia, it seemed as if an explosion had gone off. She whimpered, then pressed the toy rabbit against her lips.

No one came to investigate.

Daddy had told her to be quick and quiet. But Lydia wasn't being quick or quiet. And everything was happening too slowly. If the bad men came out of the kitchen they would see her and Snuffy. She had to move.

Lydia picked up the fallen coat and, standing on tiptoe, slipped it back over the hook. She crawled into the small space on her hands and knees. More jackets and coats hung on a rail inside, and they brushed against her face.

Daddy had said to close the door behind her, but Lydia left it ajar. She knew what came next, and couldn't bear the thought of doing it in the dark.

She found the loose floorboard right away, hooking her finger into the hole to lift it. The board pivoted on the wooden dowel positioned halfway along its length. Lydia lowered herself into the darker space beneath, heart hammering.

Inside, there was enough room to lie down, but no more. Daddy had left an old sleeping bag down there to make it more comfortable. A piece of string hung above her. All Lydia had to do was pull the string, and the floorboard would slide back in place. But then it would be completely dark. She grabbed the end of the string, but pulling it proved beyond her. She was still breathing too hard. Someone might hear her gasps. Lydia did what Mom did when she practised yoga. She breathed in, held her breath for a count of five. Breathed out.

The voices weren't muffled any more. Lydia listened. The bad men said bad words. Dad was using the laptop, his fingers tapping on the keys.

When the bad men said her name, Lydia squeezed her eyes shut, as if doing so would make her invisible. If she had been afraid before, this was ten times worse.

The three bangs were gunshots. Lydia hated guns. Dad couldn't walk because someone shot him.

After the gunshots, only the bad men spoke. Part of Lydia knew what this meant, but she wrapped that thought into a tiny parcel and pushed it deep down into the dark. Everything would be all right. It would all work out.

She stroked Snuffy's back. She was too young to remember when Snuffy lost his legs, but Mom had told the story so many times, it was almost like remembering it. At three years old, Lydia found out her father would never walk again, so she had pulled off the toy rabbit's legs and thrown them away. Mom sewed up the holes without comment, although she cried as she did it.

When the kitchen door opened, Lydia knew the bad men were coming for her. She reached for the string, screwed her eyes shut, and pulled the floorboard into place.

Darkness.

Lydia waited.

When the bad man opened the closet door, she held her breath. He pushed the coats aside, grunted, and left. She listened to his footsteps grow fainter.

In the kitchen, the second bad man was talking on the phone. He stood so close, she heard the voice on the other end. This second voice said her name.

In the dark, Lydia's eyes opened wide.

She knew that voice. She recognised it. The bad men were talking to one of Dad's friends.

The front door opened as one man left. The other walked around the house. A sudden noise above her made her press Snuffy hard against her face to stop herself screaming. The man pulled coats and jackets out of the closet.

Then the first man came back. Both men walked towards her bedroom.

Strange sounds came from the end of the hall. A hiss, a click, a roar. A lion? No. A dragon. It had to be a dragon, because when it roared, her hiding place filled with light—orange light, red light, yellow light. And with the light came heat.

The voices receded. The bad men were gone.

She was alone with the dragon. Dragons were enormous creatures. A dragon could never squeeze into Lydia's hiding place. She would stay here. She closed her eyes again as the temperature rose.

Ten seconds later, animal instinct took over. With no conscious thought preceding the action, Lydia pushed the floorboard away, climbed out, and pushed the closet door open.

She stepped out into a nightmare. The hallway was bright with flames. Every room was burning, and the shadows cast by the fire shrieked at her. Wood splintered, glass exploded. It got hotter and hotter. Fat drops of sweat on Lydia's forehead dried as soon as they formed, skin tightening.

She wouldn't use the front door. The bad men might be waiting. Lydia's best chance was the backyard.

She walked the wrong way. Towards the kitchen.

Her body tried to disobey, but Lydia was stronger. Mom and Dad were in the kitchen.

At the doorway, Lydia's eyebrows crackled as they burned down to her skin. She stepped inside.

Underneath the large kitchen table, a fiery pile of clothes provided extra material for the flames to consume, and they were already burning through the heavy wood above. On the far side of the table were two figures.

One burning body, yellow-red, purple-black, fizzed and popped like the marshmallow Lydia dropped into the fire at camp. A scrap of red material floated up from the body to the ceiling, and Lydia recognised the pattern from Mom's dress.

Dad sat in his wheelchair, face tilted backwards, staring up. The chair glowed, and his blackened fingers were stuck to it, the flesh on his hands and arms sloughing off in strips.

The kitchen smelled like barbecued pork.

Lydia tried to scream, and doubled over. There was no air, just lungfuls of super-heated dragon breath, hacking and slicing at her insides.

She stumbled out of the kitchen in agony. At the end of the hall, her bedroom door stood ajar, her bed burning, flames licking up to caress the ceiling. Beyond it, the window had blown out, and the night air fed the fire.

She picked up speed, forcing her body to straighten as she ran.

When she burst into her bedroom, Lydia was running at top speed. During the four steps between door and window, the right side of her pyjamas caught alight. Her hair crackled with flames. She held Snuffy to her chest.

Lydia hadn't taken a breath since that last horrible attempt in the kitchen, and her lungs were crumpled tight pockets of pain.

She reached the window. Jumped.

Lydia hit the ground hard, rolling over loose stones and dirt. This extinguished the flames in her hair and pyjamas. Smoke rose from her small body as she got to her feet. She shouldn't run anymore. Her body was damaged, every step making her injuries worse. But stopping meant facing the dragon or the bad men, so Lydia ran, and kept running. Out of the gate, across the street and along the dusty track behind the scrapyard to the blue pool where she and her friends paddled every summer.

When she saw the moon reflected in the water, Lydia threw herself in without slowing. Even at its deepest point, the liquid only reached her shins, so she kneeled down, scooping up water and throwing it onto her face and neck.

This time, Lydia screamed. The pain was too immediate, too great, and although she was terrified it would bring the dragon, she couldn't prevent it. But her scream emerged as a whisper, a distant wind howling through a narrow street.

Lydia became aware of parts of her brain shutting down, but she had enough strength left to crawl out of the pool and collapse. She stroked one of Snuffy's ears over and over as the world darkened.

When she next opened her eyes, the world was grey: black snowflakes falling. Her body—oven-baked clay, rigid and foreign—a badly formed sculpture. Not designed to move. After a couple of attempts, she crawled up the side of the hollow, and looked back at the town of Eagle Springs.

Her street lay under a pall of black smoke. Some buildings still burned. Blue and red lights strobed underneath the artificial cloud. Distant shouts, and the crackle of radios, underscored the sounds of destruction.

Police cars, she thought. *Ambulances.*

"Help." The word emerged so quietly she barely heard it herself, and the effort cost her. She tried a second time, but speaking felt like coughing up burning coals. She concentrated instead on crawling, making it as far as the scrapyard fence. Lydia leaned against it and waited to die.

The voices, when they found her, sounded kind enough, their tone suggesting concern and care, but Lydia's brain couldn't translate the sounds into words. The hands that lifted her were gentle, but they might as well have hammered nails into her flesh, the pain was so great.

She must have slept, because when she became aware again, she was in a moving vehicle. One of the kind voices spoke, and Lydia focused on a face. A woman. Younger than Mom. A uniform. A doctor or a nurse.

"You've been in an accident. We're taking you to the hospital, okay? Don't try to talk, sweetie."

Her right hand wouldn't move, but the fingers of

Lydia's left hand found the familiar contours of Snuffy. She closed her eyes. She would take Snuffy back to visit the dolphin, and they would dive deep as deep, far, far away from here.

Maybe they would never come back.

Chapter Two

EIGHT YEARS **later**
Charlotte, North Carolina

MID-SEPTEMBER, ten forty-five, and Donny's Bar pulsed with its slow, Sunday evening rhythm. Sports on the big screens, sound muted. An AOR radio station through the speakers, volume low. Six customers, two of them now shrugging on coats and heading into the night.

In the parking lot, three vehicles. A dark SUV, Tina's ten-year-old sedan, and Don's pickup.

Don Tashman was tidying the bar, dropping rubber nipples onto the liquor bottle pourers to stop fruit flies crawling in. Donny's Bar closed Mondays for a thorough clean, ready for another week welcoming the Charlotte's drinkers. Sundays were Don's favourite night, winding down after a busy Friday and Saturday.

He scribbled in the notepad he kept at the bar.

Give a younger band a try midweek? he wrote. *Let them keep the door?*

Donny's Bar occupied the hinterland between fashion-able Wesley Heights and Seversville. Close enough to be visible from the gleaming glass buildings of Charlotte's centre, but the bar might have been in another state for all the custom it attracted from uptown.

Tina slid a tray of empty beer glasses onto the bar. "Same again, Don."

He took fresh glasses from the tray, tilted the first under the tap. Nodded Tina to come closer, away from George, a regular and dedicated drinker, currently staring into his sixth beer. "You told them we close at eleven?"

"I told them." Tina worked weekdays at a downtown coffee shop, weekends at Donny's. Her son was seventeen. His father had skipped town a six months before Tina answered Don's help ad eleven years ago.

"They gonna be any trouble?"

The three men were strangers. Don had worked in bars all his life, and there was something off about the men in the booth next to the stage. No band tonight, and subdued Sunday lighting kept the table half in shadow. The three men had barely exchanged a word since sitting down. He didn't like it. This week's takings were in the safe. Monday morning, Don took the money to the bank. He picked up a glass to polish.

"Relax, Don." Tina placed the beers on the tray along with the tab. "They're quiet, is all, and they've only drunk two beers apiece. Just passing through, I guess."

"You know me too well."

"You're a worrier, Don. When did you last take a vacation?"

Don answered her question away with a smile. He could afford a vacation, but why bother? He could be alone here, cheaper.

Tina smothered a yawn. Mondays were as close as she

got to a day off. She worked at the coffee shop until mid-afternoon. He wondered how she filled the rest of the day. Sleeping, mostly, he guessed.

He watched her take the drinks to the table. About two years after Tina started working for him, he'd fallen for her. Nearly twenty years her senior, with one failed marriage behind him, he told himself not to do anything stupid. If he asked her out, he'd risk losing a friend, and a great worker, too. So Don said nothing. Lately, he wondered if that might have been a mistake. A year ago, Tina had won a school raffle. Dinner for two at a new Italian place. She'd asked Don if he wanted to go, and he'd laughed, thinking she was joking. She'd laughed too, said she would take her kid, treat him.

Don often thought of that moment. He'd turn sixty next year, and Tina's kid would leave for college the same summer. She'd be lonely, too. Maybe she wasn't joking about dinner. Maybe, if he asked her on a date, Tina would say yes. Maybe.

"Mm. Mm. D-Donny?"

The voice was behind him. Don jumped, swivelled around.

"Tom. You startled me. Everything OK back there?"

For a big man—and Tom, despite habitually hunching to avoid attention, must have stood six foot two or three in his bare feet—Don's bar-back had a knack for fading into the background.

"Mm. OK. I c-cleaned the, the, mm, kitchen."

"Great." Don surveyed his domain. George was draining his last beer. Tina had taken cash from the strangers and was fishing out their change from her apron. Eight minutes until closing.

"Come on, Tom, I'll help move the fridge so you can get behind it with the mop."

"N-n-no need. Mm, I, mm, did it."

"You did?" The fridge in question, industrial, full of bottles, could usually only be shuffled forward by two strong individuals working together. "Right. OK. Good. Thank you. Why don't you wipe down the tables? We'll be closing up in a few minutes."

He eyed Tom's broad shoulders and massive forearms as the young man walked away. He didn't look like a gym rat, didn't walk with that bowlegged bodybuilding narcissist gait. Tom's strength seemed natural. Like a bear, Don often thought. Unlike a bear, though, Tom radiated no sense of threat. The opposite, in fact. When Don took him on, he offered Tom the role of bouncer at weekends, to boost his pay. Tom refused, and, after a couple weeks of fetching, carrying, clearing tables, and clearing up spillages, it was obvious why. Tom did everything he could to avoid confrontation. Every bar had a scuffle or two weekends, but Don's new bar-back scurried away at the first sign of trouble. And Tom barely spoke unless addressed directly. The only way to ensure eye contact was to look at his ID card.

Don didn't mind. The same bar owner's instinct that had him monitor the table by the stage told him he could trust Tom. A loner, yes, not the smartest guy in town, sure, but a hard worker: reliable, and strong as an ox on steroids.

All of which was in Tom's favour. If someone that size and strength had a mean streak, Don wouldn't want him within five miles of his bar. However, when the strangers stood up to leave, and one of them pulled out a heavy revolver and pointed it at Tina's chest, Don wouldn't have minded if Tom had become even averagely aggressive. Instead, when the other two men also pulled guns, the bar-back looked up from the table he was wiping, and froze, the cloth dripping in his hand.

"Let's keep this civil, folks," said the oldest of the three, evidently the leader. He spoke to Don but kept his gun trained on Tina, who was doing that thing with her lips women do when they put on lipstick; rolling them over her teeth, then back, over and over.

The leader was in his fifties, his stubble streaked with grey. Average height. He looked like Brad Pitt might have looked if he hadn't won the genetic lottery. Mouth too narrow, lips thin. Cheekbones prominent, but giving the hollowed features a gaunt rather than striking quality. Blue eyes too close together. On his wrist, the faded blues and greens of a prison tattoo. "Stay smart, and you'll live longer. We clear?"

Don's brain slowed. His solar plexus, never an area of his body warranting much attention, had gone cold and heavy, like he'd swallowed a frozen stone the size of a bread roll. His fingertips buzzed. He put the glass he'd been holding onto the bar top.

Ugly Brad Pitt moved the barrel of his gun until it touched Tina's chest.

"Talking to you, boss. I said, are we fucking clear?"

"Yes. Yes, sir." The vibration in Don's fingertips had spread to his skull, and his voice made it buzz more. "We're clear. What do you want?"

"Any firearms back there, boss?"

Don didn't even consider lying. In twenty years of owning the bar, he'd only taken the Winchester off the bracket behind the bar once. It was a deterrent.

"A shotgun."

The leader nodded at one of his companions. This man shared the too-close eyes and thin lips. Siblings? Father and son? No grey in his stubble, and he vaulted the bar with little effort. Don stepped back to let the younger man retrieve the shotgun. Brad Junior checked it was loaded, then tossed it to the third man, who brandished his new firearm with satisfaction. Brad Junior produced a hunting knife and held it loosely in his left hand, a challenge in his expression. Don looked away.

"Hands behind your back, sweetheart." This to Tina, who complied. Ugly Brad tucked his gun behind his back so he could zip tie her wrists together. While he did it, Tina looked at Don. He gave her a small nod. Hoped it was reassuring. Doubted it.

"Your emergency exit connected to an alarm, boss?" Don looked at Ugly Brad, then over at the exit behind Tom.

"No, sir." Not even a silent alarm, like the sales fellow from Raleigh had tried to sell him last fall. Should have listened.

Ugly Brad called over to Tom, who was still immobile, staring at a patch of floor.

"Busboy. Go open the fire door."

Tom didn't move, but his eyes flashed briefly to Don's. The poor kid looked terrified.

"It's OK, Tom. Go ahead. Just do as they say."

"That's right, Tommy," said the leader. "Do as we say. Wouldn't wanna have to shoot you."

The third man's skin was an unhealthy, pasty grey. Thickset, with rotten teeth which he displayed often, smiling every few seconds for no apparent reason. Probably high, thought Don, the icy stone in his gut weighing heavier by the second. High, and carrying Don's loaded pump-action Winchester. When Tom shuffled towards the exit, Bad Teeth followed, ten feet behind the bar-back. He didn't need to be closer. If Bad Teeth fired the shotgun, the spray of pellets would take out Tom, smash the windows, and shred the upholstery of the booths along the west wall.

"Own it, mofugger," growled Bad Teeth. His diction was sloppy as all hell. Tom looked back, confused.

"Own it," repeated Bad Teeth, lifting the shotgun for emphasis.

"Open it," called Don. "He wants you to open it."

"Wah said." Bad Teeth jabbed the gun with each word. "Stoop-ass mofugger."

Tom pushed the handle, and the emergency exit door swung open. Outside, a fourth man waited. Even as the door opened, he was in motion, swinging a baseball bat towards Tom's head.

Tom pivoted to his right, meaning the bat caught the back of his neck instead of his chin. The shocking smack of wood on flesh made Don recoil, and Tina turn away. Tom took a half step before he fell—to his knees at first—face forward onto the wooden floor.

The new man bent down, picked up a gym bag. Then he stepped inside, handed the bat to Bad Teeth, and kneeled on Tom's back, inducing another, quieter, groan. He cable-tied Tom's wrists together, then—looking at the size of the bar-back—added a second zip tie, pulling it tight.

"We good?" The new man aimed the question at Ugly Brad. He retrieved his bag and bat before approaching the bar. Bad Teeth followed. The new guy was about the same age as Ugly Brad, but stocky, black, bearded, bald. He wore jeans and a leather jacket. Don guessed he'd arrived on a motorcycle. Meaning none of this was opportunistic. These guys had a plan.

"No problemo, buddy," said Ugly Brad. "Easy meat." He put a hand casually on Tina's breast when he said this. She flinched, and Don's icy stone grew hot with a raw anger that surprised him.

"Hey!" The word was out before Don could stop it. No one touched Tina. No one.

Ugly Brad noticed the change in him, smiled, gave Tina's breast another squeeze, his eyes on Don. "She your girlfriend, boss? Or do you just wish you could cop a feel yourself?"

Tina gave Don a tiny shake of her head. He took a long, shaky breath. *If we live through this*, Don promised himself, *tell her how you feel. You ain't getting any younger. What's the worse that can happen?*

The newcomer barked at Ugly Brad. "We're here on business. Got it?" Ugly Brad gave the bald man in the leather jacket a sour look, but he took his hands off Tina. So Leather Jacket was the leader.

"No one needs to get hurt," said Leather Jacket. He pointed his baseball bat at Don. "Open the register."

Something's different, something's changed. Don didn't know what, but the voice in his head nagged at him. *What's different? Think.*

Brad Junior backed away so Don could get to the register. Don was aware of the knife inches from his back as he laid the bills out on the bar.

"Sundays are slow," he said, as Leather Jacket placed the gym bag on the bar and unzipped it. He scooped up the couple of hundred dollars and dropped the money into the bag. He gave Don his instructions.

"My friend here will accompany you to your office, where you'll open your safe and give him the cash. Then we're gonna take your wallets, purses, and cell phones, tie you up, and leave. You're in for an uncomfortable few hours, but we can't have you calling the cops on us. We'd prefer to be out of state by the time anyone finds you. I'm sure you understand."

Brad Junior picked up the gym bag. Waved the knife. "Move, asshole."

Don moved. Then everything went dark.

"What the fuck?" This from Brad Junior, who moved in close enough that Don smelled beer, gum, and stale breath.

The tip of the knife poked into Don's side, and he gasped, a trickle of blood running down to his belt. "Power cut. It must be a power cut."

"Nobody panic," said Leather Jacket. He pulled out a phone, but the light wasn't powerful enough to reach the shadows. "You got a flashlight, man?"

"In the office," said Don, listening to the short breaths of the man holding the knife.

"Good. We carry on as planned. This changes nothing."

But Don knew different. Don knew this was no power cut. Because now he knew what the nagging voice had been trying to tell him. When Leather Jacket had given his orders, Don had looked right at him. And, behind him, everything was normal. The chairs and tables, the coasters, the booths. Nothing unusual. And that was what had triggered Don's subconscious. Because, four feet from the exit, a zip tied bar-back should have been lying on the floor.

But he wasn't.

Tom had gone.

Chapter Three

TOM LEWIS HAD BEEN in Charlotte for six months, working at Donny's for four of them. He rented a cheap, clean, one-bedroom apartment over an antique store where the items on sale were around the same age as the couple who ran it. The bell announcing customers rarely rang, and the street, a quarter-mile north of the university campus, was quiet enough that—every Sunday morning— Tom heard the amens and hallelujahs from the church on the corner.

The walk to Donny's Bar took twenty-five minutes. Tom couldn't drive, but he enjoyed walking. Jimmy Blue could drive. Tom sometimes dreamed his hands were on the wheel, engine roaring and tyres screaming, buildings flashing by on either side.

He saw Blue sometimes, during the walk home after late shifts at the bar. At night, small groups lingered on street corners, or in the shadows, figures in hoods laughing, shouting, drinking. Sometimes they went quiet when he passed on the far side of the street; a bad kind of quiet. Twice, strangers followed him for a while, but, as they came closer, so did Jimmy Blue, a man made of dark smoke becoming solid, matching Tom's footsteps stride for stride, coming alongside. Some instinct made his pursuers lose interest. And Blue dissolved as if he'd never been there.

Tom liked Charlotte. He liked the contrast between the frenetic shops, bars, business, and eateries of uptown, and the quieter, poorer neighbourhoods less than a mile outside its perimeter. He liked the parks, where he watched dog walkers, keeping treats in his pockets for any friendly canines who said hello. He liked to walk around North Davidson, where an unofficial competition ran between buildings vying to be the most colourful. Everyone called North Davidson NoDa, which was easy for Tom to remember.

Mostly, Tom liked Charlotte because people were often kind to him, waiting patiently while he struggled to find words in cafes, stores, or on the train.

As the weeks passed, Jimmy Blue kept his distance. Tom's anxiety about this unfamiliar city, in a country he'd only ever visited before, faded. One side of his life—the side Blue took care of—became more dreamlike with every passing day.

It was Tom's turn now. Tom's chance to live. Last summer in London, after years of preparation, Jimmy Blue had taken bloody revenge on those who killed Tom's parents, and—when the authorities closed in—he had fled Great Britain for America. A fresh start, where no one knew him. Jimmy stayed in the shadows in Charlotte. Maybe he would stay there forever.

Tom's favourite place in Charlotte wasn't the bustling centre, the trendy arts district, or any of the parks. It was Donny's Bar. He'd known right away that he'd like it. Right from the moment he'd walked in with the help wanted tear-off in his hand. He couldn't read it, but Iris—who ran the bakery across the street—had read it to him, and directed him to the bar.

Donny had been unloading crates of beer bottles from the back of a truck. Tom handed him the tear-off, and started lifting crates, three at a time. Donny's smile had broadened. Ten minutes later, Tom had a job as a bar-back, a title which held no meaning until Don explained it.

Although Tom didn't need money, he found he needed work. He gained satisfaction from completing tasks, such as mopping floors, changing kegs, or wiping tables. He liked being around people if they didn't engage with him much. Which made bar-back a good fit. Used to being stared at because of his size, or because of the bandanas he wore to cover the bullet scars on his bald head, Tom found that bar-backs were granted the power of invisibility. As long as he held one of the magical items—glass holder, brush, or trash bag—he could move through Donny's unnoticed, even at its most crowded.

He had his job, his apartment, and he had the city. Tom didn't remember how it felt to be happy, but he suspected it might be like this.

Then someone pointed a gun at Tina, another pulled a knife on Donny, and Tom knew it was all about to be taken away.

Chapter Four

WHEN TOM OPENED the emergency exit and caught the reflected light flash from the polished baseball bat as it swung for his head, he didn't know if the instant reaction was his or Jimmy Blue's. But his pivot meant the bat caught the back of his head and neck, rather than his face.

It still hurt, though, rattling his teeth, and the *smack* echoed in his skull as he pitched forward, shuffled a few steps before dropping, and lay still.

A tear fell from Tom's left eye onto the swept wooden floor. The teardrop filled most of his field of vision, a saltwater lake in the mountain-range shadow of his forehead.

When the man kneeled on his back, forcing his hands behind him, Tom stayed limp. He watched the lake, fascinated. From the depths, dark smoke coiled as if—in defiance of natural laws—an underwater fire had been lit and now burned fiercely. The tendrils of smoke coalesced into dark heavy clouds, a threatening weather system, rising. As if the lake reflected a gathering storm. No, that wasn't it. The storm came *from* the darkness hidden far beneath the lake's surface.

As the man pulled first one zip tie, then another tight, forcing his wrists together, Tom witnessed the dark clouds rise, entering his body through his eyes, nose, and mouth. It flowed into his pores, a rush of power, knowledge, purpose, and rage.

The dark clouds swept Tom away, a microscopic figure caught in a storm, subsumed by it.

It was all over in seconds. Tom was gone. Jimmy Blue was back.

———

BLUE HALF-OPENED HIS RIGHT EYE. Turned his head an inch.

Four hostiles. One had Tina. Two stood behind the bar with Don. Three still held the baseball bat. Four—with Don's shotgun—stood closest, twelve to fifteen feet away, his back towards Blue.

Remaining motionless, Jimmy waited for his moment. It came when hostile one put a hand on Tina, provoking Don. Everyone turned towards the bar owner.

Blue moved fast, bringing his knees up under his body, his head staying on the floor. He lifted his arms back and up, relaxing his shoulder to gain an extra inch. He pulled his hands apart to tighten the zip tie, the plastic cutting into his flesh. Then he brought his hands down fast, onto the small of his back. Both ties gave way with a snap.

Blue rolled onto his front, raising himself onto the tips of his fingers and toes of his sneakers. He exited the main bar using a simian all-fours lope that looked ridiculous, but was very effective. He stayed low, and the speed of his progress meant, if anyone had looked, they would have had 2.56 seconds to witness his escape.

Once out of sight, Blue ran for the bar-back door

leading to the storerooms, kitchen, and office. Once inside, he made for the fuse box on the wall. An archway led to the bar and the armed men.

He removed the cover and flipped the master power switch. Everything went dark. Blue prised out every fuse, throwing them in the trash. Don's heavy-duty flashlight hung on a hook next to the fusebox. Blue retraced his route to the bar, the flashlight solid and heavy in his hand.

His eyes burned dark, and his head fizzed. Strength flowed into his body like wet clay hardening in a kiln, and it felt good. It felt right. Poor Tom might try to hide from it, but there was evil in the world. Violence, savagery, and death. Jimmy Blue didn't hide from it; he fed on it. The men who wanted to rob Don Tashman were bullies in need of education, and Jimmy Blue was ready to teach them.

He couldn't help himself. He started singing.

Chapter Five

EVERYONE HEARD the voice at the same time. Don tried to swallow as his throat dried.

Ugly Brad spoke first. "What the fuck?"

A male voice. Singing. Creepy as all hell. The voice's owner moved fast. Even in the dark, he didn't collide with furniture, and Don couldn't make out any footsteps.

"I killed a man they said
And I left him layin' dead
'Cause I bashed his bloody head
Blast his eyes
'Cause I bashed his bloody head
Blast his eyes"

Brad Junior leaned in. Hissed into Don's ear. "Who else is in here?" He pushed the knife and it bit Don's skin again, half an inch of metal slicing into the roll of flesh over his hip. For once, Don was glad of his few extra pounds.

There wouldn't be a better chance. "Run, Tina!"

He slammed his fist down onto Brad Junior's forearm, smashing it into the side of the metal basin under the bar. The knife fell into the ice and water. Don raised his fist and smashed again. Something snapped audibly. Junior shouted with pain and rage.

"Bitch!" Ugly Brad had evidently grabbed Tina. A punch landed somewhere, and Tina cried out, half-coughing.

Don could navigate his bar in the dark, but these men couldn't. He moved without hesitation or thought.

He scrabbled away from Brad Junior towards the hinged bar-flap and Tina. He took two steps before the lights flashed on. No, not the lights. A firework display behind his eyes, as a heavy blow caught him. Don's legs gave out, sending him sprawling. He ended up on his knees, head full of sand, the room tilting beneath him, not sure which direction he was facing.

"Gonna cut you, asshole." Brad Junior was fishing for his blade in the ice. "Shit!" Don guessed he'd found it.

"No one's cutting anyone. Calm the fuck down." Leather Jacket.

Brad Junior fired back, "Motherfucker broke my arm. I'm gonna kill him."

"Do that and I'll put you in the ground myself. How you gonna open the safe if the guy with the combination is dead, shit for brains? Now shut the fuck up. Kenny? Where you at?"

Kenny was evidently Bad Teeth.

"Here, man. Mofugger is close, man, I—"

Bad Teeth wheezed suddenly. A smack of flesh on flesh, then the heavier sound of a body hitting the floor.

"Kenny?"

No answer. And the singing stopped.

A small square of light appeared. Leather Jacket's phone. He swung it around. The light didn't reach the shadows, but it did illuminate the unmoving form of Bad Teeth.

"Come to the bar," said Leather Jacket. "Bring the woman. We stick together, find a flashlight, take this guy out. Got it?"

"Got it."

Don's head was clearing, but blobs of light drifted across his vision like floating lanterns. He gritted his teeth, forced himself to focus. Tina needed him. Her breathing came ragged as she struggled to get the air into her lungs. He guessed Ugly had punched her in the stomach. Impotent anger rose with his bile. He crawled forward a few inches, then a foot found his back and pushed him down onto the freshly mopped floor. He smelled chemical lemon.

Brad Junior didn't sound happy. "If I can't cut you, I'll cut your girlfriend instead, asshole. What do you think?"

Before Don answered, the pressure disappeared from his back and Brad Junior hissed in surprise. The hiss became a yelp, then a kind of strangled, choking cough. Two bangs on the bar top, then something heavy fell across Don's legs.

The light from Leather Jacket's phone swung towards them. Don saw an ice bucket sail over the bar, then the light was out, and Leather Jacket was cursing.

Don extracted himself from what he suspected was the unconscious Brad Junior, but a hand gripped his shoulder, and a voice whispered directly into his ear. "Stay down. I'll take care of it."

Don stayed down. He hadn't recognised the voice, but it could only be Tom. the unfamiliar voice had been anything but reassuring. Not the words, but the emotionless way he delivered them. No fear, no adrenaline.

With Brad Junior and Bad Teeth out of the picture, two dangerous individuals remained, one of whom had Tina. Don hadn't been to church since his teens, but he remembered the Lord's Prayer right enough, and he mouthed the words now. When he reached *but deliver us from evil,* he pictured Tina, and said the words over and over again. *Deliver her from evil, deliver her from evil.*

The voice spoke again. This time, it came from somewhere behind Leather Jacket.

"Wanna take another swing with your bat, buddy?"

The voice chuckled.

Leather Jacket didn't waste any words. Don heard the *sssss* of the bat passing through the air.

Another low laugh.

"Strike one."

The voice moved as Leather Jacket swung again.

"This spirit white as lightning
Would on me travels guide me
The moon would shake and the stars would quake
Whenever they espied me"

Swings of the bat punctuated the words, none of them finding their target.

"Strike two… and strike three. Maybe strike four and five, too. I lost count."

A gasp from Leather Jacket, then a grunt of surprise and pain.

"My turn," said the voice.

Sssss—crack.

It sounded like a mallet tenderising meat.

The third gang member hit the floor hard, making no attempt to break his fall.

Don disobeyed instructions, and got to his knees, then pulled himself upright, hanging onto the bar. His skull throbbed and his legs shook, but he had to check on Tina.

"It's all in the shoulders," said the voice. "Gotta keep them relaxed and make sure to follow through."

This was the moment Ugly Brad made his move. With his comrades indisposed, self-preservation won the day.

Brad opened fire with the handgun, seemingly at random, sending bullets in all directions as he headed for the door.

Seeing as the enemy had just played baseball with Leather Jacket's skull, Ugly Brad backed towards the main entrance, firing as fast as he could pull the trigger. Muzzle flashes illuminated a small area around him. The result made the scene a surreal, jerky horror movie, the shooter's face a rictus of fear and panic.

Tina was curled up on her side. Terrified. Alive. Relief flooded Don. A muzzle flash lit up the six-foot wide mirror outside the restrooms, and he saw the man who'd saved them.

It was Tom, of course. Who else could it be? But it wasn't Tom. Not the shy, gentle bar-back who swerved out of the path of customers. This was Tom possessed by a demon, strutting and leaping, capering and crouching, dodging and sliding, closing in on Ugly Brad.

Flash. Tom dived into a roll under the mirror.

Flash. The mirror exploded, and Tom had vanished.

Flash. Tom weaved between tables.

Flash. Tom crouched behind a two-person couch, concealed from Ugly Brad's point of view.

Flash. Brad fired towards the mirror, the last place he'd seen Tom.

Flash. A shape rose silently behind Brad, looming over him like the Angel of Death.

Flash. This time, the bullet hit the plastered ceiling, and flakes of plaster fell as the muzzle flashed one last time.

Don's stomach flexed. He gagged, swallowed, regained control. The final image had revealed Ugly Brad's arms above his head, still holding the gun. Both arms bent the wrong way. The flash had reflected brightest on a piece of white bone jutting out of Brad's left elbow.

Ugly Brad screamed like a trapped animal until a solid thump suggested he'd passed out.

Silence. Don swallowed. "Tina?"

"I'm OK, I'm OK. How about you?"

Although Don had quit drinking after his divorce, he still recalled some epic hangovers, and this was worse.

"Peaches and cream," he said, although he wasn't sure why. He didn't think he'd ever said it before. It produced a pained, shaky giggle from Tina, so he was glad he'd said it, whatever it meant.

The voice materialised two feet away, and Don nearly screamed.

"Put your hands out, palms up, Don."

Don obeyed without thinking.

A heavy object landed in his right palm.

"Flashlight," said the voice.

"Fuses are in the office trash. Go turn on the lights. We have some cleaning up to do."

Don turned, mumbled, "I—I should call the cops. Right?"

"Wrong. No cops." The voice stayed flat. There was no explicit threat there. But Don didn't consider ignoring the instruction, not for a millisecond.

Out back, he replaced the fuses, then flipped the switch.

———

IT TOOK thirty minutes to clean up, by which time three of the four gang members were awake.

Tom had barely said a word other than to correct Don's use of his name.

"Call me Blue," he said. Considering the bar-back had just disarmed and beaten up four dangerous men in complete darkness, Don decided Tom could go by any name he liked.

Blue used the gang's own zip ties to immobilise them, adding several loops of gaffer tape to make sure. No need to tie up Ugly Brad. With two broken arms, he represented little threat. Bad Teeth and Brad Junior glowered as Blue examined items he'd extracted from their pockets.

Leather Jacket opened his eyes occasionally, then closed them again, head sagging. Don suspected something worse than a simple concussion.

Blue returned Don's shotgun and unloaded the men's handguns. He destroyed their cell phones with the baseball bat, which had a long streak of blood up one side.

Tina, still wincing at the punch which knocked the wind out of her, was more concerned with Don's well-being. She insisted he sit down, and they shared a half-pack of Tylenol while she held a bar-towel full of ice against his face. He soon felt better under her ministrations, but suspected it might be psychosomatic.

Blue took the car keys from Leather Jacket's pocket and left. Thirty seconds later, an engine reversed up to the exit door. The SUV's trunk popped open.

Blue came in, flipped Leather Jacket onto his front, grabbed his belt, and dragged him to the car. Once there, he picked Leather Jacket up like a beer keg, and slung him in the trunk.

"Don, Tina, wait in the office." Again that flat tone. Again, that immediate compliance from Don. This Blue guy, whatever the hell else he was, wasn't someone you argued with.

In the office, Don let Tina steer him to the couch, smiling when she sat alongside him. "Does Tom have a twin?" she said.

"No. It's him. I think." Tina's knee pressed up against

his as she checked the developing bruise on his head. Don knew she was only worried about his health, but he enjoyed having her so close.

They looked at each other when the screams started in the bar, but neither of them spoke.

A few minutes later, a car drove away.

"What the hell?" Don got off the couch, pulled up the blind. The armed robbers drove away, Brad Junior at the wheel.

Tina followed him back into the bar. Blue had locked the emergency exit and was washing his hands. Don looked into the basin. The ice cubes ran red and pink.

"You hurt?"

Blue didn't turn. "No."

Don pointed. "Sure? I have bandages in the first aid box out back."

"Not my blood, Don."

"Oh."

Blue dried his hands. "I quit, Don."

"Where will you go?"

"Someplace quiet. Someplace Tom can start again."

"But those guys..." Don's voice trailed off. He didn't want to seem like an ingrate.

"What about them?"

"Well, look, Blue, ah, thank you. For saving our lives. Thank you. But those guys won't stop just because they got a beating. They'll pull the same trick someplace else, is all."

Blue smiled. As smiles went, Don mused, it was kind of unique. No humour in it, no reassurance, no friendliness. It scared the crap out of him.

"They won't do it again, Don. They promised me they would change, that their lives would follow a law-abiding course from this night on."

"And, ah, you believed them?"

"I did. I said I'd keep my eye on the news. Especially robberies."

"Oh. Ok, OK, I see. But, ah, well..."

"Yes?"

"How would you know it was them? I mean, if a bar gets robbed, it could be anyone, right?"

"Because of their unusual distinguishing features, Don."

Don thought back. Drew a blank. "Distinguishing features?"

"That's right. Each of them is missing the index and middle fingers of their right hand."

The door swung closed behind Blue. Don watched the last of the pink liquid swirl through the melting ice and disappear down the drain.

Chapter Six

AFTER DROPPING TINA BACK HOME, Don didn't think he'd sleep at all. He made himself a strawberry milkshake and slumped in front of the television. The black and white movie had a leopard in it, but Don couldn't have named a single actor or summarised the plot if his life depended on it, as his thoughts kept returning to the moment Ugly Brad pointed a gun at Tina.

No more pretending. No more procrastination. He would tell Tina how he felt. Next morning, for sure. Although Monday was Tina's day off. Best wait until Tuesday. As long as they weren't too busy at work. Maybe when they locked up. Or Wednesday. But soon.

He must have drifted off, because when he looked at the window, dawn had highlighted the edges of the drapes.

He got up, put on a pot of fresh coffee, and by the time he'd finished the first cup, changed his mind about Tina. No point letting the pipe dreams of an old man ruin a perfectly fine friendship. Nope. Better to leave well enough alone.

Besides, there was something else he needed to do. He

slid the pickup's keys from the table and headed out into the morning.

He'd never visited Tom's apartment, but he knew where it was. Don parked up at a quarter to seven. An outside staircase led to the apartment. After raising his hand to knock, Don hesitated. Who would he be talking too—Tom? Or the other guy? For a second, he considered creeping back down the stairs and going home.

He was still standing there when a voice spoke from below.

"That boy in trouble?"

Don gave his hammering heart a couple of seconds to settle before turning and looking over the handrail at a small octogenarian in a robe with a towel wrapped around her head.

"Ma'am? Sorry to disturb you. I'm Don. Donny. From the bar. Tom's boss."

"He lit out, son."

"He's gone?"

"Unless someone has changed the meaning of 'lit out' without consulting me, that's correct."

At this time of day, Don could only think of one option for someone leaving town with limited funds.

It was only a few blocks to the bus station, and it took Don all of three minutes to spot Tom, sitting on a bench, backpack beside him, head down.

"Tom?"

The head tilted a little, and a pair of green eyes shot him an appraising glance. Not Tom.

"Mr Blue?"

"Just Blue. Why are you here, Don?"

Don sat down uninvited. His mouth dried up and his throat tightened as Blue tracked his movements with those cold eyes, but he held his nerve.

"Where are you heading?"

For the longest time, Blue didn't answer. Acutely aware of those eyes still on him, and unwilling to meet their challenge, Don kept his eyes on the passengers waiting for the next bus. Of various ages and races, they all shared a hangdog weariness.

"I don't know. South, maybe."

It wasn't much of an answer, but the fact he'd spoken at all gave Don some encouragement. "Look, Blue, I don't mean to pry—"

"Then don't."

No trace of anger, but Blue hadn't sounded angry when he took the armed gang apart last night, either. Don rubbed his sweaty palms on his knees.

"Tom is real, right? I mean, you weren't, ah, pretending, ah pretending to, ah—"

"Pretending to be slow? Stupid? A retard?"

"No! No." Don looked at Blue. "I like Tom. I would never describe him that way. Kind, gentle, hard-working. Don't put words in my mouth."

Blue half-smiled, broke eye contact. Stood up, swung his backpack onto his shoulder. "Goodbye, Don."

"Wait."

Don dangled the pickup keys from his finger. "You want someplace remote, someplace quiet where there are good people who'll treat Tom right?"

Blue didn't answer, but he didn't walk away either.

"I know a place," said Don. "Can I give you a ride?"

———

AFTER AN HOUR and a half driving west, Don turned north towards the Black Mountains. Another twenty minutes winding through tree-shadowed, sunlight-dappled roads, and the pickup pulled over just short of a narrow trail. A wooden sign announced three miles to Pike Point.

"The back way to town," said Don. "I figured you'd prefer it."

Conversation during the journey had been light to non-existent. Don scribbled the name of a hotel on a receipt.

"Connie—my sister—lived in Pike Point until she was too ill to get out of bed. She loved it out here. Full of rich folk, but rich folk need regular folk around to keep things running, and that's where Connie fitted in. She arrived in her thirties and never left. Not until those last couple weeks in hospital."

Don had shared this with no one. Why he had chosen Blue to hear it, he couldn't say.

If he'd expected any normal reaction, he was disappointed. No comforting words, or empathetic hand on his shoulder. Just that blank, unreadable gaze.

Don counted out some bills from his wallet.

"I don't need your money." When Don pressed him, Blue shook his head. "Put it away. Thanks for the ride."

Blue got out of the pickup. Paused with his hand on the door.

"About Tina." These were just about the last words Don expected, and he gaped open-mouthed in confusion.

"Tina?" he croaked.

"Tom doesn't understand much, but he saw what was going on."

"Going on?" Don had become an echo.

"Don't piss away your chances, Don. You never know what's coming. You could lose everything in a heartbeat."

Don watched Blue walk the trail until it curved left and he disappeared behind the trees.

He swung the pickup around and began the descent to the main highway, back to Charlotte, the bar, and Tina.

Chapter Seven

BLUE WALKED the three miles to Pike Point through the forest rather than along the trail. He climbed through a light drizzle that fell onto the canopy of the pine trees, filtered through the branches and needles, before hitting the soft earth below.

Tom would have found the rain refreshing and cool. He might have noticed the way it brought out the myriad shades of green, the rainbow hints coalescing and fading in the patches of sky visible between the top branches. If Jimmy registered any of this, the information didn't reach his forebrain. Instead, he noted that the rain might cover the footsteps of anyone sneaking up on him, so he increased his three-sixty checks to once every ten seconds. He stayed alert to any movement, any sudden bird flight or animal breaking from cover. His eyes constantly flicked from the middle distance to the ground ahead, looking for the best foot placement, avoiding recently fallen twigs that might snap and reveal his location.

A distant whine got louder and louder as he walked. A chainsaw. Someone felling a tree ahead. Blue stayed out of sight of three men in hard hats tackling a rotten trunk. He stayed south of them, then circled north-west to stay downwind.

When he reached the edge of the tree line, Blue hung back in the shadows. He couldn't hear the stream that ran alongside the town over the noise of the chainsaw, but he smelled fresh, running water.

The trees ended on a slight rise twenty yards short of a well-maintained street running west to east. The town lay ahead, nestled in a shallow depression on the mountainside about half a mile from its peak.

Pike Point was bigger than he expected. Big enough for a diner, general store, timber yard, and a bar. The smaller streets had the usual businesses—auto engineer, laundrette, clothes store. Just beyond the main street, the houses were substantial, well kept. The biggest property of all, sunlight bouncing off at least a dozen windows, regarded the town from its perch further up the mountain.

Blue checked the back of Don's receipt. *Mountain View Hotel.* Not the most imaginative name, considering the peak was visible from anywhere in Pike Point.

He walked out of the trees onto the road.

———

BLUE ATTRACTED a few curious glances as he walked Pike Point's main street, but everyone he encountered gave him a nod or a, "G'morning."

Instead of making straight for the hotel, he made a circuit of the surrounding blocks. Within fifteen minutes, he'd seen most of the town. When he walked past the diner —busy serving breakfasts—the smell made his stomach growl.

The principal route out of Pike Point led west along

the mountainside, then north, heading—according to the sign—to Rutherford Spring, which boasted the nearest school and hospital.

Pike Point Police Department sat between a cafe and a hardware store, and was half the size of its neighbours. One cruiser parked outside.

A park one block south of the main street had a basketball court and a grassy area with a faded diamond. No one was playing. Blue sat on a bench facing Pike Mountain, which climbed another thousand feet before reaching its peak. A handful of dwellings nestled in small clearings close to streams, which followed well-worn routes before converging north of Pike Point.

Blue took out a satellite hotspot, a device a few inches smaller than his laptop, connected to a rechargeable power bank. The low-orbit satellites he pinged for a signal were military, his access the result of a debt owed by a high-ranking Japanese politician.

He browsed realtors in the area, emailed some with enquires about nearby properties, then opened his satellite phone.

"Mountain View Hotel, Carla speaking."

"Hello, Carla, my name is David Kincaid."

"How can I help you, Mr Kincaid?"

Jimmy had considered picking up a new identity after last night in Donny's Bar, but decided it wasn't necessary. Don was the only one who knew Tom's last name. Mrs Kenwick—the antique store owner who'd given him lodgings—had glanced once at Tom's social security card, not noticing it was upside down.

"I'd like to book a room. Not for me, for my brother. He's arriving in Pike Point this morning, and may have to stay in the hotel for a few weeks. I'd like to pay for a month upfront."

"Of course, Mr Kincaid. I have the perfect room, a junior suite with a wonderful view, and—"

"That sounds fine. I'll take it."

He gave his credit card details.

"Carla? My brother has mild learning difficulties. He's shy, and he can't read or write. He's perfectly capable of looking after himself, but if you could email any paperwork direct to me, I'd appreciate it."

He thanked her as she promised to look after his 'brother'.

His stomach growled again. He folded up the hotspot, stashing it and his phone in his backpack.

At the diner, the breakfast crowd had gone, and the lunch shift was yet to arrive. The concept of brunch had yet to trouble this corner of North Carolina. Tables ran parallel to the window, freshly wiped down.

He picked a spot at the end of the counter, affording him a view of the entire room. Ordered coffee, orange juice, a three-egg omelette, French toast, and fresh fruit. All from a waitress in a lemon yellow fifties-style outfit.

He avoided eye contact, spoke very little, and stuttered when he did. Pam, this morning's waitress, waited patiently while he found the right words. When he asked, she read the menu to him without a hint of condescension. She looked to be in her forties. Brown hair pulled back, no make-up.

The food was good. Plenty of it, too. Fresh coffee, with cream and sugar. Blue took it black, but Tom didn't. He managed not to grimace as he drank it.

"P-p, p-Pam?" She came over with the check.

"Whenever you're ready. No hurry." She looked out of the window. "Might could rain later, likely."

Blue unpicked the sentence. Tom would have to adapt to the local dialect.

"C-can I a-, a-ask you s-s-something?"

"Of course, hun. What d'ya need to know?"

"You l-like it here? P-p-Pike p-Point, I mean?"

Pam considered the question, smiling. She poured herself a coffee, leaned on the counter. Waved out at the street, a gesture which encompassed the forest, stream, and mountains beyond.

"I'm a second generation Piker. My folks moved here back in the mid-sixties. Some folk might call them hippies, but they weren't the pot-smoking, tune in and drop out types. They saw the way the wind was blowing. Vietnam, Nixon, big corporations... OK, no politics, else you'll be here all day."

Blue sipped his coffee, forgetting how milky and sweet it was. Pam grabbed the pot.

"Almost done? Let me top you up. Cream and sugar, right?"

"R-right."

"Anyhow, my folks liked it well enough up here. They bought the diner from an old couple and never left. I couldn't wait to get out, of course. I wanted to travel, live in a city, meet glamorous men. And that's what I did. Worked in a bank in Miami for near enough ten years. Got married, got divorced. One day, my boss offered me a big promotion. Gave me a week to think it over. I was so excited, I drove back here to tell Mom and Dad. I arrived Saturday night. Monday morning, I got up early, took my coffee outside, watched the birds chase the mist up the side of Pike Mountain. I swear, I knew there and then I wasn't leaving. Not then, not now, not ever."

She laughed, put a hand on Blue's arm.

"Well, don't you just have a way about you? About spilled my entire life story, didn't I?"

Blue nodded. "M-mm." This was no place for him. But he felt Tom's presence flutter like a caged bird.

Pam called after him at the door.

"This place is the closest thing on God's good earth to paradise. That answer your question?"

Chapter Eight

"I ALWAYS THOUGHT this place was paradise. I was wrong. Dead wrong."

The retired police chief hitched his belt up an inch, then pushed it down again before bringing his hand to his face and touching his chin. It was a curious gesture—reflective, sad. It might have seemed comic for anyone who hadn't seen photographs of Chief Lou Braden four years ago.

Patrice Martino had seen the photos. Back when Chief Braden looked after the remote community of Greenhaven, Alaska, he sported a white-flecked beard and an expansive belly. Both were gone now, but he didn't look healthier. Just the opposite.

In every old photograph, the Chief was smiling. He'd lost that along with the belly and beard.

"Most days, I would have been a ninety-minute drive away. But that weekend, I was in Sitka," said Braden, staring along the main street towards the distant lake. Looking past the charred, blackened husks of the church, grocery store, and hollowed-out houses.

Braden's silence stretched long enough, Martino worried he'd forgotten he was speaking. "Sitka?" he prompted.

"Police training. I was on a course. Mandatory." The retired police chief spat on the ground. "High-level financial fraud. Hacking. Nothing useful. Identity theft, so help me."

He spat again, and found something to stare at on his shoe. Avoided the fire-scarred remains of what had once—according to everyone Martino interviewed—been an idyllic community. "Don't misunderstand me, Mr Martino. We have our share of crime. Domestic violence. Homicide. But not in Greenhaven."

Martino knew why. Unlike most of the tiny rural towns along the Klutina River, Greenhaven was—had been—affluent. Until 1967, it was little more than half a dozen rudimentary dwellings, and cabins for hunters. Then a retired oil baron named Orville Brown, with a hankering for peace and quiet, bought a piece of land and commissioned a ten-bedroom mansion. The eccentric millionaire, unmarried and childless, lived there alone, apart from one week every summer, when the only road that led off Richardson Highway hummed loud with the approach of rented off-roaders.

One of Brown's summer retreats for his rich friends incorporated his marriage, which—at sixty-seven years old—marked somewhat of a U-turn in his previous attitude to the institution.

Thirty years his junior, his new wife brought energy and ambition to the Brown residence, and—a year after she arrived—the construction crews were back.

Until then, if you wanted to send a letter to Orville Brown, you addressed it to Bear Paw Creek. But Daisy

Brown had a town sign painted, planting it by the main road. Greenhaven was born.

Over the next decade, the community swelled to between thirty and fifty, depending on the time of year. Alaska's hard mountain winters drove some residents to seek solace in warmer climes, but others grew to love the wilderness.

The residents of Greenhaven's twenty-three beautiful Main Street houses never experienced the hardships associated with frontier life. Local families in more modest dwellings made sure the Browns and their friends were comfortable. They maintained the generators and water supply, cut back the forest to discourage bears from straying too close.

After Orville Brown's death, Daisy sold up and moved to New York, where celebrity parties and string of lovers suggested her enthusiastic embrace of the quiet Alaskan life may not have been wholly sincere.

But Greenhaven prevailed. It never expanded much beyond its exclusive single street. The annual summer parties became low key, and, by the nineties, fizzled out. Magazines ran occasional pieces about the lifestyles of the rich, and the tiny Alaskan community got a mention, but —mostly—people forgot it existed.

Until September four years ago.

Now Main Street cracked and crumbled. Once-glamorous houses were burned-out ruins. The old Brown residence—built on a slight rise at the north end of the street —was a shell, its upper storeys gone, the remaining rooms open to the elements.

"Those bastards cut every method of communication before they got started," said Braden. "The Browns never had telephone lines installed. He enjoyed the quiet. Even his wife couldn't change his mind about that. But things moved on. The Van Haagens built a cell tower a mile out of town fifteen years back. Back over that rise, out of sight. No one wanted their view spoiled."

He made that gesture with his belt again, trying to hoist it over a gut long since gone.

Martino had read the police reports. "They took out the cellphone tower with explosives?"

"That's right. And they set a fire to draw out the younger locals. They knew what they were doing."

Martino nodded. The intruders left nothing to chance. It was a meticulously planned assault. With the cell tower destroyed, the alarm could only be raised with satellite phones. Two residents owned one, as did the town caretaker, who also maintained Greenhaven's only fire truck.

The police report stated that the caretaker tried calling Chief Braden twice during the drive to the cell tower. Neither call connected, blocked by a satellite jammer available online for thirty dollars.

The caretaker, plus his son, his daughter, and the town doctor's son, showed up to put out a forest fire. What they found instead was arson, the cell tower burning. The gang sprayed the fire truck with over four hundred rounds of machine-gun fire, then used flame throwers to reduce it— and its occupants—to a smouldering husk.

Ex-chief Braden walked back to his battered Ford pickup, took out an equally dented thermos. He poured himself a coffee.

"Only got the one cup," said Braden. "Sorry."

Martino pulled his hat brim lower and almost wished he'd worn something warmer. Almost, but not quite. He didn't consider himself a vain man, but he'd first worn a hat in his teens, and the habit had stuck. If he left home without one, he felt naked. Today's model, a dark grey teardrop fedora, offered little protection against the wind.

He looked at the silent, dead town. "OK if I look around?"

"That's why I drove you up here."

Martino didn't know exactly what he hoped to find, or —if he did—it was buried too deep to speak aloud. Over decades, he'd learned that his subconscious was best served by doing his due diligence: visiting crime scenes, watching, listening. Not reaching for angles or conclusions prematurely. They'd reveal themselves in their own time.

He walked Main Street. Stopped in the middle of the heat-cracked road. Other than the wind, the calls of birds, and the river, he heard nothing. No traffic. Greenhaven had been self-sufficient. Set apart. Exclusive. And—finally —alone, when the worst happened. Alone when a well-prepared gang visited, late afternoon, early September. Alone when night fell, and the gang moved house to house, laying out their demands to the terrified townsfolk.

As Martino passed each torched house, he reminded himself of the occupants, and of their fate. They all died from bullet wounds to the head. Executed once the gang had what they wanted, which was—predictably, depressingly—money. Three of the residents had been tortured, possibly because they resisted giving up bank codes and passwords. No one resisted for long.

The police report suggested that the gang turned off their satellite phone jammer to access the internet and transfer money. They kept the sums low enough not to trigger concern. No individual amount over a million dollars. For most Greenhaven residents, this represented a month's interest on capital, and the transfers went through without a hitch. The total haul came to around eighteen million dollars.

Martino walked the devastated town without judgment. He made a few notes, and he took a handful of photographs. Every murder scene he'd attended bore the same hushed intensity. Despite making his living as a writer, Martino had never put that atmosphere into words. Impossible to pin down how it felt, standing among the ghosts of the murdered. He associated the word *sacred* with a Catholicism long since abandoned, but it was as good a word as any.

Sixty-five souls perished in Greenhaven that night, including those ambushed at the cell tower.

Martino let a familiar sensation envelop him. He could almost hear the dead, almost see them standing in the ruins as he passed. Every rotting window frame, every piece of old police tape fluttering in the wind, every fractured, blackened brick, was a reminder, and an accusation. The killers were still out there, breathing, eating, fighting, loving. Alive. Where was the justice in that?

Chief Braden was pissing up a tree when Martino returned, but he'd picked a spot out of sight of the dead town.

"Seen enough?" The old man pulled his belt tight as he approached, and didn't glance back at Greenhaven before climbing behind the wheel.

"Maybe," said Martino. "Hope so."

———

THEY STOPPED at a diner on the way to Valdez. In a badly lit corner booth, ex-chief Braden addressed his words to the table, his voice coming from some place far off. Martino pushed his phone closer, so the recorder picked up every word.

"Police work out here can be tough. Not enough of us, not enough money to recruit and train the next generation. Sometimes, we had to accept we'd fail."

Braden nursed his beer. Martino sipped a bourbon, which cost five dollars more than it should.

"Fail how?" he said.

Braden stared out of the window.

"Me and Janey were the only cops folk in Greenhaven ever saw. Which meant we had to decide where to focus our time. Petty crime rarely got reported. Drugs? Sure, they're a problem, but how do you police a fifteen hundred mile border? Even if you tried, alcohol's the biggest killer, and it's legal."

Braden took an unironic swig of beer. "So we ignore some crimes. That's a failure. We focus on the more serious stuff. Big ticket theft. Assault. Homicide."

Martino noted the omissions from Braden's list: sexual assault and rape. The correlation between reported rapes and subsequent arrests in rural Alaska was low, the offenders' DNA rarely harvested.

But he'd save that piece. This trip was about four affluent communities. Eagle Springs, New Mexico. Whitney Bluff, Maine. Powder Creek, Oregon. Then, four years ago, Greenhaven, Alaska. Each town burned down, no survivors.

Braden was looking at the window again. "We failed Greenhaven. I arrived an hour after Janey. She took the call from a trucker who saw smoke. She found it all first."

Martino let Braden talk.

"The town was still on fire when she got there. Too late to do anything about it. No survivors. No witnesses. No evidence. Nothing. The FBI choppered an experienced investigator in, followed by her team. They interviewed me and Janey, then told us to stay out of their way. Didn't want our help. Screw them. They didn't solve shit, did they?"

"What happened to Janey?" Martino already knew, but he wanted to hear it from Braden. Jane Holden chose a career in rural Alaskan policing, straight out of the academy.

"It killed her. Literally. Janey lived closer to Greenhaven than me. She loved it up there. Never complained about the isolation. Said if she never saw California again, it'd be too soon. And Greenhaven folks liked her. They liked her plenty. The town kinda adopted her. She used to fish there weekends, go hunting. No family back home, so Greenhaven became her family. It hit her hard."

Martino knew how hard. Jane Holden had quit the police two months after the Greenhaven tragedy. True to her word, she hadn't returned to California. She made it as far as Anchorage. The last confirmed sighting put her in a dockside bar where she'd been drinking most nights. Her body washed up five days later, twelve miles away.

"Shot herself with her police revolver," said Braden. He raised the beer bottle to his lips. "On the end of the dock. If she screwed it up, she knew the water would finish her."

Martino said the inadequate words people say, but Braden wasn't listening.

They headed back to the car in silence. As Braden drove, his forefingers tapped the wheel. Occasionally, he drew in a sharp breath. He didn't speak until he drew up in front of Martino's hotel.

"You sure Greenhaven wasn't the first? They've done this before?"

"Yes."

New Mexico. Maine. Oregon. Alaska. All small communities. All wealthy. All remote. The FBI had tried to track the stolen money. Significant sums transferred to offshore accounts, then moved again, multiple times, automatically. The cash trail went cold in countries with a less than respectful regard for America. The FBI suspected the money ended up in US mule accounts, fake bank accounts using synthetic identities to launder cash.

Publicly, the FBI claimed there was no provable link between the four attacks. The media disagreed, but no one had found any evidence.

"And they'll do it again," said Braden.

It wasn't a question, but Martino nodded, and Braden finally met his eye.

"You need anything at all, call me. Let's get those bastards. For Janey."

"For Janey," agreed Martino. He got out of the pickup and walked up the steps to his hotel. One last miniature bottle of bourbon, five hours' sleep, then the flight home to Rochester, where he'd write up the latest section of a book he might never complete. A modern gang of outlaws selectively pillaging rich communities without leaving witnesses or a shred of evidence? To prove anything, he needed more than his instinct and what remained of retired Chief Braden's gut.

Chapter Nine

SIX MONTHS **later**

WHEN THE AXE bit into the first log, a disparate crowd of
birds broke cover from the surrounding trees, and left in
search of quieter perches. Tom stared after them. Thinking
of them as a *crowd* of birds was wrong, he knew, but the
correct word—flock—didn't seem to fit here. These birds
weren't together, they weren't all the same species. All they
had in common was choosing to settle in trees near his
cabin. So maybe *crowd* worked, under the circumstances.

He hefted another log onto the hickory pine stump,
and repeated the process, over and over, working up a light
sweat as the new day rolled up the slopes to the northwest,
bathing the scene in golden light.

Tom thought about words more often lately. This
unusual sensation both excited and disturbed him. As a
child, words had been important. Magical, even. He
remembered the way the local bookshop smelled when he
was ten or eleven. Overhead lights reflecting on glossy

fantasy or science fiction titles. Picking up a potential purchase, careful not to crack the spine. Tilting the book open to read that first page, peering into an unknown world.

He'd long forgotten that excitement, that anticipation. When his parents were murdered, Tom spent months in hospital, first in a coma, then—as a long-term patient in a specialist institution—learning to walk, feed himself, and go to the toilet without help. The bullet which sent tiny shards of skull into his brain changed him forever.

His body continued to grow as normal. He'd hit puberty while still being fed liquids via a drip. When he'd made his first sounds after the machines had been removed, he didn't recognise the deep rumble that emerged from his throat. When discharged from super-vised care, he stood head and shoulders above most other adults, and his body had thickened and broadened.

At six foot three, Tom rarely encountered anyone taller, even with his habitual hunching of shoulders, head held low, eyes down. And there was no hiding his size. He didn't work out, didn't have that strange, symmetrical body of bodybuilders, all sharply defined muscles and shaved pecs. Tom's stomach and upper body were a mat of wiry light brown hair, and there was no marked definition to the slabs of muscle that shifted across his chest like tectonic plates as he swung the axe. He'd met no one stronger than him. In some ways, that was good. Most people found his bulk intimidating, and kept their distance, which suited Tom. Some men, however, interpreted his existence as a chal-lenge to their masculinity. He ignored verbal abuse, and didn't respond to being challenged, or shoved, by those men. Sometimes, though, they wouldn't stop. Jimmy Blue often stepped in to help at that point. They always stopped after that.

In the second hospital after waking from his coma, Tom learned to talk again—after a fashion. He avoided speaking if possible, but if it was unavoidable, he did so haltingly, with a stammer. Even in his early thirties, Tom's vocabulary was that of an eight-year-old.

Being shot in the head halted his mental development. Worse, it sent him backwards. He had grown into a child man. He had once encountered a toddler in a supermarket aisle, lost. Before the frantic mother arrived to snatch the kid up, flashing a suspicious look at Tom, he recognised himself in the three-year-old. The boy stared wide-eyed at his surroundings, stretching out a hand to touch the shiny packets. He was tentative, shy, and the moment he saw Tom, he froze, looked away, and cried.

Tom had learned to hide his own bewilderment and anxiety, pushing his feelings down into his gut. He took jobs that involved little interaction with others; cleaning, warehouse packing, stacking shelves. Even when he worked on building sites, carrying bricks, he kept his own counsel, and—mostly—his co-workers left him alone.

His desire for solitude, fear of being noticed, and the constant hum of anxiety as he negotiated society, defined his life. Which made his current situation strange and unnerving, but also exciting and... delightful. Again, Tom couldn't be sure this word correctly described what had happened since he arrived at Pike Point, but if a few birds could be a *crowd*, maybe his life could be *delightful*.

He piled the chopped logs onto a square of tarpaulin and dragged them over to the cabin, stacking them with the rest in the covered store on the side of the building. Then he went inside to wash up and make breakfast.

From the outside, the cabin looked like any other unsophisticated, practical mountainside dwelling. The diamond importer who'd built the place liked his privacy. He'd used a quad bike—the locals called it a four-wheeler—to get back and forth to town, leaving his car in a rented space behind the hotel. Jimmy Blue had followed his lead, and Tom, having never driven a car, spent his first few weeks learning to operate the unfamiliar bike.

Tom's stomach growled. Food first, then a shower.

The cabin's interior belied its rustic exterior. The entire space was one large room. A light wood floor dominated the open-plan living quarters, stretching out towards the feature that had drawn Jimmy Blue to buy the cabin. Three-quarters of the northwest facing back wall was a single pane of glass. Beyond it was the deck, then nothing but trees, mountains, and sky.

The interior decor adhered to a minimalist aesthetic. Underfloor heating. One couch, two chairs. No television. Bare walls. Closets built almost invisibly into the walls. A bathroom hidden behind a sliding door on the south wall. A brushed steel desk in the corner with a powerful computer connected to satellite broadband. Simple wooden stairs accessing the southeast corner mezzanine, which contained a king-sized bed under a skylight.

The bookshelves lining the east wall held a single book.

Tom made a three-egg omelette, brewed tea, and breakfasted on the deck. He shared his solitude with unseen white-tailed deer, black bears, minks, otters, bobcats, racoons, wild turkeys, woodpeckers, hawks, and a hundred thousand insects.

The cabin belonged to Tom now. Tom *Kincaid*, he reminded himself. Bought by his fictitious brother, David, who'd organised everything so that when Tom arrived, the new quad bike waited in the garage, along with fishing and hunting equipment.

Before Jimmy Blue returned to the darkness, he had left a message. He had done nothing like this before, but after Tom first closed the door in his new home, he had taken out his phone, opened the memo app, and hit play.

He did it again now. As he ate, Blue's voice emerged from the phone's speaker.

"I know this place is beautiful. Everyone says so. The river, the mountains, the wildlife. The people are friendly. And this cabin is, according to the realtor's description, a *once in a lifetime opportunity to live in a modern property that combines stylish interior design with a view to die for.* Not that anyone has to die, Tom. Not this time."

Tom knew the voice spoke with his own vocal cords, used his own brain to form ideas, then put them into sentences. No one would ever be closer to him than Jimmy Blue, yet he felt only an uneasy, distant kinship, or connection, to the voice that spoke with such ease and conviction.

"You know what I saw when I came here? I saw problems. The window is too big. Anyone approaching from the north or west could watch you from the cover of the trees. They could coordinate an attack with others covering the main door, boxing you in. So I set up an alarm system on the perimeter. But who's going to attack me, or you? Our enemies are dead. I avenged your mother and father. Tom Lewis is dead, too. Lost at sea, trying to escape to America. And Jimmy Blue doesn't exist. It's over. I don't need to be here. I can rest. Time for a fresh start, Tom. Time for a new chapter."

At this point in the recording, Tom looked at the nearly empty bookcase. Jimmy could read and write. Maybe Tom could learn to do the same.

"I'll be in the dark if you need me. But I don't think you will."

The recording stopped. Tom warmed his hands on the mug and sipped his tea. He watched a distant hawk wheel in tight circles, rising to a height where it might pick out its prey, extend its deadly talons, and drop silently onto it.

———

FROM THE CABIN to Pike Point was a fifteen-minute ride, but Tom preferred to walk, only using the bike and trailer when picking up groceries. He wore lightweight all terrain running shoes and carried nothing other than a canvas backpack. He liked to run the return journey, the muscles in his legs burning as he covered the uneven ground.

Snow had fallen in the Black Mountains over winter and, in the shadiest spots, an occasional flash of white remained to remind him of the colder months. Even now, in March, the temperature rarely reached the sixties. Tom thought in Fahrenheit these days, a sure sign he was settling into this unfamiliar country.

The first building he passed was the microbrewery, an outbuilding behind Dolores Avery's house. The telltale malty tang on the breeze was absent today, as was the battered Ford pickup she drove. Tom remembered Mrs Avery—"call me Dolly, Tom, you make me feel old"—telling him she was visiting her sister in Charlotte.

The next residence was a more typical Pike Point residence. A big house on a generous plot, two SUVs and a Porsche out front. Well maintained, from the whitewashed picket fence to the European-style wooden shutters on its windows. To live up here, you were rich, or you ran a business serving those who were. Mrs Avery fell into the second category. Her Pike Point IPA, porter, and various seasonal brews were popular with her neighbours and the tourists.

No one had bothered Tom after he moved into the diamond importer's cabin last fall. Pike Point folk respected each other's privacy. "Not snippy, just happy with their own company," was how Miss Honey described the town's inhabitants.

Don't call her Miss Honey, Tom reminded himself. *It's Miss Huxley. Anna Huxley.* Not that he thought he'd ever call her Anna. Just so long as he didn't call her Miss Honey to her face. That name came from a book Tom had read as a child, and it belonged to a pretty, kind teacher. If Miss Huxley heard him say it aloud, the embarrassment might kill him.

As he turned onto Main Street, Tom looked back up the mountain. Although his cabin couldn't be seen from town, he could pick out the subtle trail which led there, and knew which treetops concealed his home. Only one property was clearly visible. It stood a mile and a half east of Tom's place. Dexter Millbank's faux-Georgian twelve-bedroom mansion made no attempt to blend into its surroundings.

'Tech Dex', as the media referred to him, only spent a few weeks a year in the town. Semi-retired from his software business at thirty-six, he owned more houses than any one human could need. The stars and stripes fluttering above one corner of his landscaped lawn meant he was in residence.

Tom headed straight for his destination. Saturday was about the bookstore, Miss Huxley, and the best few hours of Tom's week.

Chapter Ten

"TEA?"

Miss Huxley's voice came from the kitchen out back.

"P-p-please."

No American yet made tea the way Tom liked it, and Miss Huxley was no exception. Her version involved dangling tea bags on a piece of string over cups of hot water. The result was almost undrinkable to Tom's British palate. But he would never say so. The first time they met, Miss Huxley brought up the subject herself, perhaps picking up Tom's mystification at the strange brew in front of him.

"We Americans have a complicated relationship with tea, Tom. We disagreed over it a while back. Your country and mine, I mean. Ended up in a war."

Tom had grown up in Richmond, London, close to the Thames; the Houses of Parliament were only a few miles east. He had no problem believing two nations would go to war over tea.

"But I like it," continued Miss Huxley, "and no country should have a monopoly on a drink. Do you agree?"

Tom's nod registered his alignment with her position, although he wasn't entirely sure what he was agreeing with. Miss Huxley was the only Pike Point resident who had correctly identified him as British. Since then, he had been more careful around others, making the few words he spoke as generic in tone as possible. Easier to be invisible with a vague mid-Atlantic accent.

Despite the cramped surroundings which made him constantly aware of his big, broad, clumsy frame, the dust that made him sneeze, and Butler—Miss Huxley's ancient tabby cat—who regarded all interlopers with a look of haughty derision from his cushion on the top shelf, *The Book Place* was Tom's favourite spot in Pike Point. It might, he secretly acknowledged, even be his favourite place in North Carolina, in America, and in the entire world.

Miss Huxley sipped her tea. She actually seemed to like it.

A small part of the reason for his rapid, deep attachment to the bookstore was, of course, the books themselves. Miss Huxley stocked a few new titles, mostly maps, guides, or spiral-bound poetry. The rest of her stock arrived at Pike Point after passing through the hands of at least one other reader. The sign on the door read *Come in and find new worlds. Part-exchange welcome. Donations of books are more welcome.* Every few weeks, a truck brought boxes of assorted books from house clearances. Novels, novellas, plays, short story collections, poetry volumes, and non-fiction titles from *Teach Yourself Bridge* to *The Illustrated Kama Sutra*—often browsed, but never purchased—filled the walls and the freestanding shelves. Hundreds more waited out back, and Miss Huxley kept volumes circulating between the front and back rooms. Her promise of *new worlds* was never an empty one.

No music played in Miss Huxley's store, no radio or

television disturbed her customers. "If you're not giving your entire attention to a book, you're not doing it right. You should be lost in it, not skipping along the surface while half your brain is listening to some pop song. Books are for living in. Find yourself a good story, and climb inside. You'll come out changed. The same folk who don't read don't believe in magic, either. Readers do, because they have a foot in two worlds. Three or four worlds, sometimes."

The main reason Tom loved the dusty bookstore with every atom of his being was, of course, Miss Huxley herself.

When he'd first met her, she'd been a surprise. Everything about *The Book Place* led expectations in a certain direction. The handwritten signs, the smell of old books, the higgledy-piggledy arrangement of shelves and eccentric labelling of sections—*Mostly Good Poetry, Trashy Romance, Classics that aren't boring, Overrated but possibly fun bestsellers, The Good Stuff*—and, of course, the baleful presence of Butler, all added up to a preconceived idea of the owner. Old. White hair pulled back into a bun, Short-sighted, with spectacles on a chain. Dumpy, plump, eccentric.

But Anna Huxley was young, and—by any standard Tom understood—beautiful. In her mid-thirties, she had olive skin, and dark, wavy hair that fell across her face like a curtain while she read. Her brown eyes were so dark, Tom thought of them as eighty-five percent cocoa, like the chocolate she kept in a drawer, a shared treat that helped take away the after-taste of the tea.

When they first met, Tom feared he wouldn't be able to speak at all. The moment Miss Huxley reversed out of the backroom with a pile of books, slid them onto the counter, straightened up, and smiled, his lips seized up tight. Then she chatted about the weather, the state of the track leading up the mountain, the fact that Butler always knew when a storm was coming, the disappointing novel she'd just given up on, and—without stopping to wonder how it was possible—Tom joined the conversation as if he spoke to beautiful women every day. If she even registered his stammer, she showed no sign. Ten minutes later, Tom was taking his first sip of horrendous tea.

Saturday was their private book group. Miss Huxley nodded at his backpack. "How are you getting on?"

Tom pulled out the novel, laying it on the counter between them. *The Adventures of Tom Sawyer;* hardback, illustrated, battered, and torn.

"Mm, s-slow. But g-g-good. Tom is f-f-funny."

"That he is. I figured you'd enjoy it."

Miss Huxley had offered to help Tom after watching him browse the shelves, pick up book after book like holy relics, replacing them unread.

He moved his finger along the page, sounding out each syllable, looking up for confirmation. After the first ten minutes, he relaxed, as some words stopped looking like puzzles to be solved, instead communicating meaning directly to his brain. He couldn't have described how this worked. Somehow, the words stepped aside.

He reached the point at which Tom Sawyer had to whitewash a fence, and—abruptly aware Miss Huxley was looking on with an expression of quiet wonder—stopped. The words swam back into focus, once again concealing their secret world.

"I don't want to pry, Tom, but can I ask you something?" He dropped his gaze to the counter. When people said those words, it meant one thing. They had seen his scars. Tom put his hand to his head, but the bandana hadn't slipped. Maybe she'd seen them on a previous visit. The bookstore, for the first time, seemed claustrophobic.

When he didn't answer her question, Miss Huxley put her hand on his, where he was keeping his place in the book.

"I'm not teaching you to read, am I? You're remembering how to. Something happened. An accident? Illness? You don't have to tell me. But you could read once, right?"

Tom nodded. Sometimes, fragments of dreams remained when he woke, his father's voice fading as if, a moment ago, he had been reading to his boy. Since Jimmy had taken revenge on their killers, Tom could sometimes picture his parents without reliving their violent deaths. His mother in the car, muttering curses at every other driver; his father listening to the traditional folk music he favoured, occasionally dropping the needle on something more contemporary, perhaps to include Tom. But his son shared his greatest passion: reading. Bedtime stories, followed by Tom picking up his own book until his eyes grew heavy with sleep.

"Y-yes. I, mm, I loved b-b-books."

"I knew you were one of us the first time you walked in. And I'm glad I've been some help. But I don't think you'll need my help for long. You can read fluently already. It's locked away, that's all."

Tom must have looked aghast, because Miss Huxley laughed, blushed, and coughed, all at once. "Oh. Oh, that won't mean you have to stop coming here. However good a reader you are, you can still help me stock the shelves, price up the books... if you'd like."

Yes, he would, very much.

"Good. That's good. Now, let's carry on. I've always loved the chapter where Tom flirts with Becky Thatcher. A gift of a peach and a portrait in chalks. Show me any girl who could resist such romantic gestures."

Tom thought he could probably rustle up a piece of

fruit, and his drawing skills couldn't be any worse than his fictional namesake, but he imagined Miss Huxley might not be as easy to impress as she claimed.

He turned his attention to the book, and within minutes, both teacher and student were consumed by the story.

Chapter Eleven

LIGHT RAIN FELL as Tom ran home, cooling his face with a fine mist. He left the track and made his way through the trees, lengthening his route, zigzagging his way up the mountain. He kept the tightly bunched group of pines that concealed his cabin in sight, and concentrated on the air in his lungs, the warm burn in his leg muscles, and the big, open sky beyond the treetops.

For the first time he could remember, he ran untouched by Jimmy Blue's memories. Physical activity often provoked an involuntary response, triggering images of other mountains, other landscapes. Often, he'd remember carrying a heavy pack, a rifle in his hands. Sometimes, instead of trees surrounding him, he'd remember buildings; a hot, exotic city full of strange sounds and smells. Blood drying on his shirtsleeve. Tossing a handgun over the wall of a junkyard, sending it sailing into a towering heap of rusting metal.

Not today. Today was about Tom's connection to his own body becoming more assured, his stride easier, his mind clear. Just him and the mountain.

Until he rounded the final long curve to begin the final

flat quarter-mile to the cabin, and saw an unfamiliar quad bike standing outside, a tall man in dark clothes sitting on his steps, keeping dry in the shelter of the overhanging roof.

The man was drinking from a canteen. Tom stopped running. For a fraction of a second, he considered circling around the cabin to approach downwind. But that was a vestige of Jimmy Blue's paranoia. It had no place here.

Tom slowed, then walked out into the open. The man raised a hand in greeting and stood up. When Tom recognised the police uniform, his adrenaline level rose. He was glad of the run he'd just completed. His ragged breath and the sweat trickling down his forehead would look natural. He reminded himself he had nothing to hide. At least Tom Kincaid had nothing to hide.

Unless Don had spoken to someone back in Charlotte about the incident in his bar. Tom didn't think Don would do that.

"Mister Kincaid," called the man. He was black, his features symmetrical, an easy smile on his face. Fit, lightly muscled, in his late twenties. His gun still had the holster strap in place. Not expecting trouble. Tom relaxed a fraction.

"H-hello, mm, off-o-officer."

The policeman looked Tom up and down, his smile never faltering. He kept his lips over his teeth. There was tension in his jawline. The cop's eyes moved to a spot a couple of inches above Tom's left eyebrow. Tom put his hand up to his bandana. It had slipped up, exposing the edge of his bullet scars. He pulled it back.

"Perfect weather for a run. The rain and all. Better than sweating your ass off in the heat come summer."

The cop's short-sleeved shirt was tight over his upper

arms. Wiry, nearly the same height as Tom, but around thirty pounds lighter.

Tom took off his backpack. The cop watched him the way boxers eye each other before they exchanged the first blow, estimating their opponent's reach, their power, looking for weaknesses.

"You work out a lot? Got a roomful of free weights up here someplace? Home gym?"

Tom shook his head. If the cop had hoped for a longer answer, he hid his disappointment well.

"I'm Paul Geary. Sheriff's Deputy in Pike Point." The cop looked over Tom's shoulder towards town. "The only law enforcement officer for twenty miles in any direction."

He spoke mildly, his voice free of any inflection, and his body language remained open and unthreatening, but Tom stayed tense. There was no good reason for his discomfort. No trace of Jimmy Blue's presence, either. But Tom's first impression of Geary, for whatever reason, was unfavourable. He didn't like the man.

"I make a point of introducing myself to newcomers, but I've been a little tardy getting around to visiting you, Mister Kincaid. My work takes me all over the county. I've been meaning to drop by. You've been here—what?—four, five months now?"

"S-s-, mm, s-six. Six m-m-months." Tom's stammer, which had faded in Miss Huxley's company, was back.

"Whew. That long already? And how are you liking our beautiful town, Tom? Mind if I call you Tom? And you must call me Paul."

Social niceties had never been Tom's strong suit, but he understood that avoiding them sometimes led to the wrong kind of attention. He took a step forward and held out his hand for Geary to shake. This meant the cop had to descend the steps to his level, and now looked up, instead of down, at Tom.

"P-pleased to m-meet you, P, mm, p-Paul."

"Likewise."

"W-would you, mm, like t-tea? C-coffee?"

————

TOM LED Sheriff's Deputy Geary around the outside of the cabin, and the cop sat on the deck while he brewed coffee inside, bringing the jug out with two mugs. When Geary took his mug, Tom noticed an old, angry scar in the middle of his palm.

Geary saw him look. "Your momma ever tell you not to run when you're holding a glass? Guess I didn't listen so good."

Conversation was stilted. Geary asked questions any curious neighbour might ask, but the uniform he wore gave them a different weight. Tom's new sense of confidence dipped, and he temporarily retreated to the stammering, scared Tom Lewis he'd been most of his adult life. He met Geary's questions about his past with short answers and never elaborated. The cop left long silences, trying to draw him out. Tom was no stranger to silence, and Geary always broke it first.

"I can see I'm making you uncomfortable with all these questions, Tom, and I'm sorry." He wasn't. "But we have a friendly, safe community up here; our own little patch of heaven. I get paid to keep it that way. Which means grilling newcomers, just a little. Your brother looks after you, right? Financially, I mean. Bought this house, had it cleaned out and refitted."

"Y-yes."

Geary looked back through the picture window at the

sparsely furnished space within. Pointed at the computer at the desk.

"Nice computer. Looks state-of-the-art."

Although it wasn't a question, Geary waited for an answer.

Tom hadn't turned the computer on. A believable lie presented itself. "I p-p-play g-, mm, games."

Geary nodded. "Games, huh? Well. Sounds like fun." It obviously didn't.

Tom followed the cop back to the quad bike, returning the man's wave as he rode away.

He cleared the outside table, bringing in the mugs and coffee jug. He knew Geary had wanted to check inside, but no one other than Tom had stepped into the cabin since he arrived. It was his place. Before the cop's visit, he hadn't acknowledged how quickly, and how deeply, he had become attached to the mountain, the town, and this cabin.

Pike Point felt like home.

Chapter Twelve

OF ALL THE attacks Patrice Martino had researched, only one yielded a potential witness. The town of Eagle Springs, New Mexico, scene of the gang's first raid, eight years ago. Seven-year-old Lydia Garcia had hidden while two of the gang killed her parents. She escaped from the fire with serious burns, scarred lungs, and mental trauma. Lydia hadn't spoken a single word since that night. Eighteen months ago, Martino visited the Albuquerque institution taking care of her. The girl he'd met—uncomfortably close to Hannah's age—gave him a thousand-yard stare that still came back in his dreams. Lydia Garcia hid in the dark the night her parents died, and she'd never really come back.

Martino topped up his bourbon. It was his fourth or fifth, and still early evening. Drinking when stressed was a habit he'd formed in his newspaper days. The hard-drinking writer with a failed marriage and writer's block. How had he become such a cliché?

Martino's ex-wife blamed the breakdown of their marriage on his work and his trust issues. Trusting Helen became a challenge after he caught her with her legs around a podiatrist's neck. Still, he had to admit her feet looked great.

The sun was sinking over the river, the water now red-orange.

He walked over to his desk, his laptop docked with a forty-two inch screen. He scooped up the pile of paper in a plastic tray and returned to the couch and his bourbon.

Books, and most of his feature-length pieces, came from the spike. Although it was a tray, he still called it the spike, in tribute to his journalism days. Whenever something caught his eye online, he printed out the relevant page, making notes on the reverse side. He clipped articles out of magazines and newspapers on his travels. Other ideas arrived by email, sent by readers who'd seen his byline, hoping he'd expose some real or imagined scandal. He took his notebook to coffee shops, bars, and restaurants, sitting alone, looking as if he was working, but actually eavesdropping, noting any topic of conversation that engaged his imagination.

Ninety-nine percent of everything that landed on the spike ended up in the recycling box. Martino thought of it as a filtration system. Every so often, he skimmed the spike's contents. The ideas he liked came to the top. Anything left at the bottom of the pile for long was discarded.

This evening's trawl allowed him to discard six ideas. A few moved up the order. Blue-chip companies accused of racial profiling in their recruitment process. A high-placed political advisor implicated in an assassination five years ago. Kids—mostly girls—supplementing their income in college through online porn, years later getting targeted by blackmailers. One printed email came from a London cop convinced that a dangerous vigilante, officially deceased, was actually alive somewhere in America, and about to wreak havoc.

He stared at the sheets of paper with his scribbled ideas, but the fire in his belly refused to ignite.

He replaced the tray on the desk. The motion woke up the laptop, and the screen displayed a photograph of Greenhaven's blackened ruins. The book's working title sat below the photograph.

Burn It Down. Four American Towns Left In Ashes.

The fifty thousand words that followed provided details of the horrors, but no answers. Who, and where, were the culprits? Who, as the media had taken to calling them, were the Firestarters?

And that, mused Martino, as he watched the colours fade from the sky and the river, leaving the view smudged a muddy blue-black, was why he was blocked. Somewhere in the pile of research, in the hundreds of photographs, interviews, recordings, coroners' reports, FBI press releases... somewhere in that haystack of words was the answer.

Martino washed, brushed his teeth, went to bed. Stared up into the darkness, willing the pieces to fall into place, knowing the more he wanted it, the less likely it would happen. He cursed the ridiculous human mind—his own in particular—for its frailties and idiosyncrasies.

Perhaps he just need to get laid. Then he remembered the podiatrist's pudgy fingers on his ex-wife's back.

"Screw it," he muttered, and closed his eyes.

Chapter Thirteen

"WEATHER'S pretty settled right now. Last week, you might've got your boots wet, but I ain't heard an owl this side of the mountain since the last storm. How many nights you planning being away?"

"Th-three nights, s-sir."

Harpo smiled and placed one thick finger on the map. The deep dirt stains around his cuticles were probably older than Tom.

"Good. This route ain't the fastest, but you'll see most of Pike mountain, and it keeps you away from the shiny-boots, no-brain, selfie-stick, Instagrammy idiots. The path less taken. Sound good?"

Tom nodded his assent. Harpo bent back to the map.

"That's your cabin, see? You set off after breakfast tomorrow, head north by northeast, then cut due north once you've cleared the forest. You can't miss it, cos it's marked by the stream. Follow that for four hours or so and make camp. Mid-morning day two, you'll hit the summit, so take a peek at the view, then move on. It's pretty up there, sure enough, but I ain't one for standing around gawping like I deserve a medal for dragging my skinny ass up there. Thing is, folk treat a mountain like it's something to cross off a list. Out come the phones, gotta update their Facebutt page, make sure the whole world knows they're capable of putting one foot in front of another long enough to get to the top of a goddam hill. Next thing you know, they're in the diner back in the Point, taking pics of their mashed avocado on sourdough, posting that on Facebutt too. Hashtag *blessed*, hashtag *back to nature*, hashtag *awesome North Carolina*, hashtag *you'd think they'd never seen a goddam tree or a goddam avocado before.*"

Tom began to wonder if Harpo might not be a fan of social media. Or tourists. Which was odd, considering the business he ran. Every surface was piled high with camping, fishing, and hunting equipment. Out back, a brick barn held the rental equipment: mountain bikes, dirt bikes, kayaks, and canoes; fishing rods, reels, tackle boxes, and nets.

When Tom asked Miss Huxley why everyone called Henry Crabbe, proprietor of Crabbe's Hiking Supplies, Harpo, she had played him a video on her computer. The old black and white Marx Brothers film featured a character called Harpo who never spoke. Tom had frowned at this, because Henry Crabbe never *stopped* talking. But then he remembered how the men on the London building sites often called Tom *Tiny* despite his bulk. People sometimes used a nickname which was the opposite of what they meant. People were strange that way.

Having sold Tom a tent, bedroll, sleeping bag, compass, flashlight, cook pot, water bottle, cutlery, multi-tool, mallet, hunting knife, and map, Harpo was now sharing his knowledge of Pike Mountain, and the best routes for an extended hike. No one knew the mountain better. Harpo grew up in Pike Point, spending every free hour of his childhood and adolescence exploring the region. Now in his seventies, he showed no sign of slowing down. Out of season, he closed up shop and disappeared into the wilds. People speculated that Harpo's love of his own voice was the result of half a year with no one to talk to. He was making up for lost time.

"Anyhow, head across the summit northwest, and spend the second night on the west side. Next morning, follow the trails in and out of the forest, but keep bearing south, then east. You'll be circling back towards Pike Point. Keep going until you pick up the stream at Skinned Rabbit Rock. Follow the stream and it'll lead you to the Jacob Fork River, but you don't want to go that far. When you reach a little waterfall, that'll be your camp for the third night."

Tom squinted at the map. Much easier to make sense of than rows of words crammed onto a page. A map was like a picture, and his brain could more readily grasp its secrets. But there were no words next to the thin blue line representing the stream, no icon representing a landmark.

"Sk-sk, mm, Skinned Rabbit Rock?"

"It ain't got no official title, see? But that's what I call it. It's just a big old rock with a flat top, like a table."

"Wh-why did you call it, mm, that?"

Harpo gave Tom a sharp glance.

"Because that's where I skin rabbits."

"Oh."

Finding no hint of guile in Tom's open expression, Harpo grunted, and turned back to the map, walking his fingers along his recommended route.

"Come dawn, turn your face back towards town. You won't be able to approach directly, see, because the south side is rockier. A couple of steep sections you're better off avoiding. Climb down a ways before heading back up when things level out. Beyond the line of tall pines all on

76

their own, watch your step. You'll be back in the trees there, so give yourself a minute to let your eyes adjust. Wouldn't want you falling into Brown Pants Ravine."

Tom thought about asking, but another sharp look stopped him.

"You hunting, boy? Fishing? What are you doing for chow?"

"Canned f-fish," admitted Tom. "R-raw veg. Fruit. R-, mm, ramen."

"Hashtag *tourist*," concluded Harpo in an uncharacteristically pithy summary, refolding the map. He took Tom's bank card and relieved him of several hundred dollars.

When Tom reached the door, his new, bulging rucksack on his shoulders, Harpo called after him. His deeply lined face looked as dirty as his fingers, years of sun leaving a dark brown web of tan lines.

"You ever been alone, son? I mean, really alone?"

Tom, who never had an actual friend, or felt the touch of a lover, thought of Jimmy Blue. "N-never."

"When you're on the mountain, it's just you, the good earth, and the creatures that live on it. You might get a little scared. Nothing to be ashamed of, neither. A little scared is good. If there ain't a knot in your belly first time you find yourself totally alone, then you ain't been paying attention."

Wondering what this alarming speech was in aid of, Tom was surprised to find the old man pressing something into his hands. A small black case. Waterproof. Heavy.

"Know what I do when I gets the lonesomes? I look at the stars. The planets. Once you're ten miles out of town, ain't no light pollution to speak of. You can see the milky way, boy. This time of year, on a clear night, you can pick out Mars, Jupiter, Saturn. These are my spare binoculars.

Bring them back next week sometime. No rush. Have a good time out there."

With that, Harpo slapped Tom's back, pushed him through the door, and scuttled back to the counter.

Tom tried to wave his thanks at the store owner, but the glass door was so dirty, it rendered the interior as an abstract study in brown.

He headed for *The Book Place*, wanting to show Miss Huxley his purchases. One pocket on the rucksack now held his copy of *Tom Sawyer*.

Jimmy Blue had hiked across many countries, especially in the seven years Tom spent mostly asleep. Blue had crossed deserts, lived rough for weeks in forests, climbed mountains, swum across wide, angry rivers, scaled trees as tall as high rises. Some mornings, before the fog of sleep had entirely lifted, dream fragments from Blue left tracks in Tom's mind before evaporating.

Yes. Jimmy Blue had hiked. Jimmy feared nothing. Tom was afraid of everything. But he could change. The process had already started. The hike was another step on the path.

The window display of the bookstore gave potential customers fair warning of the eccentric chaos within, comprising ever-changing shelves of fiction. This meant John Irving rubbing shoulders with the sermons of Meister Eckhart, which leaned up against Robert Pirsig's *Zen and the Art of Motorcycle Maintenance*. Not every book was displayed on shelves. Miss Huxley used the transparent plastic covers favoured by libraries, punching a hole in their spine, then hung books from the ceiling, where they twisted all day.

The cram of shelves within meant the counter could only be seen from one spot outside, which afforded a clear line of sight between *Political Shenanigans* and *Leave These Lying Around And Your Friends Will Think You're An Intellectual.*

Tom stood in that spot now, hoping for a glimpse of Miss Honey—he didn't correct himself this time—before she knew he was there. His reward was immediate. Miss Huxley sat at the counter, her long dark hair swept to the side. She had a book in her hand, but it was closed, her fingers drumming on the back cover. Tom recognised the gesture. She did it when customers stayed too long, preventing her from getting back to her story. Too polite to say anything, she couldn't prevent her unconscious show of impatience. Tom loved to watch her read, her dark eyes moving down the page, her lips parted, her breathing deep, her body still.

From this narrow angle, he couldn't see the customer who had caused the drumming fingers. Then a shadow moved behind Miss Huxley and Sheriff's Deputy Paul Geary emerged from the backroom, carrying two mugs of tea. He set one beside Miss Huxley and she smiled up at him. He sat on the second stool behind the counter— Tom's stool—and they talked. Geary seemed quite at home, his jacket hanging on the hook on the end of *Children's Books Adults Secretly Read For Pleasure, But Don't Worry, I Won't Tell*. He said something and laughed, the sound loud enough to carry outside. Miss Honey smiled, but her fingers still drummed.

She wants to read. Can't you see that?

Tom watched them talk, unable to move. The tall policeman made conversation look easy, often illustrating a point with his hands, pointing, shrugging, wagging a finger. Twice, he put his big hand on her shoulder. She didn't move away. Once, he used the backs of his fingers to brush Miss Huxley's hair away from her face. Tom thought she looked uncomfortable. She did nothing to stop him, but she couldn't be happy about him touching her. Could she? Tom swallowed, blinked, tried to think clearly, and ignore his clenching stomach and dry throat. Miss Huxley was still smiling. Her fingers were no longer drumming along the book cover.

Tom didn't like Sheriff's Deputy Geary. But it looked as if Miss Huxley liked him. Tom was a grown man. Adults must negotiate this kind of issue all the time. His feelings for Miss Huxley complicated things. She and Tom could never be more than friends, he guessed. Even with his growing confidence, Anna was so far beyond him, she might as well be a fictional character in one of her books.

If life became this complicated with one friend, how did people manage with two, three, four... or dozens? What about friends, colleagues, and acquaintances? The idea of this web of relationships literally made Tom's head ache, and, as he stared through the window, he brought his left hand up to his bandana, resting his fingers on the hard skin of his scars beneath.

He wanted to move, turn away. Go home. But the new Tom, who could make decisions and act on them, had retreated. The Tom who remained was confused, hurt, and rooted to the spot.

Then Geary broke the spell. Miss Huxley took his empty mug and went into the back room. All at once, Geary's demeanour changed. The easy smile disappeared, and the cold intelligence Tom had seen up at the cabin replaced it. Butler, Anna's pampered tabby, dropped lightly from a shelf and padded into view, coiling around Geary's angle, asking for affection. The cop didn't kick him, exactly. Nothing so dramatic. He just moved his foot, firmly sliding the cat back the way he'd come.

When Butler leapt up into the window display, Geary's eye followed the movement, and he saw Tom. The two men looked at each other. For a long second, Geary's face was tight with unconcealed dislike, his eyes glittering marbles. Then the smile returned, along with a mock salute.

Behind the cop, Miss Huxley appeared. He half-turned towards her, one hand gesturing towards the window.

Tom stepped smartly to one side, out of the narrow corridor visible from the counter. He walked away, fast, and took the first turning on the right, listening for the sound of the bell above the bookstore's door, meaning Miss Huxley had come out to find him.

He heard nothing, even after he'd waited around the corner for a full minute.

Chapter Fourteen

FOLLOWING HARPO'S DIRECTIONS, Tom set out next morning, striding into the trees behind his cabin, the rising sun warming his right cheek and turning the spiderwebs golden. No piece of jewelry ever looked as beautiful as those transitory artworks between branch and trunk.

Birdsong rang out from every direction. As Tom passed through their territory, the closest took to the wing and wheeled away to a safe distance, or found a higher perch until he passed, but they never ceased their various calls. Tom listened as he picked his way through the hickories, red maples, and chestnut oaks, his brain finding patterns in their staccato song, attributing human meaning where there was none.

"Who are you? Who are you? Who are you?" came a challenge from a bird in the leaves above. Tom had learned the names of some of his new companions. Red crossbill, pine siskin, dark-eyed junko, brown creeper. So different from London's birds, the stunning song of the blackbird never far away, long summers accompanied by a sound-track of dove coos blended with distant lawnmowers. But the sounds weren't so very different, not when he listened closely. He just wished the phrases were a little more welcoming.

"Where are you going? Where are you going? Back back back back back."

After two hours of hiking, Tom entered a small clearing. He leaned his pack against a rotten tree stump. Although the pack must have weighed forty pounds, he'd barely noticed it. Harpo warned him it would be too heavy, before looking Tom over, and adding, "maybe".

Not given to introspection, Tom had rarely considered his own body; its size, its power, how it compared to others, but he did so now, sitting with his back against the stump, taking a long drink of water.

He put the flask down and looked at his big, wide hands. The old callouses from building work were barely more than patches of rougher skin now. His nails were short, not cracked, and none of his knuckles bore scabs from recent injuries. His long arms, hard with muscle, hung from shoulders so broad he sometimes had to turn sideways to enter a room. At six foot three, Tom was no giant, but his solid frame, broad chest, and thick neck combined to give an impression of great strength. Physically, Tom had a presence people couldn't help but notice. Jimmy Blue might use his physique to intimidate, threaten, or dominate, but Tom did everything to create the opposite impression. On rare occasions—now being one of them— he found himself reminded of his physical body, and how different it was to the scrawny twelve-year-old Tom he remembered.

He stood up. Straightened his back. Raised his head. Reached up and pulled the bandana away from his bald skin, allowing the sun to shine on the light sheen of sweat it found there. With no human being anywhere near, he could be himself. Or, more accurately, he could learn what that might mean without Blue.

He tipped his head back, took a big breath. Roared like a lion. Every bird within a mile scattered, and hidden animals revealed their presence by tearing away from the sound.

Tom beamed with pleasure. He roared again, a primal affirmation of his existence. *I'm here. I'm alive.*

After a full minute of release, throat hoarse, the last echoes fading, Tom picked up his pack, smiling a little sheepishly. He tucked his bandana into his pocket. It felt strange to walk around bare-headed; daring, even. He liked it.

He didn't stop for lunch, instead eating two bananas and a cheese sandwich as he walked. Hiking used different muscles to running, and he enjoyed the subtle burn in his quads as the day wore on.

He heard the stream before he saw it, then caught glimpses through the trees; a narrow splashing rush plunging down a steep section of Pike Mountain. He crouched to fill his flask with fresh, cold water, then turned directly north to follow the water to its source.

Harpo's estimate of a four-hour hike turned out to be fairly accurate. Tom did it in three and a half. His natural pace tended towards the brisk, so he paused often, taking in his surroundings, the ever-changing sound of the stream, the scents of wood and bush, of newly uncurled leaves, of a rain shower from the day before still soaking the more shadowed spots. Tom allowed a quiet joy to seep into him as he followed a circuitous route to the summit for its own sake; a traveller with no fixed destination, and no rush to get there.

He made camp above a natural horseshoe carved out by the stream as it meandered around a rocky outcropping.

After pitching the tent, he swung his legs over the edge, dangling over the water fifteen feet below. He opened *The Adventures of Tom Sawyer*.

The light faded as he caught up with the misadventures of a boy he wished he'd had for a friend when young. Or, even better, Huckleberry Finn, who had nothing, needed nothing, a free spirit who breezed through the lives of so-called civilised folk. Tom had heard a lot of talk about freedom ever since he'd arrived in America, but in the character of Huck, it made sense to him. The people who talked about freedom on television looked angry. Freedom meant more money, or more guns. As Tom often struggled with abstract concepts, he'd assumed he lacked the capacity to grasp the meaning of freedom. But here on the mountain, as it grew too dark to read, and he closed his book, he understood what it might mean for him. He tasted freedom in the cool evening air, smelled it in the green and brown and silver, saw it in the stars glimpsed through clouds. This kind of freedom meant having less, not more. Tom had nowhere to be. No one expecting him. He could wake up tomorrow, pick a direction, and walk. Disappear into the landscape.

He thought of Miss Huxley then, of the bookshop. Of Harpo and his maps, of Carla in the diner with fresh coffee always brewing. Of the owls he heard from his deck some evenings as the sun dipped behind the mountain. And he knew he would continue as planned, return to Pike Point. It was a different freedom, to know he could walk away, keep moving, but choose not to.

Tired by this rare period of thought, Tom crawled into his tent, pulled out the sleeping mat and lay down under the vast sky, pulling the blanket over himself. He slept for seven dreamless hours straight.

Chapter Fifteen

AFTER WEEKS SPENDING every waking hour obsessing over the Firestarters, nights anaesthetising himself with bourbon, and writing an average of thirty words a day on the book, Martino needed a distraction. And the best distraction, the only one guaranteed to dispel the creative miasma, was Hannah.

Before a bestseller about genetic experimentation made his name, Patrice Martino was best known for a Pulitzer shortlisted essay on the opioid addiction crisis in twenty-first century America. The irony of his own daughter's slide into drug addiction hadn't been lost on him. Hannah, now eighteen, was clean, but he'd been here before, and any parent who's watched their child repeatedly fall off the wagon can never rest entirely easy, ever again.

Prising his daughter out of Brooklyn for a long weekend in Rochester meant going big. When Hannah answered her cell with the usual drawled, "Pops," he came straight to the point.

"HP Marvello?"

"When?"

"This weekend. Fly up here. I'm paying."

"Dad, I can't. I have a meeting Friday afternoon."

"They have meetings here too. It's Rochester, not the moon."

She hesitated. He went in for the kill. "I'll let you do *The Godfather*."

"Kidding me."

"Scout's honour."

"You were never a scout, Pops."

"Irrelevant. You coming or not?"

He heard the smile. "*The Godfather*? For real?"

"I'll transfer the air fare. How's your mother?"

"Dad, seriously, you don't have to keep asking. You two can't stand each other. That's OK. I'm not a kid. I can deal with it. Just don't pretend."

"Hey, Han, I'm not pretending, I swear. We were together a long time. I still care for her. I mean, when I say 'care', not like I care for you, or my folks. Or my friends. Or my casual acquaintances. Or a stranger on the street."

She laughed. "I get it, Pops, I get it."

He ignored the interruption. "Or a stranger's dog. It's more like—how shall I put it?—I care about her the way you'd care about someone you'd met once at a party who owned a hamster, and they told you their hamster wasn't feeling so good. About as much as you'd care for a casual acquaintance's ailing hamster."

"I'm hanging up now, Dad."

"I'll see you Thursday night. Love you, kid."

"Love you too."

———

HANNAH EMERGED from the bathroom wearing Martino's robe, a towel wrapped around her head. She was on the phone.

"I'll be there. Yeah. I got it, Jan. Cool."

Did kids say *cool* again now? Patrice remembered Hannah, aged ten or eleven, sniggering at an adult using the word. And now it was back. What next? *Daddio? Right on?*

Patrice handed his daughter a coffee when she hung up. Jan was Hannah's agent. In a year of trying to break into television or movies, Hannah's best-paid role so far had been as a tomato in a kid's show skit encouraging a healthy diet. "Good news?"

"The best. *Zen Cake* wants me for *A Zombie and a Gentleman.*"

"As much as I hate fulfilling the clichéd role of bewildered father, I do not know what you just said."

"*Zen Cake.* Tommy Gryme's production company." She took a sip and exhaled in pleasure. Hannah was her father's daughter when it came to appreciation of a well-prepared cup of freshly ground coffee.

Martino nodded as if the name might mean something to him. "And?"

"And I went to an open call for their next movie. Then a recall last week. They want me for the role."

"Fantastic. What's the movie about?"

"They only gave me the scene I was in at the audition. I mean, it's a low budget zombie movie, but I get some dialogue. If it makes the cut, I mean."

"Well, that's something, right? What's the dialogue?"

Hannah rolled her eyes. "Hoping you wouldn't ask."

"Too late."

Composing herself, Hannah frowned, looked past

Martino's left shoulder and broadened her New York accent.

"Tony? Tony? I told you we were finished, you cheap bastard. Give me back my key and get out of my apartment. Tony? You drunk? What's wrong with your face? Tony? No. Stay away. You stay away from me. No!"

Hannah screamed in terror. Martino flinched and grabbed the back of the couch. "Wow. That's great, Han. Scared the hell out of your old man, anyway. And that's all your lines?"

"That's it. Tony eats my brains after I scream."

"Right. Sure. Of course he does."

"It's a start, Pops. That's what this means. It's a movie credit. Jan says she can put me forward for more interesting roles once I have that first credit."

"No more tomatoes?"

"No more tomatoes."

"You think you have a shot at asparagus?"

"Well. Let's not go crazy, Dad. One step at a time."

Hannah had slept through breakfast, so Martino took her for an early lunch. There was a salad place she loved, its menu full of words like *artisan, responsibly sourced,* and *drizzled.* Patrice favoured dimly lit joints with red and white checked tablecloths and a pepper mill you could assault someone with, but he only had one daughter, so sacrifices had to be made.

After lunch, he found a good espresso bar and read the paper while she attended a Narcotics Anonymous meeting in a church basement off Howell Street.

They didn't talk about the meeting. It was an unwritten rule. Hannah was clean, and nothing else mattered.

Back home, he lined up the DVDs on the table. *The Shining. 2001: A Space Odyssey. Midnight Cowboy.*

Hannah gave him the look.

"What?" he said. "I thought you might change your mind."

"Funny guy. Come on. You promised."

Martino sighed, shaking his head in mock despair. He took two yellow legal pads and two pencils from his desk drawer, put them on the couch between them. Picked up the remote and thumbed on the television. The title screen of *The Godfather* appeared.

"A promise is a promise," said Patrice. "You ready, Ms Marvello?"

"You know it."

He pressed play.

———

FOUR HOURS LATER, Martino sat at his computer, putting together the review as Hannah lay on the couch, dictating copy.

"Ponderous, self-important, and bloated. I'm expected to care about this dysfunctional family because every white male critic for the last four decades tells me I should, but when the Corleones aren't being irritating, they bore the shit out of me. I mean, what the hell is that first scene all about? Was that wedding party filmed in real time? I aged ten years watching these tedious assholes walk us through the most soporific family event in history. Then we have to endure a near-unintelligible Marlon Brando mumble about favours while some moron kisses his ring, which is nowhere near as interesting as it sounds, trust me."

Patrice waited for the next paragraph. He missed the customary glass of bourbon at his elbow, but the couple of bottles he'd had in the apartment were in a suitcase under his bed. Not that alcohol had been Hannah's chosen poison, but she had often washed down her pharmaceutical experiments with beer, vodka, or—on one memorable occasion involving an emergency room and a stomach pump—crème de menthe. He rarely drank in front of her now.

Hannah swung her legs off the couch and stood behind him, putting her hands on his shoulders.

"You sure about this, Pops? I mean, if it's too much for you…"

"I'm sure."

"I mean, it's your favourite. I don't mind skipping it. Seriously."

"Trust me, Han, even HP Marvello won't stop people loving *The Godfather*."

"Well, OK then. New para. 'Critics have worshipped at the feet of Pacino's Michael Corleone for too long, calling it an acting masterclass. Studied, intelligent, calculating. Nah. He's half-asleep in most scenes. He was a pretty boy back then, but if were any more vacuous in this role, the black hole he creates at the centre of this movie would have sucked cast, crew, and scenery into nothingness. Which, although tragic for the families of those affected, would have at least spared generations of movie lovers from this coma-inducing waste of time, which spawned two sequels—one marginally less crappy, the other as preposterous as it is laughable—and a generation of prematurely balding losers who corner girls at parties to give them their TED Talk on how *The Godfather* is perfect in every way'."

Patrice stopped typing. "Prematurely balding losers?" He checked the mass of text. "Was that all one sentence?"

"Punctuate later." Hannah picked up a bowl of potato chips and threw a handful into her mouth. "Now then. Onto Fredo Corleone, played by John Cazale."

Martino's fingers remained half an inch above the

keyboard. "John Cazale? You're gonna take a dig at John Cazale?"

He swung around to face his daughter, his eyes wide. Hannah let the moment last a few seconds, then burst out laughing.

"You fiend."

She grinned. "Even Marvello wouldn't diss John Cazale."

Hannah came up with the name *HP Marvello* when, aged twelve, she announced her intention of becoming a novelist. The name faded along with Hannah's novelist ambitions.

Three years later, in rehab, Hannah started writing savage movie reviews, eviscerating classics with sadistic glee. She'd sent them to her father, who edited them, sent them back, and said he thought they'd sell. And so a writing partnership was born. The movie reviews, skewering baby boomer favourites, became a cult success on a comedy website. Some went viral when a backlash in the comments section doubled the website's traffic.

HP Marvello's secret was that the father and daughter behind the pseudonym both adored the movies HP sneered at.

"Got a title for this one yet?" said Hannah. The titles were Martino's responsibility.

"Sure, kid. How's this? '*The Godfather Made Me An Offer I Was Able To Refuse.*'"

"Damn, you're good."

"I know it. Too early to eat ice cream straight out of the tub?"

"Never."

Hours later, the phone rang, and Martino's racing heart only settled when he remembered Hannah was asleep next door.

"Martino?"

"Yes."

"It's Braden. Lou Braden."

Patrice waited for his memory to fill in the information. It always did, though not necessarily in time to help. Then a hangdog expression, and a shrinking waistline swam into focus. "Chief Braden. What can I do for you?"

Even as he asked, Martino knew there could only be one reason for the retired cop to call. The next sentence, delivered in that rough, low wheeze, confirmed it.

"Heard from the feds. It's happened again. A town is burning."

Chapter Sixteen

THE THREE DAYS and nights of Tom's hike passed without incident. He stuck to Harpo's suggested route. As he walked, he allowed his thoughts to roam free; from North Carolina to Richmond, London, encompassing slivers of memory from California, Germany, Thailand, and the perilous ocean crossing that brought him from Thames Gateway, London, to the port of New Jersey.

After the second night, the images swimming through his consciousness faded, and he walked for long periods, thinking of nothing much. Tom didn't recognise this period as a happy one until much later.

If it hadn't been for what followed, the hike around Pike Mountain might have marked the beginning of a new stage in his life.

A change had begun in Tom. Before now, Jimmy Blue had all the smarts. Jimmy took care of Tom, kept him safe from those who might hurt him. Killed his parents' murderers. But Jimmy had returned to the darkness so Tom could live. And out here, with birds, trees, rocks, and the telltale snuffles and growls of an occasional animal for company, Tom had begun to sense this change.

Halfway through the second afternoon, the rain Harpo claimed wouldn't arrive started to fall. Tom's route took him northwest across the summit, and when the first drop of water splashed onto his head, he was already in the trees on the west face, the mountain now lying between him and Pike Point.

For a few miles, he followed an old, overgrown trail made by animals rather than humans. The trail avoided open spaces and led west, down the mountainside, before turning south to stay within the trees, close to the route Harpo had suggested.

Tom's previous experience of rain had been that of a city dweller. Rain drove people indoors. Rain meant watching the world blur and shift on the other side of a window, the yellows, whites and reds of cars, vans, and buses, headlights on, sending water across the pavements in brown waves to drench the legs of pedestrians. A rainy day meant a day inside, which brought its own pleasures: a warm bedroom with comics or books, the smudged grey world outside fading as the fictional world enfolded him.

But this rain on Pike Mountain couldn't be avoided. As the initial drops got heavier and more persistent, Tom pulled the waterproof jacket from his pack. For a while, he walked like the remembered pedestrians on waterlogged streets; bent over, eyes on the ground. When the rain increased in intensity, Tom responded by searching for a tree with dense enough foliage to shelter him. He spotted a big chestnut oak and diverted towards it, then stopped. Asked himself what he would gain by standing underneath a tree instead of continuing his hike. His boots were water-proof, as were his jacket and pack. His trousers, from mid-thigh to mid-shin, might get wet, but so what? He had another lightweight pair with him.

Mind made up, he continued along the trail. As he walked, his posture straightened. He paid attention to the changes wrought by the weather. The afternoon darkened, visibility reduced to ten yards. Beyond that, an out-of-focus grey curtain. But the sound of the rain captivated Tom. The water didn't fall straight down; it arrived in wet slants on a north-easterly breeze. Drops, large and small, hit every leaf and every branch on the way through the forest, before smacking onto dirt, stone, mud, or Tom's boots. This percussion section surrounded Tom, and he experienced its music in a way no headphones could ever replicate; the sounds arriving from above, below, and from every point of the compass. And, along with the soundtrack, the rainwater brought an explosion of fresh smells as it woke the trees, bushes, leaves, and rocks.

Tom slowed, walking with a smile on his face, tilted towards the sky.

Towards evening, the downfall stopped. Tom camped fifteen miles from his cabin, still preferring to sleep in the open. After the rain's music that afternoon, the small waterfall ten yards from his sleeping mat provided that night's concert. Other than that, all was silence, apart from the wingbeats of birds passing overhead.

When Tom lay on the mat and stared out into the vastness, he saw nothing. Nothing at all. The entire world lay before him—the whole universe—but it hid in impenetrable blackness. And, for the first time he could remember, it didn't scare him. Where once he would have looked for Jimmy Blue for reassurance, checking the deepest shadows for that deeper silhouette, the watcher who never abandoned him, now he remained content to be a tiny part of a greater landscape. A human being on a mountainside.

Here in North Carolina, or somewhere else in this enormous country. Or anywhere else in the world. Wherever he was, he was alone. Anonymous. Unprotected. Content.

If the wind hadn't been north-easterly, things might have turned out differently. If he hadn't camped next to the waterfall, the constant rush of liquid on rocks wouldn't have drowned out the distant gunshots, or screams. And if Tom had known enough about the natural world to question the rise in numbers of birds flying southwest, away from Pike Point, he might have cut his hike short to investigate.

As it was, Tom didn't know anything was wrong until Saturday morning, when, after avoiding Brown Pants Ravine and picking his way through the dense forest, he emerged from the pines a mile from home, and witnessed the aftermath of a nightmare.

―――

A BLACK PALL of smoke drifted away from what remained of Pike Point. Not a single building had survived the night. Blue and red lights flickered among the blackened husks where the people of Pike Point had lived, loved, and worked.

Tom closed his eyes, rubbed them. When he opened them again, nothing had changed. The remains of the town seemed oddly blurred, the lights of the firetrucks, ambulances, and police vehicles unfocused.

He remembered Harpo's parting gift. Dropped the pack from his shoulders. Dug out the binoculars, brought them to his face. Found the notched wheel that changed the focus. Twisted it backwards and forwards, the scene never sharpening, the town existing in a dark bubble; the sunlight unable to penetrate the grey shroud.

Tom realised why the binoculars struggled to focus, why the scene appeared to be in motion. Flakes of ash, most too tiny to see, but some as big as his fist, had turned Pike Point into a snow globe from a horror movie.

Uniformed figures walked through the grainy streets. No one ran. No siren punctured the heavy silence.

He counted four firetrucks. There was no urgency in the firefighters attending the scene. Nothing but smouldering rubble remained for them to pick through.

Miss Honey. The bookshop.

Tom's hands shook so badly, he couldn't see the east side of Main Street. He put the binoculars down as his vision swam, and he dropped to his knees, his breathing ragged. His head ached as if someone had tightened an iron band around it. Tom's fingers prickled with pins and needles. The skin on his face tightened and his lips dried. He tried to suck in more oxygen, gulping at the air, gasping, acutely aware his chest was tightening, his ribcage compressing, his heart fluttering like a moth in a lampshade.

He knew. In that first glimpse from his position a few hundred feet above the town, maybe three miles from his cabin, he knew. The diner was gone. The hotel, too. Harpo's place. The tiny police department. The logging company, the auto repair shop. The heat had been so intense, the blacktop along Main Street was buckled and split in places.

And no one except uniformed emergency services personnel moved among the rubble.

He knew.

The Book Place was gone. His first glance confirmed it. The novels, the plays, the short stories, the poetry. All crammed into wooden shelves. The fire must have burned hot, fed by the ideas and dreams of writers, bound into paper kindling.

And Miss Honey? Miss Huxley, he corrected himself.

Anna.

He knew.

There could only be one explanation for the solemn, unhurried movements of the police, firefighters, and ambulance crews.

They weren't attending an emergency. As they raced up the mountain, they might have thought they could still help. They might have run from house to house, looking for survivors. But they were too late. And so was he.

Chapter Seventeen

TOM MOVED through the trees towards Pike Point as if in a dream, with no conscious control of his body.

He left his pack, and Harpo's binoculars, beside the tree where he had first seen the pall of smoke over the town.

Although he must have passed within a few hundred yards of his cabin, Tom didn't register the moment. Time passed, but mental activity had ceased, shocked into a numb blankness by the scale of the tragedy.

When he next became aware, Tom was behind the microbrewery. The incinerated malt in the outbuildings gave the already acrid stench a savoury top note. A sickly barbecue odour accompanied the other smells, but Tom didn't think about that. Wouldn't think about that.

He jogged to the rear of the building, the back wall still intact. The bricks were hot to the touch. Before crossing to the next smouldering house, he checked the driveway. Mrs Avery had been away for a few days, but the old Ford pickup outside suggested she'd returned. A stab of pain penetrated the numb fog of his mind for a moment.

He moved on, making his way parallel to Main Street through the backyards. The ash found its way into his lungs, and cops and paramedics coughed as they checked the buildings.

Tom tied his bandana over his mouth to create a makeshift filter. Better than nothing. He headed towards *The Book Place.* The ash cloud was thinner there, and a police cruiser sat nearby, with two male, and one female, officers talking.

Tom's mind started up as reluctantly as a twenty-year-old car on a cold day. He had to see for himself. But the police would spot him before he reached the bookstore, even with the blanket of ash making visibility poor.

An idea came to him. Simple, but it might work. Such was Tom's numbed state of mind, he didn't acknowledge that ideas were Jimmy Blue's province, not his. Blue would have been in motion from the moment he spotted the black cloud over Pike Point. He'd have a plan and would carry it out without hesitation. Not this time. It was down to Tom.

He ran behind the smoking ruins, staying low. When he came alongside the fire truck he had spotted through the binoculars, he darted out from cover, climbed up to the cab, and lifted a heavy-duty high visibility jacket from the back of the driver's seat.

He put the jacket on as he walked. Too small. Tight across the shoulders, and no way to zip it up across his chest. Outside the hotel, he scooped up a handful of ash—still warm—and rubbed it over his face, covering his scars.

As he passed the police cruiser, the oldest cop looked up. Tom froze for a split second, then kept moving. The cops stopped talking. He had hoped to walk past, listen in. He hadn't expected to attract attention.

"Hey, bud."

Tom briefly entertained a wild hope that the older cop

was talking to someone else, but when he glanced up, the man waved him over.

A flutter of alarm threatened to turn into full-blown panic. Tom approached the group, his big frame hunched, eyes down, mouth drying.

"You OK?"

As Tom looked up, he took in the handguns on the hips of all three cops. His plan didn't seem so good now. He knew the words he needed would never come if they questioned him. The rush of anxiety made him gasp, and he inhaled a lungful of ash, coughing. He stopped walking, put his hands on his knees, and spluttered, half-turning from his audience.

Now he saw *The Book Place*. The frontage, blackened, smoking, and making strange creaking and cracking noises, remained. Behind it, everything else had gone. Nothing remained to show this building had once contained shelves, books, and a storeroom. The misshapen black lumps inside could have been anything.

Tom, still coughing, looked up at the wall where Butler usually perched, but it had gone. He wondered if the cat had escaped the devastation. One black shape drew his eye. Not in the burned store, but on the street. A long, black object. A bag.

A body bag.

Tom dropped to one knee. Stared. Forced himself to look away, then wished he hadn't. More bags lay in front of every store, every house, as far as he could see, until the ash hid further horrors.

That was what the paramedics were doing. Following the firefighters as they checked each building. Then, once they were able, moving inside. Not to save lives. Too late for that. They brought out the dead. Laid them in front of their houses, or businesses.

When a hand gripped Tom's shoulder, he didn't flinch.
"It's OK, son." Tom stifled a sob.

"Here, take this. Come on." The older cop pressed a water bottle into Tom's hand and, steadying him by the elbow, led him back to the others.

The police cruiser's trunk stood open, and the cop guided Tom in that direction.

"Take a seat. Have a drink. No shame in struggling with—". He waved a hand at the smouldering buildings and didn't finish his sentence. "I've been a cop thirty-six years. Never seen anything like it. Take all the time you need. You want anything else?"

Tom shook his head, meeting the cop's eyes for a moment. The man gripped his shoulder and squeezed, then went back to his colleagues.

"When's the local deputy getting here? What was his name?"

The woman answered. "Geary. Should be here in thirty minutes, give or take. Jesus. He's been fishing at Lake Norman while his whole town burns to the ground. Everyone he knows is dead."

Tom heard this through a haze of shock and disbelief. This wasn't a random tragedy. It was murder. He forced himself to tune into the voices. They said Geary would be here soon. He remembered the way the local deputy had looked at him.

"They find any survivors yet?" said the older cop.

The second man answered this time. "No. They sabotaged the cell tower. Poor bastards couldn't call for help."

"Jesus. The Feds are welcome to this. It's a fucking war zone. I don't... I can't even..."

The cop fell silent. No one spoke for a while. The car radio crackled into life. Tom couldn't understand the distorted voice, but the older cop leaned in through the window and answered. A brief conversation followed, during which Tom caught one word. Geary.

Tom needed to leave. Now, without drawing attention to himself. While he considered how he might accomplish this, a crack echoed down the street, followed by a deep rumble, then a crash, as the front of the *Mountain View Hotel* collapsed, sending fresh grey dust billowing into the ash cloud.

The cops all looked towards the fresh devastation.

Tom moved, walking, not running, putting a burned-out truck between him and the cop car. Once he'd covered enough ground to become near invisible in the ash, he dodged between two blackened properties and turned north. No one called after him.

Chapter Eighteen

DEXTER MILLBANK'S mansion hadn't escaped the horror of the previous night. It no longer looked 'Gatsby-esque', as Miss Huxley described it. It was a blackened, smoking hulk. A single fire truck was in attendance, but there was little left to salvage.

Tom kept walking.

They had spared his cabin. Upwind of the devastation below, it looked just as Tom had left it three days earlier. The birds still sang. A woodpecker drummed its greeting as he crossed the clearing to his door.

Whoever did this went after Dexter Millbank's place, but ignored his cabin. Why?

His hand shook as he put the key in the lock. Stepping inside, he let the door swing closed behind him. The enormous window offered the usual unspoiled view across the mountainside. If he looked through the smaller window behind him, he would see Pike Point. Tom's mind slid away from that idea, and he unlaced his boots.

His next conscious thought arrived in the shower as ash swirled around the plughole.

"What do I do now?"

At the kitchen counter, he poured a glass of orange juice, stared at the familiar room. The question was too big to answer. Well, too big for Tom Lewis to answer. But he didn't want to consider the alternative. Not now. The memory of the body bag outside the bookstore forced him to blink away tears.

He needed to eat, so he made a tuna sandwich, sitting on the deck to eat it.

Much later, Tom's stomach growled again. He blinked at the darkening mountainside. Looked at his watch. The numbers took longer than usual to make sense. He spoke them aloud, something he hadn't done for months.

"Six forty-two."

His voice sounded harsh and raw inside his head.

How did it get so late?

He opened the fridge. Stared inside. Pulled out a box of eggs. He'd bought them in the grocery store, now gone, its owners lined up in bags on the sidewalk. He cracked six eggs into a bowl, whisked them with a fork. Oiled and heated a skillet, dropped the mixture into it, added a handful of spinach leaves, then folded the omelette and turned off the range. Added salt and pepper, and ate it out of the pan, standing in semi-darkness.

Later, Tom must have gone to bed, because that's where he was when the computer screen turned itself on and a low chime brought him awake.

The screen provided the only light as Tom swung his legs over and put his bare feet on the wooden floor, padding quickly down the stairs.

He kneeled in front of a drawer he'd never opened. Did it now, removing the clothes he found inside. Took them over to the computer, picking up his boots on the way.

106

He dressed fast, standing close to the computer. Felt the long knife in the trouser pocket press against his thigh. Wrapped a Velcro sheath around his ankle for a second, shorter blade. Found the in-ear monitor in the jacket pocket. Hooked it around his ear, pushing the bud into place. His actions were fast and precise, but he took no conscious part in what was happening. He watched himself doing it. Blue wasn't in control, not yet, but Tom sensed him so clearly, he averted his eyes from the mirror in case he found two figures looking back at him.

Tom leaned over at the computer's big monitor. The screen had divided into six boxes, each showing a different black and white film. Sometimes the films changed, first in one box, then another. The films showed trees, bushes, the mountain, or a view of the cabin. Figures moved through these scenes. Some in uniform, others not. All armed. Some had handguns holstered at their hip, but one or two carried rifles. They moved cautiously.

Tom stayed back from the screen. Instinct told him to stick to the shadows. He looked out of the picture window. Clouds scudded across the sky, obscuring then revealing the distant stars.

He blinked.

Knowledge fell into his brain, arriving randomly like a game with ping-pong balls he'd seen online. People bounced the ball towards paper cups. Most missed the target, but some bounced just right and settled inside a cup. Like the information bouncing into his consciousness now.

Eighteen. Nineteen. Twenty.
Proximity alarms.
Early warning system.
Twenty-three. Twenty-four.
Hidden cams, ordered online.

A sequence of numbers. 896667242 ENTER.

Thirty seconds.

Thirty seconds to punch in the code and press ENTER if this was a false alarm.

Twenty-seven, twenty-eight.

One of the uniformed figures turned his head as he walked through one of the boxes on-screen. Tom knew him. Sheriff's Deputy Paul Geary.

He laced his boots, backed away from the desk. Thirty seconds were up, and he hadn't entered the password to prevent the endgame program running. All images blinked off as he moved, replaced by a black screen. Boxes of scrolling text appeared and disappeared. Another ping-pong ball plopped into a cup, and he knew the hard drive was being overwritten. A hidden battery ensured that, even with no power, the corrupting program would run, overwriting every file, every folder, and every line of code countless times with random words and numbers.

The next minute was crucial. Tom crossed the room fast, staying low, close to the walls, keeping the table between himself and the window.

Just as he had planted the hidden cameras, and programmed the computer to wipe itself clean, so Blue had left instructions in Tom's brain.

Go to the walk-in closet. Push aside the hangars. Slide the shoes aside, two inches to the left. Hook a finger into the metal ring revealed in the floorboards. Pull.

A hinged section of floor came up.

Tom looked down into the blackness under the cabin.

Jimmy Blue waited there.

Tom hesitated. Pike Point had given him a taste of being alive, fully alive. For a man who had lived a half-life since childhood, he was reluctant to step back into the darkness. Would he lose all the progress made since moving here?

And why run? He had done nothing wrong.

More ping-pong balls found their cups.

Tom was a new arrival in Pike Point. His fake ID couldn't withstand the scrutiny it would be given if he were arrested. Then what? If his fingerprints and photographs were ever shared with the UK police, his new life would fall apart. Jimmy Blue had left a trail of corpses back home.

Five seconds passed while he stood above the open trapdoor. He thought of Tom Sawyer's love for Becky Thatcher. He thought of Miss Honey's smile, and of Butler curling around his ankles in *The Book Place*.

They were the last thoughts Tom could call his own.

He stepped forward, mind emptying as if a powerful arm had swept all the paper cups away, the ping-pong balls bouncing into the gloom.

The man who dropped through the trapdoor into the gloom underneath the cabin wasn't Tom Kincaid, or Tom Lewis. He was nothing. An absence, a hole where a person once existed.

But the man who landed on the soft earth beneath and, staying in a crouch, moved purposefully to the rear of the cabin, was the opposite of absence. He flowed into Tom's frame with a grim inevitability, putting on that heavy muscular body like a favourite suit.

Jimmy Blue stared out into the blackness beyond the cabin. The story the cameras told was that he was surrounded. Geary headed up a team approaching from the front. There were fewer hostiles at the rear, but little chance of Blue breaking through their line without running into at least one of them.

Why had the arsonists left his cabin untouched? Probably to frame him. Blue put the thought aside to be examined later. He had more pressing problems.

He reached up under the cabin and found the waterproof bag he'd shoved between its raised wooden footings. He unwrapped it and took out the handgun and ammunition inside. Blue put the gun in his pocket.

In the trees, a dog growled.

They were coming for him.

Time to leave.

Chapter Nineteen

BLUE PUSHED the ferns aside and stepped out into the darkness, crossing fifteen yards to the trees north of the cabin. The cameras showed this was where the closing circle of hostiles was stretched thinnest.

He heard the thin crackle of a radio, the squelch of heavy boots through mud. He smelled aftershave and sweat. Blue slowed his breathing, and his pulse, listening.

The closest hostile offered little threat. His heavy footsteps and quick breaths suggested someone bulky, but out of condition. A flashlight beam strobed through the dense foliage ahead. From his position, Blue spotted five more lights, two to his left, three to his right.

If he stayed where he was, the nearest hostile would walk directly past him.

He waited. Close enough to pick up the stale cigarettes and gum on the man's breath.

Four more steps, and Blue would be clear.

The man drew level with his position, oblivious to the motionless figure three feet away.

Blue's heart rate remained steady at fifty-two beats per

minute, each breath a slow trickle through his nostrils, his diaphragm rising and falling almost imperceptibly.

Directly in front of the hostile, a bush shuddered as something exploded from within. A cottontail rabbit thudded away through the undergrowth.

"Shit!" The hostile took a step backwards, his flashlight swinging wildly, then dropping to the ground. The beam caught the bobbing tail of the rabbit as it bolted for cover. A relieved laugh ended in a cough.

A low voice from ten yards away. "Clyde?"

The smoker finished coughing and spat, responding in a rough whisper. "I'm fine. False alarm."

The hostile—Clyde—picked up the flashlight, his fast-fading burst of adrenaline prompting a relieved chuckle. A chuckle that stopped when the beam of light revealed a pair of hiking boots.

Jimmy spun anticlockwise from the tree trunk. He chopped down and sideways with the edge of his right hand on Clyde's neck, his left hand ready to follow up if needed. But the first strike hit the intended mass of nerves. As the man fell, Blue caught him, lowering him to the ground. He wedged the flashlight in the lowest branch of the tree. Enough to convince Clyde's colleagues he was still there. If they looked hard at the unnaturally steady light, they'd know something was wrong. But Blue didn't need long.

Clyde would be unconscious for between thirty seconds and two minutes.

Blue closed his eyes for three seconds to acclimatise to the dark.

He loped through the trees, zig-zagging uphill, keeping his footsteps as near silent as he could, jumping from one tree's roots to another, avoiding the telltale squelch of boot in mud, leaving few footprints. He followed the route Clyde had taken on the way in, ensuring his own scent would merge with the other man's stale breath and aftershave. The dogs would have little to go on.

He was a quarter-mile clear when his earpiece buzzed into life. He stopped to listen. Much further, and he would lose the signal from the cabin.

Someone pounded on his front door.

"Thomas Kincaid, this is Sheriff's Deputy Paul Geary. Open up!"

Geary repeated himself, then tried the locked door. He muttered something Blue didn't catch. They'd come prepared. The cabin door was three inches thick, solid wood, but the cops swinging their battering ram knew their job, and their second attempt got them inside.

The next minute and a half consisted mostly of shouting. Blue smiled, remembering Macbeth's take on humanity. *A tale, told by an idiot, full of sound and fury, signifying nothing.* The noise they made covered their fear, gave them the illusion of strength and power. Sound and fury intended to make Tom cower in fear. It had no effect on Blue. His power lay in silence and shadows. Fear was for the other guy.

The shouting continued for a while. Once they'd searched the place, the noise level dropped, and Blue picked out two voices he recognised. One was Geary's, the other belonged to the cop who had given Tom the water. Their conversation was interrupted three times. First by a shout when the searchers found the wiped computer, next when they uncovered the trapdoor. Finally—and Blue cursed Tom's naivety when he heard this—one cop found an unwashed skillet containing the remains of an omelette.

"The bed's been slept in," said Geary, "and that unwashed plate looks like it was used today. He can't have gone far. If we organise search teams, bring in some choppers—"

"I don't think so." The older cop's voice was measured. "He's a person of interest, Geary, not a suspect. His ID might not be genuine, but there's no evidence he was involved."

"How much evidence do you need? We all know this was the Firestarters. You spoke to the FBI. There was an insider in every other case. An insider! This guy appears from nowhere six months ago, using a fake name, now he's on the run... you shitting me?"

"Calm down, son."

"Calm down? My town has burned to the ground. I've been here six years. They were my friends. You want me to calm down? I'll calm down when we catch that asshole, or I put a bullet in him."

"I'm serious, Geary. Calm the fuck down right now. I get it. This is hard for you. Maybe you're too close to think straight. If so, stand down, let my team take care of things. Get some rest."

"No way. You saw that trapdoor in the closet. He had prepared for this. I'm not going anywhere until we find Kincaid."

"You need to listen. And you need to consider the evidence. Yes, Kincaid's behaviour—the bricked computer, the trapdoor, the lack of any personal item that might help identify him, all points to someone hiding something. Wouldn't surprise me if Mr Kincaid turns out to have a criminal past. But none of the evidence connects him to what happened here."

"Not yet. But—"

"But nothing. If he was involved, why murder everyone in town, make himself eggs, then go to bed? He could have been a thousand miles away if he'd left this morning. No. I repeat: for now, he's a person of interest. If we find any evidence linking Kincaid to the Firestarters, or whoever did this, then it becomes a statewide manhunt. But I don't see it. We should get back to town. The first twenty-four hours are crucial. Let's not waste any more of them."

"Sir." Geary's tone was flat. There was something cold about Paul Geary. Tom hadn't liked him, and Tom's instincts were good.

Blue pocketed the earpiece and jogged away.

By the time he realised he'd underestimated Geary, it was too late.

The sheriff's deputy had posted sentries further out, in case their quarry made it past the cordon closing in on the cabin. As Blue jogged through the trees, he emerged into a clearing. Halfway across, his eye caught a flash of moonlight on a rifle.

If the cop had been alert, things might have gone very bad, very fast, but he wasn't. The man was leaning against a tree on the far side of the clearing, rifle slung over his shoulder.

Blue's attention snapped back to the uneven ground under his feet, the patches of shadow and dark, the grunt of surprise from the cop as he looked up.

Rather than ready his rifle, the cop went for the handgun in its holster.

"Stop!"

Everything happened too fast for anything but instinctive actions informed by years of training, combat, and survival. Jimmy upped his speed. Adjusted his course to head for the nearest trees and their concealing shadows.

As he sprinted, his mind ran a real time movie of the cop behind him, based on the glimpse he'd got. The holster's safety strap had been hanging loose, meaning the gun would emerge in one smooth action. The man was in his forties or fifties. Slower than someone in their twenties, sure, but more considered, too. No panic in his voice when he ordered Blue to stop.

The gun would be nearly level now, aiming at Blue's back. Only time for one shot, and the cop would want to make it count. Jimmy allowed an extra beat to give the cop time to get a bead on his centre of mass, before diving right.

Blue had been punched and kicked before. His body had been hit with bricks, baseball bats, truncheons, nunchucks and—on one occasion—a microwave oven. He'd been stabbed in the side. But this was the first time he'd been shot. The old bullet wound on his head belonged to Tom Lewis, not Jimmy Blue.

The impact—which tore a gobbet of flesh from his left shoulder as he hurled himself away—registered as a slap, a wasp sting, nothing more, but it pushed and spun him as he fell.

Blue let his momentum carry him out of the clearing. He rolled behind a tree, putting the trunk between him and the cop. Got to his feet immediately and calmed his breathing. Became still.

His mind remained clear. His attention sharpened, noting the wound, disregarding it for now. A trickle of blood ran down his shoulder blade.

The armed man approached. No more shouted warnings.

Blue deepened his breathing further. His body relaxed in readiness. From the cop's point of view, the injured man had fallen when shot, crashing into the bushes and trees beyond the clearing. After that, silence. Unconscious, perhaps.

The cop slowed as he entered the trees. Steady.

Blue stopped breathing entirely and closed his eyes.

He listened.

A creak of shoe leather on the soft ground. Rapid inhalations and exhalations. The muted crackle of cartilage in middle-aged knees.

His timing needed to be perfect. Placing his feet with care, toes first, checking for loose twigs or leaves before committing to each step, Blue inched his way around the trunk to keep it between him and the advancing cop.

For his age, and considering the evidence of his worn knees, the cop reacted fast when Blue stepped out behind him. But not fast enough to avoid the heavy fist that hit his kidneys with two hundred and twenty pounds of brawn behind it.

The cop staggered half a step and crumpled, eyes rolled back in his head with pain.

Blue unclipped the radio from the groaning man's belt and stamped on it.

When he resumed his jog, he upped his speed considerably. The cop's injury and the wrecked radio might buy him fifteen, twenty minutes before they came looking.

———

SOME OF NORTH CAROLINA'S old gem mines had been transformed into tourist attractions, complete with refreshments, gift shops, and a 'guaranteed gem find every time'. Others, often not much more than a long abandoned shallow cave scraped into the rock, were barely identifiable as mines.

Jimmy's fake IDs were concealed all over America, hidden in the back covers of hardback books sold to unwitting buyers. A phone chip and battery in each book meant Blue could locate his nearest cache and steal it. This particular ID ended up on the shelf of a used bookstore in

Atlanta. During his first week in Pike Point, before handing control back to Tom, Blue stashed it up here in case of emergency.

Tonight, he searched an area two miles from the cabin. He found the old dig—surely the work of one individual— a half-dug old tunnel two feet in diameter, and four feet deep.

From the mouth of the shallow hole, Blue walked north, turned left at the first tree he reached, then right after another four paces, stopping after passing a further six evergreens.

He'd chosen a spruce tree. The fold-up shovel was wedged in its branches. He pulled it down, unfolded it, and dug between the roots. The wound on his shoulder bled more freely as he worked, and the T-shirt he wore stuck to the blood and sweat on his back.

Forty seconds later, he brushed the soil from a hermetically sealed resin case. Inside was a backpack. It contained a fresh social security card and driving licence, cell phone, satellite phone, laptop, portable charger, plugs, two thin T-shirts, a pair of nylon-spandex mix lightweight trousers, and a water bottle. A large zipped pocket held make-up, a hand mirror, skin glue, packets of coloured contact lenses, and two wigs plus facial hair.

Also, and most useful, a small first aid kit. Painkillers, antiseptic wipes, a bandage, and three self-adhesive dressings. He stripped to the waist and cleaned the wound. The chunk of flesh missing from his shoulder muscle measured less than half an inch in diameter, and was still bleeding. He needed to stitch it up, but it would have to wait. The dressing would soak up any bleeding for now.

Blue hiked in the opposite direction of his intended destination for ten minutes. He smeared blood from the used antiseptic wipes on the trunks of trees, finally wedging them into a knothole. That should distract the dogs.

He followed the contours of Pike Mountain south until he found the stream, where he filled the water bottle, drank the contents, and filled it again. Only then did he turn back to the town.

The usual warm dots of light from windows and street lamps had gone. Instead, arc lights powered by portable generators were positioned along the main street. Forensic tents, erected to house the charred remains of Pike Point's residents, dotted the scene, and investigators in hoods and gloves, shoes protected by plastic bags, walked between them.

Blue considered walking away. This wasn't personal. No one knew Tom Kincaid's true identity. No one had heard of Jimmy Blue. If what the older cop said was correct, this was the latest of several raids on small towns.

He thought about the future. A new name, a new home. A big city. Somewhere he could lose himself.

But when he tried to picture that future, all he saw was a body bag outside a bookstore.

Maybe this was personal, after all.

Somewhere out there was an organised gang who had swept into Pike Mountain like Viking raiders, minds black with avarice, hearts soaked in hate, hands already red with blood.

An attack like that took planning, preparation. Pike Point had residents with firearms. It had a police department. Whoever did this knew the best time to strike, and how to eliminate any potential resistance. And they must have known billionaire Dexter Millbank was at home.

Blue scanned Tom's memories, looking for any clues. Pike Point's residents would have run if they had been able to. Meaning they were dead before the fires were set. Shot in the back of the head, the cop said.

A precisely executed attack by a team working to a schedule, each with tasks to perform at allotted times. They had done it before. Unlikely that Pike Point would be the last town to suffer this fate.

Unless someone stopped them.

Blue shouldered the backpack and started the descent towards town.

Chapter Twenty

A FINE RAIN shower began next morning, starting as the sun rose, lasting for an hour before giving way to a cool, sunny Spring day.

As the first drops hit the iron roof of the open-sided barn, Jimmy opened his eyes. He lay still for a full minute. His makeshift bed for the night was a roll of tarpaulin tucked between horizontal stacks of felled trees.

Birdsong provided a melodic counterpoint to the rhythmic scratches of the rats, mice, and various unidentified rodents who shared his accommodation. When Blue arrived in the night, an owl dropped from the rafters and, with a few silent wing beats, powered away in search of prey. It hadn't returned during the night.

It was quiet. The quietest, Jimmy imagined, since humans first built a settlement on the mountainside. A few generators chattered in the distance and, at intervals, vehicles passed the timber yard.

No one came close to his hiding place. The last place the cops would look for a man on the run would be in the town he was running from.

The rain had become lighter still, falling like a curtain of mist. Blue scuffed his feet in the sawdust to avoid leaving obvious footprints. Visibility was poor in the early half-light. The house by the timber yard, like the rest of Pike Point, had burned, but the fire hadn't consumed the entire building. Some rooms at the rear had survived relatively intact.

He jogged across to the house. The back door was unlocked, and Blue entered a large high-ceilinged kitchen with two fridges and a table that could seat ten.

He found a glass in a cupboard and filled it with water. The power was off, but the first fridge—the size of a sentry box—yielded butter, cheese, ham, and half a cooked chicken. A quick search of the cupboards produced a loaf of bread and a jar of peanut butter. Blue breakfasted in a kitchen that smelled like an old barbecue. On one wall, a television, on the other, a photograph showing the timber yard's owners, their three children, and two dogs.

Blue ate until certain he'd consumed enough calories to last the day.

The wound on his shoulder was bleeding again. A search of the kitchen didn't produce any medical supplies, but—in a drawer containing odd screws, nails, and batteries—he found a tube of strong glue.

Bending over the kitchen sink, Blue washed the top half of his body, using a dishcloth to sponge away the dried blood. He dried his torso with his T-shirt. Antibacterial hand soap stood in for antiseptic, and he washed the bloodied hole in his shoulder, patted it dry, then squirted glue into the wound. He held the edges of his skin together for five minutes before releasing them. The makeshift fix held.

He washed up the plate and cutlery, and replaced

everything where he'd found it. He wiped clean everything he'd touched with a dishcloth, including the door as he left.

Back in the barn, Jimmy plugged in the laptop and connected the satellite phone. Internet searches were slow using the satphone, but Blue found the confirmation he was looking for. Pike Point wasn't an isolated attack. It had happened before. New Mexico. Maine. Oregon. Alaska. And now North Carolina. Remote communities. Wealthy. Residents robbed, killed, and their homes set on fire. Five attacks in under eight years. No arrests. No real leads. An ongoing failure by all branches of law enforcement.

A bit more digging uncovered a handful of conspiracy theories, with the culprits being variously identified as government agents, aliens, and—on one forum—as a hith-erto undiscovered species of intelligent, if psychotic, bear.

There were links to articles in the local, national, and international press, but a quick scan revealed the media were as short of ideas as the police and the conspiracy theorists.

Jimmy had almost given up when he found something that convinced him it was worth staying close for another day or two.

Blue propped his mirror against a log, and took out his make-up kit, unzipping it to reveal brushes, combs, four shallow tubs of foundation, skin pens and pencils for fake tattoos and spots. Moisturised tissue to remove it all.

Of the two wigs, the blonde one would be quickest, as his stubble was naturally light. He added a goatee. Removed his bandana, applied tape on his scalp and tape on his chin, positioning his new hair carefully.

He chose grey-blue contact lenses. Subtle, not striking. He didn't want to be memorable. There was no disguising his physique, as he had no clothes other than hiking trousers, T-shirts, and a lightweight jacket.

Once satisfied, he packed everything into the backpack, dropping the handgun into an inside pocket. He set out towards town, taking to the trees until he was a hundred yards from Main Street.

He paused behind a delivery truck, using its side-view mirror to scan the street. Police cars blocked any access. Yellow and black *tape* marked a makeshift border between law enforcement, press, and the first rubberneckers. Local news vehicles had parked as close as possible, their occupants out and jostling for position. Only two national television network vans so far.

Blue waited for an opportunity to move.

Twelve minutes after he took position, a large van with a satellite dish on top emerged from the road snaking between the trees and headed for Main Street. As it slowed, Jimmy stepped out behind it and followed at a brisk walk.

When it stopped at the barrier, he took his phone out of his pocket, held it up to his mouth, and started talking. He added a German accent. Not heavy, but enough to add another layer of disinformation to his disguise. Jimmy had worked with acting coaches and could convincingly inhabit the characters he played. As he didn't intend using this current disguise for long, he wanted to leave anyone he encountered with a few easy-to-remember features. Tall. Blonde. Goatee. European accent.

"But yesterday morning dawned unlike any other for the town of Pike Point," he said as he walked. "Now it looks like a war zone, or the aftermath of a wildfire. Burned-out buildings, some still smoking. Bodies on the street, covered by tents as forensic teams search for evidence. But isn't a war zone, and this fire didn't spread from the nearby forests."

Blue exchanged nods with a cameraman setting up a

tripod. A reporter held her head steady for make-up to be applied.

"No," he said. "Human beings are responsible for the devastation I'm looking at today. They came to this small town two nights ago, and they brought death with them. They moved from house to house like a plague, killing everyone they found. And when they were done, they burned Pike Point down."

No one challenged Blue, or gave him more than a cursory look as he continued his fake dictation. Journalism, like almost every other business, had changed as the internet grew. Even a decade ago, Jimmy might have found it hard to pose as a reporter, since most crews knew each other. Now, news often emerged from social media before being picked up by traditional networks. Bloggers and vloggers provided content for their subscribers, and Blue looked like another freelancer hoping to generate enough clicks to pay the bills.

As he talked, he scanned the journalists for a face he'd memorised from last night's online search. Jimmy had found an online interview with a respected freelance journalist turned author. The interviewer asked: *It's been nearly three years since your exposé of opioid addiction and big pharma malpractice. What's next? You were seen in Whitney Bluff, Maine, earlier this year. Can we expect a book about the tragedy there?*

The answer was the reason Blue had risked staying in Pike Point today.

I never talk about work in progress, Connie. You know that.

Whitney Bluff was the second town raided and burned to the ground. The interview's subject was a writer with a reputation for exhaustive research. A man who, once he'd got his teeth into a story he thought needed telling, didn't stop until he told it.

Blue knew all about single-minded tenacity, and this

man reminded him of himself, just without the talent, or capacity, to deliver violent justice to wrongdoers. Well, nobody was perfect.

If this writer was researching towns that had fallen victim to the same brutal raiders, he would be on his way to Pike Point.

Jimmy Blue looked forward to meeting Patrice Martino.

Chapter Twenty-One

MARTINO DIDN'T ENJOY FLYING. He wasn't afraid of it.
Bad turbulence made his palms sweat, but so did dentistry,
neither of which were statistically likely to kill him. He
hated the sterile homogeny of airports. The lighting, the
squeaky floors, the bored hostility of security guards and
customs officers. The routines of ticket checks, the shuffling dance of grimy humanity from one pen to another,
the inevitable disassociation from reality. He listened to
music or radio, read books, made notes on whatever piece
he was writing, but nothing prevented the grey fog from
descending. He always ended up walking out of Arrivals
shop-soiled, tired, dry-lipped, and staring.

While fine rain blurred the view through the car rental
window, he filled in the paperwork for a bland sedan. He
checked his phone while he waited. An email from his FBI
contact contained attachments, so he opened his laptop,
connected to the Wi-Fi, and downloaded the initial reports
from Pike Point, scanning for any fresh information.
Nothing leaped out, other than a potential witness reacting
to a heavy-handed attempt to bring him in by running

away, leaving one cop unconscious, and another with severely bruised kidneys. The witness—Tom Kincaid—hadn't escaped unscathed. The second cop claimed to have winged him.

Twenty minutes later, Martino followed the GPS instructions out of the airport complex onto the highway, heading west. The tree-lined blacktop drew him across the state towards the mountains, which he reached in a little over two hours. It was only as he turned onto the smaller roads snaking up the mountainside that he shook off his airport torpor.

Pike Point waited. Another town destroyed. Another chance to find something linking the tragedies. Or another chapter in a book with no insights, no revelations, no conclusion. And no point. The customary spike of adrenaline competed with the heaviness in his gut at his lack of progress. And behind it all lay a dull, numbed horror at another small community laid to waste.

The adrenaline pulled ahead of other emotions the closer he got. Maybe, this time, there might be something to get excited about. Why had Kincaid run? Had they finally found the insider?

———

"HEY, Martino, who do we need to screw to get in there?"

The shout came from a reporter as a cop let Martino through the barrier. Patrice waved non-committally. He took off his hat as he followed the cop. The rain had stopped.

The cop handed him over to a lean man in a suit and raincoat.

"It's a fair question," the lean man said, nodding over at the reporter who'd shouted.

"Patrice Martino." Martino put out his hand. The agent shook it as if it were a rotting fish.

"Agent Salton," he said.

Martino replaced his hat, pulled it square, and looked up at the taller man. Salton had walked away. Patrice didn't move. When the agent noticed his absence, he gestured for the writer to catch up. Instead, Martino started speaking. To hear him, Stanton had to retrace his steps, which he did with ill grace. When he was back in front of him, Patrice made eye contact.

"Mr Salton. In another life, I might have pursued a career in law enforcement. Maybe even ended up in the Federal Bureau of Investigation, like you. I'm good at assembling information, noticing details, and finding patterns."

"Well, that's fascinating as all hell, but if you'll—"

Martino continued, never raising his voice.

"But I enjoy writing. Not fiction—I could never come up with an idea I liked. But I worked my way up from junior reporter to feature writer at The New York Times. Picked up a few prizes. Went freelance. Published some books. Specialised in crime. White collar, blue collar, fraudsters, murderers, war criminals. Over the decades, I've worked with the police, the CIA, the NSA, the FBI, the Secret Service. The contacts I've made in these agencies don't call me because they like the quality of my prose, Mr Salton. I help with investigations—even cracked a couple —so they offer me a level of access which irritates some of their employees. I get it, I do. But have you given any thought to why Associate Deputy Director Pimm called you?"

The FBI agent flinched. Martino's contact at the Bureau had been a rookie when they first met. Now Sky Pimm was two promotions away from running the outfit.

Without his help, she would be a decade away from that kind of seniority. She owed him.

Agent Salton would have made a terrible interrogation subject. His emotions were writ large on his gaunt, equine features. Martino had given variations of this speech before. At this point, the obstructive agent was rethinking his dismissive attitude.

"Don't get the wrong idea, Salton. I won't complain about you. But you should treat my involvement as an opportunity. I have extensively researched previous attacks. I can help find the assholes who came to Pike Point the night before last and killed every man, woman, and child. We want the same thing. Let's start again, shall we?"

This time, when Martino held out his hand, Salton shook it like he meant it. Whether he did, Patrice didn't really care.

An hour later, Martino finished his tour of the town. Agent Salton answered questions, and offered some ideas of his own as they walked the grim thoroughfare, occasionally asking police or forensic officers about their findings. The final fifteen minutes passed in silence. Salton had no new information, and Martino had no more questions. Patrice made notes, but, as the minutes ticked by, he fought a rising wave of hopelessness.

So far, Pike Point offered little more than a fifth name in his research folder. He viewed today's horrors with the journalistic detachment he'd spent years building, but some scenes would haunt him. Another good reason to finish the book. The uneasy dead, their murderers unknown, alive, and free, would visit while he slept, or when he was tired, guard down, and they wouldn't stop until his writing reached a conclusion.

The first twenty-four hours might be crucial for the cops, the FBI, and the forensic teams, but not Martino. His epiphanies, when they came—*if* they came—arrived, without fanfare, often days, weeks, or months later. Walking by the river, having a shower, eating lunch, mind drifting. That was when his subconscious pulled a piece or two of a puzzle together, and show him the beginnings of a picture.

He was here to find more pieces. Enough to suggest an outline, at least. But North Carolina had yielded nothing more than Alaska, Maine, Oregon, or New Mexico.

Except for one potential breakthrough.

He stood outside the *Mountain View Hotel*. The sign, stencilled in sheet metal, was all that survived. It had dropped from its position above the main doors and lay face up in the street.

"The witness," said Martino, finally. "The man who ran. Tell me about him."

Salton shrugged, pointed up the mountainside. Patrice could just make out a track winding through the trees. At its end, a dark roof. "Bit of a loner. That's his place."

Martino nodded up at the remains of an ostentatious mansion to the north. "The gang hit that place. But they didn't bother with…?"

"Kincaid," supplied Salton. "But most of the smaller buildings out of town are seasonal lets. They were untouched. They only torched the big house up there. It makes sense when you know whose place it is. Whose place it was. The poor bastard got barbecued along with everyone else."

"Who was he?"

"Dexter Millbank."

"The tech guy?"

"Yup. One of his vacation homes. According to his PA, he came here two or three times a year. He paid a couple in town to act as caretakers."

Martino looked up sharply at that. "How long in advance did they know he was coming?"

"Already been down that road." Salton took out a cell phone as big as Martino's childhood television. Tapped the screen a few times. "Millbank's PA phoned through the date a month ago. That's when the Hudsons—the couple who cleaned the place—shopped for his supplies. Everyone knew when Tech Dex was inbound."

"Damn."

"Yeah."

If everyone knew, anyone could be the insider.

"What can you tell me about Kincaid?"

"Not much yet, but the backroom guys are running checks. He didn't spend much time in town, kept to himself. You heard what happened when they tried to take him in?"

"Yes. Sounds like he can handle himself."

"Still got shot, though. He won't get far."

A police car trickled towards them along Main Street, weaving between forensic tents.

Salton put his phone away. "I asked the local cop to take you up to Kincaid's cabin. He thinks Kincaid is our man."

The agent's tone suggested he believed otherwise, and Martino was inclined to agree. If Kincaid was involved, why hang around after the attack, then run when the cops show up? Still. Many of Martino's best pieces had come down to a change of mind. He'd listen to what the cop had to say.

The police cruiser rolled to a stop ten yards away, and a tall, fit man levered himself out of the driver's seat. He put one hand on the car roof and stayed where he was.

"You the writer?"

"That's me." Martino caught the scowl the cop directed at Salton, who ignored it.

"Ever ridden a four wheeler? It's the fastest way up there."

Martino shook his head. He liked his transport sedate, comfortable, and air-conditioned.

"Guess I've got myself a passenger, then."

———

DOUBTLESS, four wheelers were useful in remote communities with poor roads, but the fifteen minutes Martino spent behind Sheriff Deputy Paul Geary were torturous. Maybe the machine offered reasonable comfort for a solo rider, but the pillion seat seemed designed to vibrate along with the howling engine at a frequency that numbed his genitals.

Ghosts of those vibrations continued after he dismounted. Martino was glad he was already a father, as he suspected he'd just lost whatever remained of his fertility.

The cabin looked designed to blend into its surroundings; the yellow and black police tape spoiled the effect.

Patrice followed Geary into a large, airy, light space. An enormous piece of glass offered a stunning view across trees to the mountain.

Martino recalled the single paragraph on Kincaid in the initial FBI report. A big man in his mid-thirties using a false identity. No employment history, but he lived well up here in his three million dollar hideaway.

Geary liked Kincaid as a suspect. He walked around the minimalist cabin, pointing out the desk where a computer—now with the FBI—had wiped itself clean. Hardly the actions of an innocent man. Then the trapdoor, an unusual emergency exit, added by Kincaid, hidden in a closet. And, the sheriff's deputy pointed out, not a single personal item or piece of paperwork left behind.

Geary described Kincaid as private to the point of evasion on the one occasion they met.

"I came up here to welcome him once he'd settled in. I like the residents to know who I am. Asked about his background—he's Australian, I think—but he didn't talk much. Kincaid couldn't get his words out. Kinda useful when you don't wanna answer questions, am I right?"

Martino took a few notes and watched Paul Geary. The Pike Point cop had been away fishing, returning to find his town gone, and his neighbours murdered. He must be in shock. Deep shock. Martino wondered if Geary should be here. The cop was a stranger to Martino, so it was hard to know if his current behaviour was normal. The sheriff's deputy sometimes stopped talking, his thoughts elsewhere.

Martino broke into Geary's reverie.

"What are you going to do? Personally, I mean? Do you have family here? What happened to your home?"

"Burned with the rest," said Geary, still staring out of the window. "No family. I'm giving a statement in Asheville, then reporting back to Charlotte. They say I should take a leave of absence."

Martino thought about the cops from the other destroyed towns. All psychologically damaged. The Alaskan cop killed herself. The others left the police force and moved away. Patrice had emailed all three. None had agreed to be interviewed. How did life continue after something like that?

"What will you do after that?"

Geary shrugged. "Haven't thought that far ahead." He rested his hand on the butt of his holstered gun. An unconscious gesture. "Only wish I'd been in this room when Kincaid ran. He's involved. I can feel it. Find him, and we'll find the rest of the killers. And you'll have your story."

Martino turned down a lift back on the four wheeler. He wanted to give his subconscious time to breathe, and his testicles time to recover.

Chapter Twenty-Two

AN HOUR'S drive from Pike Point, the town of Asheville surprised Martino; far from being merely an outpost from which to explore the Blue Ridge region, it was buzzing with activity as Martino followed the car's directions to his hotel. If a street corner didn't boast a bar, with music drifting out onto the street, it usually had an art gallery, or a micro brewery.

He parked the car in the lot behind a bland six-storey building. He'd booked this mid-range hotel not because of the ambience, or reviews, but because the FBI and out-of-town cops stayed there. Experience taught him the atmosphere in the bar would be like those of war zones back in his newspaper days. Some people clammed up after witnessing horrors. Others talked. Most drank. Martino wanted to be around the most useful subset: drinkers who talked.

He checked into a room that—other than a framed photograph of the nearby Blue Ridge Parkway—could be anywhere in America.

Martino had a shower, gradually reducing the temperature of the water until each breath came as a gasp, then turning it up to something more civilised to wash and shave.

Standing by the desk, a towel wrapped around his damp body, he sucked in his middle-aged paunch. It didn't hang over the waistband of his pants yet, the way he'd seen on some guys, but it was time to get back to long walks, and maybe add some sit-ups and push-ups into his morning exercise routine. Which meant starting a morning exercise routine.

He called Sky Pimm, Associate Deputy Director of the Federal Bureau of Investigation, and the reason behind his early access to Pike Point. A few years back, newly divorced, he'd spent a long weekend with Sky in the Hamptons. They'd never spoken of it since, and—he had to concede—their fling hadn't affected their working relationship. But whenever he heard her voice, Martino felt a teenaged flutter of nerves.

"Martino."

"Pimm."

Business as usual, but he could hear her smile.

"Give me your gut reaction, Patrice."

"I'm not hopeful."

"Shit."

"Yeah. Whoever they are, they're too good to leave anything useful. If they were going to make a mistake, they'd have done it the first time, in Eagle Springs."

"If it's the same gang, they did make a mistake. They left an eyewitness."

"An eyewitness who'll never speak again."

Sky chewed her bottom lip while thinking. Martino imagined her doing it now.

"Sky, if we could find the link between the towns, get one step ahead of the Firestarters..."

"Don't call them that. And we've tried, trust me. We've narrowed the list of potential future targets to thirteen hundred and sixty-two small, affluent towns, spread across a potential territory of three and a half million square miles. And that's assuming these assholes stick to the mainland."

"I'm sorry, Sky. I wish I had more to give you."

"Yeah. Me too. What do you make of Kincaid?"

"As the insider? I don't buy it. He's a loner who barely spoke to anyone. Hardly the actions of a man gathering intel for a criminal gang. And he stuck around after the attack. Makes no sense. What about the sheriff's deputy? You have anything on Geary?"

"He's one of the good guys. Went through police academy in Fayetteville a decade ago. Clean record, not a single complaint against him. He turned down promotions so he could move to Pike Point. Said it was a dream job, living in the mountains, hiking, fishing, hunting."

"Did you check out Geary's alibi?"

"You don't trust anyone, do you?"

"One trait we have in common."

Sky laughed. "Fair. Yes, I checked. Multiple witnesses put Geary a hundred miles away. His phone pinged off a nearby cell tower. He was fishing Lake Norman while his town burned. Your cop theory doesn't stack up, Martino."

Patrice rubbed his temples with the corner of his phone. If an epiphany was on its way, it was taking its sweet time arriving.

"Martino, I'm going to bed. You?"

Hearing Sky talk about going to bed triggered an echo of their long weekend of sex. It had left Martino with a hangover he was yet to shake off.

"I'm going to the bar," he said.

———

UNFORTUNATELY, it looked like tonight wouldn't be good for information gathering.

When Martino walked into the bar, it was nearly empty. A couple shared a bottle of wine opposite two teenagers hunched over their phones. The few FBI agents occupied a corner booth, and their body language telegraphed an unwillingness to be disturbed.

Patrice pulled up a stool at the bar and ordered a large bourbon on ice. When it arrived, he caught Agent Salton's eye in the booth, raising his glass. The agent nodded and returned to his conversation. They hadn't made the best start, although Salton had warmed as the day wore on. Martino hoped to cultivate that relationship. It would help to have the lead agent on board.

While he nursed a second bourbon, a stranger entered the room, scanned its occupants, and made his way to Martino.

"You are Patrice Martino, yes?" The newcomer was tall and broad, dressed in an off-the-peg suit that looked tight over his shoulders and upper arms. He was blonde, with a goatee.

Martino nodded. "That's me."

The man smiled. Not much of a smile. The muscles of his mouth moved, but the grey eyes didn't join in. The stranger dragged a stool closer and sat down.

"May I?"

"I guess you already did."

The man looked pained. "I am sorry. I don't wish to presume, but it's very important that I speak to you."

There was an odd, uneven cadence to the stranger's speech. European. Martino had spent time there, chasing stories. He tried to pinpoint the accent. Dutch, perhaps? No. Not guttural enough.

"You're German?"

The blonde man nodded. "Very good. Yes, Germany. My mother was in the US military. My father was German."

That quick-fade smile again. "I live in Berlin now. I run my own private investigation business. Every year, I come here to visit my sister."

Martino couldn't figure out where this was going.

"Your sister lives in Asheville?"

"No. Not here." The man looked away. When he turned back, he held Martino's gaze. "She lived in Pike Point."

Martino had been in this situation before, sometimes as the first person outside close family to speak to the bereaved. He had learned it was best to be sympathetic, but professional. "I'm sorry for your loss."

"Thank you."

"What was her name?" Martino took a small notepad and pencil from his pocket. "You mind if I…?"

The man nodded. "Of course. This is why I have come to you. Her name was is… *was* Anna. Anna Huxley. She ran the bookstore in town. My name is Edward. Edward Huxley."

Martino called the barman over. Huxley ordered a light beer.

"How can I help you, Mr Huxley?" said Martino.

"I vacationed in Atlanta for a few days before coming to see Anna. Then I saw the news. I flew in this morning."

Huxley's bottle of beer looked tiny in his hand. "I saw you go through the police barrier this morning, Mr Martino. I didn't think you were a policeman or FBI agent. You don't look, that is… well, it's just—"

Martino smiled, held up his hands. "It's okay, I'm not offended. I look like an out of condition writer, which is fine, because I am.

"Oh, sorry. Ah, this is good that you understand. One of the reporters said you were writing a book about similar attacks all across America. He told me you were lucky to get access to these cases. He, this man, he was not full of compliments for you. Jealous, I think. He said you were a, what is the word? Hick?"

"Hack," corrected Martino. "I've been called worse."

The man leaned forward. As he did so, the tight suit shifted on his bulky shoulders frame and Martino noticed a small splash of red on the white shirt beneath. Huxley straightened his collar. "I cut myself shaving. My hand shook."

Martino was amazed the man had even bothered, given the circumstances.

"I looked for you on the internet."

"How did you find me?"

"I called hotels this afternoon, and asked if you checked in yet, and this one said they expect you this evening. So here I am."

"You're a good investigator, Mr Huxley. And I really am sorry for your loss. But I can't share any information with you. I don't work that way. I'm sorry."

Huxley took a sip of beer. Put it down on the coaster, adjusting it until it was dead centre.

"I do not ask as a grieving brother. I make you a business proposition. I am, as you say, a good investigator. Thorough. I work the details. Also, I work alone, like you. I may find information you do not, and the same is true for you. If we share, we will not duplicate our work. We will get results faster."

Patrice finished his bourbon. Huxley carried himself

with the same alert wariness Martino had seen when interviewing elite soldiers. Although sitting with his back to the
room, Huxley shot regular glances at the mirror behind the
bar. When the FBI agents stood up, he followed their
reflected progress.

"Mr Huxley."

"Edward, please."

"The way I research and write is tried and tested, and
it works, Edward. One reason it works so well is because I
keep myself apart. I allow nothing to colour my judgment.
Here's what I can do."

He took his business card out of his wallet and handed
it to the investigator.

"If you find something we missed, call me."

"You will accept my help, but will not offer me the
same?"

"I'm sorry."

Huxley took a cheap cell phone out of his pocket and
dialled. Martino's phone buzzed on the bar.

"Now you have my number, too. I have extended my
stay for a few more weeks."

Huxley stood up. Martino did the same and was
abruptly conscious of the six-inch height difference.
Huxley's shoulders, arms, and hands looked capable of
breaking bones—and heads—should the urge take him.

"I hope you change your mind," said Huxley. "I'm good
at getting results."

He tossed a bill onto the bar for his beer and left
without shaking hands.

Martino decided against a third bourbon, but stayed in
the bar for another few minutes, his mind itching with the
familiar sensation of an impending idea. When it came, it
wasn't an idea at all, but an observation.

The last thing Huxley said, about getting results. He had spoken without a trace of an accent.

———

A LONG DAY followed by two large drinks meant Martino drifted into sleep within a minute of lying down. Having delivered one useful subconscious observation already, his mind remained in that supple state of readiness as he bobbed along in the currents of his untethered thoughts.

Then he sank into dreams.

Two Hannahs: one laughing as he tickled her, the other hollow-cheeked and staring in a hospital gown.

Hannah walking the charcoal streets of Pike Point, as ash fell like snow around her. A waiting car, engine idling. His old car, the Buick. Helen in the front seat. Martino got in, and Pike Point vanished, replaced by a hospital parking lot. Martino remembered this moment. Eight months before the podiatrist's bony ass gave him a reason to leave, this was the day he knew his marriage was over. In a hospital parking lot, sitting next to each other, neither of them saying a word about what had happened. It should have been raining, it should have been dark and cold, that's how a movie would show it, but life had other ideas, and, minutes after seeing his baby girl hooked up to a drip, he sat with a woman he no longer understood, as the midmorning sun hit the Buick like a searchlight, exposing every smudge of dirt, piece of trash, and speck of dust.

Martino looked out at the parking lot. It had gone. The Buick was now parked in the centre of the Asheville hotel bar. FBI agents, led by Salton, came out of the car, guns drawn, shouting something.

He put his fingers to his shoulder. They came back covered in blood.

Martino woke up. Picked up his phone. Pressed redial. Sky picked up.

"I sleep five hours a night, Martino. Tell me you have a good reason for waking me up."

"I need information, and you're the fastest way to get it."

Pimm listened, said she'd get someone to call him back.

"Now let me sleep, Martino."

His phone rang twelve minutes later.

"This is Harry Iverson at Quantico. In answer to your query, I can confirm Anna Huxley is an only child. No siblings."

Three minutes later, Martino banged on Salton's door, dressed in the hotel's thin towelling robe.

An irritated-looking Salton opened up.

"I've found Kincaid," said Martino.

Chapter Twenty-Three

JIMMY BLUE WOKE EARLY. He'd chosen a cheaper hotel than Martino's, but it gave him relative anonymity and an ethernet connection. Tonight, he would leave Asheville. Today, he had a new identity to learn, money to transfer to new accounts, and travel arrangements to make.

There was a mall across the street. He ate a burger from a gas station and went shopping.

Back in his room, he emptied the bags onto the bed. Tom Harper—the name on his new social security card—favoured cheap, ill-fitting suits, plus jeans and polo shirts for evenings and weekends. In the driving licence photograph, he had dark hair. He'd checked in as blonde Edward Huxley. Tomorrow, Tom Harper would be born.

Most financial transactions took place automatically, but Blue needed to authorise transfers, entering account numbers and passwords when necessary. It was finished by early afternoon, and he raided the bag of food, eating a cold taco, looking out of the room's only window.

He shook a bottle of lidocaine spray. According to the label, it took about twenty minutes for the numbing effect to peak. He sprayed it on his shoulder, sat at the desk, and waited.

In the desk drawer, next to the expected Gideon Bible, Jimmy found dusty cardboard boxes containing a shower cap, shoehorn, and sewing kit. Once the twenty minutes were up, he boiled the small kettle, poured steaming water over the sewing kit needle, and threaded it.

He rubbed the worst of the grime away from the mirror by the door, brought over the desk lamp, and angled it at his shoulder. The wound had proved too deep for the glue to hold, and it had pulled itself open over the course of the previous evening. The T-shirt he'd worn during the day and the shirt he'd chosen for his meeting with Martino were both stained with blood.

Blue tore open a packet of antiseptic wipes, using two of them to clean the wound and. He leaned close to the mirror and pushed the hot needle half an inch into his flesh.

Some mental techniques allowed practitioners to transcend pain, but Jimmy sometimes preferred to feel it. He gritted his teeth as he pulled and pushed the needle through his skin. Five stitches closed it, and he used a Band-Aid to keep the end of the thread in place, unable to get both hands onto it to tie a knot.

During the afternoon, Blue stretched out on the sagging bed and allowed himself a light doze.

Tonight, he planned to steal a car and put some miles between him and the North Carolina mountains.

Tiredness tugged at him. Blue closed his eyes. He bypassed the early stages of sleep, heading straight to the dark centre of consciousness, letting the black cloud envelop him.

After fifty-five minutes, he shook his head and sat up.

The numbing spray had worn off and his shoulder pulsed with mild pain. A good sign—it meant it was healing.

He checked the laptop. A message from Bolsteroni, his pet hacker, confirmed a prepaid bank card in Tom Harper's name would be waiting in a locker near Charlotte bus station.

He caught sight of himself in the mirror and pulled up a chair. Stared at his reflection. He hadn't put the wig and goatee on yet, and the old scars from the bullet wound and subsequent brain operations caught the late afternoon light.

Blue let his mind uncouple, and looked inside. He looked for Tom Lewis, who wished no one harm, however evil. Tom Lewis, who'd read comic books as a kid, where law-abiding characters forged a secret identity to deliver justice.

"I could still walk away, Tom. What do you say?"

He sank deeper, finding no trace of the boy from Richmond, South London. Instead of Tom, images of Anna Huxley appeared, handing over a cup of awful tea, helping Tom pronounce a tough word. She didn't wear perfume, but the cream she used on her skin had the faintest scent of sandalwood. He could smell it now, as she pushed her hair behind her ear, bending over a novel, lost in its fictional world.

"Tom?" she said.

"Tom?" echoed Blue.

No one answered. Tom had retreated from what he'd seen in Pike Point, unable—or unwilling—to process it.

"That's right, Tom, you run away. Leave it to Jimmy Blue to sort out. I'll enjoy it. But take some responsibility, Tommy boy. It was your choice."

Blue continued to stare at his own reflection. It was rare for him to be absent for so long. He'd ducked out of

Tom's life for months before, but never completely. He'd come back at night, steal a couple of hours of sleep from Tom, stay connected to the physical world. But this time, he'd kept his promise and stayed away. Time had unravelled, lost its meaning, and Blue's self-awareness had dissipated like smoke from a bonfire. He'd snapped back into the present moment in the cabin as Deputy Geary and his team closed in, but he had been clumsy, edges blunted through lack of use. Lucky to have escaped with only a minor injury. He needed to let the old pain fill his veins, charge his system with poison-spiked adrenaline.

His phone rang, the tiny screen lighting up on the desk. Blue picked it up.

"What?" He spoke as himself, without thinking. Only one word, but enough of his true identity came through to make the caller recoil with a gasp.

Blue blinked at his reflection, then swivelled away to look out of the window. For a second he couldn't remember who he was supposed to be, the fake identities he'd used over the years swirling around him. This was a new phone, a burner. Who had this number? Only Martino. Which meant... Edward Huxley.

"Hello? Is anyone there?" He brought the subtle, lilting quality back into his voice.

"Mr Huxley. It's Patrice Martino."

"Ah. Mr Martino. This is a surprise."

"Yeah. Maybe I was a little hasty last night. It might make sense for us to work together on this. Just so long as you respect my boundaries. I'm used to working alone."

"Of course. You have made a very good decision, Mr Martino. I am certain my skills will be useful. We will find those who killed my sister. I am sure of it."

"I've been working this story too long to share your

optimism, Mr Huxley, but I hope you're right. I'm leaving Asheville tonight. Can you get back to the hotel?"

"Yes." Blue looked impassively at his face in the mirror. "I can be there in an hour."

"Perfect. I'll see you in the bar."

Chapter Twenty-Four

BY THE TIME a man reaches his mid-fifties, Martino mused, he's probably a long way through his personal list of *firsts*. First proper kiss—Mandy Hartman behind a fake tree during a high school drama rehearsal. First fight—also Mandy, forty seconds later, who broke off from sucking his neck to punch him in the face after Martino's thoughts strayed to the girl across the street, and he whispered 'Alison'. First time he got laid—now that *had* been Alison, whose family moved to Nevada at the end of a glorious summer of exploration, meaning he never saw her again, accounting for his first broken heart. First proper job—junior writer on a short-lived Brooklyn arts paper. A bagful of firsts before the age of twenty. Now the bag was nearly empty, and when he shook it, the items left inside didn't hold the same appeal. The later firsts hadn't been much fun. First close death—a heart attack which came with no warning—took his father from him thirty years ago. Martino's first marriage had ended in his first divorce. Fifteen years after the first child, he'd witnessed the first stomach pump, the first suicide attempt, the first rehab program.

But tonight's first was, he admitted, exciting. He'd never been involved in a sting. Martino nursed his bourbon, swirling the liquid around the melting ice cubes. *Relax, and act normal.* That had been Agent Salton's advice. Easy for him to say. He didn't know how bad an actor Martino was—a fact which had been painfully clear to anyone who witnessed his shambolic performance as a soldier in his high school staging of Macbeth. He tripped during a fight scene, fell offstage, and knocked over the drum kit in the orchestra pit. Everyone laughed. Lady Macbeth—played by Mandy—had laughed longest and hardest.

Still. That was a long time ago, and he'd been carrying a wooden dagger while wearing tights. Tonight, he just had to be himself. Which shouldn't be a challenge, but somehow was.

Martino checked the mirror behind the bar. Thirteen customers. Six of them were cops—two by the entrance, two by the fire exit, and two at the end of the bar. Four FBI agents occupied a table in the middle of the room. By the window, an old couple, both frowning, sharing a happy hour pitcher, unaware they were about to get some free entertainment.

He checked his watch again. Seven thirty-seven. Exactly a minute later than the last time he'd checked. Edward Huxley, or Tom Kincaid, had been due at seven thirty. How long should he wait?

The door opened. He caught the movement in the mirror, heart racing. Two couples entered, laughing, one of them approaching the bar. They ordered a bottle of wine, and the barman said he'd bring it to their table.

After the false alarm, Martino lifted the bourbon to his lips and took a tiny sip. Another first: he'd never made one bourbon on the rocks last twenty minutes before.

The barman flipped up the hinged part of the bar—a

writer should know its name, thought Martino... *barflap?*— to take the tray of glasses and wine bottle to the new customers.

Another barman took his place. "Another bourbon?"

"Uh, no thanks, I—"

Martino looked up into a pair of green eyes, then down to the handgun pointing at him. Kincaid had lost the goatee, and his hair was dark. A wig. He wore the same black apron as the rest of the bar staff.

"Sit tight and don't move. I'm going to make you a drink, Martino," said Kincaid, putting the gun down and filling a fresh glass with ice. Martino's eyes flicked back up to the mirror. The real barman had reached the table and was pouring wine into the first glass. The old couple were halfway through their pitcher, still drinking in silence. The cops and FBI agents remained at their posts.

Look up, he thought. *He's here. Kincaid. He has a gun, and he's standing in right in front of me. Look up.*

Nothing.

Martino tried to keep his voice steady.

"Why the gun, Mr Huxley?"

Kincaid's expression didn't change. He put down the glass, added a splash of bourbon, and placed it in front of Martino.

"We don't have time for games, Martino."

The German lilt had gone; replaced by a generic accent that could be from anywhere or nowhere.

"You're sitting in a well-lit bar," said Kincaid. "It's dark outside. And your law enforcement friends have taken up positions straight from the field manual, covering the exits. They put two in a car at the rear, but they're currently indisposed."

Martino swallowed. That promoted a small smile from Kincaid. "Relax. I gagged them and left them handcuffed to a fence. There's a risk they'll die of embarrassment, but I didn't hurt them. You noticed the blood on my shirt last night."

It wasn't a question.

"And you remembered that Tom Kincaid was shot up on Pike Mountain. I guess you checked on Anna Huxley's brother?"

"She doesn't have one," confirmed Martino.

Kincaid shrugged. "I assumed I'd be walking into a trap. For the record, I didn't buy your change of heart for a second. You're no actor."

No shit, thought Martino. *You should have seen my performance as fifth Scottish soldier.* He swallowed again, and—still thinking of Macbeth—screwed his courage to the sticking place.

"Mr Kincaid, I doubt you had anything to do with what happened at Pike Point. It makes no sense. But I want to discuss what you saw."

"As do your friends in law enforcement. But they'll put me in handcuffs first. Between you and me, I was hiking on the mountain. I saw nothing."

Kincaid glanced across the room, and Martino checked the mirror. The real barman was still filling glasses.

"My offer stands," said Kincaid. "I want access to your research into the other attacks. You've worked on this for years, and I need to get up to speed. Only this time, I'm not asking nicely."

"My answer is the same."

"What?"

"You heard me." Martino looked at himself in the mirror, as if to confirm those words had actually come out of his mouth. He put his right hand on top of his left to stop them shaking. "I work alone. Occasionally, *very* occasionally,

I share information if it'll help me with a story. If you think pointing a gun at me will scare me, you're absolutely right. I'm in imminent danger of soiling these pants, and they're my favourite pair. But threatening my life won't change the facts. I'm not handing my research over to some thug. What the Firestarters did is public knowledge. Go read the reports. Visit the ruins. Talk to the families of the dead. I did."

Martino looked up. The barman was on his way back.

"Nice speech, Martino, but I don't give a shit about your principles. People who get in my way regret it. I'm not some thug, but I do get results. With or without you, I will find the people who did this. If you want the same, you'll help me. Don't waste your time,"—he nodded towards Salton—"chasing me. We'll speak again."

"Excuse me. Who are you?" The real barman stopped just short of the counter, staring at the imposter. Martino looked for the gun, but Kincaid had dropped it into the apron pocket, and was wiping his hands on a bar towel. He gave the barman a warm smile.

"I'm Kenny. Trial shift." He stuck out his hand. The barman took it, still not sure.

"Shane. No one said anything to me. I supervise all the new hires. Who did you speak to?"

"HR," said Kincaid. "The one with the hair."

"Tara sent you?"

"Uh-huh. Tara. Sorry, man, sounds like a screw-up. I don't want to start on the wrong foot here." He untied the apron, backing away. The thug had gone, replaced by a warm, friendly guy you'd trust to care for your sick grandmother. The tone of voice, the angle of his head, the way he held his body. Everything was different. This guy would have been a knockout as fifth Scottish soldier.

The barman shook his head. "Look, man, I guess

someone forgot to pass on the message. I don't have time to show you the ropes tonight, but what say you come back tomorrow morning around eleven?"

"Appreciate it."

"Looks like you know what you're doing, anyhow." The barman turned to Martino. "How's the drink, sir?"

"Fine," squeaked Martino. He coughed. "It's fine."

"Tomorrow, then," said Kincaid, and was gone.

Five minutes later, Salton got off his bar stool and came over. "Guess he's a no show. You think he guessed you were onto him, Martino?"

"Maybe." Martino couldn't have said why he didn't raise the alert when Kincaid left. With every passing second, the opportunity to do so faded.

"Early night," said Martino. He threw a bill onto the bar and left.

———

THE EXPECTED knock on his door came forty minutes later. Salton looked unhappy.

"Problem?" said Martino.

"He was here. Kincaid. Pepper sprayed two of my guys, stuck duct tape across their mouths, and handcuffed them behind their car. Weird, though."

"Weird how?"

"Jumping my guys, then not even trying to get a message to you. Heard anything since?"

"No." Technically, not a lie.

"I guess he figured he'd be outnumbered and bailed."

"Guess so."

"Shit," said Salton.

"Shit," agreed Martino.

"You going to repeat everything I say, like a goddam parrot?"

Hannah would undoubtedly have answered that question with the words, 'goddam parrot'. Martino smiled.

"This funny to you?"

"Not at all, Agent Salton. I was thinking of something else. I'm sure you'll bring him in soon."

"Bet your ass I will, Martino. Bet your ass."

Salton stumped off without another word. Martino shut the door and went back to his minibar bourbon. He hadn't bothered with ice this time.

He tipped the glass, letting the smooth fire warm his throat.

And admitted to himself why he'd said nothing to Salton.

It was because when Kincaid had said he'd find whoever had attacked Pike Point, Martino had looked into his eyes, and seen a depth of conviction he'd never witnessed before, so powerful it brooked no dissent.

Kincaid didn't *hope* he would find the gang responsible for the murderous destruction of five quiet American towns. He *knew* it.

And Martino, who had walked through the remains of those five towns while the entire American law enforcement system spun their wheels, believed him. Or, at least, he wanted to believe him. And that was enough.

Chapter Twenty-Five

THE MUD-SPLATTERED white Toyota pickup truck Blue stole had a faded baseball cap on the passenger seat. He put it on. A man in a baseball cap driving a pickup truck in North Carolina made him close to invisible.

Blue spent the first thirty minutes of the drive to Charlotte free-associating, filtering Tom's memories of Pike Point, hoping something Tom might not have consciously noticed would rise to the surface and give him a place to start. A weak point in the gang's methodology. But nothing came. Jimmy returned his attention to the road spooling ahead of him, winding down the window an inch to let the cool night air in.

He found the locker near Charlotte train station without incident, driving past the location twice to make sure it was clear. Three minutes after parking, he was back in the pickup again, with a cardboard box addressed to Tom Harper. He tipped the contents onto the passenger seat. Driver's licence, social security card, and a prepaid credit card with a couple of thousand dollars ready to use. He could top it up by electronic transfer when necessary.

Blue reached under the dashboard, twisting the wires back together to restart the engine. Three a.m. He'd need to eat soon, but food could wait.

Time to head north. He needed information on the gang who destroyed Tom's new home town, and he knew exactly where to find it.

Chapter Twenty-Six

AFTER FOUR DAYS IN ASHEVILLE, Martino drove away from the North Carolina mountains towards the airport.

Oblivious to the scene of destruction on the mountainside, the state of North Carolina greeted Spring in its usual optimistic fashion. Fresh green leaves opened on the trees, green shoots pushed through the soil with the promise of summer flowers, and the local wildlife—birds, chipmunks, rabbits, and white-tailed deer—had shaken off their winter torpor and were celebrating nature's annual renewal.

Martino was giving up on the book. Temporarily putting it aside, at least. He couldn't think straight. And he was waking nights, two or three times, sitting up gasping, staring into the dark, still seeing shrivelled, burned corpses reaching towards him.

As he drove, he allowed the beauty of his surroundings to lift his spirits. Whether it was the onset of spring or the decision to stop working on the Firestarter's story, his mood lightened with every mile he put between himself and Pike Point.

He was allowed one failure. No one could accuse

Patrice Martino of not doing his bit for serious journalism. His stories and books had exposed wrongdoing, had brought justice and, sometimes, provided peace of mind to the victims of crime. He kept a folder of emails and a drawer full of letters from people thanking him. He never reread them, but he knew they were there.

Time to write something lighter. Surely he'd earned it. He might even get Hannah interested in a co-write. Perhaps bring the clickbait movie reviews of HP Marvello to a wider audience. Compile the best into a novelty book for Christmas. Why not?

According to the rental's GPS, the airport was fifty-five minutes away. His flight left in four hours. Martino had been so keen to leave Asheville, he hadn't considered the timing. He'd booked the first available flight, checked out, and driven away.

Martino eased off the accelerator and turned on the cruise control. He flexed his fingers and rolled his shoulders, trying to ease away some of the tension. Then a name on the GPS screen jumped out at him. A turn-off for Lake Norman. Why did that mean something? Martino shrugged, turned on the radio and scanned the local stations, hoping that in between the nineteen-seventies rock and country selection, he might find some classic fifties swing.

Lake Norman. The sheriff's deputy. Geary. That's where Geary went fishing while his town burned.

Martino's first Firestarters theory was that the local cops were the insiders. The lack of any evidence wasn't the biggest hole in his hypothesis. It was this: one cop might be morally corrupt enough to exchange their neighbours and friends' lives for money, but five of them? It didn't add up.

However, ignoring his hunches never worked out well.

He sighed, recognising a subconscious compulsion.

Martino watched his hand flick the stalk to signal. He slowed the car and took the exit.

———

MARTINO'S subconscious pulled another trick when he reached Lake Norman. The lake was the largest body of water on the Catawba River, meaning there were dozens of places Sheriff's Deputy Geary might have chosen for his base. But the turnoff Martino took led him south of the lake, and the first buildings he saw—alongside a seasonal cafe with a large parking lot—displayed a sign announcing *Angler's Paradise*. Martino remembered the name from the FBI notes. This was Geary's vacation spot.

A wooden building stood close to the water with its own jetty. A second sign advertised boat rental, fishing supplies, groceries, and bait sales.

The door was open. Martino found a middle-aged woman behind the counter and asked if she was the boss.

"Not me." She pointed out the window. Martino looked along the wooden jetty towards a lean man in his sixties, sandy-haired, wearing a checked shirt.

The proprietor of *Angler's Paradise* was kneeling over an upended canoe when Martino reached him.

"Excuse me?"

The man in the checked shirt looked up, acknowledged Martino, and straightened, rubbing his hands on paint splattered overalls. Martino revised his estimate of the man's age upwards. Late seventies, perhaps even early eighties. His blue eyes nestled within folds of wrinkles, and his neck displayed hollows and folds.

"The lady in the shop said you might help me."

"That's no lady, that's my wife. Always wanted to say that."

Deacon was British and spoke with a dialect Martino couldn't place.

"Well, I'm glad I could oblige, Mr—"

"Deacon." The man stepped forward and shook Martino's hand. "Norman Deacon."

"Norman?" he asked.

Deacon chuckled. "Yeah, I know. I've heard them all before, so don't bother. Am I named after the lake? Is the lake named after me? When we moved here thirty years ago, I even thought about changing my name. But then I thought sod it, why the bloody hell should I? It's my name, after all. The real question is, what kind of idiot calls a large body of water Norman? That's the question you should really ask yourself. I mean, it's not like there are rivers called Jennifer, or mountains called Colin, is it? Bloody daft. Sorry, here I am dribbling on. I didn't get your name."

"It's Patrice. Patrice Martino."

"And how can I help you, Mr Martino?"

"I'm a writer." After leaving the employ of a newspaper, Martino had been quick to stop introducing himself as a journalist, which had the same cachet as a debt collector, or IRS investigator. "I'm currently working on a—"

"Martino?" Norman Deacon pointed a dusty finger at Patrice's chest. "I read one of your books. You're the guy who brought down that Ponzi scheme in New York, right?"

Martino nodded. It would be ten more years before the ex-banker behind that disastrous pyramid scheme got parole.

"Shit a brick," commented Deacon. Martino filed the expression away for potential future use. "And you're writing a book right now? You think I can help you?"

Martino nodded again. Deacon responded by adding

another conversational nugget to his growing collection. "I'm gobsmacked, proper gobsmacked. Fuck."

He pronounced both *book* and *fuck* to rhyme with Luke, a bizarre twist of pronunciation Martino had never encountered.

"Well, ask away," said Deacon. "Anything you like. Will I get my name in there? Do you need a photo? C'mon then. Right this way."

Martino smiled. It wasn't always this easy to convince someone to open up.

Deacon set off towards the wooden building. Martino jogged to keep up. Deacon was probably thirty years his senior. Martino reminded himself, not for the first time, to start some sort of fitness regime.

"We'll talk inside," Deacon said over his shoulder. "Have a chat over a brew."

A brew, Martino discovered, referred to hot tea rather than cold beer.

Martino opened his phone. He found Paul Geary's official picture on the town's website and showed Deacon. Mrs Deacon—Teresa—poured the tea, then sat alongside her husband.

The hot liquid—served in a chipped mug—was the deep brown of a muddy river, and, to Martino's palate at least, didn't taste much better.

"Lovely tea," he said, and tapped the screen. "His name is Geary. He came out here just over a week ago, fished for a few days."

"Aye, I remember him. He were a bit of an odd duck."

Martino waited for some elaboration. Teresa nudged her husband to comply. "We get loads of blokes come out here on their own, needing a few days peace and quiet, getting away from the wife, you know? A break from the nagging." He caught the eye of his spouse. "Present company excluded, obviously."

"Obviously," repeated Teresa. "Biscuit?" She offered a plate full of cookies. the one Martino took had the words *Rich Tea* stamped into it. He took a tentative bite and discovered it was neither rich nor made of tea. Its only unique quality was a lack of any discernible flavour.

"An odd… duck?" prompted Martino. "In what way?"

"Well, we didn't see much of him after he'd popped in for a few bits of food and some bait, like. But last week were quiet, so I took me own boat out most days."

"A break from the nagging, Norm?" said Teresa. Her husband winked at her, and Martino got a glimpse of the affection between them.

"Any road up, I were out there nice and early, best time of the day. Lovely. Quiet, like. You know. Saw your pal. He weren't concentrating on his fishing. He had a line in the water right enough, but the float were snagged on some weeds when I went by first time. I came back about five hours later, and the float were still there. Hadn't moved an inch. He hadn't paid it any mind at all."

"What was he doing if he were—*wasn't* fishing?"

"Nowt, far as I could tell. But he were a pacer, know what I mean? Couldn't keep still. Ants in his pants. No wonder he didn't notice his line were snagged. Spent most of the time walking up and down the bank. I reckon he'd had a fight with his bird."

"His… bird?"

"Yeah, you know, wife, girlfriend. Or boyfriend."

"What makes you say that?"

"He were on the phone when he were pacing up and down. Why come out to a spot like this and waste all your bloody time on the blower?"

Martino wished Deacon had a subtitle function. "Could you hear what he was saying?"

"Nah."

Martino washed down his last bite of cardboard with a sip of hot, muddy water.

"Thanks for your time, both of you."

Martino stood up, as did his hosts.

"This guy gonna be in a book, then? He a wrong 'un?" Deacon looked hopeful.

"No, no, nothing like that. I'm writing about Pike Point."

Mrs Deacon shuddered and folded her arms across her chest. "Terrible business. Those poor people. Terrible."

"Yes, Ma'am."

"And this Geary bloke?" Deacon didn't want to let it go just yet. "How does he fit in?"

"He's Pike Point's police officer. He was fishing here when the town was attacked. I just needed to fill in the details, make sure I got the facts right."

"Poor bastard. You mean he got back home and..." Deacon's voice faded.

Teresa took her husband's hand. "Those poor people," she repeated.

Chapter Twenty-Seven

BY THE TIME he reached his Rochester apartment, Martino was ready for bed. A truck had jackknifed on the freeway near the airport. From the back of a cab, he'd watched traffic officers shouting, waving, and placing cones around the stricken vehicle, his eyes stinging through a mixture of exhaustion, and the sterile recycled air of a plane's cabin.

When he finally dragged his suitcase inside the apartment, leaning on the door to close it, he felt ninety years old.

Martino headed straight for the shower, discarding his clothes between the front door and the bathroom. He stood under the hot water until his skin wrinkled.

No bourbon tonight. A mug of herbal tea might lull the busy brain that had spoiled his rest.

Halfway across the main living space, he stopped. Something was different. In his exhaustion, it took Martino a slow count of ten to realise what it was. The ergonomic chair wasn't tucked under his desk the way he always left it. It faced the room, as if an invisible guest was watching him.

"Shit."

Martino checked his desk. To the casual eye, it looked a mess, with papers, pencils, and magazines strewn across the surface. But that was a trick he'd learned from a paranoid colleague two decades ago.

One piece of paper on the desk—marked with a coffee ring—should line up perfectly with a particular scratch on the wood beneath. He checked it now and exhaled in relief. It hadn't moved.

Great. He was exhausted, drinking too much, and now, apparently, succumbing to paranoia. Martino swung the chair to face the desk and pushed it in.

The moment the chair touched the wooden surface, his monitor blinked into life.

Martino took an involuntary step back and turned to check the empty apartment. He always turned off the computer when he left home. The note-taking program he used on the road wouldn't sync up properly if this computer was still running. He always powered down the computer. Always.

Holding his breath, Martino walked sideways to his right, never taking his eyes off the open-space room. He'd only turned one floor lamp on when he got home, and his apartment seemed full of shadows large enough to conceal an intruder. He stepped back until his heel contacted the wall, still moving sideways, extending his hand to reach for the dimmer switches. His fingers scrabbled on the smooth surface. He slapped his hand on the switches and twisted them fully clockwise. Recessed ceiling lights came on and the shadows disappeared. He was alone.

Martino exhaled. Took one shaky breath, then another. He eyed the bourbon bottle on the shelf.

He checked the apartment, opening closet doors, even

looking under the bed. When satisfied, he returned to the desk. The computer monitor showed the logon screen asking for his password, a six-digit number. Whoever had been here, this was as far as they got.

Martino pulled out the chair and sat down, tapping in the password. Maybe he had left the computer on after all. What kind of intruder broke in, took nothing, and left without disturbing his papers? The lock on his front door was intact. Nothing was missing. He could relax.

He double-clicked the last document he'd been editing —his visit to Greenhaven, Alaska. When the screen displayed a new sentence, written in a large font, he pushed away from the desk in shock.

Your work will save me time. I'll be in touch.

Nothing else, no signature. Kincaid had broken into his home and copied all the research and draft chapters of a book Martino had been working on for thirty months.

"No." Martino got up from the chair and, with shaking hands, poured himself a large bourbon, draining half of it immediately. He'd just realised the worst part of the intrusion. Far worse than someone taking his work.

His passcode was Hannah's birthdate.

Kincaid knew about Hannah.

Chapter Twenty-Eight

FIVE MONTHS **later**
Los Angeles, California

JESSE WAS on the treadmill when the alarm sounded. Fitness played an important part in her life, and the home gym reflected her commitment. Besides the treadmill, she had an exercise bike, rowing machine, cross trainer, and a selection of free weights. Current medical thinking suggested a link between physical fitness and mental flexibility, capacity, and potential. A healthy body empirically contributed to a healthy mind. She ran five days a week. When the buzz of the alarm and its flashing light interrupted her, she was twelve kilometres into a fifteen kilometre run.

Jesse noted her irritation at being interrupted as she rubbed a towel over her face, shoulders, and hands. In the habit of regularly observing her own mental state, she saw this irritation for what it was: a weakness. She took self-knowledge more seriously than anyone else she'd ever met.

Most people took little interest in their own flawed person-alities. How could anyone improve themselves if they didn't understand the raw material they had to work with? Jesse had avoided that omission.

What mattered, she thought as she jogged up the metal stairs to the next level of the apartment, was that she recognised and acted on any personal weakness or bias that might affect her judgment. Her negative reaction to the interruption of her exercise was an excellent learning opportunity. It showed an over-reliance on the exercise routines she had set up. Yes, it was vital she remain fit. But the daily mental and physical exercises existed to serve Jesse's work. Not the other way round. So, her annoyance at not completing a run was a weakness to overcome.

Having worked through the logic, she allowed the irri-tation to evaporate.

She jogged across the enormous, main living space—once a warehouse—windows deliberately left uncleaned, giving the place a subdued, dirty light until she closed the metal shutters at night.

At the far end of the room, she punched in a six-digit combination to open her panic room. The company that fitted it was accustomed to lone females as customers. They thought she was paying them a small fortune for protection against home invasion. But Jesse didn't need protecting.

Jesse still referred to the sealed and secured space as her panic room, though. She liked the irony of the name. From the spot in which she now stood, she had planned raids that brought in tens of millions of dollars, and ended hundreds of lives. And, shut inside her panic room, she had completed the arrangements for the next attack. The final raid. Afterwards, she would destroy the contents of the panic room and start a new life. Not the clichéd new life people droned on about when they switched jobs or

170

partners. Jesse's new life meant a new country, a new name, a new history.

She sat at the bank of computer monitors, used her thumbprint to open the software, and identified the source of the alarm.

Oh. An unexpected emotion. Surprise. And, she noted dryly, a second layer of surprise at her own initial surprise.

A live cam feed appeared on the largest monitor. Albuquerque, New Mexico. A private bedroom in an institution offering long-term care to post-traumatic stress disorder sufferers. The patient occupied a suite of rooms. She could afford it. The patient inherited a considerable fortune when her parents died.

Jesse tapped on the keyboard again, flipping between cameras in other rooms. All empty except the sitting room, where Lydia Garcia sat at a small dining table, a glass of water in front of her. Opposite, a stranger. A man; his back to the camera. Big, his back broad, arms slabbed with muscle. Jesse tapped the volume key, and a deep voice emerged from the speakers on her wall.

She listened for a few minutes, her initial surprise morphing into a cold shock she had never experienced before. Then something impossible happened. The patient —Lydia Garcia—spoke. Barely more than a whisper, and never in full sentences, but she spoke. And when Jesse heard what Lydia said, she picked up her phone. She called a number she had never expected to use, but, as remote a possibility as this situation was, she had planned for it.

Jesse thought about the next raid. She could call it off. Or, if this problem could be contained, bring it forward. There were too many variables to reach a logical decision. She needed to reduce those variables.

"This is Jesse," she said into the phone. "Yes, I'm watching it now. How quickly can you be there?"

She listened while zooming in closer to the man on the screen.

"Good. No. Alive, for now. Call me when you have him."

Chapter Twenty-Nine

ALBUQUERQUE, **New Mexico**

THIS HAD NEVER HAPPENED BEFORE. At first, Tom couldn't grasp what was expected of him. Often, when scared, threatened, or desperate, Tom called on Jimmy Blue for help. Tom never thought it might happen the other way around.

His head hung down. As he blinked his surroundings into focus, he saw his hands first, big, solid. Underneath his hands, a wooden surface.

Blue needs me.

As if someone pulled a veil away, the room brightened. Tom looked left, where a shuttered window opened onto a dark night. That was how Blue got in. The breeze from outside was warm and dry. Pinpricks of light at regular intervals suggested the edge of the city, but he could be anywhere on earth.

Albuquerque.

Blue had called him, Blue needed him, and Blue had

left information behind for him, which dripped into his brain, wax from a candle into a saucer.

The room was plain, but tastefully decorated, with bright paintings of sunlit landscapes, a shelf full of books, fresh flowers in a vase, a pair of headphones lying on the couch. It didn't look like a hospital, but Tom knew this was an institution for patients needing long-term care. Tom had spent most of his teens in buildings like this. Not so nicely decorated, but the same.

The patient in question was sitting opposite.

Lydia. Her name is Lydia.

Despite the circumstances—the unexpected awakening, the unfamiliar surroundings, the usual disorientation, the dizzying dislocation from time and space—Tom didn't panic. The sense of calm flowing through him, settling his fear, was an unusual gift from Blue. There must be something important, something *really* important Blue needed him to do. Something to do with the girl. Lydia was looking right at Tom, and not screaming for help, despite the fact a stranger had climbed into her room at night. What had Blue said to her? And what could Tom do?

Lydia Garcia. Along with her name, more information slotted into place. Tom knew she had lived here since the age of seven. Legally still a child, at fifteen, but somebody stole Lydia's childhood. Somebody devoid of empathy or compassion, who killed without compunction. Evil human beings. Tom Lewis had met similar human beings.

And now he knew why he was here.

Tom pulled the bandana away from his scalp, revealing the old scars. Only then did he finally look properly at the girl sitting opposite.

Lydia Garcia might have passed for a woman in her early twenties. Long, dark hair, tied back in a simple ponytail. High cheekbones, a slender neck, symmetrical features. Burns on her neck, across her face, and into her hairline, leaving the flesh there shiny, hard, and red. She left the scars of her trauma uncovered.

Lydia held a stuffed rabbit—tatty and worn, both legs missing. And her eyes remained those of a seven-year-old child. A scared, lonely, betrayed seven-year-old child.

She had seen her parents die. She watched her parents burn.

"It, mm, h-h-appened to m-me too, Lydia. I watched, mm, my, mm, m-mother and father d-d-d-die, mm, in front of me."

Lydia looked up, and Tom saw a faint spark in those lost eyes, a glimmer of understanding and hope. Someone lived in the same hell she did, and—somehow—had found a way out. A way back.

———

LYDIA LISTENED IN SILENCE, staring out of the window. She didn't flinch once, not even when Tom described hearing his mother's screams when they set her on fire. Or the moment a would-be gangster raised his gun to shoot a boy in the head.

The change she underwent during the time Tom described that night was subtle, but unmistakable. Lydia Garcia existed in a place no one could reach her, so no one could hurt her again. Tom Lewis knew that place well. He had spent months there alone. Maybe he would never have returned if Jimmy Blue hadn't found him. Now, meeting someone who'd been through horrors matching his own, he wondered why Blue had come to him. No one had come to Lydia.

When he stopped talking, Lydia looked out of the window towards the city. She hadn't spoken for eight years.

Perhaps Tom's testimony wasn't enough to unlock whatever kept her silent.

Lydia pushed her chair back from the table and stood up. She crossed the room to the small kitchenette. After filling two glasses with water, she placed one in front of Tom. She drank hers without taking her eyes off him, then sat down.

When she spoke, the hairs on the back of Tom's neck lifted. Her voice was soft, not much louder than a murmur. A little rough, but perfectly audible. Heat and smoke had damaged her lungs, throat, and vocal cords. Doctors concluded that Lydia's lack of speech was both physiological and psychological. This moment proved them wrong.

"Why did you come?"

Tom swallowed. He watched Lydia's thin fingers worry at the faded fabric of the toy rabbit. An aching sadness, close to despair, threatened to overwhelm him. This girl had never resumed a normal life after her parents were killed.

"The people that attacked, mm, y–y–your t-town. They are, mm, s-s-still, mm, d-d-oing it. You c-can, help, c-c-catch them. You're the only, the, mm, only one, who ever s-saw anyone."

Lydia slowly shook her head. "I didn't see anyone. I hid like Daddy told me, and I didn't come out. When I did, it was too late to save them."

"You were, mm, s-seven." Tom leaned forward, but Lydia turned to the window. He spoke to the side of her face. "I was t-t-twelve. We were, mm, children. We, mm, we c-couldn't s-stop them. It wasn't y-your fault. The b-bad people d-did this, mm, to us."

Tom's speech had regressed since Jimmy Blue had come back. The months at Pike Point improved his vocabulary, understanding, and communication skills. But those skills were slipping away.

"P-please." This felt like a last roll of the dice for Jimmy Blue. He had never needed Tom before. He must be desperate. But what if Lydia remembered nothing to help Blue find the gang? What then?

"I heard him," said Lydia. She for reached her glass of water and found it empty. After refilling it, she returned to her chair. Once again, she looked out towards the lights of Albuquerque.

"W-who did you, mm, hear?"

The institute was situated in extensive grounds. Which meant Tom could hear the approaching engines.

Lydia's room had no shadows. Nowhere for Jimmy Blue to wait, watch, and listen. But Blue was close, and getting closer as the car engines became louder.

Blue was waiting. Waiting for Lydia to finish what she was saying.

The cars were coming for him.

Lydia seemed not to notice. "The man who killed my mom and dad. He made a phone call. When he couldn't find me. He knew I was supposed to be there, so he called someone. And I knew the man who answered. I recognised his voice. I didn't want to believe it, not then, not now, but it was him."

The first vehicle reached the gravelled area outside the institute's main entrance, skidding to a halt.

Tom held his breath.

"My dad's buddy," she said. "Sheriff Donnelly."

Tom stood up, pushed his chair back. Took two steps towards the window. The dark shape outside came to meet him, flowing through his eyes, nose, ears, slipping under his skin, pushing him out, back to the holding place without time, without pain, an emptiness containing nothing and no one.

Blue watched the driveway. One police car, one unmarked saloon. More vehicles approaching down the long drive.

"Sheriff Donnelly wasn't their leader, though."

Jimmy backed away from the window. Lydia stared through him. "He said a name. Jesse. Jesse was in charge."

Noises outside. Blue looked over his shoulder. The driver's door of the cop car opened, and a uniform got out, looking immediately up to the window.

Blue ducked out of sight. His fingers were on the door handle when Lydia spoke again.

"Wait."

He turned. Her expression had changed. She looked directly at him for the first time. Eyes wide in recognition of the transformation, Tom giving way to Jimmy Blue. There was a hardness in her expression. "Will you kill them?"

"Yes," said Blue, and left.

Chapter Thirty

THE ROTHWELL INSTITUTE was four storeys high. From a central lobby, two lifts served the entire building, next to an echoing stairwell. Blue used neither, climbing a rear fire escape to access the roof, then lowering himself to Lydia's fourth-floor window. He couldn't exit the same way, as the reception committee outside would see him.

The internal stairs were in the rear corner of the building. Jimmy had memorised the layout, as well as the surrounding streets.

Before opening the stairwell door, he stopped, placed his ear against the wooden surface. Hearing nothing, Blue pushed it open with his foot, stepping backwards to check for danger before continuing. No one waiting. No footsteps from the lower floors. He reached through the door to the wall, flicking off the light switches. A more modern building would have automatic lights, motion activated, but the last electrical overhaul had been a decade ago.

As he slipped through the door into the darkness, a radio crackled into life outside, and—two seconds later—

someone kicked the ground floor door open. Beams of light played on the walls four storeys below.

Despite the uniform he'd seen, no one shouted a warning, no one announced themselves as police officers.

Instead of retreating, Blue ran down a flight as the men below began ascending the stairs. They had spotted him at a fourth-floor window, so they would start there, leaving backup at ground level.

Blue, keeping to the edge of the stairwell, brushing the wall with his fingers, silently opened the door to the third floor, easing it closed seconds before his pursuers reached it. He ran around the corner, flattened himself against a wall, and waited. As the men passed, one kicked the door open and checked the corridor before continuing up to Lydia's room.

Jimmy darted down the corridor without hesitation. The only light came from a faint glow around emergency exit signs. He had identified three ways of escape, and the one he intended to use required access to a window in the rear north-west corner. The window was in a resident's bedroom.

Blue twisted the handle, and the door swung open. Maybe the room was unoccupied. Once inside, he stayed completely still, listening and watching.

This was no suite, but a good-sized bedroom with a door leading to a separate bath. The bed was occupied; a frail figure in his forties or early fifties was sleeping, propped up on three pillows. There was nothing peaceful about this man's rest—his face gleamed with sweat. The sleeper twitched and mumbled.

Blue took out his phone to check the signal. Not good. The speed of the response to his visit suggested someone had bugged Lydia's room. Whoever had been listening didn't want the conversation to go public.

Blue tapped out a brief email and attached the audio file he had recorded. He had hoped to edit it first, but there was no time. He could already hear voices. They were searching this floor.

The figure on the pillows stopped moving. A pair of glittering eyes followed his progress as he crossed to the window.

"Who —" began the man, but stopped when Blue raised a finger to his lips. It still surprised him how often this technique worked. Like a small child, the man in the bed obeyed, pressing his thin lips together, his eyes still tracking Jimmy's every move.

"What's the Wi-Fi password?" Blue's voice was calm. The man swallowed.

"Rothwell2000. All one word."

"Imaginative."

With the email sent, Blue opened the back of the phone, removing the battery and the sim card. He pushed the sim into a pot plant on a low table, shoved the battery under a sofa cushion, and snapped the phone between his hands, destroying as much circuitry as possible. He went to the bathroom, lifted the cistern lid, and dropped the pieces into the water.

Back in the bedroom, Jimmy pulled the window up. After three inches, it stopped. Two metal bolts screwed into the frame on either side prevented the window from rising further.

"To stop us jumping," whispered the man in the bed. Lydia obviously wasn't considered a suicide risk, as her window had lacked these modifications. *Lucky*, thought Blue. If Lydia's window had stuck at three inches, he would have had to smash it.

Jimmy put both hands under the frame and applied pressure. He looked back over his shoulder.

"You likely to jump?"

The man on the bed shrugged. "Nope. Not high enough. I'd wind up back in this bed with two broken legs for my trouble. "

"Good," said Blue, and heaved the window up. The metal bolts ripped away from the frame as the wood splintered. They clattered on the wooden floorboards. Blue climbed onto the sill.

"Crazy bastard," said the man on the bed. "Good luck."

Blue reached with his left hand. The brickwork was old, much of the pointing crumbling and soft, which created a useful, if precarious, series of shallow finger and toe holds. Blue pushed his fingers hard into a gap, shuffling left to make room for his right hand. No one shot at him, meaning they were only monitoring the building's regular exits. But someone might be walking the perimeter. He needed to make this fast.

Blue took his weight on his fingertips and stepped off the windowsill, his body swinging like a pendulum. If the brickwork was in worse condition than he expected, or his fingers slipped, he would drop three floors.

The brickwork held. The seven fingers he had jammed into the crevice took his weight for three seconds, then he found a toehold below.

His descent was straightforward after that. Six inches around the corner, on the north-facing wall, a drainpipe offered an easier descent. As he clambered down, he watched and listened for his pursuers. They hadn't yet reached the room above.

The grounds of the institute were dotted with trees, bushes, and hedges, providing a series of walks for its residents to take, with paths ringing the main house, leading off to landscaped areas. Blue could taste moisture, but there'd been no rain. The hiss of automatic sprinklers confirmed the reason behind the lush display of planting.

The sprinklers were useful tonight. The night was quiet, but the hiss and patter of the nocturnal watering system helped cover any sounds Blue made as he jogged to the trees beyond the main building. From there, he moved south towards the cars in front of the Institute. The uniformed policeman was still there, three other men standing by their vehicles. All armed. Blue's car—stolen earlier that evening—waited half a mile away on a residential street.

He couldn't see the Institute's main gates from here, as the grounds sloped away towards the city. Other hostiles would wait there. His best option was to take one of their cars. His high-speed driving training had come at the hands of one of the most experienced police pursuit drivers in Germany, and Blue had proved a keen and talented pupil.

He doubled back towards the Institute.

The quarter-mile driveway ended in a half-circle of asphalt in front of the building. There was room for three cars. The fourth was parked behind.

Blue used the hedges to cover his approach. When he stopped, he was fifteen yards away from the target. The rearmost car was an old Dodge—big engine, bad handling. The door was open, the driver standing beside it, a shotgun held loosely in his left hand. He was smoking. The keys were in the ignition. Sloppy.

Blue let himself become part of the night as he waited for his moment, his body maintaining a preternatural stillness. He waited for his cue.

Two minutes after taking position, it came. A shout from inside the house, the simultaneous crackle of four radios, each man listening to the report from their colleagues. The main cop waved over one of his friends and they headed in a direction of the north-west corner and Blue's escape route.

Two hostiles remained. When the uniformed cop disappeared around the corner of the building, Blue struck. He didn't waste energy on subtlety. He crossed the gap fast, building speed, his body low. The man turned. Blue's shoulder cracked two of the man's ribs as he barrelled into his side. The hostile went down hard. Jimmy didn't stop to look. He was already behind the wheel, twisting the key, throwing the shift into reverse, and stamping on the accelerator.

The Dodge shot backwards, and he twisted the wheel, throwing the gear shift into drive, the engine howling at the demands he put on it. Gravel spat back towards the building as he accelerated away, spraying the remaining pursuer with tiny stones. When the wheels stopped spinning on the gravel and bit the surface beneath, the resulting burst of speed slammed the driver's door shut. He pulled the seat belt across and clicked it home, then checked the mirror again. The hostile reached for his radio. No doubt warning his colleagues at the main gate.

The speedo's needle passed fifty as the Dodge crested the hill. Jimmy sang over the music the eight cylinders made.

"Well what is this that I can't see
With icy hands takin' hold of me
Well I am Death, none can excel
I'll open the door to Heaven and Hell"

A pickup truck and a van blocked the main gate. Their drivers crouched behind open doors, weapons ready. Blue stood no chance of getting through, particularly as the van driver held a semi-automatic weapon. Even if he survived the hail of bullets, hitting two vehicles head-on would push a thousand pounds of engine through the footwell and out of the back of the car, taking Blue with it. They'd be scraping bits of him off the driveway for days.

Luckily, he didn't intend leaving via the main gates.

These boys were professionals. They didn't waste bullets while he was out of range, and they didn't break position, even with the Dodge barrelling towards them at close to seventy miles per hour. When Jimmy picked his spot, yanked the steering wheel right, and left the drive, racing across the manicured lawn, they responded quickly. Both men were inside their vehicles and on the move in under four seconds. Too late to stop him.

He'd checked locally available public records for the Rothwell Institute, and checked the last time they replaced the fence. Over two decades ago, with eight-foot wooden panels. The Dodge would tear through them like cardboard.

The ground sloped upwards briefly before continuing to drop towards the city, so Blue didn't see the fence until it was too late. Weeks old, by the look of it, its metal panels sparkling in the moonlight. Not yet in the planning records. Unlucky. He had time to pump the brake twice, scrubbing perhaps twenty miles an hour from his speed, and he jerked the wheel, prompting the car into a slide. This spread the impact across the passenger side of the car when he hit the fence. The corner of the car crumpled in an explosion of glass and metal. The suspension, compressed beyond endurance, gave way. The Dodge pivoted, its rear now smacking the fence, and—for a moment—Blue thought he would have a chance to get away on foot. But a ditch caused the front corner to dip and, as the passenger side crumpled, the car flipped forty-five degrees, coming to rest with the roof pushed against the fence, the driver's-side wheels spinning as the engine coughed out its last breath.

Blue was only dazed for a second, hanging from the seat belt. He tried the door handle, but the roof had wedged it shut, and he couldn't exert enough pressure to move it. Instead, he leaned back against the seatbelt, brought his left leg up to the window and kicked, hard. On his second attempt, the window gave way. Blue slipped a knife from his ankle sheath, swivelled to brace his right foot against the steering column, and cut through the belt. As soon as he was free, he climbed through the open window and dropped to the ground.

Two sets of headlights lit him up like a karaoke singer on Saturday night. The armed men were silhouettes, but one of them put a few rounds into the undercarriage of the Dodge to make his point.

"Lose the knife, asshole. And, if you're carrying, take your gun out nice and easy, and drop it on the ground. We're not supposed to kill you, but no one said nothing about shooting you in the legs. Show's over. You're coming with us."

Chapter Thirty-One

JIMMY BLUE'S email pinged into Patrice Martino's inbox at one a.m. The two-hour time difference between New Mexico and New York State meant Martino was asleep. Genuine sleep, too, rather than a drunken stupor.

Next morning, Martino made himself breakfast at seven-fifteen, after a twenty-five minute jog along the river. Martino hated running. He glared in disbelief at the pairs of joggers who passed him, chatting as easily as if they were sitting on a bench, rather than putting their limbs and respiratory system through hell. Martino never attempted conversation during exercise. On a good day, he might manage a one-syllable answer, especially if the question was, "Enjoying yourself?" If his mood was particularly bleak, he might answer that question with two words.

He downed a glass of fresh orange juice, flipped the switch on the coffee maker, and stood at the counter, eating oatmeal straight out of the pan.

Shortly after returning from North Carolina, five months earlier, Martino had given himself a long look in the mirror after stepping out of the shower. His pallor was grey, his body sagging and paunchy, his eyes red-rimmed. Not a great look, and one he could do something about.

That day in the bathroom proved to be a turning point. And Hannah's unfeigned delight when she visited—"Wow, Dad, what happened to you? Had some work done?"— only reinforced his decision.

Letting go of his obsessive pursuit of the gang behind the attacks on small American towns over the last eight years had been good for his health; physically, and mentally.

Five minutes of admin, then a second pass of a book review for a Canadian magazine. Emails first. After deleting spam and marketing, nine emails remained, three of them interesting. One from Hannah, which he saved until last as a treat. One from his agent.

But the email that jumped out, he didn't want to open. The subject line read *Lydia Garcia*. The only witness to the first Firestarter attack in New Mexico. A traumatised and injured seven-year-old, who never recovered from what she heard and saw. A witness who ended up institutionalised, unable to speak. Martino didn't recognise the sender—*Darkman_808*.

He hovered over the delete button.

Martino rubbed his eyes with the backs of his hands and sighed. *Who the hell am I trying to kid?*

He read the email.

I'm in Albuquerque. Listen to the recording. Your cop theory is right. Find the link. Email me.

Underneath the text, a cell phone number and an audio file.

Martino took some deep breaths. Since Tom Kincaid broke into his apartment and stole his research, he'd jumped at every phone call, every knock at the door. His sleep suffered, and Hannah became increasingly annoyed by the amount of times her father checked on her. Kincaid was smart, capable of violence, and secretive. Martino thought a little paranoia was justified.

And now this. When Martino heard nothing more from Kincaid, he assumed he'd reached the same conclusion as Martino: that the gang made too few mistakes to be caught. There were no leads. Nowhere to start.

Martino clicked on the audio file and listened through the small speakers on either side of his screen. Then he plugged in his headphones and listened again. He took no notes, sitting with eyes closed, hardly daring to believe it was true.

The initial part of the recording featured Kincaid himself, speaking in the halting fashion Sheriff's Deputy Paul Geary described: stammering, hesitant, struggling to string together a full sentence. It didn't sound like an act. But what he spoke about made Martino regret his vow to reduce alcohol consumption to one evening a week. Second time around, he skipped the first part of the recording. Kincaid's testimony—as shocking and fascinating as it was—could wait for another day. He turned up the volume and listened to Lydia again.

He didn't question the veracity of the recording for a second. He had never heard her voice, of course. Lydia Garcia hadn't spoken for eight years. But this was her. He felt the truth of it in his writer's heart. What she described matched the police reports in Martino's folder from when he first researched the attacks. More than that, it was the way she spoke, as if it had happened a week ago, the terrified little girl still close to the surface.

When he took off his headphones, Martino's face was wet with tears. He went to the window and watched the river slide by. He paced his apartment for half an hour, his state of mind moving from grief and horror, to a dull anger which sharpened minute by minute.

Lydia Garcia had identified Sheriff Donnelly, Eagle Springs' local cop. A voice on a phone, feeding information to the gang as they stole from, then killed, her parents. A police officer. A public servant sworn to serve and protect the residents of Eagle Spring. He betrayed them all.

When he returned to his desk, Martino considered his options. He could give the recording straight to the FBI, but that brought its own problems. Sky Pimm would point out that the voice on the recording could be anyone.

Unless, of course, Lydia Garcia was still talking.

Martino picked up the phone. He'd been to the Rothwell Institute once himself, two-and-a-half years earlier, and looked into the eyes of the teenage girl who had seemed so distant from reality, she existed in a parallel universe.

He opened the Albuquerque notes, found the name he needed.

A distracted receptionist at the Institute treated him with the usual suspicion, before transferring his call to the senior consultant.

"Mr Aldis? Not sure if you'll remember me, but—"

"Of course, of course. You visited Lydia a few years back. I've been waiting for your book. Did I miss it?"

"Still a work in progress. Has Lydia's condition changed in any way? Has she spoken?"

"As I think I promised, Mr Martino, I'd let you know if that happened. There is very little chance of Lydia ever speaking. Her trauma runs too deep. I'm sorry."

"When did you last see her?"

"An hour ago. I checked every patient this morning, as there was an incident last night."

"An incident?" Martino pressed the phone closer to his

ear. After the trick Kincaid pulled at the Asheville hotel bar, he assumed the man could get in and out of a private hospital easily enough. "What happened?"

"An intruder. Never happened before."

"Do you know why he was there?"

"No. He disturbed a patient on the third floor as he left, but nothing has been stolen, and no other patients reported seeing anyone. I've instigated a review of our security procedures."

Martino called the Albuquerque Sheriff's department next. Used his journalistic credentials to prise a little information out of the brusque young man who answered the phone. Yes, an incident occurred at the Rothwell Institute the previous evening. Yes, an officer responded. No, the perpetrator was not in custody, as he escaped during his transfer to the station. A press release would follow, but the Albuquerque police department was confident they would catch the man quickly.

Martino ended the call and stared towards the window. Tom Kincaid wasn't the enemy. He'd been doing the legwork while Martino hid in Rochester, writing restaurant reviews.

Kincaid had found the key to unlock the identity of the Firestarters.

Chapter Thirty-Two

THERE WERE TWO OF THEM. They came in the night, after leaving him to sweat for twenty hours. They'd cuffed his ankles, and locked his left wrist to a heavy iron wall bracket, so all Blue could do was to take the beating.

The two men concentrated on his torso, arms, and legs, working him for about ten minutes, landing heavy blows that caused pain, but did no permanent damage. They used their feet, breathing heavily while they worked. They talked about sport, and one of them complained his girlfriend didn't like him watching football.

Blue did what he could to minimise the damage. He kept moving, as if trying to escape the blows raining down on him, but that wasn't his intention. Torn skin, muscle and tissue damage—they would repair themselves, given time, and they wouldn't slow him down. But he wanted to avoid broken bones, so he twisted and turned, making sure their boots never hit the same spot twice.

He held on for a long time before feigning unconsciousness. Too soon, and they'd guess he was faking.

They left him slumped on the floor in the dark, double-locking a heavy door behind them.

Ignoring the agony, Jimmy stretched out his limbs, testing his range of motion, checking for damage. It was all superficial, if painful. His body would be a Picasso of bruises for a week or two, but he'd ignore the pain until his body repaired itself. He'd done it before.

His best recourse was sleep. Give his body time to recuperate. Some people might struggle to nap after a savage beating. Blue had no such problem.

Three hours later, Blue opened his eyes, lying on his side on the concrete floor. The room had no windows, but light crept in around the edges of a large rectangle. He picked out some details. A pool table. Shelves on both walls. On the left side of the room, the shelves held a mixture of home improvement supplies—bags of cement, spades, a spirit level, toolboxes. Hammers, saws, and drills hung from hooks on the wall. On the right-hand side, sporting equipment. A dusty football, a couple of baseball mitts, balls, and bats. The most prized items, judging by their condition, were a gleaming set of golf clubs.

Next to the pool table, an indoor putting practice set showed signs of regular use, a golf ball resting in the plastic cup. There were more golf balls scattered around the space.

Blue pushed himself up into a sitting position. Not the easiest manoeuvre with his left hand chained behind him. His leg cuffs were uncomfortable. Not so tight he couldn't feel his feet, but enough that they fizzed with pins and needles.

A few hours of sleep had left his arms numb, so he waggled his fingers, rotated his wrists, flexed the muscles in his forearms, biceps, and triceps. Shrugging his shoulders and rolling his neck, he noted the dull, pulsing ache at the back of his skull. They'd hit him pretty hard.

He was in a garage. A garage alongside a single-level house, twelve to fifteen miles outside of Albuquerque.

He'd been in the back of the van for the journey, so Blue didn't know if they travelled north, east, south, or west. When the two men had opened the van's rear doors, guns drawn, beckoning him out, he'd tried to take in as much information as possible about his surroundings. Neither of his captors seemed concerned that he might describe the house later. Not a good sign. It meant they didn't believe their guest would live long enough for it to matter.

After his initial capture, Jimmy assumed he'd be delivered to the nearest police department. He reassessed this when the van left the city streets for quieter roads. Despite the cop at the institute, Blue wasn't being arrested. This was something else.

After he stepped out of the van, the younger thug had delivered a heavy blow to the back of Blue's head. Jimmy drifted in and out of consciousness while they trussed him up and cuffed him, meaning he learned little about his captors. But he recognised the type. These guys didn't look like cops. More likely local muscle, organised crime, enforcers. The Albuquerque cop had poor taste in friends.

The beating had been workmanlike, certainly for the older one, who seemed bored. They were doing a job.

Blue swallowed. His mouth and throat were dry. There was a plastic bottle of water on the shelf. He reached over with his free hand, taking three greedy swallows.

He reviewed the previous evening's events. He'd bypassed the Rothwell Institute's alarm system, so the cop and his crew were alerted some other way. Blue spent fifty minutes in Lydia Garcia's room, and they arrived while he was still there. Conclusion: her room was bugged. The Firestarters. They were smart. Despite knowing she'd survived, they didn't kill Lydia: why draw the heat, why risk leaving any clues that might lead back to them? Even if Lydia recovered, there was a good chance she'd remember nothing about that night in Eagle Springs.

But the response came fast when she started talking, so they must have prepared a contingency.

All of which meant they were going to kill him soon. The routine came straight out of *Henchperson 101*. A first beating to soften him up, so he would talk during the second beating. They would employ some basic but effective torture methods next time. After which they'd shoot him, dump the body into some hole in the desert, and go back to moaning about their love lives and golf swings.

Chapter Thirty-Three

RAMIRO WAS asleep when his phone rang, the vibrations rattling his gold chains on the glass table beside the bed. He'd tossed back a few cold ones when he got home after he and Johnny whaled on bandana guy. Funny. The thrill never really kicked in at the time. It was always an hour or two later that his blood hummed, and his hands shook. A beer or two meant he wouldn't be awake all night, reliving the choicest impacts of bat on flesh, the most satisfying grunts of pain from the man on the garage floor.

On the five occasions Ramiro had killed someone, this delayed response had been even longer. First time, it took him by surprise, kicking in at four in the morning, six hours after he'd stuck a hunting knife in Manuel Alonso's heart. Rita had been over that night, and when the adrenaline ripped through his body, Ramiro hadn't stopped to ask before flipping her on her front, grabbing her ponytail in his fist, and taking what he needed.

Rita wasn't his girlfriend now.

He picked up the phone. It was the boss.

"Hey, Andy. Yeah, yeah. No problem. What do you need?"

Ramiro smiled, scratching his belly. "Sure. That's pretty generous. Of course. I'll call Johnny now. I'll let you know when it's done."

He checked the chunky watch on the table. 09:10. Time for pop tarts and coffee. Bandana guy would be dead before lunch, and he and Johnny would have twenty large to split between them. An easy morning's work.

He called Johnny. "Get over here in a half-hour. There's five grand in it for you."

Ramiro was pouring his second cup of coffee when the van pulled up.

Ramiro wasn't sure how old Johnny was. Twenty-six? Thirty-nine? The kid had one of those faces. He had all of his hair and good skin. The girls liked him, even the nice ones. Gangster groupies gravitated to Ramiro, so he played on his image. Chains, rings, gold watch, ink on his neck—it all sent a message. The women who let Ramiro buy them a drink looked past his flattened nose, small eyes, and barely existent neck. Ramiro was ugly, but dangerous, which was the best kind of ugly. The women who wanted him didn't complain about being slapped around a little.

With his pretty looks, Johnny could have been a movie star, but he didn't have the aptitude. Johnny got off on violence. When he wasn't dishing it out, he was thinking about it. He tried not to let it show, but Ramiro noticed the little things. The way Johnny wet his lips when he held a knife, the way his nostrils flared and his pupils dilated when he shot someone. When Johnny strangled Giorgio Kendra's mistress, he had a boner the whole time. Didn't even try to hide it, rubbing up against her as she gasped, cried, and went still.

"Five grand." Johnny shook his head, swinging the van onto the desert road. "Shoulda negotiated."

"You're looking at it wrong, Johnny. We chained this guy up in a fucking garage. We won't break a sweat. Five grand ain't bad at all."

"Maybe." Johnny liked to argue. Ramiro was the senior partner, but Johnny didn't like anyone to take advantage of him. Naturally, Ramiro took advantage whenever possible. That was how things worked.

When they reached the house, they headed straight to the kitchen and listened at the door leading to the garage. Nothing. Ramiro flicked on the light, took a pace back, and drew his gun. Johnny turned both keys and pulled the door open.

"You gotta be shitting me." Ramiro used his gun to point inside.

Johnny drew his own gun and entered the garage first.

Bandana guy lay where they left him—on his side, legs drawn up to his chest to avoid the baseball bats.

No need for any wet work today. Nature had beaten them to it. Bandana guy's pallor was an unnatural grey. Vomit, streaked with blood, had pooled under his sagging head, and dried in clumps around his mouth. He wasn't breathing.

Johnny took a step closer. Ramiro hung back, gun still drawn. "Check his pulse."

Johnny spread his palms and raised his trimmed eyebrows. "I look like a fucking nurse to you, Ramiro?"

Ramiro shrugged. "Just make sure he ain't faking."

Johnny put his foot on bandana guy's hip and pushed. The body rocked. "He's not breathing. If he's faking, you better get the Oscar committee on the line."

"Just take his pulse, Johnny."

Johnny holstered his gun, squatted alongside the body.

Pushed the handcuff away from the body's wrist and rested his fingers on the veins. He waited half a minute before standing up.

"No pulse," he said.

"Good," replied Ramiro. "This is good. We bury this guy, and if even if someone finds him, he died of natural causes. They probably won't even bother investigating."

"Sure." Johnny smiled. "The cops will figure this guy walked into the desert and buried himself?"

"Smart ass. I'll go move the van. You drag him to the door."

Johnny looked pained. He tapped his shoulder. "Look, man. I pulled a muscle when we were smacking this guy around. I'll get the van."

Johnny liked to challenge Ramiro's authority. Ramiro thought of the fifteen grand he'd pick up later. He could afford to be magnanimous. "Sure," he said. "Why not?"

When Johnny left, Ramiro freed the man's ankles, unlocked the handcuffs, and left them dangling from the shelf. He rolled the corpse onto its back and put his hands under the armpits.

"Jesus. How much do you fucking weigh, pal?"

The corpse opened his eyes and punched Ramiro under his right ear.

Chapter Thirty-Four

JIMMY BLUE HAD no illusions about the limits of his body. He had a genetic head start: Tom's father would have made the English rugby squad if not for a knee injury, and Irene Lewis had been a tough, wiry woman. But Blue pushed an already powerful body as hard as any Olympic athlete. Harder, in fact. Athletes were specialists, their bodies reflecting their chosen discipline. Swimmers were broad, hammer-throwers heavy, long-distance runners lithe. Blue was an all-rounder. He could run a marathon, but he would finish it an hour behind the winner. The difference was, at the finish line, Blue could still beat the crap out of a heavyweight boxer.

More important than his fitness and strength was the dispassionate mental focus that made Blue unique. Jimmy didn't consider himself human. This otherness gave him a clarity that kept him a step or two ahead of his enemies—who thought along predictable lines, however innovative they considered themselves to be. Blue could anticipate an opponent's next move seconds into a fistfight. He fought without errors, analysing every feint, every dodge, every punch and kick. But this advantage extended beyond physical conflict. It enabled him to reason his way through problems such as the one in the New Mexico garage.

After the two thugs left, Jimmy analysed potential strategies, examining likely outcomes. As he thought, he worked through some yoga and Pilates exercises. The cuffs on his ankles and his left wrist prevented him from completing the full set, but careful stretches kept his muscles warm, preventing cramp. A middle rib on his left side was cracked. He breathed from his diaphragm to ameliorate the pain.

By the time he finished his routine, Blue had settled on a plan.

He just had to die.

Cicadas chirped their endless song outside, and something howled and yapped in the distance. Blue crawled as far as the limits of the handcuff would allow. His mind held a perfect representation of the surrounding space—the shelves, golf clubs, and pool table, the location of every item on the dusty floor. Blue reached out, his cracked rib howling its dissent. He stretched half an inch more, unable to stop himself hissing in pain, and placed his forefinger on top of a golf ball, rolling it towards himself. He slid it under his T-shirt into his armpit.

That was step one of three. Step two was easier. He dragged his hand along the floor and rubbed the detritus into his face and neck. The concrete dust was gritty and dry, making his skin convincingly corpse-like.

Stage three would have been familiar to any teenage binge drinker. Blue stuck his fingers down his throat, gagged, and retched. He put his fingers in the acidic puddle and transferred some to his face—smearing it on either side of his mouth and down his chin.

Then he waited.

Jimmy heard the pickup truck minutes before it reached the house. He lay his head next to the pool of vomit, and slowed his breathing, putting himself into a light trance. An average person can hold their breath for between forty-five seconds and a minute. Blue could manage nine minutes. He had once held his breath for over eleven minutes, but he hadn't had a broken rib then. Even allowing for his injuries, he thought he could manage five minutes. That should be enough.

He hyperventilated when the van pulled up outside. His ribs sent increasingly urgent messages to his brain demanding he stop. When his lungs were full, he forced in another half dozen tiny gulps of air, taking the final one when the key turned in the door. At the same moment, he positioned his right arm close to his side, the golf ball a hard lump in his armpit. He squeezed it into place, stopping the blood from pumping into his limb.

The two thugs weren't immediately convinced, but his lack of a pulse clinched it. One returned to the van, while the other unlocked his handcuff.

The man didn't have time to react before Blue's fist caught him. The back of the thug's head broke his fall, and the resulting crack of skull on concrete echoed around the garage.

Henchman number one wouldn't bother anyone for a while.

Blue relieved his erstwhile captor of his gun. Walked to the front of the garage. Listened to the van reverse towards him, then the crunch of boots as henchman two approached. Blue pressed the garage door button and dropped to the floor, pistol gripped in both hands.

As the slit of light grew wider, he saw steel-capped boots, blue jeans, and the wheels and fender of the van beyond. When Blue saw the man's knees, he shot both of them. The scream was high-pitched and loud as the hostile fell backwards in a cloud of blood and bone. Blue stood up and shot the man twice more in the chest. He walked back to henchman one and put a bullet through his head. A cursory search of the body and he had the keys to unlock the cuff on his ankles.

Blue used a rag from the golf bag to wipe the cuffs clean, along with everything he had touched. He went out front to relieve henchman two of his weapon. They both favoured the same handgun—a Sig Sauer nine millimetre, easy to tuck into a pocket.

Crouching next to the corpse, Blue fired six rounds back into the garage, two of them hitting the first body. After wiping the gun, he placed it in the second man's hand.

Back in the garage, he emptied henchman one's clip through the open garage door. He wiped the second gun, leaving it on the floor close to the first body. Two lowlifes fought and killed each other. No need for the cops to look for anyone else.

A quick search of a house yielded little of interest. One bedroom contained a bed, observed by three concealed video cameras. He found his wallet and new ID card in the kitchen, along with a well-stocked fridge, if you liked beer and microwave food. He'd need new ID soon.

He microwaved a frozen pizza, carried it outside on a plate with a litre bottle of water tucked under his arm. Ate it looking out at the desert, then washed the plate, and replaced it in on the shelf.

The Albuquerque thugs' only mistake was not killing him immediately. Whoever bugged Lydia Garcia's room hoped their paid muscle would beat some information out of Jimmy before ending him.

Blue thought about Martino's extensive research, his

commitment to uncovering the truth. Once the writer had listened to Lydia's recording, he would surely put every effort into finding the connection between the cops in each burned town. Jimmy ha*d r*ead Martino's draft book. He wanted justice. But Martino's version of justice meant— depending on the State which tried the Firestarter case— the death penalty, or life in prison. Blue didn't want anyone going to prison. They didn't deserve to live.

He left the house. His broken ribs and bruised body became irrelevant. A distant noise, a radio turned low. The darkness lifted him.

Jimmy Blue is coming for you.

Blue climbed into the van. He'd dump it, steal something anonymous.

Next stop, North Carolina, and Sheriff's Deputy Paul Geary.

Chapter Thirty-Five

MARTINO MADE himself a pot of coffee and paced while he drank it. After months with the Firestarters folder unopened on his hard drive, the book untouched, today had left him reeling. He knew himself too well. No point pretending he wasn't about to renew his obsession with the gang who'd pillaged their way across America.

He called Agent Salton. After exchanging minimal greetings, he got to the point.

"Paul Geary. Anything new on him? He still a cop?"

"I can check. I'll call you back. Anything specific you're looking for?"

"Yes. The records of the phone calls he made at Lake Norman."

Martino made a second pot, standing in front of the stove until the liquid bubbled over and hissed. He turned the heat off. After a few minutes, he refilled his cup, looked at it until it went cold, then poured it down the sink and resumed his pacing.

His phone rang.

"Salton?"

"Guess again."

"Ah."

"Yes."

He hadn't spoken to Associate Deputy Director Sky Pimm since a semi-drunken call he made to her Easter weekend. His cheeks reddened at the memory. The mostly one-sided conversation had gone much better in his head —after several very large drinks—than it did in reality. When, next morning, he reviewed the key points, he winced.

—*Sky. We went to bed, and it was good. So we should go to bed again. Doesn't have to be your bed. I have a bed. And a shower. Chairs, too. It's an apartment, Sky. You'd like it.*

—*It's very late, Patrice, and I have an early flight.*

—*Thing is, how often do people like us meet someone, y'know, who, well, who....?*

—*Who is intelligible? You're drunk, Patrice. Good night.*

He had sent a contrite email the following day, but Sky hadn't responded. "You got my email?"

"Yes. I accept your apology, Patrice, but this isn't a social call. Agent Salton reached out. I thought you'd dropped the Firestarters book."

"I put it aside for a while."

"So what's changed? We have no new information. Is there something you want to share?"

Well, yes. An audio clip from a wanted felon claiming to contain the voice of Lydia Garcia, a young woman who hadn't spoken for eight years. He knew what Sky would say. He didn't want to look incompetent, as well as love-sick and desperate.

"I'm just tying up loose ends, Sky. Making sure I didn't miss anything."

"Why focus on the cop? We've been down that route. The gang strikes when the main law enforcement officer is away. It's highly likely an informer tells them the best time to strike. Is the local cop the informer? We've checked for any financial transactions before or after the attacks. Nothing. Every cop has an exemplary record. They are all well thought of. They had no motive to betray their towns. Patrice, we are the Federal Bureau of Investigation. We did our job. We investigated them. The local cops did not help a gang of criminals to murder their neighbours and burn down their homes. It's a dead end."

And that, thought Martino, was a lecture.

"OK, I get it. But—"

"But what? But Pulitzer-shortlisted writer Patrice Martino knows better than dozens of FBI agents and five state police departments? Must be tough to possess such prodigious talents."

"Come on, Sky, don't be like that. I'm just trying to stop these—"

"And we're not? *I'm* not? Jesus, Patrice. You've lost your way. Drop this. And don't waste my agents' time again. Are we clear?"

"We're clear." He looked out across the Genesee River towards the east side of Rochester and Upper Falls. "Sky? Just one more thing. I promise. Did Salton get what I asked for?"

He held his breath. She didn't end the call. But her tone was icy.

"Yes. I have it in front of me. A record of all the calls made from Sheriff Deputy Paul Geary's cell during his stay at Lake Norman."

Martino still wasn't breathing. Sky let him hang for a couple of seconds.

"He made a two-minute call to his Pike Point office when he arrived at the lake."

"And?"

"And that was the only call he made the entire trip. Don't bother me again, Patrice."

She hung up.

Martino placed his phone on the counter. What had Norman Deacon said about Geary? That he didn't fish much, and spent a good deal of time on the phone. Geary's registered cell phone had only made one call. So he'd used a burner. Why would a police officer need a burner?

He considered calling Sky back. Put his finger on the *redial* button. But it wasn't enough. Not yet. He needed more. He needed evidence of the connection between the cops. If he could prove they knew each other, she'd take it seriously. She'd have to.

Martino poured a glass of water and sat down at his computer. An email from Agent Salton confirmed Geary's phone record, along with some new information. Sheriff's Deputy Paul Geary had taken compassionate leave a month after the Pike Point attack. After three months, he'd asked for an extension of that leave. He hadn't shared his current whereabouts with the police department.

Martino stared at his list of the five law enforcement officers who were absent while their towns burned.

Ed Donnelly, Eagle Springs, New Mexico

Ryan Leto, Whitney Bluff, Maine

Hennie Castello, Powder Creek, Oregon

Jane(y) Holden (deceased), Greenhaven, Alaska

Paul Geary, Pike Point, North Carolina

The rest of the day was likely a long, tedious internet search. This time he'd go back further, look for links in their teens. If nothing emerged, Martino planned to turn up on the doorsteps of the surviving cops, their families, and friends, asking questions, hoping to shake something loose.

If the voice on the recording really was Lydia Garcia's, he'd be deliberately provoking multiple murderers. He'd need to be cautious. Not give them any hint of his true intent. Tread carefully.

He hoped Google would come through.

Chapter Thirty-Six

JIMMY BLUE PLANNED to visit Paul Geary and beat the shit out of him until he talked. As plans went, it was simple and direct. Often the best way.

First, though, he needed a vehicle that didn't belong to a criminal connected to the Albuquerque Police Department. He also needed a phone, a laptop, and some cash. Fortunately, the owner of the van—one Ramiro Spinoz, according to the unopened bills stuffed in the glove box— had programmed his home address into the GPS. Blue shook his head in mild disbelief as he drove through the desert back to the Albuquerque suburbs. You just couldn't get the thugs these days.

The van, grey and anonymous, attracted no attention, but Blue hadn't survived this long by taking unnecessary risks. He parked a quarter mile from the Spinoz residence.

Jimmy walked past the property and circled around the rear before returning to the van. No one was watching the single-storey house, and there were no signs of movement within.

Blue opened the van's rear doors. Empty apart from a

couple of boxes. He unhooked a baseball cap from the rear-view mirror and tucked a box under his arm. Walked back to the house. Rang the doorbell. No answer. Blue let himself in with the house key on the van's key chain.

He searched the house. Ramiro, an inconvenience while alive, made up for it in death. A big man who favoured loose clothing—common among those who carry concealed weapons—Ramiro had closets full of clothes to replace Blue's vomit-stained outfit. He took a quick shower, then dressed in sweatpants, a T-shirt, and a lightweight army-green jacket.

Blue found six thousand dollars in cash stuffed in a gym bag, along with a snub-nosed Beretta with packets of ammo. Ramiro owned a small laptop, the password for which he'd written on a scrap of paper in his bedside drawer beside a roll of cash.

Blue left by the back door, the laptop and cash in the gym bag, the Beretta in his jacket pocket.

Using the van again was a calculated risk. Ninety minutes had passed since he killed the two men in the garage. He dumped the vehicle on a side street three blocks from a used car dealership on the edge of town. He paid four thousand dollars cash for a ten-year-old Mustang worth half that, for which the dealer agreed to lose the paperwork.

Blue visited the airport next, specifically the long-term parking lot. He parked opposite a family unloading enough luggage for a two-week vacation. When they left, he traded their number plates for the Mustang's. He made one last stop at an out-of-town mall for a burner phone and a roadmap.

He used the stolen laptop to connect to the Wi-Fi, and sent a coded message to his pet hacker Bolsteroni, asking him to track down Sheriff's Deputy Paul Geary.

He joined the interstate at noon, figuring it would take three long driving shifts to reach North Carolina, with two breaks for sleep. The Mustang's suspension was soft and saggy, the steering pulled to the right, but the engine farted like an angry elephant, and that was all Blue cared about. It would get him to where he needed to be. Then the Pike Point cop would give him the information he needed.

Three hours into the drive east, Blue's new burner pinged with a message. No one but Bolsteroni had the number.

your guy Geary is holed up in alabama
hes in a cabin on the blackwater river for a month
no phone no email
beer and fishing
sounds gud

Jimmy typed a new message.

Geary was a cop at Pike Point, North Carolina. What's the link between him and the cops in other towns targeted by the Firestarters?

He pulled over and checked the address Bolsteroni had sent, tracing his finger along the map. Made some rough mental calculations, and figured he would be there a few hours earlier than his estimate for Charlotte. Bright and early, Saturday morning.

He couldn't wait to see Geary's face.

Chapter Thirty-Seven

A MOMENT of serendipity unlocked the Firestarters' secret. It arrived as many such moments do: unexpectedly. It was so satisfying, so perfect. Martino repeated the steps leading to it, making sure he hadn't made a mistake.

Three-and-a-half hours earlier, he started with the most unusual name on the list of cops. Hennie Castello had been a police officer in the tiny community of Powder Creek, Oregon, an idyllic settlement on the forested edge of a state park. Martino uncovered a handful of people with the same unusual first name. A surgeon in Bolivia. A music producer in Washington. But nothing at all for Hennie Castello. So he tried Ryan Leto, who had looked after the coastal village of Whitney Bluff in Maine. This generated thousands of hits. He combined the name with other words. Ryan Leto baseball, Ryan Leto football, Ryan Leto school, Ryan Leto arrested (a bit of a long shot, considering the guy ended up as a cop). He worked down a list of possibilities. Nothing.

Martino moved to the next name: Jane Holden, the

young cop who assisted Chief Braden in Greenhaven, Alaska. Now deceased, which was one reason the corrupt cop theory never caught on. Holden had been so devastated by the destruction of Greenhaven, she had killed herself. If she was a member of the Firestarters, her suicide made no sense. And it broke the pattern. The other officers from devastated towns left the police force, moved away, most becoming loners. None had reintegrated into society. With them, it might be an act. But sticking a police revolver in your mouth and pulling the trigger? That was the real thing.

He copy/pasted Holden's name into the search box, and scrolled through the first ten pages of results.

Martino took a break every twenty-five minutes, forcing himself to stand up, walk around the room, stare out the window as the afternoon sun lit the river.

He checked his watch. Three-twenty. The hinterland between coffee and bourbon, neither of which would help.

Martino paced instead. Pacing helped. Something about getting the body moving, the blood flowing. Instead of focusing on the task, he indulged his mental whims, observing his mind's tangents without censure or judgment. Predictably, his thoughts turned to his daughter. Hannah, enjoying the success of their savage movie reviews, had turned out a few solo efforts, all good. Hannah wrote well. Martino, remembering the way Hannah reacted to every suggestion he made during her teens, held back from giving too much encouragement. He didn't put her in touch with his agent, although he wanted to. She would find her own way. Hannah always did.

He smiled, remembering the day he found her halfway up the side of a warehouse, egged on by her friends. Hannah never turned down a dare. Martino spotted her edging along a narrow ledge, ten feet up.

At the sight of parental authority, Hannah's friends scooped up their school bags and abandoned her, giggling. Although she denied it later, Hannah was stuck. The gap between the ledge and the window frame was too far, but Hannah hadn't wanted to quit in front of her friends. Martino borrowed a ladder from a neighbouring store. Hannah climbed down, muttering darkly that she was practically an adult and shouldn't be treated this way. Martino grounded her for a week. Three days later, Hannah broke her left leg in two places, trying to climb the outside of the school gym.

The write-up in the school newspaper—not the official one handed out to parents, but a cheaply printed sheet put together by students—featured the headline *Spidergirl Breaks Leg In Death Plunge*. A sensationalist and inaccurate headline, but Hannah liked it. After she moved out, Martino found it tucked between the pages of a Stephen King novel.

He stopped pacing. An accident. Some accidents got reported in the news.

He typed Jane Holden's name and added the word 'accident'. Filtered the results by years, concentrating on anything picked up before she joined the police force.

And there it was. Serendipity. Oh, happy day.

Local Students Pulled Out Of Car Wreck On Ventura Freeway.

Four students from Woodbank High School were treated for their injuries after the car they were traveling in crashed near Sherman Oaks. None of the students were seriously injured, but the driver, Connor Pasternak, was kept in hospital overnight with a suspected concussion.

There wasn't much else, just a namecheck of the students involved. Two were familiar: Jane Holden and Paul Geary.

They attended the same high school in Los Angeles.

This was it. Martino knew it. He recognised the signs, the rare and welcome sensation of supposition and speculation making the leap into the world of facts and truth.

He had them.

Chapter Thirty-Eight

DOROTHY REES–"PLEASE call me Dorothy, dear. Mrs Rees makes me feel like I'm back in a classroom"—hadn't made it far out of Van Nuys after retiring. The cab from Los Angeles Airport had dropped Martino in front of a tidy bungalow on a well-mannered street lined with mature trees. The birdsong nearly drowned out the sirens to the north.

"Dorothy, yes, of course. And you must call me Patrice."

Dorothy, the retired principal of nearby Woodland High School, stood five feet in her stockinged feet, and her dark skin stretched across angular features, which made her eyes appear unnaturally large. Her face was lined and her hair grey, and she carried herself with old-fashioned grace and dignity. When she opened the door, Martino wondered how this diminutive figure could have run one of the largest high schools in Los Angeles. Five minutes in her company showed him how. Dorothy had a way of commanding respect without uttering a word. And she behaved as if there was no one she would rather speak to, nowhere she would rather be.

She brought two glasses and a jug of iced tea. She motioned Martino to sit down, folded her bony hands, and gave him an encouraging smile.

"How can I help you, Patrice?"

He put his hat on the chair next to him.

"As I explained on the phone, Miss Rees—sorry, Dorothy—I'm a writer. I'm working on a piece about police officers who survived trauma. How they cope, what strategies they use. I researched their childhoods. That's when I discovered something surprising."

Dorothy took a sip of tea and raised her eyebrows. "Do tell."

Martino flicked through the pages of his notebook. "Two of the police officers attended Woodland High School. You were their principal."

"Oh, my." Dorothy smiled more broadly. "How exciting. And you hoped I might remember them? Might supply an anecdote or two?"

Martino returned the smile. "Something like that, yes. They would have left the school in 2006 or 2007. Jane Holden and Paul Geary."

He placed the notebook on the table facing her, but Dorothy didn't look at the names. She closed her eyes.

Martino had caught the earliest flight that morning. He was hungry, tired, and probably beginning to smell. He had hardly slept, because he was on the verge of exposing the Firestarters. Of stopping them. He bit his lip as he waited for Dorothy to speak.

"When I took charge of Woodland High, the gang situation in Los Angeles was at its worst. And our school was in the middle of it."

He sipped his tea. The old lady evidently intended to

provide some background colour before getting to the point.

"Running any school is tough. Running Woodland High is a vocation. To win over any of those students, they had to trust me, and I them. I made honesty the keystone of my school. And, believe me, every student knew better than to lie to me. I could sniff out a falsehood in a second. So I would prefer it if you stop lying to me."

For a moment, he thought he'd misheard. Martino's cheeks reddened.

"Ma'am?" he croaked.

Dorothy Rees fixed him with a look, pinning him like a Victorian butterfly.

"I will not stand for dishonesty, Mr Martino. When you called, I did a little research of my own. The internet is an amazing resource, is it not? Your credentials are impressive, as is your writing, although—judging by the small sample I read—you overuse the semicolon."

"Um."

"But when I examined a list of your published work, some rather obvious questions came to mind."

"They, er, did?"

"Indeed. The first was why a writer who uncovers wrongdoing and corruption on a grand scale is writing about police officers with trauma."

"I write about a broad range of subjects, Mrs Rees." This, at least, wasn't a lie.

Dorothy sighed. Martino became acutely aware of his unshaven face and rumpled suit; his unkempt hair no longer hidden beneath his hat.

"Whatever you really want from me, it's urgent enough for you to skip a night's sleep, get on a red-eye, and come straight to my house from the airport. You casually place a list of names in my line of sight, hoping to provoke a reaction. Am I making sense?"

"Yes, ma'am. I'm sorry. I misjudged you."

"You're not the first. Now start again, Patrice. And this time, no horseshit."

Point made, she picked up the jug. "More iced tea?"

"Thank you. Mrs Rees—Dorothy—I can't tell you everything. But I promise to cut the, er, horseshit."

"Thank you. That's all I ask."

He admitted he was researching a criminal gang made up of serving police officers. He told her this gang had stolen a great deal of money and committed a string of murders.

When he had finished, Dorothy took Martino's notebook from the table. "Thank you for your honesty. Would you excuse me for a moment?"

"Of course." Martino stood as the retired principal left the room.

A few minutes turned into fifteen. Twice, Martino crossed the door, thought better of it, and returned to his seat. He picked up his hat, passing the brim through his fingers. He made notes about the room—unfussy decor, lack of ornaments.

When she walked back in, he shot to his feet.

Dorothy carried a yearbook under one arm, and a folded newsletter headed *Woodland High School Journal*, which she opened to a page of grainy photographs and small print. She placed Martino's notebook, with the list of cops, next to it.

Then she leaned forward, uncapped a fountain pen, and added two more names.

Al Critchen

Dionne James

Martino stared at the names, then across at the photograph Dorothy's finger rested on. It showed a dark-suited man handing a pile of books to a young Hispanic woman with a shy smile. The caption read: *Surprise For School Group As Local Baptist Church Donates Bibles.*

"She was in tenth grade then, but you won't find any other pictures. That girl was camera-shy to the point of phobia. Dionne may have been the most intelligent student who ever walked the halls of Woodland High. A brilliant mind, quite brilliant. But when that photograph was taken, she'd set her sights on academic mediocrity. Her grades trended resolutely towards the average soon after puberty hit, and that's where they stayed, despite her teachers'— and my own—best efforts."

"What happened, do you think?" Although this seemed to be another tangent, Martino doubted it. He'd already badly misjudged Dorothy Rees once. He wasn't about to compound the error by asking her to get to the point.

"I can't tell you the whys and the wherefores. But I do know Dionne lied to me. And—at the time—I had my suspicions regarding her reasons. When her grades slipped, I called Dionne in. She promised she was doing her best. I knew better, but nothing could convince her to apply herself. But what she lacked in academic prowess, she made up for in piety. She started a Bible study group and did a power of good for her fellow students. So maybe I was wrong to feel the way I did."

"Which was?"

"Betrayed."

Martino scanned the room again. The oak bookshelf held a range of non-fiction titles, ranging from philosophy to houseplant care. No Bible.

He risked going back to her first name. "You're not religious, Dorothy?"

She smiled at that. "In neighbourhoods where drug

deals happen at the end of the street, and cemeteries fill up with teenagers, religion reveals itself as the opiate of the masses. Distracting flim-flam."

She leaned forward. "Probably best not to quote me on that. I guess you're wondering why I've told you all about someone who isn't on your list."

"A little, yes."

Dorothy opened the yearbook to the pages listing Woodland High's clubs and societies. She ran her finger down a page and swivelled the book on the table.

Senior Bible Study Group
Leader: Dionne James
Members: Ryan Leto, Ed Donnelly, Jane Holden, Al Critchen, Hennie Castello, Paul Geary

Two things jumped out at Martino. He addressed the first. "Bible study? They all belonged to the same Bible study group?"

"Not what you expected?"

"Not exactly, no." Dionne James was a pretty Latino girl with a ponytail and a demure smile.

"I don't suppose you have a photograph of the study group? Or separate photographs of the others?"

"No, I'm sorry, I don't. They used one of the meeting rooms every Friday evening, and they kept themselves to themselves."

"You said Dionne's grades slipped, but she became more religious. Are the two things linked?"

"Dionne is an only child, and her parents are devout. Vocal about it, too. Quick to complain about anything they considered heretical in their daughter's education. Geology, evolution, pretty much any novel written since nineteen hundred. That kind of thing. So when Dionne's schoolwork slipped, I wondered if they were to blame. It couldn't have been easy for her, being taught one theory in school, then hearing it refuted by her own parents. I admit, I hoped her stunning brain would reject the flawed circular logic trotted out by her folks. When she started the Bible group, I knew I had lost her. But even I will admit, what she did with that group was nothing short of astounding."

"Astounding? In what way?"

Dorothy tapped the list of names. "Show that list to any of her contemporaries at Woodland High, and they'll say the same. Bullies, every one of them. Gang members, truants, in and out of my office for their first few years. Bad kids."

"Bad?"

"You sound surprised. Educators can't judge children so harshly, but I'm retired, Patrice, so I can say anything I damn well like. Some kids are just born bad. And every teacher knows who they are. The school shootings we've seen in recent years? I guarantee the identity of those gun-toting idiots did not surprise their teachers. Were they shocked? Of course. Traumatised, devastated. But not surprised."

Martino remembered his glass of iced tea. He took a sip, barely tasting it.

"The kids in the Bible study group. How bad were they? Potential school shooters?"

Dorothy Rees held his eye as she nodded.

"Every one of them, apart from Dionne. A shame she wasted such intelligence, compassion, and drive on religion, but I admire the way she turned those lives around."

"You say she sought them out?"

"She did. Her teachers and I worried for her safety at first. Our scepticism turned to amazement when we saw the change in them. They stayed out of trouble. Even applied themselves to their studies. Not one drop-out, and

—for the rest of their school career—no member of that Bible study group showed up in my office again."

Dorothy frowned. "And now you tell me their transformation was temporary."

"I'm afraid it's likely, yes."

"That poor girl. Dionne brought them together, focused so much of her time and energy on changing their lives, and they've thrown her kindness in her face."

Her shoulders sagged, and—for the first time since he'd arrived—Dorothy Rees looked like an old woman.

Martino stood up, put his hat back on his head.

"Thank you for your time. I'll, er, see myself out."

He stood awkwardly, feeling much like a naughty schoolchild in the principal's office, waiting to be dismissed.

"The photographs you wanted," she said.

He waited, unsure if he should respond. Dorothy put both hands on the arms of her chair and pushed herself upright, before crossing to the window overlooking the street. When she said nothing more, Martino joined her. She pointed west through the branches of an ash tree.

"Two blocks over, take a right and you'll see the church. Dionne's father still preaches there. He and his wife live in the bungalow next door. They might have a photograph of the study group. And they can put you in touch with their daughter."

Chapter Thirty-Nine

GEORGE AND CARLA JAMES, caretakers and preachers of the Holy Light Church, welcomed Martino like a long-lost friend. Halfway through his explanation for turning up on their doorstep, they ushered him into a large kitchen, handed him a slice of chocolate cake large enough to satisfy two hungry weightlifters, and offered a bewildering selection of hot and cold drinks.

"Water's fine, thank you." The sound of the running faucet reminded his bladder of all the iced tea sloshing around inside it. "May I use your bathroom?"

George James—tall, bald, and bearded, his capacious belly preventing him from sitting close to the table—answered incoherently around a mouthful of cake.

"George!" His wife tutted affectionately. "I'm sorry, Mr Martino. First door on the left."

The bathroom was a shrine dedicated to two people: Jesus Christ, and Dionne James. Pictures of both covered the walls. The most recent photograph of Dionne showed her between her parents. She had grown into a striking woman, her long hair now cut short, her body lean, her pose assured. Her smile wasn't as broad as her parents' grins. A politician's smile, which didn't reach her eyes.

Mrs James was on the phone when he returned. "Wonderful," she said. "See you soon, honey."

She put the phone on the counter and clapped her hands. Small and skinny, she could have used one leg of her husband's trousers as a dress. The fact she never stopped moving probably accounted for her lack of middle-aged spread. She didn't cut herself a slice of cake.

"Praise be, Mr Martino. Dionne can help you. She's on her way over."

"She still lives in Los Angeles?"

"She surely does. Thank the Lord she never moved away. It's a blessing for parents to have their children close, don't you agree? Especially an only child like Dionne. She still helps out at church when she has time. I just wish she'd meet a nice young man and settle down. Young people wait too long these days. Don't you agree, Mr Martino?"

"I don't know. I married young myself."

"Well, there you go."

"I'm divorced now."

Not the most diplomatic statement, but Martino was distracted. He was on the cusp of finding the evidence that would wrap up this story and finish the Firestarters.

Carla James put a hand on the cross around her neck. "I will pray for you and your wife to reconcile."

He remembered Helen's legs around the podiatrist—the little squeaks she'd made. It had been years since she'd squeaked like that for him.

"It's unlikely," he said. "But I appreciate the sentiment."

Dionne's father steered the small-talk back to less controversial subjects, holding forth on the merits of their loving and hard-working daughter.

"She sounds like a wonderful young woman," said Martino. He added, "You obviously brought her up well."

Carla's smile returned. He might have repaired some of the damage. "That's very kind, but we can't take the credit. I thank Jesus for our daughter every day."

The tilt of her head, and the colour that rose to her cheeks, suggested Mrs James believed she shared at least some of the credit with her Lord and Saviour.

"What does Dionne do for a living?"

George answered. "Computer work. For the government. She can't really talk about it, but we know she's doing well. She works so hard. Her place is incredible, and she gets to travel, too. She's in demand. Hey, why not ask her yourself?"

George stood as the door opened, and the woman from the photograph walked in. Dionne James kissed both parents before shaking his hand. Her grip was firm, her skin cool and dry. There was that politician's smile.

"And you must be Mr Martino. Mom said you're a writer. How exciting. How can I help?"

He gave her the pitch. He was working on a piece about teens who had turned their lives around, and those who had guided and inspired them.

"And you dug up my old high school Bible study group? That's a long time ago, and it was really nothing special."

"You're being modest, Ms James."

Her parents beamed, but their daughter shook her head. "Call me Dionne, please. I'm not being modest. We met Fridays after school for a couple of hours, read the scriptures, discussed what we'd read, and ended with a prayer."

"But the students who attended were involved in gangs,

getting into trouble. After they'd been to your Bible group, they changed their lives."

She shrugged. "The credit isn't mine. I showed them the Truth,"—Martino could hear the uppercase T—"and God did the rest."

"Amen," said George, and Carla contributed, "Praise him."

Martino wasn't sure he could take much more humility.

"Well," he said, "the result was remarkable. The members of your Bible group changed their lives, dramatically. Even in their choice of careers."

"What do you mean?" Dionne's brow furrowed. "What careers?"

"Well, they all became police officers."

Her eyes widened.

"You didn't know?" asked Martino.

"No. No. I didn't. We lost touch after graduation. I emailed regularly for a while, but, over time, they stopped responding. I thought I had failed them, that they had turned away from the Lord. But now you tell me they all chose to serve their communities. It's hard to take in."

Her mother handed her a tissue and Dionne dabbed at the corner of her eyes. After bringing such positive news, Martino decided against telling her the rest and ruining her day.

"Mom mentioned photographs," she said, when she had regained her poise.

"Yes. It would be great to have pictures with the article. I don't suppose you kept any?"

This time, her smile reached all the way to her eyes, and Martino saw the resemblance to her father.

"I throw nothing away, Mr Martino. There are boxes in my loft I haven't opened for years. One of them is full of stuff from high school. And there are SD cards from an old digital camera in a drawer somewhere. I took plenty of photographs of the Bible group. If you give me your address.... Unless?"

Dionne James turned the smile on him. "Are you in a rush to leave?"

"Haven't booked my flight home yet."

"Great." Dionne got to her feet and took a car key from her purse. "No time like the present. Can I give you a ride?"

Chapter Forty

DIONNE KEPT up a constant stream of chat as she drove —the surface level small-talk certain people are naturally good at. Martino, exhaustion competing with adrenaline, tried to screen it out.

As she prattled on, Martino nodded and grunted at appropriate moments while his imagination went into over-drive. One photograph would be enough to bring the Firestarters down. One photograph of them together, before they spread out over the country like a dormant virus, waiting in their chosen neighbourhoods until ready to kill their hosts.

The car journey lasted twenty-five minutes. As they joined the traffic on East Olympic Boulevard, and rolled past liquor stores and topless bars, the part of Martino's brain not involved with feigning interest in Dionne's soliloquy or imagining the incriminating photographs, did the equivalent of tapping him on the shoulder.

She hasn't spoken about herself. Not once. Her stream of consciousness has covered her parents, their church, the shameful state of the public highways. But nothing about Dionne James. Is anyone really that *humble?*

Cynicism is the journalists' curse, but it frequently saved Martino from making an ass of himself. He brought his attention fully to the woman beside him, who signalled left, bumped across a lowered section of sidewalk, and followed the wall of a warehouse, parking behind it.

Dionne turned off the ignition and got out, stretching. She smiled at Martino. "Home, sweet home."

"You live in a warehouse?"

"I have a friend in real estate. The previous owner tried to burn it down for the insurance money. Literally picked it up in a fire sale."

Martino remembered the neon sign on the bar next door as they'd turned in. Not yet illuminated—eleven-fifteen on a Saturday morning being too early for even the most committed patrons—but it featured a huge-breasted woman in a cowboy hat beckoning drinkers inside. A warehouse next to a titty bar. Not his first guess for the home of a preacher's daughter.

"It's nicer on the inside."

Martino hoped she was right. The whole area had a run-down, semi-abandoned air that didn't fit with the smart young woman now turning the key in the lock.

Dionne pushed the door open and walked ahead. An automatic light illuminated a small hallway more like an airlock than a porch. The outer door may have boasted flaking paint and a rusty keyhole, but the next door was something else entirely. Painted industrial grey, it was made of solid metal. As well as a normal lock, there was an electronic keypad on the wall. At least she took her home security seriously. Dionne entered a few numbers, and the door clicked and opened.

She smiled back over her shoulder, holding the door

open for him as she stepped through. "Come on in. I'll make you a drink while I find the box of photos."

"That would be great." Martino walked inside and stopped talking. Whatever he had been expecting, this wasn't it.

The inside of the warehouse was a large, echoing space. He looked up at a series of mezzanines to his left and right, a walkway linking them running underneath the dirty cracked windows he had noticed from the road. Staircases to the upper levels on each side. Some upper rooms were open to the vast interior space, others had stucco walls. From an open-plan mezzanine two floors up on his left, he heard voices. Either Dionne had left a television on, or people were talking. He felt a prickle of unease.

More stairs led down to a basement. But this wasn't what caught Martino's eye.

The echoing space wasn't empty. It was marked out in chalk, as if by a giant child. A wide chalk road led from one end of the warehouse to the other. In the centre, various wooden and cardboard boxes were stacked, each representing a building. Crude doors and windows were drawn on the front, along with surnames. Taller buildings used two or three stacked boxes. The tallest of these, four boxes high and the same wide, was marked *Church*. Toy cars and buses lined the street.

Martino shook his head in wonderment. A town sign stood at one end, the name written on a piece of cardboard with a sharpie.

Desolation Station.

The voices didn't come from a television. A tall man appeared at the edge of the mezzanine above. His thin, hard face looked familiar, although Martino couldn't immediately place him. Then he spoke, and Martino's world narrowed to a single, terrible realisation.

"Hi, Jesse."

He went cold. How could he have not seen it? A mind honed by years of thinking and writing; researching, interviewing, asking questions. Drawing conclusions. An instinct for story that pointed him in directions others failed to go, often bringing scoops others missed. But this—this was an error of catastrophic proportions. A fall so hard, it sent him reeling. He had accepted the humble, God-fearing, hard-working girl conjured by Dorothy Rees and Dionne's parents. But that fearsome intellect described by Dionne's ex-principal had never diminished. Dionne James didn't turn to religion and abandon her studies. She merely focused her talents in a new direction.

The skin under Martino's eyes tightened, and his skull buzzed. He wondered if he might pass out. He had made a stupid, blind assumption, deciding Woodland High's dangerous, disaffected teens had formed their gang at poor Dionne James's Bible study group.

How could he have failed to see what was in front of him?

Dionne James. Nicknamed Jesse. After the outlaw, for Chrissakes.

Martino looked again at the model town. The Firestarters' next target. This chalk and cardboard town represented the culmination of a plan by Dionne James and her cohort of corrupt police officers. And Martino had walked right on in.

He turned around with a look of resignation, unsurprised by the handgun now pointing at his chest.

Dionne 'Jesse' James winked and held out her hand. "Phone, please."

"Fuck," said Martino.

233

Chapter Forty-One

THE FIRESTARTERS WAITED for Jesse to speak. Four of them sat around a boardroom table on the first mezzanine level, glasses of water alongside their legal pads. Al Critchen joined the meeting remotely through the conference phone speaker. Of the original Bible study group, only Janey Holden was missing. Holden had succumbed to an attack of conscience after the raid on Greenhaven. Guilt sent her looking for oblivion in alcohol and crystal meth. She became unreliable and unpredictable. No one protested when Jesse flew to Anchorage, shot Janey Holden in the face, and pushed her body into the Gulf of Alaska.

Their leader stood at a whiteboard, sharpie in hand, Martino's cell phone beside her. The scene mirrored a billion other office meetings around the globe, but this one was different. The agenda didn't feature budget plans for the fourth quarter, maintenance issues in the executive bathroom, or potential salary cuts in middle management. Instead, the notes they'd made outlined a detailed plan to rob Desolation Station, then incinerate the place along with its residents.

A relatively straightforward task, as—officially, at least —no one in Desolation Station owned a cell phone, since there was no cell tower to provide a signal. Communication with the outside world was discouraged. The single official satellite phone belonged to Dwight Hardleman, a retired electrician from New Jersey.

Dwight Hardleman didn't go by his given name anymore. He and his followers used the name he'd adopted after being electrocuted fourteen years earlier, when the ladder he was on touched a power line. When he opened his eyes seconds later, flat on his back, Dwight had vanished, replaced by Om, an avatar of the Godhead, and prophet of the imminent apocalypse.

The Firestarters could give two shits for Om's belief system, but one aspect of his philosophy brought him to Jesse's attention. The charismatic prophet's electrically induced epiphany attracted a growing number of disciples prepared to sell everything they owned, give him the proceeds, and move to Desolation Station, Nevada. Banks represented the corrupt old world, so donations were converted to a currency likely to survive the breakdown of society: gold.

Desolation Station—an old stagecoach stop and home to around thirty pioneers in the eighteen hundreds—was little more than a collection of rotting buildings twenty miles from the highway when Om discovered it. But his first disciple—an artist who'd enjoyed a great deal of success in the eighties—handed over twenty million dollars, and the transformation began. A short online documentary about the prophet building a new Eden in the Nevada desert went viral. Desolation Station reached saturation in months, and plans were made to accommodate future growth with modular housing. Two hundred and eighty disciples currently occupied the simple dwellings, and numbers continued to rise.

"I'm calling it off," said Jesse, holding her hand up when the others protested. "Someone broke into a medical facility in Albuquerque two nights ago. The voice you are about to hear is Lydia Garcia."

That got their attention. Everyone remembered the survivor of Eagle Springs. New Mexico. When the Garcia girl made it out of her burning house alive, it almost scuppered the entire elaborate plan Jesse had laid out in high school.

She tapped in Martino's cell phone code and pressed play. They listened in stunned silence as Lydia Garcia's voice, tinny and small, unravelled their world.

Afterwards, the conference phone on the table crackled into life, and Al Critchen muttered, "Jesus."

A cop in Eureka, Nevada, Al lived eighteen miles from the Desolation Station. He cleared his throat, but Jesse leaned in towards the phone.

"Al, I hope you're not thinking about interrupting."

"Of course not, Jesse."

"I always said no plan is set in stone," she said. "If we can't adapt, we get caught, or killed."

No one argued. Dionne 'Jesse' James' plan would have seemed crazy to the teenagers she'd recruited for her study group if she hadn't begun with a demonstration of her capabilities. She'd asked Paul Geary to step forward. Geary was the meanest of a mean bunch, with a growing reputation for violence. A quick temper and a body that had matured faster than most of his contemporaries meant he was universally feared at Woodland High. Which made it even more surprising when Dionne James—nearly a foot shorter and at least fifty pounds lighter—spun him round, slammed his hand on the table, and put a knife through it, pinning him to the wooden surface. She clapped a hand over his mouth to stop the scream and, when she spoke, everyone paid attention.

"Everyone in this room thought Paul was the most dangerous person here. You assumed I was the weakest. I'm a quiet, studious, *What Would Jesus Do* nerd in a room full of psychos. But you're wrong. I'm the most dangerous person here. Do you know why?"

No one answered. She took her hand from Geary's mouth. He had paled and was trying not to move. Dionne looked at the blade, and the growing pool of blood on the varnished wood beneath.

"You'll live," she said. "I used a stiletto. A slender blade, extremely sharp. If I'd stabbed you between your ribs, you'd be dead by now. Quit whimpering while I'm speaking."

Geary, who'd been humming involuntarily, shut up.

"That's better. By now, I hope you've guessed we're not here to study the word of the Lord. Today's lesson is about perception, and about patience. And how, if you manipulate perception, and practise patience, you will become very, very rich."

It was almost a decade since that first meeting. Jesse had long proven her point. When she told them they'd be rich, but it would take ten years to happen, they might have laughed if it hadn't been for the blood pooling under Paul Geary's hand.

To everyone who knew her—even her own parents—Dionne James was a quiet girl with strong religious convictions. She'd just shown them it was a sham. A part she played every second, and every hour, of every day. She'd pulled back the curtain to let them see backstage, showing them the real Dionne. It had been Geary, after she pulled out the knife and sent him to his seat with a first aid kit, who suggested they call her Jesse. "You know," he said. "Jesse James."

"Yeah, I get it, Paul. Nice idea. Jesse. I like it."

And everything Jesse had promised came to pass. The Firestarters had learned her lessons concerning patience and perception. Patience, because Jesse's plan wouldn't be complete until they were approaching their thirties. Perception, because who was more trustworthy than your friendly small-town cop? Even if the investigations into the gangs' raids meant a little suspicion initially fell onto the absent law enforcement officer, Jesse had correctly predicted how quickly that suspicion would dissipate. None of the gang ever contacted each other. When they called Jesse, they used a burner, destroying it after a single call.

The only individual still seriously considering the police insider theory wasn't a Fed, or a cop. He was a journalist. And, currently, that journalist was locked in a room beneath them.

Al's voice emerged from the speaker.

"You're gonna quit because of Martino? Why not just kill the guy?"

Jesse laughed. "What have I told you about sharing your suggestions, Al?"

The others smirked. Jesse took a long swallow of water from a sports bottle. She was big on hydration.

"I'm not going to touch Martino. He won't say, or write, a thing. He's not the reason I'm calling this off."

Just like in a classroom, no one wanted to be the first to ask the question.

Jesse replaced her bottle on the table. "There's another voice on that recording. The man who got her to talk. The man who broke out of a safe house in Albuquerque yesterday morning, killing two experienced guys. The man whose ID says he's Tom Harper. In Martino's phone, he's

Tom Kincaid. He's the reason I'm bringing our retirement plans forward. Go tidy up any loose ends and wait for my call. When it comes, it'll be time to cash in your chips and leave the casino."

A cough from the far end of the table broke the silence.

"Jesse, I, er, I have some news about Kincaid."

Jesse became still. Not a good sign. The man who'd interrupted swallowed before continuing.

"I had a call from my boy, Cure LaCroix in Louisiana while you were downstairs. Kincaid showed up there today. Cure shot him. He's dead."

Chapter Forty-Two

MARTINO HAD BEEN SHUT inside the small office for two hours when a key turned in the lock. He'd spent his incarceration alternately berating himself for his failure to identify Jesse, and looking for a way out. She'd taken his phone. The computer on the metal desk needed a fingerprint to log in, and he had the wrong fingers. He wasted a few minutes in a desultory search for a weapon. People in movies overcame their captors and escaped. In real life, they got shot.

Patrice eyed Jesse warily when she walked in. No gun this time, but he doubted an out of condition putz could overcome the leader of the most notorious criminal gang in the country.

Jesse tossed his phone at him. She'd made him unlock it before locking him in. The Lydia Garcia recording was there, plus emails to Agent Salton and Sky Pimm.

"Sit down," said Dionne. He made a mental note to think of her as Jesse. Then he made a second mental note to disregard the first note, since he was about to die. Finally, he made a mental note overriding all previous notes to stop making mental notes and spend his final few minutes thinking about the people he loved. Which, now he found himself *in extremis*, turned out to be only Hannah. Sky warranted a brief thought, as did his agent, Ron. Even Helen got a half-second of acknowledgement. But it was Hannah he pictured, from the first time he saw that crumpled, angry face, to the last time he'd spoken to her, signing off the phone call with a casual *ciao.*

"What's it gonna be?" he said to Jesse, doing as she'd instructed, and lowering himself into the chair behind the desk. He folded his arms so she wouldn't see his hands shake.

"What's what gonna be?"

He cleared his throat. Didn't want to squeak. "How are you gonna do it? Shoot me? Strangle me? Stab me and dump my body in some shitty neighbourhood so it looks like I got mugged?"

Jesse waited for him to finish. "You're an intelligent man. What would happen if you disappeared or turned up dead?"

The question came out of left field. Martino, doing his damnedest to face his death with some dignity, gaped like a freshly landed dogfish.

"Er..."

"Think it through quickly. I bore easily."

Martino found, to his surprise, that he was capable of coherent thought. Maybe it was the unexpected nature of the question.

"The police, the FBI, my agent, some of my colleagues... they know what I'm working on."

"And?" prompted Jesse.

"And if I vanished, or died tragically young"—what was this? A joke? Gallows humour?—"people would ask questions. They'd check my emails and phone records. They'd follow the same trail that led me to you."

"Exactly. Good. Look, relax, will you? I've already said I won't kill you, and you've just reasoned out why."

Martino had been folding his arms so tightly that when he removed his hands from his armpits, the fingers were numb. He flexed them to get the feeling back.

Jesse leaned against the door.

"I've kept tabs on you for nearly three years."

"Should I be flattered?" Bravado now? Martino was drunk with adrenaline.

"You're thorough, and—like I said—smart. You pieced the facts together from very few clues. But I doubt you would have got here without your friend Kincaid and his visit with Lydia Garcia."

"He's not my friend." *Shut up*, Martino told himself, literally pushing his lips tightly closed to prevent his mouth flapping about.

"Whatever. He's not a problem anymore."

"Why not?"

Jesse nodded to herself. "Because his body is at the bottom of the Blackwater River in Alabama."

She put her hands on the desk, staring at Martino. He couldn't have felt more intimidated if she'd been seven feet tall and holding an axe.

"You're on your own now, Patrice."

Hearing her use his first name made his skin crawl.

"Like I said, he's not my fr—"

"Yes. Whatever. But you need to understand no one has your back. There's been no new police chatter about the Firestarters. Kincaid only sent the recording to you. You're a lone voice. Let me tell you what your future holds."

Here it comes. All this talk of not killing me, it means nothing. There's no way I'm walking out of here.

"You've been an irritant up to now, Patrice."

"I've been called worse. Ask my ex-wife."

The adrenaline had turned him into a wise-cracking asshole from a nineteen-eighties action movie. His mouth was dry and his heart was pounding. He was a plump journalist who wore a hat, not Bruce Willis.

"Maybe I will. Or maybe I should ask Hannah."

Martino's heart fluttered like a butterfly in a cupped hand. His reaction to hearing his daughter's name on Jesse's lips was visceral. He couldn't speak. Couldn't move. Worse; he couldn't think.

"Finish your book, Patrice. I hope it'll be a bestseller. But drop your cop theory. Mention it among other possibilities in an early chapter, then abandon it after building a convincing case for another theory. It'll be a compelling read, but there will be no satisfying conclusion. By the time it's published, my colleagues and I will be enjoying new lives. I've had a long time to plan our retirement. Your book, and its lack of any conclusion, will further reduce the already tiny odds of us ever being found. And now you know why you'll do this for me."

He croaked out the word. "Hannah." Martino's body and mind belonged to someone else. Someone heavy, slow, and very, very old. His voice emerged as if phoned in, long distance.

"Yes, Patrice. Hannah. I'm a planner, Patrice. I don't like surprises. And I understand the importance of leverage. Move."

"Excuse me?"

Jesse waved him away from the desk. "Move. I want to show you something."

Martino stood up, shuffling aside while Jesse took his place and logged in to the computer with her thumbprint.

The sensation of detachment from his own body continued.

Photographs of Hannah appeared on the large monitor. The first was a studio head shot from her portfolio, the same picture that appeared on her agent's website. But the rest were different. Candid shots, most taken at a distance with a long lens. Hannah crossing a New York street, looking in the window of a deli, buying coffee in Central Park. Someone had been watching her. Following her. Martino's stomach lurched.

They had taken the last set of photographs through Hannah's apartment window. Sprawled on her couch. On the phone, standing at her window, looking out towards the Brooklyn Bridge. Eating takeout noodles in her underwear. Towelling her naked body after a shower.

Martino retched. Jesse handed him a metal trash can. He threw up, eyes stinging with tears, legs threatening to give way. A terrible sorrow flooded his system, along with horror and fear. Rage, too.

Jesse handed him some tissues. Martino wiped his mouth.

"Don't underestimate my access to her," said Jesse. "My power over her. One phone call is all it would take. Christ, Patrice, will you sit down before you fall over?"

Even as he dropped into the chair, a detached element of Martino's brain noted Jesse's choice of curse word, and wondered how she kept up her pretence of devout faith without ever raising suspicion. Dionne James hadn't just fooled her peers and teachers, she'd fooled parents who believed their daughter piously followed their version of Jesus. To maintain the act through her teens, while making detailed long-term plans in opposition to everything she professed to care about... that took a level of resolve Martino had rarely encountered. He'd seen absolute commitment in sports people, business leaders, and politicians, but never in a criminal. Not that this meant he admired her. Or, at least, only in the way you admired a poisonous snake in a nature documentary.

Jesse took the trash can and left, returning with a glass of water.

"Drink." Martino did so. He kept a semblance of control by thinking no further ahead than the next action. He drank the water, returned the empty glass when asked to, and followed Jesse back through the warehouse with its model of Desolation Station, and out through the steel door.

It was evening. Martino had forgotten what day it was, let alone what time.

Warm city perfume of gasoline, sweat, beer, and rotting trash. Warehouse exterior illuminated only by the lap-dancing bar's flashing coloured lights. Strobes of mortuary blue, vomit green, blood red.

Jesse handed him his bag. He'd forgotten he'd brought it. A change of clothes, toiletries, laptop and chargers. He hung onto its handle and stared blankly, waiting for instructions.

"I called you a cab to the airport. Go home. Visit your daughter. Go to the movies. Forget any of this ever happened. If you don't..."

Jesse leaned in close. She smelled great—soap, subtle perfume, and her hair carried a faint tang of apples. How could she smell good? She should stink of rotting flesh and corruption. Her breath tickled his earlobe.

"I'll torture Hannah. I'll keep her conscious through the worst pain imaginable, until she forgets what it was like to live without pain, to breathe without agony. And, while I'm doing it, I'll tell her why it's happening. I'll tell Hannah you betrayed her. Afterwards, I'll send you videos, so you can see everything I did to her."

The flashing neon lights were washed out by the headlamps of a cab. To the driver, they probably looked like a couple saying goodbye, her face tilted up to his. Jesse opened the door and Martino got in. She handed the driver a hundred.

"My friend isn't feeling so great. Drive smooth, ok?"

"Sure thing, lady."

The last glimpse Martino got of Jesse was her bare arm as she turned to walk back inside. A normal woman's arm, brown, lightly muscled, smooth. As if it belonged to a human being.

Chapter Forty-Three

FOUR HOURS before Patrice Martino realised—too late—that Dionne James was Jesse, Jimmy Blue approached a remote fishing cabin on the banks of the Blackwater River, Alabama.

The sun had been up a while. Blue would have preferred to wait until dark, but the clock was ticking.

Geary's fishing cabin stood two miles from its nearest neighbour. The only way to reach it was down a muddy narrow track marked by a wooden sign on the highway. Blue passed the sign, rolled the Mustang off the blacktop, and left it behind the trees.

He followed the track on foot, the Beretta he'd taken in Albuquerque swinging loose in his jacket pocket. The late summer humidity stuck his T-shirt to his back, but he didn't take the jacket off. A handgun in a pocket was easier to access than one tucked behind a back. He didn't even need to remove it to fire.

When he caught sight of the simple wooden cabin, Blue hung back in the shadow of the trees, looking for movement. Seeing none, he loped across ten yards of exposed ground, flattened himself against the screen door, and listened.

No sounds from within. He scanned the yard. Geary had arrived on a German motorcycle. Blue walked over. Laid his hand on the engine. Cold. A cobweb hung between the kickstand and the dirt.

Jimmy moved silently around the cabin's exterior. A path led to the river. Sitting in a camping chair, rod balanced on a stand, a six-pack of beer with one missing at his feet, the fisherman was oblivious to Jimmy's presence. A radio alongside on the wooden jetty played a sports channel.

Blue squinted at the figure, silhouetted by the sunlight dancing on the water. Without turning, he tried the cabin door behind him. It opened, and Jimmy stepped inside.

The galley-style kitchen was only notable for the quantity of food and drink it contained. Looked like Geary had enough provisions for a month or more. The second of two large fridges was crammed with beer cans.

Apart from a tiny bathroom, the cabin boasted only one other room, containing a bed, dresser, television with DVD player, and a stack of movies. No cable out here. A beaten-up recliner faced the screen. A quick search produced no weapons, but Blue took the box of nine millimetre bullets he found in the dresser.

Outside, the fisherman hadn't moved. The six-pack was now a four-pack.

Blue held the Beretta ready as he crossed the twenty yards to the jetty. Close to the back of the chair, he slowed, realising he could have marched up clapping his hands and singing. His prey was whistling.

The bullets Blue had found belonged to the Glock 19 on top of the bait box.

Blue considered clearing his throat, but Geary belched

loudly and got up, stretching his arms and yawning. He lit a cigarette, and the sweet, heady stench of a potent strain of marijuana drifted back to Jimmy. The fisherman took a couple of stumbling steps closer to the water, unzipped and peed. Blue placed the barrel of the gun on the nape of his neck.

"Sheriff's Deputy Geary," he said, and the man froze. "Why don't you put that away? Nobody wants to die with their pecker in their hand. Turn around. Slowly."

The fisherman did as instructed, and Blue's jaw actually dropped an inch while he tried to comprehend what he was looking at. Or, rather, who he was looking at.

"Who the fuck are you?"

———

WHO THE FUCK the fisherman was turned out to be Stephen LaCroix, better known as Cure by acquaintances, most of whom met him in prison.

"See, man, I'm the guy you come to if you need shit. When you're serving all day and a night and your only way out is back-door parole, you appreciate the little luxuries and shit. Bats, pruno, whatever you need. I'm on the other end of the fishing line, you know what I'm saying?"

"No," commented Blue, "so stop saying it and answer my question."

They were back inside the cabin, Cure in the recliner, eyeing the gun pointing at his heart.

"Jus' trying to explain why everyone calls me Cure. Because I procure shit in the joint, see?"

Blue decided on a more robust approach. He took a half-step forward and delivered a left-hand jab so fast, Cure saw the blood on his assailant's fist before he realised his nose was broken.

A surprised intake of breath and a wheeze of pain. "The fuck, man? You busted my nose."

"Correct. Another superfluous word and I'll start on your fingers."

LaCroix—the same height, build, and age as Geary— processed the sentence, got stuck on the word *superfluous,* and decided not to ask for clarification.

Blue allowed a little darkness to surface. Cure stopped whimpering. In fact, he stopped breathing for a few seconds, his body instinctively pushing back against the chair. On a deep, ancient level, the Geary lookalike had just registered his relationship to his captor. Blue was the predator, Cure the prey.

"I will ask questions," said Blue. "You will answer, using as few words as possible. You will do everything I say. If you don't annoy me, I might let you live."

Cure tasted his own blood from his ruined nose. His right leg twitched rhythmically, a movement outside his control. He didn't dare speak, so he nodded.

"Good," said Blue. "Let's begin."

It took eight minutes for Jimmy to get what he required. Cure, once sufficiently motivated, proved capable of supplying information in succinct sentences.

Sheriff's Deputy Paul Geary and Stephen 'Cure' LaCroix first met in Charlotte five years earlier, when Geary was an arresting officer in a drug bust. Cure didn't recognise Geary when he showed up a second time, two months ago. Geary handed the confused Cure a knife to examine. It was only when he took it back that Cure noticed Geary was wearing gloves, and he watched in dawning horror as the cop slid the knife into an evidence bag.

"If I found this item during a search of your house, car, or person," said Geary, "you'd go back to prison for the rest of your worthless life. Or you could do me a solid. What do you say?"

Cure was happy to help the officer. The form that help took was—somewhat surprisingly—a month's fishing in Alabama.

He'd met Geary a final time last week, on the Florida Alabama border. Geary gave him the cabin keys, and they swapped vehicles, Cure completing the journey by motorcycle.

Geary had replaced Cure's cell phone with a burner containing one number. That phone was now on the bed next to Cure's Glock. Cure's eyes flicked to the weapon as the man half-considered making a lunge, but the idea barely made it into the outer reaches of his consciousness before being swatted away by his instinct for self-preservation. Cure was stoned, drunk, and hardly in peak physical condition. Blue, built like a quarterback, black bandana over his scalp, cold lizard-green eyes fixed on his prey, clearly scared the living crap out of him.

As Cure talked, Jimmy considered the implications of Geary using a body double. Using Cure as a stand-in freed Geary up to be elsewhere. And if anyone dropped in, Cure was a close physical match.

So why did Geary need an alibi? Where was he?

"When do you leave?"

It had been a while since Blue last spoke. Cure scrambled to find the words.

"Er, ah, right, yeah, I'm gone on the first of the month, man."

There were eighteen days left in August.

Blue thought fast. The Albuquerque thugs' bodies would have been discovered by now. The Firestarters knew their captive had escaped. In their place, Blue thought he might trigger their escape plans and dissolve the gang.

He couldn't let that happen. He opened a kitchen drawer, pulled out the sharpest knife.

Blue handed the burner phone to Cure. Placed the knife on the seated man's crotch. Pushed the tip of the blade forward until it pierced the denim, and Cure whimpered.

Blue smiled at the sweating man.

"I want you to make a phone call," he said.

Chapter Forty-Four

THE MOTORCYCLE WAS A TWENTY-YEAR-OLD BMW, built for touring rather than speed, but the air-cooled flat twin gave out a throaty growl as Blue swept west along I-10 towards Pensacola.

Blue had let Cure LaCroix live. He made it clear— once the man regained consciousness—that his instructions were to be followed to the letter. As a taster of what would occur should LaCroix deviate from those instructions, he broke the ex-con's right leg. He made a temporary splint and set the bone. Before leaving, he let Cure watch him put the burner phone back together.

"I've inserted a listening device." This was a lie, but Cure wouldn't know that. "If you call anyone, it will trigger alert me. And I'll be listening to every word you say. You got that?"

"Yes, sir."

"It will also alert me should you be stupid enough to open the back of this phone. You won't be stupid, will you?"

"No, sir."

"Good, because it'll irritate me if I need to track you down and stab you to death. But I will do so if you cross me. Are we clear?"

"Yes, sir."

Jimmy pondered his generosity at leaving Cure alive as he cruised along the interstate. Maybe Tom's long stint in Pike Point had left Blue with some residual empathy and compassion. He laughed. No. Cure might yet be useful; that's why the ex-con was still breathing. If Geary called again, Cure would stick to his account of how he'd shot dead a big, bald intruder called Tom. The photograph he'd sent of Blue's 'corpse' on the cabin floor was a clincher.

When Jimmy finally came face to face with Geary, the killer cop would think he'd risen from the dead to take vengeance.

In Pensacola, Blue found a diner with decent Wi-Fi, and sat in a booth at the back. He set an online program running to find his nearest SIM card. Before leaving Britain, Blue had mailed fifty hardbacks to a New York State book distributor, which sent them all over the country. The back cover of each book held a SIM card wired to a lithium battery, plus a driving licence and Social Security card in a new name. Pure chance would dictate how close the nearest book was to his current location.

Blue didn't check the results until he'd shovelled two all-day breakfasts and a pint of black coffee down his throat. When he angled the screen back towards him, he smiled. He didn't believe in fate, but the way the encounter with Cure LaCroix had played out gave him an unexpected advantage against the Firestarters. Now this. The nearest book was four point three miles from his current position. He checked the route, left cash and a ten-dollar tip on the table, and headed out to the bike.

Eight minutes later, Jimmy fixed the young man behind

the counter of a quiet used bookstore with an easy grin, adopting a generic American accent with a slight southern bias.

"Howdy." When Tom had first moved to Charlotte, he'd smiled every time someone greeted him this way, as he'd previously believed it was a word only used in movies.

"Can I help you, sir?" The clerk eyed the huge customer a little nervously. Blue broadened his smile.

"I hope you can. My uncle Bob has developed a hankering for a little self-improvement, and as it's his birthday next week, I thought I might treat him to a book to help him in this worthy endeavour."

The clerk visibly relaxed as he unpicked his customer's wordy request.

"*Self-help* is on the back wall alongside *Crystals, Angels, and Astrology*, sir."

"You're very kind."

Blue found two copies of *Think and Grow Rich*, and one *7 Habits of Highly Effective People*. Blue lifted the dust covers, but none had the pen mark he'd made back in London. Blue picked up a *How to Win Friends and Influence People* for his imaginary uncle. Next stop was the fiction section, and the end of his search. The telltale pen mark was clear on the store's only copy of *To Kill a Mockingbird*.

"The Harper Lee is for me," he explained as the clerk rang up his purchases. "Always meant to read it, but never have. Shameful, I know."

Outside, he ripped open the back cover, removed his new identity cards, snapped the SIM, and flicked it away. He dropped the battery down a storm drain, then stuffed the books into his backpack before returning to the bike.

Blue glanced at his new name. Tom Chapman. Much better to be Jimmy Blue, named after a song Tom's father had loved. A name given by no one. A name invested with the power of myth.

He set a fire a few hundred yards back from the highway out of town, watching his previous identity become ashes along with the bookstore purchases.

Blue planned to find a cheap airport hotel, book a morning flight to Rochester, New York, and visit Patrice Martino. The writer had gone quiet since receiving the recording of Lydia Garcia. Surely, now he knew the local cops were the insiders, he'd have found the connection between them by now. Time to motivate him.

In the parking lot of an airport motel, Jimmy checked his emails. He propped the laptop on the bike seat. The first message was from Bolsteroni.

found this local old news report link

two of them went to the same high school in la

maybe they all went there?

Blue clicked the link and scanned a newspaper report about a car wreck, unaware it was the same report Martino had read. During the ride to the airport, he stopped once to wipe his gun clean and throw it into the bushes. Couldn't check it in as baggage without a licence.

The news report changed everything.

The first flight to Los Angeles meant changing at Dallas, arriving in LAX in time for breakfast. He could sleep on the plane.

Chapter Forty-Five

ALL INTERNATIONAL AIRPORTS are impersonal to varying degrees, but LAX, to Martino at least, epitomised disinterested, soulless corporate contempt for anyone with more empathy than a lugworm.

This evening, the oppressive atmosphere matched his mood perfectly.

He came back to himself as if waking from dreamless anaesthetic. He sat on a plastic chair at the gate, placed his elbows on his knees, and pushed the heels of his palms into his eye sockets, rubbing until red and yellow shapes throbbed across his field of vision.

His flight left in ninety minutes.

A sign on the wall showed an arrow below one of the most welcome words in the English language.

Bar.

An hour later, Martino was drunk. Or most of him was. His legs certainly were, which they revealed by taking an oddly circuitous path on his third trip to the bathroom. The rest of his body still felt like a loaner, limbs too loose, skin on his face stretched too tight. His eyes slid slowly away from anything he tried to focus on. Despite this, his mind refused to embrace this attempt at oblivion. Much of his brain conceded a temporary loss of control, substituting a temporary, fuzzy haze for rational thought. But, to his distress, a small part of Martino's consciousness spoke up, and it said things he didn't want to hear.

—*Time to face facts, Pat, don'tcha think?*

Helen had been the only person ever to call Martino Pat, and then only when angry. He'd always hated it. Pat wasn't a name, it was something you did to dogs or small children.

—*There are people out there who think you're a big shot, Pat, but you and I know they're schmucks, right?*

—Shut up.

Martino tried to ignore the voice by looking at the screens dotted around the bar. Most showed football games. One displayed a scrolling list of stock market prices. In the corner, a screen no one watched showed some back-patting documentary about an old TV show. One actor looked familiar, but Martino couldn't place him. He gulped bourbon, but the voice in his head was far from done.

—*Shortlisted for the Pulitzer, bestselling author, respected journalist. Yeah, yeah, quite the success story, Pat.*

—I'm not listening.

—*But what makes a man a success, Pat? Is it a numbers game? I sure as hell hope not, cos you're not gonna trouble the Forbes list this century. Over fifty years on this planet, and whaddya got to show for it? A half-paid-for apartment—in Rochester, of all the goddam places —a failed marriage, a sex life only a monk would boast about, and a daughter you're terrified will start using again.*

Martino took out his phone, brought up Sky Pimm's number. Stared at it, blinking every time it blurred and drifted away.

—*Who ya trying to fool, Pat? You're not calling Sky. You're not calling anyone. You're on your own.*

Martino put the phone down. Looked back at the television. Bill, that was the name of the half-remembered actor. Bill someone.

—*Stop trying to distract yourself. It won't work.*

—I said shut up.

—*I'm you, Patty boy. You can't stop me talking. Can't stop me pointing out the obvious. Here's something to chew on. Hannah's been clean for years. So why do you still go cold if the phone rings at night, picturing her cold and grey on a mortician's slab, scabs on her arms and legs, the hit that killed her being flushed out of her veins to make room for formaldehyde?*

—I swear to God…

—*To who? Oh, sorry, you pedant—to whom? Would that be the God you reasoned out of existence in tenth grade? The God you sneer at when other people take comfort in religion? The God you caught yourself praying to when Jesse threatened to kill Hannah? That principle crumbled pretty fast, didn't it?*

Martino ordered another double bourbon, along with the strongest imported beer they carried. He couldn't taste it anymore.

Bill Bixby. That was the actor.

—*Considering how you earn your living, Pat, it's ironic that you lack character. You made your choice. Hannah's life over a town-full of strangers. They'll die, but Hannah will live. Accept it.*

—I can't.

—*You can. You have to. I see that cowardly little thought floating around your drunken skull. Forget it. You'll never kill yourself. You don't have the balls. Even if you did, you'd never leave Hannah alone. Better a weak excuse for a father than none at all, especially as losing you might send her in search of a fix. No. You'll live. You'll wake up every morning, eating, breathing, talking, looking like a regular human being, all the while knowing you condemned everyone in—what was*

259

its name?—Desolation Station. Yeah, Desolation Station. Knowing you condemned them to die, so your little girl can live. That's the trade. And I'll never let you forget it.

Bill Bixby. *The Incredible Hulk.* That was the TV show. Martino had loved it as a kid. Mom would let him watch it in the kitchen while she made dinner.

—You're reminiscing about old TV shows now?

Something about that show. Something important. Martino's inner voice faded as he attempted to bring his alcohol-impaired faculties to bear on the relevance of a fictional green monster to his existential crisis.

He stood up, almost fell over, and flopped back onto the bar stool. The television in the corner was playing a clip. Even though the late seventies special effects were laughable compared to what any kid with a laptop could do now, Martino still felt an echo of the excitement he'd experienced watching the mild doctor transform into a musclebound green, raging creature, who could lift cars, uproot trees, even throw a bear clear across a river.

Martino's body was still slow with booze, but his mind shrugged off the stupefying effects of the bourbon and beer as it tried to interpret the flares his subconscious was sending up.

His email filing system flashed up in his mind. He grabbed the thought like a lifebuoy. For over two decades now, since his first book hit the stands, Martino's weekly inbox always contained at least a dozen ideas for an article, or book. He had a reputation for digging out the truth, and bringing the powerful to account. People liked to see justice catch up with those who thought the law didn't apply to them. So folk emailed him. Recent emails ranged from a Detroit schoolteacher accusing her neighbour of stealing her underwear to harvest her DNA, to alien abductions of Postal Service workers in Georgia.

Martino pushed the bourbon aside and opened his laptop. He looked at the four folders of unsolicited emails. Whatever was nagging at him lay in one of them.

CRANKS

NOPE

UNLIKELY

MAYBE

Each folder contained hundreds of emails. He disregarded *CRANKS*. The DNA underwear and Georgia abductions were in there, along with an even mix of conspiracy theorists, the clinically unstable, and religious fanatics, with a big overlap between the three categories.

The *NOPE* folder was also unlikely to hold the answer. *CRANKS* emails didn't warrant replies, but the *NOPE* folder did. Usually a one-liner along the lines of not having the time or expertise to help them.

So the answer lay in either *UNLIKELY* or *MAYBE*. Martino regularly scanned the *MAYBE* folder. Over time, he either moved them into *UNLIKELY* or *NO*, or started researching the story.

He opened *MAYBE* now, scanning subject lines, hoping one of them would jump out. None did.

Which left *UNLIKELY*. Emails with ideas not flat-out crazy, or liable to provoke a lawsuit, but not a good fit. Usually, they represented too much work for too little reward. Martino had bills to pay.

"Espresso, please. A double." The bartender raised an eyebrow at Martino's sudden change of heart, but brought him a small cup of mediocre coffee for six bucks. He tossed the bitter liquid back and squinted at the laptop.

There were over two hundred *UNLIKELY* emails.

He ordered another double espresso and sent it after the first, wincing at the aftertaste. There really was no excuse for terrible coffee anymore, particularly when, apparently, it was more valuable than gold.

Martino glanced at the TV, but the documentary had finished, replaced with a cartoon.

The message from his subconscious refused to come into focus, so he stopped trying. Instead, he put himself back in the kitchen with Mom in Brooklyn, making himself a pastrami sandwich while the green creature on screen lifted unconvincing-looking boulders and heaved them towards terrified onlookers, never causing serious injury. After each rampage, the monster calmed and transformed back into the quiet doctor. The doctor had to keep moving, Martino recalled, because there were people hunting him. One guy in particular. A journalist.

At this point in his reverie, Martino's subconscious did the mental equivalent of slapping him around the face with something cold, wet, and heavy. This was it. The journalist looking for the monster, not knowing he was hiding inside the doctor.

Oh.

Martino checked dates on the emails. The one he wanted was sent less than a year ago. He half-remembered the cop who wrote it. Harper? Burton? Barber. *Barber.* He found the email and opened it. Detective Inspector Barber, of the London Metropolitan Police. Rare to get an email from Britain, so he'd looked her up. A high-flyer, tipped for the top job in Scotland Yard. Until she got demoted from Detective Chief Inspector to plain Detective Inspector.

He scanned her long email. She'd taken a risk sending it, since her obsession (or, as Barber claimed, legitimate interest) was the reason she got demoted. As she wrote in her opening paragraph, if her boss found out Barber was still pursuing Tom Lewis, her career would be over. She ended by appealing to Martino as her best hope to see justice served on a brilliant, extremely dangerous criminal.

Tom Lewis. The name meant nothing to Martino, but —even dulled by alcohol—his journalistic senses tingled. He read the email a second time. When done, he rubbed his temple with his fingers like a mime portraying deep thought.

Tom Lewis. Six foot three. Around two hundred and twenty pounds. Shot in the head at twelve, the same night his parents were executed in front of him. Brain damaged. Learning difficulties. A stammer, and he could barely read or write. Now in his early thirties.

Sounded a lot like the Tom Kincaid on the audio file with Lydia Garcia.

Barber claimed Lewis had another side, an alter ego. A killer, who—twenty years after being shot—took revenge on the gang who murdered his folks. A man who, last year, became a brutal vigilante, picking off some of London's most feared criminals.

This man was a ghost. The police had no more success finding him than the beleaguered criminals did.

A good match for the Tom Kincaid who evaded a police raid, injured two cops, and melted into the North Carolina mountains, resurfacing in an Asheville bar filled with FBI agents.

Barber had another name for Tom. Jimmy Blue.

———

MARTINO BOUGHT A VENDING machine burner phone, over-paying for a piece of shit handset with a week's worth of pre-paid calls and data.

For the second time that evening, he thanked the god

he didn't believe in when he powered the device on and it had thirty percent battery life.

On his laptop, he found the email containing the recording of Lydia Garcia, and copied the sender's address into the burner. *Darkman_808.* Darkman? Jimmy Blue?

He typed the email as fast as a middle-aged man using his thumbs could.

———

MR KINCAID,

Delete this email after reading it.

I found the Firestarters. All cops, like you said. Six of them, including Dionne James—she calls herself Jesse. If she finds out I betrayed her, Jesse will kill my daughter.

The Firestarters' final target is Desolation Station, Nevada. They are planning the attack now. It'll happen soon, and when it's done, they will disappear forever.

I've been told you are dead. If you are who I think you are, you've been dead before. You're hard to kill, it seems. I hope that's true. I need that to be true.

I can't go to the police or the FBI. So, Tom Kincaid, Tom Lewis, or Jimmy Blue, save these people, if you can. Do what you have to do. But please, for the sake of my daughter, and for all the lives these assholes have taken, do one thing for me.

Kill Jesse.

———

THEY WERE CALLING his name when Martino got back to the gate. He mumbled his apologies and followed the last passengers through to the plane. Before boarding, he took the battery and SIM out of the burner, dropping them into the trash. On the plane, he reached under his seat and shoved the phone on top of the stowed lifejacket. He stared out at the criss-crossed coloured lights, the grey, utilitarian buildings, and the other taxiing aircraft; swollen, slow, and clumsy when not in the air.

When Tom Lewis became Jimmy Blue, he had no learning difficulties. Barber described Blue as ferociously intelligent, deadly, and utterly devoid of mercy. When Martino had met Kincaid in the Asheville hotel bar, the same intelligence had been on display.

The engines roared as the aircraft accelerated along the runway. Its nose lightened and tilted towards the sky.

When the plane levelled off, Martino closed his eyes. He put a hand on his gut. An unfamiliar sensation churned at his innards, something heavy and dark, a bitter seed planted by Jesse, already putting forth its sick buds.

He hoped Barber was right about Jimmy Blue. He hoped the man he'd emailed would show no mercy.

———

JIMMY BLUE and Patrice Martino were in the air simultaneously for about twenty minutes, Blue's flight on its final approach into Dallas Fort Worth as Martino's left Los Angeles.

It wasn't until Blue reached LAX, a few hundred yards from the bar Martino had got drunk in hours earlier, that he opened his laptop, and read the email.

Martino knew his real names. How? Tom Lewis had been lost at sea between London and New York. Officially declared dead.

He frowned. Refocused. Now wasn't the time to dig into how Martino had pieced together his true identity. Tom would never be Tom Lewis again, and Jimmy Blue was a visitor to this reality, not a resident. Blue had no passport, no Social Security card, no bank accounts, no records of any kind. No birth certificate because he had never been born. He arrived fully formed, a coalescing of energy, purpose, and intelligence. His name was a meaningless label.

Blue turned his attention to a map of Nevada on the laptop. Found Desolation Station, a speck in the desert. An online search led him to the Ommers, an eschatological cult based in Desolation Station, once an abandoned trading post. Now it was expanding, new homes added as fresh disciples sought enlightenment.

None of which interested Blue, until he discovered that Om, their revered leader, was a Prepper. Convinced of an imminent apocalypse, Preppers made sure they were ready for it.

The map showed one road leading to Desolation Station. A century and a half ago, the settlement was a trading post, a rest stop for travellers. Now, only one road led in. Or out.

Blue closed the laptop. Preppers hoarded guns. Lots of guns.

Good. Blue could work with guns.

Chapter Forty-Six

MONDAY

SHERIFF AL CRITCHEN had done everything possible to avoid promotion to the top job, but the town of Joshua, Nevada only supported seven police officers, three of whom were close to retirement when Al moved there nine years earlier. A clean record, plus a reputation for fair dealing and patience—neither quality coming naturally, but he was trying to play a long game, after all—meant that when the old Sheriff hung up his hat, they gave Critchen the badge. He would have preferred to keep the relatively anonymous role of Undersheriff. Still, it wouldn't be for long. Once he'd helped wipe Desolation Station off the map, he'd brush the desert dirt off his boots for good. Al Critchen planned on emigrating to Ireland, the land of his ancestors, and somewhere he hoped he'd never see another fucking cactus.

Monday afternoon found him with his feet on his desk, and his office door shut. Without wanting to draw attention to it, Critchen's attitude to work had become slipshod these past few weeks. Jesse would be displeased—even this close to payday—but what Jesse didn't know couldn't upset her.

Truth be told, Al would be glad to get away from Dionne 'Jesse' James. She'd proved her brilliance, her commitment, and her brutality over and over, and—granted—without her, Al would almost certainly be dealing drugs in some shitty LA neighbourhood, in jail, or dead. Instead, he was less than a week away from being eye-wateringly rich. But Al hated every second of police work. If Jesse had her way, the only fun he'd have was when the Firestarters burned down a town. Which didn't happen nearly often enough for Al's liking. Even then, he had to rein in his urges, and follow orders. Jesse's orders. Yes, he killed people, even knocked them around a little first, but he didn't have enough fun. Pulling a gun always gave Al Critchen an erection, and a quick trip to the bathroom after wasting some rich assholes didn't really scratch his itch. But 'no rape' was one of Jesse's rules. Not that it would be rape. Every woman responded to a powerful man the same way, however much they tried to hide it by screaming and fighting back. Critchen had satisfied his urges privately on a handful of occasions, and the women had enjoyed the things he did. They couldn't hide their true feelings from Al.

He opened his desk drawer and swigged from a pint bottle of whisky, followed by a fresh breath-spray chaser.

When he took his stress-relieving trips out of state, Al pictured Jesse when he smacked the women around. Maybe he'd track her down once this was over. It would give him something to do in his 'retirement'. But until she transferred the money, there were over ten million reasons to keep his fantasies to himself.

The phone rang. He ignored it.

Critchen wondered how the rest of the department would react when the truth came out. When Desolation Station finally resembled its name, when the fire had died down, and they'd counted the bodies, what would they think when they found out their sheriff wasn't on vacation at all, but had vanished?

Someone knocked on the door. "Sheriff?"

Critchen shook his head. Patrolman Harry Stoke. Possibly the dumbest man in Nevada. Twenty-seven years old, which—Al guessed—matched Harry's IQ. He shouted towards the closed door.

"Which part of 'do not disturb' don't you understand, Stoke? Go away."

Al thought about Jesse again, allowing that surge of anger, lust, and fear to course through him. What he would give for a few hours locked in a soundproof room with that woman. She'd have to be sedated first and tied up. Tied to the bed. Yes.

Al let his hand drift to his pants.

When Stoke knocked again, he almost screamed at the idiot. "I'm busy, Stoke."

"I know, sir, I'm sorry. It's just there's a phone call for you, and—"

"DO. NOT. DISTURB."

Christ, Stoke would need a map to find his own wiener.

Critchen tried to visualise Jesse naked, but the moment had passed. He had another drink, cursing Stoke, before widening his disapproval to all law enforcement officers in the state, the country, and the world. He toasted his empty office.

"Screw you all. Assholes."

He took another swig of whisky. His fellow Firestarters were scared of Jesse. Ever since she killed Janey in Alaska.

269

Bunch of pussies. Not him. Al Critchen broke Jesse's precious rules. Take her prohibition about criminal activity. When, three years back, Al had recognised a face in bodycam footage from a drug squad raid on a brothel near Reno, he had sniffed an opportunity. The terrified man keen to keep his face averted had used a false ID when arrested. Al checked the arrest records and found the man in question was bailed within an hour and never charged. No one cared who he was. No one but Al Critchen, who couldn't keep the grin off his face for three days straight. The brothel's familiar-looking client was Dwight Hardleman. Better known to the residents of Desolation Station as Om. End-of-times prophet, founder of his own spiritual movement, and final target of the Firestarters. Also, famously celibate. His belief that sex distracted the pure of heart, rendering them unable to transcend the physical plane might resonate with Om's acolytes, but Mandi, Shantelle, and Kara—the last of whom's thighs were wrapped around Om's face when the police burst in— might be less convinced by the sincerity of his convictions.

For Al, this heralded a more fruitful relationship with the cult leader. Once Om had seen the photograph Al produced, he agreed to pay the sheriff an annual stipend of five hundred thousand dollars, transferred by his accountant to an offshore account. Om could afford it.

Critchen, and the other Firestarters, would soon receive an amount far greater than the one and a half million he'd received from Om so far. If Jesse came through. In her place, Al would undoubtedly screw everyone else over. A million on plastic surgery and his own mother—if she were still alive, the crackhead bitch— wouldn't recognise him, and the combined haul from their raids would buy a small country. Jesse kept her escape plans close to her shapely little chest, maybe because they didn't include the others. Al bet he was the only one with a contingency.

His skim from Dwight, the name Al always used when he and the fake prophet were alone, much to Om's dismay —was just an insurance scheme against Jesse's likely betrayal. And Al enjoyed the thrill, keeping a secret from super-smart, always-right Jesse.

The phone rang again, and Stoke's knock inevitably followed. This time, the red-faced patrolman, his prematurely thinning hair greased across his glistening skull, opened the door wide enough to poke his ugly face into the Sheriff's office.

"Stoke! I'll have you mopping puke in the drunk tank for a month for this, you—"

"I'm sorry, sir, I really am, but the phone call, it's—er— it's, well, it's—"

Critchen spread his arms wide at Stoke's inability to reach a point. The phone continued to ring.

"It's, er, it's Internal Affairs, sir."

Internal Affairs. Keeping his expression neutral, Al waved Stoke away. No need to panic. No need at all. Internal Affairs randomly audited cops in the same way as the IRS, with the same result—making law-abiding, decent people feel like criminals. But Al Critchen was a criminal. A very successful one, days away from his final score. So screw Internal Affairs along with the rest of them.

He picked up the phone. Cleared his throat.

"This is Sheriff Critchen speaking. How can I help you?"

"You're a tough man to get a hold of, Sheriff."

"Yeah, my apologies for that. Some kind of trouble with the phones today. My extension isn't ringing at all. We have an engineer coming in first thing."

Too much detail. Every cop knows that liars go into too

much detail. Police Academy 101. Al moved his arms, his shirt peeling away from the sweat. The fan moved lazily above his head, displacing the warm air, providing no real comfort.

"Who am I speaking to?"

"My name is Frank Cawson, Internal Affairs."

The second name might have been Carson, Dawson, even Johnson, but the guy kept talking.

"Let me put your mind at rest, Sheriff Critchen. You are not—currently—the subject of any investigation by my department."

Al noticed the word *currently*, and didn't like it any.

"So, what can I do for you?" He couldn't place Carson, or Johnson's accent. Maybe a touch of a Texas drawl? Why was he focusing on the man's voice, for Chrissakes? Al sat up straighter.

"Well, it's not something I can discuss over the phone," said the agent. "I'm planning a visit to Nevada so we can sit down together. Today's Monday, and my diary's pretty full the next day or two. The officer who answered my call told me you're on vacation from tomorrow. When will you be back in Joshua, Sheriff?"

Never. "I'm away until this time next week, sir."

"Hmm. I'd sure appreciate talking to you a little sooner."

This from the guy who assures him he's not being investigated. Currently.

"Well, I can't really help you there. I'm visiting my mother. She's pretty sick."

"I'm sorry to hear that," said Cawson, sounding anything but. If Critchen's mother had really been ill, and had Al given a single shit about her, he might have been offended. "Listen, how about pushing your trip back a day or two? I could be there Wednesday or Thursday. Or you could come back earlier."

"Yeah, yeah, I could do that. Come back earlier, I mean. If it's important. How about Friday afternoon?"

"Well, I appreciate your sense of duty, Sheriff. I wish everyone could be this cooperative. Shall we say three p.m. Friday?"

"Sure. I'll see you then, agent..?"

But the line had gone dead. And Al would see the Internal Affairs asshole in hell first.

———

BLUE TUCKED the phone into his jacket pocket, smiling up at a blue sky unbroken by clouds. He'd walked away from the highway so Sheriff Al Critchen wouldn't hear any telltale traffic noises while speaking to the Internal Affairs agent.

He stretched, working through a simple series of exercises. He'd been on the road four hours, with the same distance again to cover before reaching Desolation Station. The phone call with Critchen meant Blue could stay the night in Tonopah, get some proper rest, and study the plans Bolsteroni sent through of the religious cult's settlement, built on the site of the old Nevada trading post.

Blue got back on the six-year Honda motorcycle he'd bought in LA, started it up, and rejoined the traffic heading north towards the border between California and Nevada. The road linking Yosemite and Death Valley was marked Grand Army of the Republic Highway on the map, but the name was the most interesting thing about it. The shimmering blacktop cut across the featureless desert scrub in an endless straight line, the view barely changing as the Honda ate the miles.

Critchen had been as evasive as Blue had expected, but the Nevada sheriff's preference to cut the fictitious trip to his sick mother short, rather than delay leaving by a day or two, gave Blue a useful timeline.

The sheriff and his fellow Firestarters intended to attack Desolation Station between Tuesday and Thursday night.

The Firestarters expected to ride into town with the confidence and savagery of the bandits that plagued trading posts over a century ago. A final raid to complete their brutal, and successful, criminal rampage across America. A big pay-off, followed by an escape into new identities, funded by the deaths of hundreds of innocent people, including Anna Huxley, proprietor of *The Book Place* in Pike Point.

What the Firestarters wouldn't expect was any resistance they couldn't easily handle.

They weren't expecting Jimmy Blue.

Chapter Forty-Seven

TUESDAY

IN MEDIAEVAL EUROPE, feudal lords built castles to take advantage of local geography. Most castles topped hills, with moats often dug around the ramparts. Any invading force that crossed the moat and climbed the hill encountered archers hiding behind stone walls three feet thick, aiming through windows little more than slits. Those who survived were greeted by barrels of boiling oil.

Desolation Station had no such geographical features to draw upon, but it had a watchtower. The view from the top was unbroken in every direction for miles. The watchers would spot any hostile approach so far in advance, residents would have time to visit the armoury, strip every gun, reassemble and load them, plus have something to eat before they needed to address the problem.

A mile from Desolation Station, and under observation by the watchtower, stood a single-storey building alongside the only approach road. Inside, a slowly turning fan lifted the grey-streaked hair of a woman dozing in an office chair, a folded book on her lap.

"Paula, wake up." The short man in the chair beside her put a hand on her shoulder. When her eyes opened and blinked, he pointed to the cloud of dust a few miles south-west. "Compact, I reckon. Maybe one of them Jap cars. A Nissan. What do you think?"

"I don't know, Clarence. You're usually right, anyhow." Paula had taken early retirement from teaching after a substantial inheritance meant she no longer needed the income.

"C'mon, Paulie, give it a shot."

Paula's younger sister always called her Paulie. Being called Paulie annoyed her. But, during her last workshop with Om—sitting so close to the prophet she could have *touched him*—he urged everyone to treat every irritation as an opportunity to be present, to meet reality with the unquenchable light of love. Paula knew this was just such an opportunity, and she should treat Clarence's childish enthusiasm as a blessing, but he was such a tedious dolt it proved difficult to channel much unquenchable light his way. When she made the spiritual leap Om spoke about, she would see the idiot with the eyes of an enlightened being, and everything would be alright.

"Very well, Clarence." Paula leaned forward and squinted. The vehicle approaching Desolation Station was still too far away for any kind of accurate identification, and Paula's scant knowledge of automobiles gave her a disadvantage, but as she brought her glasses up to her face, she caught a flash of sun reflected from a single headlight. She couldn't prevent a smile of triumph.

"I don't think that's a car at all, Clarence. It's a motorcycle."

Clarence, the undisputed master of the game he had

conceived, held his tongue. The young man, thought Paula, was confident of victory. Pride before a fall. She bet Om never sat next to Clarence. No, sir.

"Well, I'll be… jiggered." Clarence had resorted to the binoculars. "Paulie, you're a marvel. You're right. It is a motorbike. Congratulations! You're getting better at this. You win the round."

His enthusiasm seemed genuine, but Paula knew it must be feigned. No one enjoyed losing. She held her face still to prevent her smugness from showing.

As the bike came closer, Paula took the binoculars back. The motorcycle was smaller than average, making its rider look almost comically broad. About to share her observation with Clarence, she checked herself as she realised her mistake. The bike was perfectly normal, but the man astride it was huge. The sun bounced off a bald head, under which a thick neck topped shoulders thick with heavy muscle. His chest strained against a sky-blue T-shirt not quite capable of containing it, meaning a few inches of hard stomach were visible atop his jeans.

"Oh, my," breathed Paula. Normally, she would have tutted about the lack of helmet and protective clothing, but if the bike tipped this rider over its handlebars, the desert road would probably come off worse.

Clarence stood by the barrier. He lifted the radio handset.

"Motorcycle. Solo male rider."

Paula knew the disciples on the watchtower would monitor the situation through powerful binoculars. She also knew about the rifles with telescopic sights. She'd never volunteered for weapon training. Not because she disagreed with protecting the community, but because, as her daddy used to say, she couldn't hit a barn with a fly swatter.

She joined Clarence by the lowered barrier as the rider stopped, turning off the engine in response to the short man's hand gestures.

This was only her second shift in the gatehouse. She wondered how she and Clarence must look to the visitor. Along with everyone else in Desolation Station, they wore standard American prison apparel: cheap sneakers, jogging pants, a thin sweater over a T-shirt. The jogging pants and sweater were bright orange. It removed an unnecessary decision from the spiritual seekers. Nobody had to think about what to wear. Besides, as Om pointed out, everyone on the planet lived in prisons of their own making. The difference was, he and his disciples were aware of it.

The new arrival towered over Clarence like an adult over a toddler. Paula felt a twinge in a place she preferred not to acknowledge. The same twinge had made her fidget as a teenager whenever the TV showed wrestling bouts between large, Lycra-clad men. She blushed, lowering her head, when those dark green eyes found her own.

Clarence's dumb face wore his usual witless smile. "Welcome to Desolation Station, sir."

The rider nodded. One side of his scalp was a mess of old scars. Paula's twinge doubled, and her lips parted. She swallowed and stepped forward.

"My name is Paula. This is Clarence. We are two seekers in this holy place."

The man smiled, stretching his legs. The material stretched over his undulating muscles, and she swallowed again.

"Two seekers," she repeated, and Clarence gave her a look. "If you're carrying any weapons, you must leave them here. You can pick them up when you leave, or—should you decide to stay—add them to the community armoury."

"I have no weapons." The stranger's voice was deep, as Paula had expected. The tingle was so insistent she feared her discomfort would be plain to the two men. Odd. As she'd matured, she'd realised her attraction to the fearsome wrestlers on television was because they scared her. The glass screen separating them from the family living room made it possible for her to enjoy the sensation safely. In real life, however, her tastes proved disastrous when dating. A few nice boys asked her out, but she found their clumsy advances irritating. The only local man she'd found attractive was jailed at nineteen for killing a tourist in a bar brawl.

This was another reason for her move to Desolation Station. Violent men weren't drawn to spiritual communities with no alcohol, no drugs, no gambling, and no sexual relations. So there was no danger of Paula being led away from her holy quest by her secret urges.

The big stranger allowed Clarence to check him with a handheld metal detector, then submitted to a body search. Paula looked away when Clarence's hands moved up the man's legs. She adjusted her thin orange sweater, unconsciously pulling it tighter over her chest.

Why on earth had this stranger triggered the worst part of her? He was huge, undoubtedly, and his frame bulged with muscles that came from genetics and hard work, not gymnasiums and steroids. But his smile looked genuine, his voice was low, soft, and unthreatening. He carried no weapons, and his whole demeanour was gentle and, well, humble. No hint of violence.

Paula bit the inside of her cheek so hard it hurt. She reminded herself of Om's teaching. Every departure from the path gave you another opportunity to find your way back. But it took everything she had to stop herself picturing the stranger naked, on his back, with her astride him.

Clarence, she realised, was staring at her. Why was he doing that? With a sudden jolt of horror, she realised her gaze had settled on the big man's crotch.

She looked up. Coughed. Drops of blood from her bitten cheek sprayed her hand.

"You ok, Paula?"

"I'm fine. Fine. Don't fuss."

"You sure."

"I said I was fine, goddammit."

Clarence looked even more stupid when shocked. She forced herself to go to him, although that brought her perilously near to the stranger. Her breathing quickened.

"Clarence. I am so sorry. Please forgive me. I didn't mean that, I'm just… it's the heat. I apologise."

Clarence muttered his forgiveness, but Paula was already squaring up to the big man. Face your unwanted desires, your fears, your anger, your frustrations. That's what Om said. Face them head on, and see them as the imposters they are. Watch them dissolve.

"May I ask your first name and your business here?"

Her voice only shook a little. She could do this.

"Of course, ma'am." Tingle. "My name is Jimmy. I'm here to see Om on an urgent matter." Tingle.

"Thank you, Jimmy. Please leave your motorcycle in the parking lot to the right before you reach the Main Street. Go to the church to request a meeting with Om. You should prepare yourself for a wait. There are many demands on Om's time, and it may be a day or two before he'll see you. It's a wonderful opportunity for spiritual practice. You can work on your patience."

Aware that she was babbling like a schoolgirl, Paula stopped talking. The stranger turned that warm smile on her, and the tingle increased to such an absurd level that her legs shook. Perhaps this was a sign of progress. This man was docile, polite. Meek, even. And yet the attraction she felt was stronger than that she'd experienced when watching documentaries about serial killers. Maybe this was an interim stage between unhealthy sexual urges and the purity of celibacy. Yes. That must be it.

Clarence lifted the barrier, and with a nod, Jimmy mounted the motorcycle, kicked the engine into life, and entered Desolation Station.

Clarence let the barrier fall. "You sure you're ok, Pauline?"

Still tasting blood, Paula nodded.

"Sex," she said, walking back to her position in the gatehouse.

Ten minutes went by before she realised what she'd said instead of *yes*, and spat out her tea.

Chapter Forty-Eight

OM'S LIKING for seclusion was well-documented. Two years after moving to Desolation Station, he announced he and his followers would align their physical body's vibrations with those at the heart of all creation, enabling him to usher the community into the next plane of existence. Om's version of spiritual progress—in Blue's opinion—had more in common with video games than organised religion. The planes of existence behaved suspiciously like levels in a platform game, especially when Om warned of the spiritual enemy to be defeated in each.

Bolsteroni voiced the same suspicion in the encrypted message Blue picked up forty miles back in the parking lot of a coffee shop. He'd also sent a folder with details of every financial transaction Om had made—in various names—plus applications for Desolation Station building permits.

bolsteroni

so you have to defeat the end of level boss to get to heaven

Telling ya this om dude stole all his best ideas from an italian plumber and his bro

this is a religion id be gud at man
whatever
hes a liar anyway cos someones blackmailing him
they tried to hide where the money goes but i crack this kind of
shit in my sleep
keep safe d-man

Blue parked the motorcycle in a bay alongside a dusty, neglected Harley-Davidson. The other vehicles—compacts, sedans, soft-tops, pickups, SUVs, even one eighteen-wheeler—were all caked with yellow dust. Most sat on flat tyres. A few had rotted through their wheel arches, drunkenly facing the exit they would never use. The only well-maintained vehicles were a line of buses, standing ready for the nights their leader took them into the desert to pray under the stars.

Blue walked along Desolation Station's only street, lined with simple dwellings. The general store he passed looked like any other until he noticed nothing had a price, and there was nowhere to pay.

The lack of traffic wasn't the only odd note. There were no telephone wires, and Blue's cell phone had lost all signal. The townspeople—hard not to think of them as prisoners when they dressed like them—kept conversation to a minimum, since Om discouraged superficial communication. Even the animals seemed to understand. A huge Bernese Mountain Dog, led by a young woman in glasses, couldn't quite contain himself when encountering Blue, and let out a greeting, but it was a muffled *buff* rather than a bark. Blue rubbed the animal's large, shaggy head.

Om's presence was ubiquitous, his smiling face beaming at his followers from billboards at intervals along the street, each accompanied by one word. *Prayerful. Mindful. Loving. Awake.*

The residents of Desolation Station had rejected

America's consumerist society. That meant no televisions, no radios—other than short wave for local communication —no computers, and no phones. The town got its water from the underground river, which powered a generator. They only needed enough electricity to heat and light their small homes and cook their food. The houses were mostly single-storey dwellings with three or four bedrooms, a bathroom, and a shared living space where occupants ate and prayed together.

Blue made mental notes as he walked, returning the nods of those he passed.

Two architectural features marked Desolation Station as unusual. One was the watchtower, standing seventy feet above the town. Blue looked up as he walked. While the Ommers espoused a life of peace and love, they were far from pacifists. They expected a worldwide descent into anarchy and chaos, and—since they eschewed any outside communication—they would only know about it when the first marauding gang showed up. When that day came, the watchers in the tower would sound the alarm, the holy men and women of Desolation Station would go to the armoury for their weapons, and a well-armed small army would meet the unwelcome visitors.

Blue caught a flash of sunlight from binoculars and gave a cheery wave to whoever held them in the tower.

The second architectural feature was the church. Half as tall as the watchtower, but much wider and deeper, it squatted at the end of the street, a plain cube with too many windows, unevenly distributed. As photogenic as a nineteen-sixties government building, the church was another example of Om's detachment from earthly concerns. He rejected much that others considered beautiful or pleasurable. The file Bolsteroni had sent concerning Om's blackmail suggested the holy man hadn't turned his back on all beauty and pleasure. Particularly the beauties and pleasures found in the brothels around Reno.

Still, while it was hardly the Taj Mahal, the church was impressive. It was a big white box, sure, but it was the biggest white box for hundreds of miles in every direction.

Steps and ramps led up to the huge open doors, but Blue ignored them, following the path around the church to the left, turning the corner towards the rear, and the building Bolsteroni's hacked permit applications suggested he'd find there. A simple wooden sign confirmed the information was good.

Medical Center.

————

BLUE FOUND the medical building abutting the north wall of the church. The church's west wall, if the plans Jimmy had seen were accurate, had an extra set of rooms jutting out at right angles. Om's private domain, from which he emerged to address the faithful, like a Nevadan Pope.

The medical centre receptionist, a young woman in her mid-twenties, was writing notes on a yellow legal pad. A row of filing cabinets lined the wall to one side. No computer. An old typewriter squatted in the space a flat-screen monitor would normally occupy. Handwritten patient notes. No MRI, no CT scans. Not even an X-ray machine. Medical emergencies were diverted to Reno.

"Can I help you?" The woman looked up and registered Blue's clothing. "Welcome to Desolation Station."

The woman's accent and overly friendly disposition suggested she was Californian.

"I need to see a doctor."

"Sure. Absolutely." She picked up the radio handset.

Blue scanned the waiting area. It was spartan. A row of six wooden chairs, all unoccupied. Physical sickness suggested spiritual failure here. Blue wondered how many residents suffered with treatable conditions rather than attend the medical centre.

The door behind the desk opened, and an Asian man in his forties emerged.

"I'm Doctor Chan. Please follow me."

Chan led Blue into a corridor with doors at intervals. The doctor pushed open the first door. A treatment room with a bed, two chairs, and a locked drugs cabinet.

Blue smiled at the doctor. "It's so quiet," he said. "How many staff work here?"

Chan shrugged. "I'm one of only three doctors in Desolation Station. Today, it's just me and Cara on the front desk."

"Good," said Blue. He clamped his hand over Chan's mouth, grabbed a fistful of orange polyester, and dragged him along the corridor. At the final room, he opened the handle with his elbow, and lifted the doctor inside.

This room was a duplicate of the one Chan had shown him. The only addition was a window looking out at the desert.

Blue pushed the doctor into a chair. Chan's pupils dilated, and his breathing quickened. Blue's voice remained quiet and controlled, but the smaller man blanched as he listened.

"I'm about to take my hand away. If you make a sound, I will punch you in the face. I have punched lots of people in the face, Doctor Chan. If you're lucky, the impact might only break your nose, fracture your cheekbone, or both. If you're not so lucky—and I speak from experience—the punch will break your neck. So keep quiet."

He took his hand away. Chan drew a shuddering

breath and licked his lips. Blue pointed at the drugs cabinet on the wall.

"Do you have sedatives capable of keeping someone of below average build and weight unconscious for around fifteen minutes?"

The doctor looked up at him, confused. Blue clarified.

"It's not for me, doctor. It's for you."

Chapter Forty-Nine

AFTER CHECKING the doctor was genuinely unconscious by slapping him across the face, Blue opened the window and climbed out. He emerged at the rear of the church. A glance right confirmed Bolsteroni's information was good. Om's living quarters, jutting out of the church's rear, made an already ugly building uglier.

Dwight Hardleman, while very rich indeed by any standards, had built his church cheaply, taking as his model the warehouses of one of the world's biggest internet fulfilment companies. His place of worship looked like a massive parcel depot. A steel frame, covered in insulated panels measuring six feet by four feet.

Blue eyed the panels as he jogged along the back wall of the church. As well as mountain climbing in Scotland and France, he'd spent a few months with night-time free-runners in central London. They laughed when he asked them to teach him, pointing out his physique made him ill-suited to the flowing, fast style of parkour. But initial scepticism turned to respect as Blue dragged his heavy body over walls, under bridges, and up buildings. One night, a couple of security guards cornered the group. Blue, arriving a few minutes later, delighted the free runners by staring down the two uniformed men until they backed off in fear.

And now, as he looked up at Om's bathroom, he thought of how easily the old parkour crew would have scaled the sixty feet to the window. They were wiry, lithe, and light. But while he lacked the half-mountain goat DNA that made the best parkour exponents exceptional, Blue had something extra. He had willpower focused so tightly it defied description.

So a climb of sixty feet, even hauling his heavy frame up a panelled wall with very little purchase, caused no trepidation.

Blue pulled his sneakers off. He stuffed his socks inside, tied the laces together, and hung them around his neck. He took six paces back, mapping the best route as he did so, looking for tiny inconsistencies in the placement of the panels, where the gap between them might be an eighth of an inch wider.

His sprint ended with a leap, shoving his left foot into the first gap, then immediately pushing off to reach the first handhold, jamming his right foot into a fresh gap, ignoring the pain.

Momentum was as important as accuracy with such precarious finger and toe holds. Lose momentum, and he would fall. Worse, he would fail. Unthinkable.

Blue's last leap—sideways and upwards to the window sill—left him hanging. He flexed his bruised toes and took a deep breath before looking up.

The bathroom window was open an inch.

A little luck along the way didn't hurt.

Blue let go with his left arm, reached up, found the corner of the window, and hooked his fingers around the frame. It opened smoothly and silently. He brought both legs up to the final panel, pushing his toes as hard as he could into the gap, finding as much purchase as possible. It wasn't much.

With both hands on the sill, he pulled up, simultaneously pistoning both legs.

The third toe on his right foot caught for a split second before giving way. He heard the small, dull crack as he entered the bathroom head first, rolling onto a rug next to a huge, free-standing, roll-top bath.

Blue sat still, taking in deep breaths through his mouth and nose to maximise oxygen intake and minimise noise.

His toe was already swelling, the skin turning dark purple. It wouldn't slow him down. The break was clean, and the bone beneath hadn't pierced the skin.

Music played in the room beyond. Not the ambient, drifty, whale song, massage room choice a spiritual guru might favour, but nineteen seventies middle-of-the-road rock. The Eagles, possibly, or Neil Diamond.

Jimmy found Band-Aids on a shelf alongside six different brands of body lotion. He bound the broken toe to its neighbour. There were boxes of painkillers on the shelf, but Jimmy didn't want his senses dulled.

When ready, he stood behind the door, back to the wall. The sun was sinking, lighting the bathroom a warm orange. Blue didn't know the layout of the room beyond, or how many people were in there, but even prophets had to attend to bodily functions now and then.

Jimmy's breathing slowed, as did his heart rate. A remarkable woman had once taught him it was possible to become so still that you became almost invisible. He would never completely match her ability, but he had developed his own technique since, and—as far as any six foot three, two hundred and twenty pound man could—he faded into the background.

The light faded quickly as the sun disappeared. When he heard footsteps, Blue re-engaged his senses, like a computer emerging from sleep mode.

The door opened and a short, balding man with a wispy grey goatee, wearing a white towelling robe, entered, humming tunelessly. He left the bathroom door open, relying on the light from the main room.

Up close, Dwight Hardleman, or Om, spiritual leader of hundreds in the community of Desolation Station, and inspiration to tens of thousands beyond through videos, books, and online courses, was a disappointment. A religious leader might be expected to project an outward sign of inner enlightenment. The only outward sign Om presented was a long, loud fart, followed by a self-congratulatory, "awesome".

Blue clamped a hand over Om's mouth. "I'm not here to hurt you, but if you call for help, I will. Nod if you understand."

Om complied, trembling. When the guru looked up at the hulking bald figure, reflected light glimmering on the old bullet scars that scored his head, a second, involuntary fart squeaked out.

"Anyone else here?" Blue nodded towards the apartment beyond. Om shook his head. "Good. Here's what's going to happen. You listening?"

Om responded with a brisk series of nods, eager to cooperate. Blue looked him in the eyes, but kept the darkness back, suspecting that—were Dwight Hardleman to get any more scared—he might soil himself.

"I'm taking my hand away. Sit down."

Blue released the man and indicated the toilet. Om put down the seat and collapsed onto it.

"I'm guessing you're not a fan of your local law enforcement representative, Sheriff Al Critchen."

Om, confused by the unexpected direction of the conversation, didn't respond, although the trembling continued.

"I know he's blackmailing you, and I know why."

Hardleman's brows lowered.

"Thing is, Dwight, the situation is worse than you think. Blackmail isn't your biggest problem."

Blue left a pause. He needed to be sure the shaking man on the toilet seat was taking this in. Om cleared his throat. "What's my biggest problem?"

"Critchen is a member of a criminal gang called the Firestarters. Heard of them?"

Hardleman's already terrified expression became even more pronounced.

"Good. Because Desolation Station is their next target."

Om processed the statement, then shook his head, his breathing settling. He had some backbone, after all.

"I don't think so. I've read about them—the Firestarters. Even wondered if they might try their luck here. Our gold reserves are no secret. But we're not some gated, half-asleep retirement community popping valium, playing golf, and watching TV. We are well-armed and well-trained. Critchen knows that."

Hardleman's voice settled as he spoke, and Blue detected some of the authority and conviction that convinced hundreds of followers to sell everything and move to the desert.

"Our lives here aren't purely devoted to spiritual progress, Mister…?"

Blue maintained his silence, and, after clearing his throat again, Om continued.

"I've seen the future in visions. It's violent, and it's ugly. When society rips itself apart, and bandits come calling,

292

we will meet force with force. Anyone who knows about our gold also knows about our armoury. Outside of a military facility, I doubt you'll find a better maintained, comprehensive collection of weapons in Nevada. If the Firestarters come to Desolation Station, they'll die here."

Om had sat up straighter during his speech. "So, whoever you are, and"—he looked at the open window —"however you got in, we don't need your help. We can take care of ourselves."

Blue stared at the portly guru, who blanched and moved back on the toilet seat.

"I'm going to make a few suppositions, Dwight. Tell me if I get anything wrong. OK?"

Om nodded.

"I'm guessing Sheriff Critchen has been a regular visitor over the years, even before blackmailing you.."

Om said nothing.

"I imagine Critchen knows how the watchtower shifts work. He probably complimented you on your foresight. After all, no one can sneak up on you when you're surrounded by flat desert. Night vision devices up there, right?"

Still nothing other than a tiny nod from Om.

"Every so often, Critchen inspects permits, examines random guns, that kind of thing. Yes?"

"Yes." Om flashed a quick look at Blue. "Yes, sir."

"He knows the range of your most powerful rifle, the largest calibre weapons you have, the amount of ammunition. Right?"

"Yes."

"The Firestarters know everything about your defence preparations, Hardleman. If this were a fist fight, they'd turn up with knives. If you had knives, they'd bring guns. What do you think they'll bring to Desolation Station?"

"What do you want from me?" The guru seemed genuinely confused.

"I'm going to save your lives. You're going to take your clients on those buses of yours for a road trip. Stay away for three nights. When you come back, it'll be over."

Om stood up. His eyes were level with the middle of Jimmy's ribcage. He spoke fast, and when his hands shook, folded his arms.

"You come in here, spin some crazy story about the Firestarters. And you want me to believe Al Critchen is one of them? How? He's been in the Joshua police department as long as we've been here. He's a cop. A corrupt cop, and not a nice guy, but that's all. This is bullshit. You spin this crazy story, scare us into leaving, and then you and your friends steal our gold while we're off on this road trip. Yes, you could hurt me, or kill me, but there's only one of you, and there are a few hundred folks out there who will rip you limb from limb, however tough you are. Kill this body, and I'll go to the next spiritual level. I'm not afraid. But you should be. If you want to get out of here alive, you need to leave. Now."

Blue's answer was to grab Hardleman by the throat, lift him off the floor, and carry him to the open window. He didn't stop, instead shoving the small of Om's back against the sill, pivoting him so his body balanced—legs in the bathroom, the rest of him hanging in the warm night air, sixty feet above the desert.

When Blue relaxed his hand enough for Om to breathe, the sounds he made were those of a terrified small animal caught in a trap.

"Lots of people say they're not afraid to die," said Blue, leaning out himself to look Hardleman in the eye. The movement caused Om's balance to shift, and the guru squealed as he slipped another inch away from safety.

"Ninety-nine times out of a hundred, it's not true, and—when the moment comes—I see it in their eyes. Just like you. Am I right? Are you afraid? Because if you really believe that spiritual crap, I can send you to the next level right now. Which is it? Should I drop you on your head? Or—"

Blue released his grip on Om. For a few hundredths of a second, gravity reasserted its dominance, and the guru dropped. A muscular hand grabbed the front of his robe.

"—or would you prefer to live?"

"Yes!" squeaked Om. "Live! I want to live! Please, please. I don't want to die. You're right. Pull me back inside. Please."

A jerk of Blue's arm and the guru was back in the bathroom, curled up on the rug. Om crawled over to the toilet, lifted the seat, and threw up. Blue ran some water and passed a wet cloth to the gasping figure kneeling on the floor. Hardleman wiped his mouth and sat leaning against the tub, wheezing.

Blue flushed the toilet, put the seat down, and sat next to him.

"Good. So few people truly know themselves, Hardleman. You should have let me finish talking. I don't expect you to believe me without proof."

Om struggled to control his voice. "How can you prove it?"

"I'll bet the sheriff's last visit included a check of the armoury."

Om nodded.

"Did you meet him during that visit?"

Om found his voice again, but it was missing much of its power. "No. I, er, I try to avoid the man if I can. Joe, my most trusted disciple, accompanied Critchen to the armoury." Om's tone was hesitant.

"You have one of those short-wave radios next door?"

"Yes."

"Good. Let's go call Joe. Send him back to the armoury. Critchen left something there. A backpack, or a bag. Tell him to radio in when he finds it."

———

WHILE THEY WAITED in the apartment, Blue picked up a gold bar from a row on a shelf, weighing it in his hand.

"This real?"

Om nodded. "A kilo bar. Worth sixty-four thousand dollars. The dollar will soon collapse along with every other currency. Humanity will go back to physical currency with actual value. We are prepared for that."

"Sure you are." Jimmy replaced it on the shelf.

They lapsed into silence for six minutes, then the radio on the table crackled into life.

"Om? I'm in the armoury. You're right. The sheriff left his backpack here. I found it in the corner, under some boxes of ammunition. What do you want me to do?"

Hardleman looked to Blue for instructions. Jimmy was spooning hot chilli into his mouth. Om's apartment was more like a luxury hotel suite than a monk's cell, and the well-stocked fridge had contained a selection of meals. He motioned for Om to hand over the radio.

"Joe? I'm going to hand the radio over to a friend of mine. A… security adviser. He'll tell you what to do."

Blue took the handset. "Joe? Do you have a sharp knife?"

"Yes, sir." The clipped tone suggested ex-military.

"Don't open the backpack. Slit the middle of it so you can see inside, but do it carefully."

During the thirty-six seconds of silence that followed,

Blue finished the chilli. Om twitched with the after-effects of his trip out of the bathroom window, his second large glass of fine tequila doing little to settle him. At the sound of Joe's voice, he jerked as if jolted by a cattle prod.

"Sir?"

Blue picked up the handset. "Go ahead."

"It's a bomb. Linked to a cell phone. Enough plastic explosives to destroy the armoury. Probably half a block in either direction, too. What should I do?"

Blue handed the radio to Om, who lifted it to his lips, his right hand bracing his left.

"Don't tell anyone what you've seen, Joe. Lock up and bring the armoury keys here."

"Yes, sir."

Om replaced the handset.

"Guess we're all going for a bus ride."

Blue smiled. "Good decision."

"For how long?"

"Come back Friday. That should give me time to take care of your visitors."

———

THE BUSES LEFT an hour after midnight. Blue followed their progress through night-vision binoculars from the top of the watchtower.

Hardleman had gathered the faithful in church two hours earlier, speaking from the balcony to announce a three-night period of prayer and meditation in the desert. The snake of buses heading along the single road towards the distant highway contained every resident of Desolation Station.

Blue, listening from the apartment behind the balcony, was impressed by Om's recovery from the quivering wreck

297

of only an hour earlier. The man who addressed his disciples spoke with conviction, passion, and purpose. His followers did as he asked, and left their homes, bringing only food and water.

As the taillights faded out of sight, Blue scanned the eerily still and silent town. The armoury—minus a few of its weapons—still contained Critchen's bomb. The attack could—in theory—happen any time. Critchen's vacation began today.

Blue's gut told him they were coming tonight.

It took him three hours to prepare, which included checking the weapons he'd borrowed from the armoury.

The moon was a sliver, and the stars bathed the desert in a cold, blue glow.

Jimmy lay down in the street near the town limits. Like the trackers who crossed this landscape when Desolation Station was little more than a line of wooden buildings, he relied on senses other than sight to alert him to imminent danger. Any approaching vehicle would cause vibrations in the hard ground miles away and wake him.

He placed two handguns and the rifle within reach, leaving the hunting knife he had borrowed in its sheath on his ankle.

Sleep came easily. Rest, while not strictly necessary, was good for mind and body. No dreams disturbed him, no thoughts prevented him from sinking into the first stages of unconsciousness, ready to emerge into full wakefulness in less than a second.

Blue let the pretence of humanity he had worn since Tom called him slip away, seeping into the Nevada dirt like spilled blood. Its departure left him stronger, more present.

Om had asked a question before boarding a bus.

"What's in it for you? You haven't asked for money. You haven't asked for anything. Why are you doing this?"

Blue had thought again of the pall of smoke over Pike Point, the charred bodies in black bags in the street. Paul Geary's cold smile in the bookshop. The way Geary had touched Anna's shoulder, knowing she'd soon be dead, probably at his hand. Then he thought of Lydia Garcia. A child hearing her parents murdered while she hid, terrified.

He'd answered the guru truthfully.

"Because I can't do anything else."

Chapter Fifty

ON A QUIET STRETCH of US 93, a Nevada highway patrol car closed in on a truck. The lights on its roof came on, along with a brief wail of its siren.

Inside the truck's cab, Dionne James put a hand on the driver's arm.

"Pull over. I'll do the talking."

Hennie Castello signalled and slowed the truck to a stop.

"I was doin' fifty-one, fifty-two, Jesse. I wasn't speedin'."

"It's probably a random check, Hennie. Just follow my lead. Now switch."

The two of them swapped places. Jesse kept her eyes on the side-view mirror, watching the Ford Interceptor pull onto the dusty shoulder behind them. The sun had sunk beneath the horizon ninety minutes earlier, and, other than the cop twenty yards back, they had only encountered three vehicles in the past thirty minutes.

Jesse unclipped the walkie-talkie on her belt as the driver's door of the patrol car opened. She spoke to the passengers concealed in the truck's rear.

"Folks, we have a state trooper for company. Nice and quiet, please."

She turned off the device, leaned across to the glove compartment, and placed it there, removing a Ruger compact pistol. Jesse and Hennie wore matching uniforms: black pants, tan short-sleeved shirts with the words *Safehands Disposal, Specialist Haulage* stitched above the breast pocket.

She wound down the window. The cop was young, lean, bearded. He pulled a cap over his shaved head and gestured for Jesse to get out. His handgun was still buttoned into his holster, his body language relaxed. She killed the engine, pushed the door open with her foot, climbed down a step, then dropped onto the blacktop.

"Evening, officer. Hope everything's alright. I wasn't speeding, was I?"

The cop shook his head, looked her over. Evidently decided she looked too young to call her Ma'am. "No, Miss, you were doing a steady fifty. Did you realise you have a busted tail light?"

Jesse frowned. "No, I did not. Bob?"

Hennie's face appeared as he leaned across the cab.

"Our tail light is broken."

Hennie shook his head. "Must have happened on the road. I checked her over before we left Phoenix."

This was only half a lie. Hennie had checked the truck over in a storage facility half a mile from Harry Reid Airport, Las Vegas.

"Hmm." The cop headed to the rear. The words on the truck's side matched those on Jesse's breast pocket. Jesse followed the cop. Hennie stayed in the cab.

"Where you folks heading?"

"Chemical disposal facility in Wyoming. Just north of Green River."

301

At the rear, the patrolman touched the defective tail light with the toe of his boot. It flickered briefly on, then off again. Stickers on the back doors pictured skulls. One said *Warning: Poison*, the other *Extreme Caution: Contagious Substance.*

"What is it you're transporting, exactly?"

Jesses shrugged. "Now you're asking. They train us on how to handle this stuff, but that's all. The paperwork has the details, but I flunked science. You're more than welcome to check. My clipboard is up front."

She started towards the cab, but the cop didn't follow.

"Open her up, will you? I want to check everything is as it should be."

"Sure thing. I'll get the keys."

As she got close to the cab, Jesse called up to Hennie. "Bob, the officer wants to check inside. Can you get the keys and a spare suit, please?"

Hennie didn't answer, but when he appeared, his jaw was clenched shut. She gave him a cautionary look. Hennie's tendency to act first, think later, had been tough to train out of him.

"Easy," she said, quietly. He held out two yellow bags, dropping them through the window to Jesse. She walked back to the cop. He was stroking his chin.

"There are better routes north from Phoenix. Why are you out here?"

Jesse smiled. "Our routes take us as far from large population centres as possible."

The cop looked up at the warning symbols again, then at the bags Jesse carried. She opened one, removing a rolled up hazmat suit and oxygen tank. She started putting hers on and gestured at the cop to do the same.

"Sorry, officer. Regulations. No skin contact, and—in

302

case any of the containers have been compromised—you need your own air supply. I'll help you set it up."

Jesse took her own suit out of the bag, laying out the various items in front of her. She stepped into the over-shoes first, then pulled the suit up to her hips. The patrolman shook his head.

"Is this really necessary?"

Jesse shrugged, picked up the oxygen tank, and made a show of inspecting it, twisting the valve to release a brief hiss of gas. "Guess I can't force you. But this shit—excuse my language—can kill you. Breathe in a few particles of the wrong thing and… well. You should see the photos they showed us in training. Sheesh."

The cop took a moment, then picked up his own bag, unzipping it.

Someone sneezed inside the back of the truck.

For a second, everyone froze. Everyone but Jesse. Hennie stopped moving and gawped. The cop, whose instincts had been pretty good so far—good enough to check Jesse's cover story out—recovered fast, dropping the bag as his right hand went to his holster. His fingers made it as far as the clasp before he grunted, dropped to his knees, then fell sideways, a hole half the size of a nickel in his forehead.

Hennie joined her. Nudged the dead man with the side of his boot. Looked up and down the empty highway. No headlights visible in either direction, and the road cut straight through the flat landscape for miles.

Jesse replaced the Ruger in her pocket, and nodded at the car behind them, blue and red light strobing across the desert. "Kill the lights, Hennie."

She stepped up to the truck, grabbed the handle. The rear doors weren't locked.

"I'm opening it up," called Jesse. "Come on out. We have a mess to clear up."

Four men jumped out. No one spoke, and they all watched Jesse, waiting for orders.

Ed Donnelly, Ryan Leto, Al Critchen, and Paul Geary were so close to becoming ludicrously rich, they could almost taste it. A dead cop on a Nevada highway couldn't stop them now. Jesse would know what to do. They stood in a semicircle, looking at the corpse, and at the patrol car, its lights now turned off, idling on the shoulder.

"OK."

They all turned their attention to their leader. Hennie rejoined the group, standing next to Geary.

"Don't tell me who sneezed. In a few hours, we'll have new identities, new lives, and enough money to do whatever the hell we want. Someone nearly threw all of that away. If I knew who, I'd struggle to stop myself shooting you."

No one moved or spoke.

"I have a solution which will buy us time. Do as I say and don't ask questions. Got that?"

They got that.

"Good. Hennie, Paul, put the cop in the trunk of his car."

The two men did as instructed. Al swore when the cop's face swung their way.

"I know him. Martin Pass. Ambitious little fucker." He spat in the dirt.

Jesse used her phone's flashlight to illuminate the area around her feet. She found the bullet's casing and tucked it in her pocket. She kicked dirt and dust over the pool of blood where the cop had fallen.

To the north, a distant vehicle approached.

"We need to get moving. Al, drive the car. We'll follow you."

Critchen looked surprised. Al's was the only face someone around here might recognise. But he did as he was told.

Once the cop car pulled around the truck, Hennie followed it as instructed. They passed the oncoming vehicle six minutes later—a station wagon with a sleeping family in the back; the driver looking like he wished he could join them.

Jesse waited another five minutes before picking up the walkie-talkie.

"Far enough, Al. Pull over."

The car in front slowed and left the road, bumping to a halt on the shoulder. Hennie went to follow, but Jesse grabbed the wheel. "Stay on the blacktop. No tyre marks that way."

The truck stopped on the highway.

"Kill the lights," said Jesse. "I won't be long."

Al got out of the car, frowning. He'd evidently been thinking.

"Hey, Jesse, I don't get it. Someone is gonna see the car on the shoulder and call it in. Or the cop won't pick up his radio and they'll send someone to check. And they'll find him dead in the trunk, shot, and dumped out here. They'll call in the big guns, Jesse. Trust me on that. Roadblocks, helicopters... everything with out-of-state plates is gonna get pulled over and searched. I know you said no questions, but I don't get it, Jesse."

"You're right, Al. As it stands, this is a terrible plan. But I'm not done. Pop the trunk, will you?"

"Sure." He leaned into the car, and the trunk popped open. Jesse sat on the sill. The dead cop stared up at her. She leaned in, sliding the cop's handgun out of its holster.

She waved a hand at Al. "Move back."

He took a few steps away.

"Perfect." Jesse shot Critchen three times: the first in the gut, the second in the heart, and the third in the shoulder. The middle shot was the one that counted. The other two were window dressing.

Al took in a few wet breaths, coughed, and was still. She hoped he'd survived long enough to realise she knew about his betrayal.

Jesse wiped her prints off the gun and placed it in the cop's hand. She stepped away from the car, took the Ruger from her pocket, and shot the cop's corpse three times in the torso. Then she placed the pistol close to Critchen's body, taking his own gun and his walkie-talkie. Finally, she dropped the bullet casing she had retrieved. She spoke to her dead colleague while she worked.

"Here's what happened, Al," she said. "This cop sees someone walking along the shoulder. He knows the guy. It's a local sheriff. So he pulls over. Maybe he's concerned about the sheriff's state of mind. Turns out his concern is well-founded, since the sheriff shoots him in the gut, sticks his body in the trunk, and drives off to bury him. Thing is, the cop isn't quite dead, and when the crazy sheriff pops the trunk, the cop lets loose. There's a firefight, during which the cop gets shot in the head, but—what do you know?—the sheriff takes a bullet to the heart and he dies, too. Now, ballistic evidence won't back up that story, but by the time they find out, I'll be on a private jet. You stupid, greedy piece of shit."

Jesse went back to the truck. Hennie said nothing. At a nod from her, he put the truck into drive and continued heading north. The turning towards Desolation Station was thirty miles up the road.

Jesse spoke into the walkie-talkie.

"Al's dead. For the past few years, he's been black-mailing Dwight Hardleman, better known as Om, the man whose town is about to provide the final deposit in our retirement accounts. Al knew my rules. You all do. He broke them, and he could have ruined everything. We will split his share between us. That's all."

The truck, still sticking to a steady fifty miles an hour, headed towards their final score, the culmination of a decade of work.

Next stop, Desolation Station.

Chapter Fifty-One

BLUE WOKE UP, but didn't open his eyes. He kept his body relaxed, his pulse slow, his breaths deep.

The vibrations that roused him were barely perceptible. He pushed his left ear onto the compacted earth of Desolation Station's main street.

Blue listened past the insects and the reptiles, the breeze, the expansion and contraction of wood and brick as the night cooled.

And there it was. A distinct note, faint, but unmistakable. The rumble of an engine, the gritty hum of tyres on the blacktop. Still miles away, but no doubt where they were heading. The road from the highway ended at Desolation Station.

Jimmy stood up and performed a series of stretches to warm his body.

He tucked the handguns into the holsters that hung from his hips, scooped up the rifle, and swung it over his shoulder.

For a split second, he became aware of Tom's presence —an occurrence rare enough to make him pause, as the uncanny sensation of someone else taking the next breath with him, looking through his eyes at the starlit street and the desert beyond, came and went within a single heartbeat. Then Blue was alone.

A scrap of memory remained of a silent, traumatised boy recovering from horrific injuries in hospital. On the television, a movie played in the liminal hours between late afternoon and evening. A man in black stared down a street in the American West a century earlier, pistols in holsters, cheroot between lips, eyes narrowed. Waiting for an enemy to arrive, ready to deliver the only justice he understood.

Blue smiled. Yes. A good memory.

He jogged to the watchtower, taking the steps of the narrow staircase inside two at a time, generating a light sweat. At the top, he focused binoculars on the approaching vehicle. Judging from the style of the headlamps, a truck.

Another minute passed before the lights of the gatehouse helped fill in some details. The truck had a male driver. A woman sat alongside him. If Martino's information was good, she was the gang's leader. Dionne 'Jesse' James. Blue focused the binoculars on her face. Dark hair pulled back, light brown skin. A killer of hundreds, including the inhabitants of Pike Point. All for money.

He put the binoculars down.

The Firestarters were here. They expected a payday. They would get a reckoning instead.

Chapter Fifty-Two

"IS THAT IT?"

Hennie pointed through the dirty windshield at a distant smudge of light. He didn't have to stick to the speed limit anymore, but the truck wasn't good for much more than sixty-five miles per hour.

Jesse slid a pair of binoculars from the dash. "Yep. That's it."

She raised the walkie-talkie. "Ten minutes. Check your weapons."

Half a mile after the turn-off, they'd pulled over, changing from their *Safehands* uniform to green medical scrubs. They'd peeled away the truck's fake company logo, revealing the name of a medical supplies company.

For the final few miles, they drove in silence. Hennie's fingers tightened a little on the wheel, and his breathing became shallower. Jesse's reaction to the imminent raid was the opposite. The closer they got, the more relaxed she became. She had devoted years of her life to the Firestarters, training this team for the most audacious criminal plan in history, moving them into position in remote police departments all over the country. She had researched their targets to an obsessive extent. This made her remarkable. Unique, even. Dionne 'Jesse' James had no criminal record, no underworld connections. An invisible leader of an untraceable gang. Patrice Martino's appearance had shaken her, but she had taken care of it. She had turned Martino from a threat to an asset. The conclusion of his book would cement the Firestarters' reputation.

Five towns had burned. One remained, its lights growing closer by the second. For a town full of Preppers, the residents of Desolation Station were woefully unprepared for this. Since Om didn't trust the outside world, they had no way of raising the alarm. No telephone network, no cell phone tower.

By now, the team on duty in their famous watchtower would have spotted the approaching vehicle. The two disciples in the gatehouse would be ready to greet them. Night vision binoculars could pick out the truck's medical supplies logo, the same company used by Desolation Station's medical centre.

Jesse smiled at the thought of the backpack full of explosives in Om's precious armoury. Before anyone discovered the medical supplies truck wasn't what it appeared to be, the Nevada desert would light up with an unexpected firework display.

The gatehouse was half a mile away. "Stand ready."

On a recessed shelf above the windshield, the truck's cab had a Citizens' Band radio set. Although it looked normal, it was useless as a method of communication. Jesse had illegally imported a crate of devices from New Zealand, a country which used different radio frequency bands to the rest of the world. One channel connected the walkie-talkies the Firestarters carried. Another, at the far end of the dial, was reserved for tonight's raid. In an area with no cell phone coverage, the New Zealand CB set could signal the walkie-talkie strapped to a bagful of C4 explosives in Desolation Station's armoury.

Hennie stopped the truck at the gatehouse, just short of the dropped barrier across the road. The lights were off, and Jesse couldn't see anyone inside the low building. Al's report stated there were always two Ommers on duty.

The truck's suspension bounced as the three men in the back dismounted. They stayed out of sight of the tower.

Hennie found a note stuck to the inside of the gate-house door which solved the mystery. He peeled it off, walked inside, and came back with a radio handset. He handed the piece of paper up to Jesse.

Attending prayer meeting. Please wait here until someone can help you. If urgent, use the radio provided to contact the watchtower. DO NOT PROCEED WITHOUT CONTACTING THE WATCHTOWER.

Jesse didn't like it. The gatehouse should be attended twenty-four-seven. It must be a pretty important prayer meeting to release those on duty.

She wound down the window and listened. Up ahead, the town was eerily silent. Even at one a.m., she expected some sound, some movement, to carry across the still night air.

"This is gonna be easy," said Hennie, smiling. "They're all in church."

Jesse didn't look at him. "Too easy," she muttered. She didn't believe in instinct, in making decisions based on gut feeling, but, despite all her research and experience, this didn't *feel* right. Something was off, something didn't fit. For the first time in her adult life, Jesse doubted herself. The sensation lifted the hairs on her arms like an icy breeze across her skin. Then it faded, and she gave the tiniest shake of her head. Tonight was the last raid, the final stop on a pillaging tour of America. Not a good time to allow emotion to supersede logic.

She called softly out of the open window into the still desert air. "Leto? Your toy good to go?"

A deep voice responded from the rear of the truck.

"Sure thing, Jesse."

"Good. Fire on my word."

"Got it."

Jesse reached up to the CB radio and twisted the dial to select the channel linked to Critchen's bomb. The late sheriff of Eureka may have been a disobedient asshole, but he had been competent.

Absolute silence fell. There must have been ambient noises in the desert—wind, the rustles and creaks of plants, the whispering scuttle of lizards and insects—but none of the Firestarters heard them. The adrenaline flooding their systems affected all of them differently, but even Jesse couldn't fight it. Her body tightened as if someone had thrown a switch on some vast, powerful machine, causing vibrations in her bones and teeth.

Her voice emerged as a harsh whisper.

"Hennie, call the watchtower."

In this heightened silence, when Hennie spoke on the radio, his voice sounded unnaturally distinct.

"Evening, folks. Am I speaking to whoever is up there in that impressive watchtower of yours?"

There was a sarcastic edge to his voice Jesse wouldn't have tolerated previously, but since she wouldn't have to tolerate Hennie—or any of the others—after tonight, she let it slide. So what if the lookouts on the watchtower detected an arrogant challenge in Hennie's words? They wouldn't be alive long enough to do anything about it.

"You are. I'm looking right at you."

Hennie responded with a mock salute.

Jesse's skin was crawling again, and the doubts flooded back. Although Hennie seemed unfazed—unsurprising, since he had the emotional intelligence of a vase—the voice from the watchtower had a visceral impact on her. A ball of ice replaced her heart for a beat. Her lips unconsciously retracted from her teeth, and she bared them like a cornered animal. When the voice spoke again, the impact lessened in its intensity, but the echoes sounded in her body.

"Welcome to Desolation Station."

No threat, no aggression, either in the words or the tone. The speaker spoke almost without inflection. Why did it make her feel like someone had pushed a blade against her throat?

With an effort, she swallowed, took a breath, and pushed the unwanted, and unwarranted, reaction away.

She put her forefinger on the button and counted down.

"Three, two, one."

She pressed the button. Jesse held her breath, releasing it when a fireball lit the houses and church orange-red as the armoury exploded.

The sound came next, a dull rumble and crack of masonry violently dismantled, reduced to fragments, and hurled in all directions. The ammunition inside the building exacerbated the force of the explosion, and a series of smaller explosions, still significant, followed the first.

"You're up, Leto."

Jesse watched Ryan Leto—former state trooper at Whitney Bluff, Maine—in the side-view mirror as he stepped out with what looked like a short drainpipe braced against his shoulder. Leto didn't rush, taking a wide stance for stability, looking through the sight towards the tower, its occupants distracted by the destruction to the east.

When he pulled the trigger of the rocket-propelled grenade launcher, yellow flame shot out of both the front and back, and the weapon bucked and boomed.

The passing missile left an after-image on Jesse's retina —a yellow line, already fading, drawn between the truck and the watchtower.

The top of the tower disappeared in a yellow-white flash, then a deadly rainfall of bricks and metal fell on the surrounding streets.

The crew couldn't resist a whoop of pleasure and excitement at the sight. With the armoury destroyed, and their only armed protectors now burning inside the remains of the watchtower, the citizens of Desolation Station were helpless.

Even Jesse couldn't prevent a tight half-smile.

She turned to Leto, the rocket launcher now held at his side, a big shit-eating grin on his dumb face.

"Nice shot. Now put it away, and let's go to work."

Leto patted the launcher. "Sure thing, Je—"

His grin disappeared at the same moment as a hole materialised between his eyes, and a thousandth of a second before the back of his skull blew open. The impact of the sniper's bullet punched his corpse off its feet, and he came to rest in a sitting position, a confused expression on what remained of his face, before his body caught up with the reality of his situation, and flopped backwards.

Geary and Donnelly froze.

"Take cover!" Jesse screamed, taking her own advice, and dropping into the truck's footwell. She waited for the next shot, but it didn't come. She had been looking at Leto when he died, so couldn't locate the shooter. Almost all of

Desolation Station's buildings were low, single storey. With the tower gone, where would a sniper hide?

"Castello!"

Hennie's voice answered from the gatehouse. "I'm here. What the fuck?"

"Get back over here and drive." Why hadn't the sniper taken another shot?

"Fuck that, Jesse."

"Excuse me?" Jesse's tone held a warning, but internally she acknowledged they were all in shock. They had encountered resistance before, but her plans had always allowed for multiple contingencies. They had never been taken by surprise. Until now.

"I mean, no offence," continued Hennie, "but you saw what just happened, right? Someone just blew Leto's fucking head off, Jesse. If I run to the truck, I'm gonna get my head blown off, too. Think I might stay here."

"You stay there and I'll shoot you myself. Get ready to move."

Jesse grabbed the radio. Kept her voice low, steady, unruffled. Best to remind them who was in charge, and why.

"Donnelly, Geary."

"We're here." Geary, over the years, had matured into a reliable lieutenant.

"Take another rocket from the box. And grab Uzis, both of you. I'm gonna roll the truck forward. Stay close to the rear. Hennie, when it comes alongside, get in."

Staying low, Jessie put her foot on the brake and pulled the stick into drive. She kicked the driver's door open, then slid across to the passenger side, easing her foot off the brake. The vehicle trickled forward towards the barrier.

Hennie's lapse of loyalty proved temporary. As the

truck's fender contacted the barrier, he sprinted and dived, landing in a sprawl of limbs on the seat alongside Jesse.

"Stay down, give it some gas, and break the barrier," said Jesse. "Once you're through, maintain a walking pace."

Hennie's eyes were wide, his breaths coming fast. He did as instructed, practically sliding into the footwell to keep the engine block between him and any bullets. The truck jerked forward.

Jesse hissed at him to keep it steady, then slid out of the passenger door, hit the ground and rolled. As the truck hit the barrier, causing it to bend, buckle, then give way with a screech of metal, the rear doors came alongside her, Geary and Donnelly following on foot. Geary handed her the second rocket and waited for instructions.

"Donnelly. Run to the front and get ready to open fire on the town," she said. "East to west. Aim for the rooftops. About a two-second burst."

"East to west?"

Ed Donnelly's grasp of geography was tenuous, but he was an excellent shot. "Left to right," she said.

"Got it."

"Geary, do the same, but aim for the windows. Distract that fucker so I can kill him."

They jogged away. The truck bumped over the broken barrier. The rocket launcher lay next to Leto's corpse.

"Fire!" she shouted, and the sound of submachine gun fire punctured the night, followed almost immediately by the crash of breaking glass.

Jesse ran. She grabbed the launcher, barely breaking stride to do it, and threw herself at the gatehouse, crawling inside.

The window at the back of the building faced the

town. As she looked out, Jesse reloaded the rocket launcher and brought it to her shoulder.

A speck of dust worked its way underneath her right eyelid, but she ignored the powerful urge to blink, waiting for the enemy to respond.

The returning shot came a fraction of a second after Geary and Donnelly stopped firing. The sniper was fast. Faster than anticipated. Accurate, too, judging by Geary's hissed, "Jesus!"

But it gave Jesse what she wanted. A flash from a distant muzzle on a rooftop to the east. Only one sniper?

As she squeezed the trigger, she saw a second flash from the same position, and the window blew out. A bullet smacked into the wall behind her a millisecond after the rocket left the tube, the explosive roar of its departure painfully loud in the confined space.

She'd thought the sniper was good, but this was something else. To return fire back in response to Donnelly and Geary, then deduce it was a diversion and turn the weapon onto the gatehouse, demonstrated a reasoning process almost inhumanly fast.

The building underneath the sniper exploded in a bright flash, the sound of destruction reaching her a split second later. Inhuman or not, no one survived that.

Jesse jogged back to the truck. "Geary, Donnelly, get in the back."

She swung herself up into the driver's seat. Castello scuttled over, still ducking. When she pressed the accelerator fully, the truck lurched forward towards the town, where the burning armoury and tower had now been joined by a third conflagration on the main street.

For a moment, Jesse experienced something close to regret about the sniper. The death of such a talent seemed almost wasteful.

She kept low as they approached the parking lot on the outskirts of Desolation Station, but the truck progressed unhampered by any more gunfire. A lone sniper left to defend the town should the watchtower fall? It made no sense. Also, if the townspeople were in church, why had they stayed there, despite the explosions and gunfire? She had missed something.

Jesse brought the truck to a stop across the street from the burning building she had hit. Reflected flames danced in the windshields of the cars to her right.

She must have grunted when she worked it out, because Hennie Castello swung around in his seat.

"Jesse?"

"The buses," she said. All the photos of Desolation Station hacked from satellite images, or supplied by Al Critchen, showed the same row of vehicles lined up at the edge of the parking lot. Where they should have been, there stood a row of empty spaces. "Where are all the buses?"

Chapter Fifty-Three

TEN MINUTES EARLIER, AS THE FIRESTARTERS' truck pulled to a stop outside the gatehouse, Blue grabbed the radio and descended the watchtower stairs, keeping to the rear of the houses on the main street. As he walked, he spoke to the gang member who radioed in, keeping up the illusion that he was responding from the watchtower.

Jimmy's timing couldn't have been much better. As he climbed the ladder behind the house nearest the approach road, an explosion behind him confirmed the destruction of the armoury. He crawled onto the flat roof and raised the sniper rifle, a SIG SSG 3000.

He picked up a male through the night vision scope. The man held an RPG-7. A flash of yellow and the barrel of the rocket launcher jerked up, its payload leaving at nearly seven hundred miles per hour. The watchtower exploded.

Jesse and her cohorts had wiped out all of Desolation Station's defence capabilities. Well, not quite all.

Eye pressed against the scope, Jimmy registered the triumphant grin of the man with the RPG-7. Blue squeezed the rifle's trigger. Without waiting to see the result, he tracked the barrel towards the truck. He caught a distant yell from the woman in the truck's cab and watched two men throw themselves behind the vehicle too fast for a second shot. One of them, he hoped, was Paul Geary. He didn't want to kill Geary at a distance. He wanted to look the fake cop in the eye when he died.

No one was visible in the driving seat of the truck, but Jesse was shouting orders. Too far away to make out individual words.

The man Blue had sniped had been either Ryan Leto, Ed Donnelly, or Hennie Castello. He would have recognised Geary or Al Critchen, whose face Blue had seen in Bolsteroni's report. He hadn't bothered to memorise the others. They'd be dead soon, anyhow.

Two men stood behind the truck. A third in the gatehouse. Jesse was in the truck, and a fourth gang member was dead. If Martino's information held up, there were six Firestarters. Desolation Station was their final hit. Blue expected all of them to be here.

He waited for their next move. Now he'd find out how well Jesse improvised.

He didn't have long to wait. The truck moved, nosing into the metal barrier across the road. Jesse stayed down as she drove, presenting no target. When the barrier gave way, the man in the gatehouse sprinted the six or seven yards between him and the truck, diving through the open driver's door. Blue kept the scope on the truck. A better chance would present itself.

The truck, after slowing almost to a stop as it destroyed the barrier, revved and picked up speed, heading for the town. Jimmy smiled with genuine pleasure at the sight. Confronted with unexpected resistance, Jesse might have elected to keep her winnings. He had half-expected the truck to turn around and drive away. He would have shot out their tyres, then hunted them down.

Instead, Jesse had continued her attack. Confident of winning. Good. She and her colleagues had killed men, women, and children without mercy. Let them come.

Machine-gun fire erupted from the truck, the bullets punching holes in the building below him, and those next to it. The windows went next, the sound of smashing glass a constant refrain as the bullets sprayed across the street. They weren't aiming at him, he knew, swinging the rifle around. Their firing pattern was indiscriminate, close to random.

He found two shooters at the front passenger side of the truck. They were already moving as he took his shot, missing both.

A distraction, he realised. But distracting him from what? He swung the scope back in the opposite direction. The rocket launcher had gone. Blue brought the scope to bear on the only place where someone might aim and fire unseen. The gatehouse. He squeezed off a single shot before his body overruled his brain, acting without hesitation. He dropped the rifle as the telltale yellow flash registered on his retina through the gatehouse window.

Blue sprinted across the flat roof, ignored the ladder, and threw himself into the night. The height of Desolation Station's simple dwellings meant he only had around ten feet to fall, and the yard below was clear of obstacles. To avoid injury, Blue prepared himself to employ the same simple technique used by millions of military parachutists when dropping into enemy territory. Legs together, take the initial impact on the balls of the feet, then the heels, already falling sideways to spread the shock of landing evenly across the calves, thighs, glutes, and lats, rolling to bring him back to his feet.

It didn't play out that way.

The RPG-7's payload hit the house as he jumped, the shock wave pushing him away from the rear wall, already ripping itself apart. Like a giant hand meeting a fly, his body was swatted into the night. A piece of brick caught him on his right shoulder, and Jimmy spun as he fell, all control of his descent lost.

He mitigated the potential damage as much as possible, keeping his form, feet still together, body as relaxed as he could make it, considering the fact that he was being propelled by an exploding building, and his jacket was on fire.

The brightness of the explosion gave him one slight advantage: he saw the ground before he hit it. Unfortunately, since he could change nothing about his approach, the knowledge only confirmed the obvious. This was going to hurt. A lot.

Instead of using five consecutive points on his body to spread the impact, he had the choice of two: his head or his arm. His head may have survived a bullet, but Blue didn't fancy his chances if he allowed his cranium to break his fall. Instead, he turned his face to look along his other shoulder, meaning his right arm took all the damage. He heard the bone snap before the back of his head succumbed to gravity, hit the ground, and he lost consciousness.

Chapter Fifty-Four

BLUE'S first thought on waking was that he had been lucky. He had ended his fall face up, so his body smothered the flames on his jacket. He hadn't burned to death while unconscious.

His second thought concerned the passage of time. Periods of unconsciousness distorted perception. It might have been seconds; minutes, or hours.

Blue had flipped as he'd fallen, landing with his head towards the burning house. His scalp prickled with heat. The fire still raged. Beyond the crackle and roar of the flames, he heard the truck's engine.

Seconds, then. He'd only been out for seconds. Lucky again.

His third thought involved moving, fast, which he duly tried to do, rolling into a kneeling position. His broken arm made itself known in a flash of agony.

A broken toe was one thing. He could ignore the pain. The arm wasn't so easy. Blue, reaching across his body with his left hand, used his fingers to trace a line from his right wrist to his shoulder, squeezing as he went. He found a weak point in one of the carpal bones, then two definite breaks—the radius and humerus. Anticipating the pain as he squeezed, he opened a mental door to the darkness and channelled it there. Pain was nature's way of reminding him he had an injury that needed seeing to. He didn't need the reminder.

He got to his feet. Stood in the yard for a few seconds, checking his eyesight, a sure indicator of any brain injury. No blurring, no ghost images, just a normal backyard behind a house on fire, in a ghost town full of killers.

Using his good hand to hold his arm tight against his body, Blue jogged back along the path. Close to the smoking watchtower, he ducked inside the houses he passed, opening drawers and cupboards. He found what he needed at the third try—a roll of wide electrical tape. With no time to make a proper splint, he wrapped the tape awkwardly around his body, pinning his arm in place. In the yard behind the next house, he picked up the axe and assault rifle he'd left there. The rifle's magazine held a hundred rounds, effectively fully automatic because of an after-market alteration. A blunt instrument compared to the Sig he'd abandoned on the rooftop, but fine for his purposes. And he needed a big magazine, since he couldn't reload easily with one arm.

Back on the path, Blue ran past the remains of the watchtower, crossed behind, and looked back along the street. Jesse's truck had stopped opposite the parking lot. Two hostiles with submachine guns—Uzis, he thought—stood outside the burning house. The fire prevented them from confirming his demise. Good.

Using the dancing shadows of the fire for cover, Blue crossed the street unobserved. Fifty yards beyond the church, close to the still-burning armoury, a utility building housed the equipment that distributed hydroelectric power to the town.

Two minutes with the axe, and the town's lights were off, along with all the power. Blue emerged into a night lit only by the flames from the armoury and watchtower, the fire at the far end of the street, and the headlights of the truck. His inner darkness flowed into the surrounding shadows. He had one good arm, a rifle with a hundred rounds of ammunition, two knives, and—hopefully—the element of surprise. It would be have to be enough.

According to Om, the church housed nearly a thousand one-kilo gold bars in its vault. Current value over sixty million dollars.

Everyone in Desolation Station knew where the gold was. The steps down to the vault were a spiral leading to a reinforced door. And the steps were in the centre of the huge open space inside the church. Smart thinking, Blue admitted. The church was always milling with people. The faithful may have given up their material wealth, but by placing the vault in full view of all, Om showed the gold belonged to the community, not to him.

The truck moved forwards. The two men with submachine guns—Geary was one of them—rejoined their colleagues. They kicked in the doors of some houses as they passed, ducked inside, then returned to their position, speaking into walkie-talkies.

He wondered what Jesse had made of the deserted town. In her place, he would be wary, looking for signs the whole thing was a trap.

Blue left them alone for a few minutes. Long enough for Jesse to believe her rocket attack on the sniper had mopped up any remaining resistance.

Staying west, he jogged to the rear of the last house before the church. He didn't bother kicking in the door as

Geary had done. An unnecessarily dramatic entrance, as no one in Om's paradise locked their doors.

In the front room, Blue placed a chair near the window, giving him a clear view of the steps leading to the church. He checked the rifle, then the handguns.

The truck rumbled past his position two minutes later. Jesse must have been driving, as the figure in the passenger seat was male. Geary and another male jogged behind with submachine guns.

Four of them. With one man down, there should be five. Where was the missing cop? In the back of the truck? Acting as lookout back at the highway?

The truck passed the church, swung around to face the gatehouse, and stopped.

Judging from the way the vehicle dipped on its suspension, Geary and his colleague were back inside. Jesse and the third man jumped down from the cab.

Blue leaned closer to the window. Too far for an accurate shot. He'd have to pick his moment to get closer.

He'd wondered how the gang intended to move a thousand kilos of gold from the vault to the truck. The reappearance of Geary and the fourth man answered his question. They rolled a heavy-duty medical gurney between them—designed to carry obese patients. Where the patient would normally lie, straps held down shapes hidden under plastic sheeting. More explosives.

Geary and partner headed for the ramps, pushing the gurney into the church.

Nine minutes later, the two men re-emerged, leaving the now empty gurney near the top of the steps before rejoining the others. Even at this distance, the body language of the Firestarters was easy to read. Tension, anticipation.

Blue eased open the window, resting the automatic rifle on the sill.

He held his breath.

The explosion, when it came, sent a cloud of dust billowing through the enormous open doors of the church, and obscured the steps, the truck, and the enemy.

Blue swore. He swore again when the truck moved closer to the steps, blocking most of his view.

He heard the gurney roll back down the ramp. He glimpsed the three men around it as the last of the smoke cleared.

Blue's muscles tensed in anticipation.

Geary steered the front of the gurney, stopping it behind the truck. He stepped inside. The other two men took turns taking gold bars from the gurney, sliding them along the floor of the truck. They quickly established a rhythm, intent on their task.

Now.

Chapter Fifty-Five

BLUE LEFT the house and broke from cover, moving with the strange, loping, crouching run he learned during his time in the Bavarian mountains. Not as fast as a sprint, but close to silent.

His luck ran out.

A reflection in a window gave him away. The closest hostile—a gold bar in each hand—turned at the unexpected movement. Half-visible in the darkness and drifting smoke, Blue braced the automatic rifle stock against his upper thigh.

They locked eyes.

Blue opened fire, spraying bullets in a tight arc. The first burst caught the man in the stomach, tracing a line below his ribs as he jerked backwards, dropping the bars. The second hostile didn't have time to turn before half a dozen rounds opened him up from sternum to throat, crimson spray coating the truck door behind him as he fell. Blue sent the rest of the magazine into the truck's interior, hoping the ricochets found Geary. He would rather have finished the man up close, but dead was dead.

Reaching the end of the clip, he dropped the rifle, drew the handgun, and waited. Listened. Something didn't add up. A full second passed before he realised. The truck's sides were stretched canvas, not metal. No ricochets.

The barrel of a gun appeared at the back door of the truck. Geary must be on his belly.

The nearest cover lay behind him. The street was clear of debris. Blue jogged backwards, keeping his gun trained on the rear of the truck.

Jimmy heard a shot. His body jerked backward. His left leg stopped supporting his weight, and he stumbled and half-fell before regaining his balance.

He saw her, or rather her hands, and the gun she held. Jesse, underneath the truck, head pushed into the dirt.

Blue threw himself sideways and rolled as she fired again. He crashed to the ground behind a metal billboard displaying Om's giant face. The next shot ricocheted harmlessly away. Om had just saved him.

The word under the prophet's smiling face read *Alive*. Perhaps there was something in this spiritual business after all.

Whispers came from the truck. Jesse giving her orders.

Blue dialled the pain down. Thought fast, moved faster. Keeping low, he threw himself across the two-foot gap between the billboard and the fence. Bullets bounced off metal and bit into wood, narrowly missing his trailing leg.

When he reached the house, he pushed the door hard enough for it to bang against the wall. Rather than entering, he rolled into the shadows at the far end of the covered porch, and lay still.

Even a mind as brilliantly adaptive as Jesse's would press her advantage now. Especially with her enemy wounded. Blue lay on his side, good arm outstretched, gripping the handgun. He pushed away every thought. This, he knew, was a rare ability amongst humans. For Blue, it was like throwing a switch. His mind cleared. Sounds, sights, smells. Gun, path, billboard, flickering light. Burning wood, baking brick, night breeze lifting particles of sand, carrying them across the street. Footsteps. Two sets. The heaviest close now. Geary. Jesse hanging back.

Geary came into view, submachine gun ready. His eyes darted around the scene, but Blue, utterly still, remained invisible.

Geary took a step closer, then another.

Blue ignored him, looking for the real danger. He saw her—fifteen yards behind Geary, moving crablike in a crouch, rifle held steady.

Blue waited for his moment, wanted to be certain.

Geary was halfway along the path. Mid-step, off balance. Blue fired between the man's legs. The bullet nicked Geary's lower thigh as it passed. He staggered and slipped.

The shot found its target, knocked Jesse off her feet. She landed hard on her back. The billboard blocked Blue's follow-up shot. The first had gone higher than he'd intended, the barrel pulling to the right, tagging her left shoulder. Always a problem when using unfamiliar weapons.

Geary was still upright, grabbing the fence for support. He fumbled the Uzi. Blue squeezed the handgun's trigger, aiming for the man's stomach. He wanted Geary to die slow.

The gun jammed. The second handgun, still in its holster, was pinned to the wooden boards by Blue's leg.

Geary, hearing the unexpected and welcome sound, smiled. He knew Jimmy's hiding place.

The distance between them was too far. Blue brought his knees underneath him, pushing himself upright. His injured leg held. He made the door in three steps and dived inside.

What he did next might not have fooled Jesse, but Geary was more straightforward. Blue went right and dropped into a crouch next to the open door.

Sure enough, the burst of submachine gun fire broke the window, and peppered the far wall, at waist height. Predictable.

He heard Jesse call out a warning, but Geary ignored it. Blue slid the hunting knife from the sheath on his ankle.

Geary came in, breathing heavily, gun held tight to his body. Pumped up, high on adrenaline, certain of success.

Blue stabbed upwards with all the strength he could muster from his crouch, driving the knife between Geary's legs, then—when he ripped it back out again—angling the blade to ensure maximum damage. Geary wheezed like a deflating child's birthday balloon. His finger tightened on the trigger, but the burst of fire hit the ceiling.

Blue got to his feet in front of Geary, held the dripping blade upright under the cop's chin, pierced the skin, and paused. Geary became statue-still. His eyes swivelled toward Jimmy. Blue nodded when they widened in recognition.

"That's right, Geary. Tom from Pike Point. This is for Anna."

Geary opened his mouth as if to respond, which meant Blue saw the steel blade through his open lips as it passed upwards, penetrating muscle and cartilage.

The knife Blue left hilt deep in Geary's throat must have severed various avenues of communication between brain and body, because the cop performed a kind of perverse Irish jig, his limbs flailing spasmodically before he fell sideways, and bled out on the wooden floor.

Blue hoped the man's death had been agonising. A shame it had been so quick.

The bullet Blue had put into Jesse had winged her. He needed to finish the job.

Chapter Fifty-Six

JIMMY LEANED AGAINST THE WALL. Felt lightheaded. When he put his hand on his left leg, his fingers came back wet and sticky. The blood loss wasn't fast, but it wasn't stopping either.

He limped back into the kitchen. A medical kit hung on the wall. Blue grabbed two thick pads, bandages, and a roll of medical tape.

Hoisting his leg onto the kitchen table, he bandaged the wound as tightly as he could with one arm, using medical tape to hold it all in place. It was a pretty poor job.

Blue's head snapped up. The truck. Its engine roared as Jesse made her escape. Jimmy limped to the door. Picked up Geary's submachine gun. Headed out to the street.

Even as he swung his weapon round, he knew it was hopeless. The Uzi wasn't effective beyond two hundred yards.

The brake lights came on, and the truck shuddered to a sudden halt. Blue limped fast, narrowing the distance.

Jesse fired through the open driver's window. Muzzle flashes followed by the sound of hundreds of impacts.

Even if she had seen Blue stomping closer in her side-view mirror, Jessie didn't waste any bullets on him.

Jimmy upped his pace, stumbling, cursing.

He fired as the truck lurched away, but it accelerated out of range.

Even pushing his battered body hard, it took Blue thirty seconds to reach the edge of town. Jesse—injured, and acting on limited information—was still making smart decisions.

Her sole remaining advantage was significant. She had transport. And she had fired into the parking lot, hitting the closest vehicles, including Jimmy's motorcycle, now on its side, one shredded tyre spinning.

As the truck's engine faded, Jimmy reached the parking lot.

He found what he needed three rows back from the street; a Japanese SUV. The key was in the ignition. Blue half-fell inside. Started the engine, skidded away, the rear smashing the headlamp of another car as he left.

Once in a straight line, he straightened up, aimed at the distant taillights—Jesse couldn't risk driving blind at that speed—and floored the accelerator. She may have a head start, but Blue would be faster. He doubted she would manage much better than sixty miles per hour in the gold-laden truck. He had already hit seventy and was still picking up speed.

His focus became laser tight. There was no desert, no road, no starry sky. No scent of blood and sweat, or sweet-sour undertones of the Nevada scrub. No engine noise, no rush of wind as he wound down the window. Nothing but predator and prey, the deadly calm conviction of a lion about to pounce on a wounded gazelle, bringing her down to tear out her throat.

Blue gripped the steering wheel between his knees,

ignoring a fresh flare of pain from his bleeding leg. Once holding the SUV steady, with the cruise control set at eighty-five, he brought the Uzi to his shoulder, angled the muzzle through the open window, and waited for his moment.

Five hundred yards.

He'd set the headlamps to full beam, giving him a clear view of the truck, rear doors banging. Gold bars slid around the floor of the fleeing vehicle. Occasionally, one dropped onto the highway.

And the streets were paved with gold. Tom's father's voice, telling his son a story. Scratch of stubble, stale smoke and tea, record player turned down low.

Three hundred yards.

The SUV's headlights must be dazzling Jesse by now, as death closed in. He wondered if she was afraid. He hoped so.

Blue tried to shut down Tom's memories, an unwanted distraction.

Two hundred yards.

A hundred and fifty.

The invisible skein between Jimmy Blue and Tom Lewis stretched and weakened along with images of Tom's father, accompanied by the odour of hand-rolled ciga-rettes. Blue shook his head. Mild concussion from the RPG-7 attack.

One hundred yards.

Blue leaned left, braced his arm against the door, and aimed for the truck's tyres. The SUV hit a bump, the car twitched, and the shots went high.

Fifty yards. Closing fast. He turned off the cruise control. Brought the muzzle back into position. Held it as steady as possible. Took aim a second time.

The gold bar that hit the SUV came so fast, Blue only

registered it as a sudden flash in his headlights. A few inches further left, and it would have whistled past harmlessly. A few inches right, and it would have dented the fender. Instead, it flew under the SUV's driver side wheel arch, caught the top of the fast rotating tyre, and flicked into the shock absorbers above, neatly snapping the spring and causing the side of the vehicle to collapse.

The result was immediate. With a sound like a box full of cats wired up to the mains and given a few thousand volts, the tyre ripped itself apart under the weight. The wheel—pinned between the SUV's chassis and the blacktop—buckled and lurched. The initial impact snatched the Uzi from Blue's fingers, sending it flying into the night, flipping end over end along the road as the car slewed into a long skid, sparks flying up into the darkness.

The car clattered, juddered, and screamed, careening out of control. Although it quickly shed its speed, it was still doing forty when it left the road at the end of its diagonal trajectory, tipped its broken nose into the soft dirt ditch, and tipped, the passenger side lifting into the air.

Blue, thrown against the steering wheel, gasped in pain. As the SUV left the highway, continuing to tip, he threw himself across to the passenger side, grabbing the headrest with his left arm.

For a moment, the SUV hung there, perfectly balanced, before Blue's weight brought it crashing to the road. He took some of the impact on his broken arm. On this occasion, he blacked out.

Tom looked up at his father, who'd stopped reading. His father looked back, but his eyes didn't see Tom. They'd never see him again. What Tom thought was a bruise on his father's forehead wasn't a bruise at all. It was a hole. He smelled petrol. Someone held Tom's arms from behind, and he couldn't free himself, couldn't do anything to help, and knew that someone was about to drag him away while they burned his mother alive. He knew how this ended. It ended with a man shooting him in the head, and he wanted that moment to come now, come now, come now, because the darkness that arrived with the bullet swept away his mother, his father, and all the terrible things he had seen, and put them in a place at the bottom of a glass cliff, where he never had to go. He didn't want to remember, he didn't want to remember, he didn't—

A human body normally shuts down some of the brain, causing limbs to relax, to prevent further injury. Blue's brain didn't work quite the same way. He couldn't prevent unconsciousness, but he opened his eyes seconds, rather than minutes, later.

Concussion brought Tom close, and Jimmy could not spare him the memory of his parents' murders, and the moment a young would-be gangster shot him. The end of Tom's childhood, the end of normal development, the end of his future. The beginning of Jimmy Blue.

He kicked open the passenger door before the SUV fully came to rest. Blue looked for the submachine gun, scanning the road for it. The stricken car's engine coughed weakly, then lapsed into near silence, apart from a dull, hollow ticking. He heard Jesse's truck; distant now, the sound growing fainter.

Jimmy staggered back to watch the leader of the Firestarters escape.

Failure.

Still staring at his distant prey, he took a deep breath and roared out his rage and frustration; a sound which sent every living creature who heard it into a panic, all of them immediately putting as much distance as possible between them and whatever creature had pierced the night with its unearthly, terrifying cry.

Chapter Fifty-Seven

WHEN OTTO SCHULTZ opened his eyes in the grey, Nevada half-dawn, he wondered if the rain had woken him. He lay under the bedspread Martha had never finished and listened to the rhythmic pattern of water on his window.

He glanced at the clock. Not yet six. Otto thought he might just lie here and enjoy the sound, knowing it wouldn't last long. Not in Nevada. By the time most people were up and about, there would be no evidence of rain, everything having returned to its customary dusty dryness.

Martha had teased Otto about his love of water. Not just rain, but rivers, ponds, lakes. *If you like it so much,* she'd say, *why didn't you stay in Germany? Why settle in Nevada? You looked at the map first, right? Watched a few westerns? Did you see many umbrellas? Didn't think so.*

Otto smiled in the half-dark. His answer to her questions had always been the same. Who knows why someone ends up in one place rather than another? Opportunities arise, doors open, and before you know it, a place you only intended to visit becomes the place where you put down roots. Not because of its climate—certainly not. Not because of its potential for a thriving veterinarian practice. Laughable. The truth—as Martha knew very well—was that Otto Schultz left behind friends, family, and a more lucrative career in Dortmund, because of a girl. Martha Hilson, she was back then. Short, plump, full of smiles, unremarkable to so many others, who, somehow, walked past this treasure in their midst every day without seeing it. Otto saw it immediately. Ten minutes of talking to this laughing, teasing, freckled girl working in her parents' convenience store, and he was lost. Smitten. In love. He left the store with a can of soda, a copy of Time magazine, and Martha's telephone number.

The rain stopped while he was reminiscing.

Six years. Six years this Christmas since Martha died. Fifty-nine years together. Almost six decades. Wonderful. Not without the occasional argument, of course. Petty, unnecessary, and mostly his fault. No real rows to speak of. There was that time when the fellow who ran for mayor took a fancy to her, and Otto—bristling with jealousy—accused Martha of enjoying the attention more than she should. Her response had been to laugh in his face. Not an unkind laugh, not scornful, but an irrepressible response to Otto's stiff, formal outrage; a sound that started in Martha's throat, spread to her belly, and ended by shaking her entire body. Otto, red-faced and hurt, resisted for around half a minute, watching his wife as she whooped and groaned, then he joined in. They ended up in a tangle of limbs on the sofa.

Martha was right. We were lucky. But couldn't the cancer have left her alone for another decade or two?

Seventy-seven was no age to die. Martha missed Otto's eightieth birthday by three weeks. She'd hidden a card taped to a beautifully wrapped old Leica camera under a blanket in her sewing room. He found it two years later, while putting some of her things away.

The rain hadn't woken him. Martha had been a light sleeper, but Otto slept like the dead. A bark from Gracie might have woken him, but Gracie had been gone eight months now. He couldn't bring himself to buy another dog. Another dog was as unthinkable as another wife.

If not the rain, if not a dog barking, then what?

Otto reluctantly concluded he would have to get up. He swung his legs over the side of the bed, easing himself into a sitting position. He'd always been fit, active. These days, the walk from the house to his car raised his pulse. Otto felt every one of his eighty-five years. Slow body, skinny mottled legs, liver-spotted hands. Neck wrinkled like an underfed turkey. Otto had crossed off every box of the old-age bingo card.

He stepped into his slippers and shuffled to the bathroom. Even if it had been a nuclear explosion that woke him, radiation poisoning would have to wait until he'd taken a leak.

Standing in the bathroom, looking out the window, shaking the part of his anatomy Martha referred to as Otto Jr, the retired veterinarian worked out what disturbed his sleep.

Outside, the practice door was open. Otto had never forgotten to lock it before. Might this be the first sign of dementia? He took his glasses from the shelf and squinted at the outbuilding. He noted the splintered wood, plus the footsteps in the still-damp earth. Unless his particular form of senility induced hallucinations, he had a visitor.

Tucking everything back where it belonged, Otto washed his hands, and put on his robe, pulling its belt tight around his skinny waist. Someone was in the outbuilding. A junkie maybe, looking for a fix. Or a thief.

Martha would have called the police, but Otto Schultz had no faith in local law enforcement. He had been treated badly by the sheriff's department a few months after arriving in Nevada, when a local drunk was knifed outside a bar by a man described as having a foreign accent. Three days in a cell smelling of vomit and disinfectant—but mainly the former—before a drifter was arrested a hundred miles west with his victim's wallet still in his pocket.

Instead of an apology, the sheriff shrugged at Otto and warned him to stay out of trouble. Otto had been sure to follow that advice, and—his confidence in his adopted country's sense of fair play dented—kept his distance from all local representatives of the police from that day on.

Anyhow, he thought, shuffling downstairs and lifting his shotgun from the cabinet behind the door, *I can deal with this.*

Outside, gun held in front like a talisman, Otto's confidence dwindled with each step. By the time he reached the building, his hands shook so badly he doubted he could shoot anyone unless they agreed to remain perfectly still at a distance of three feet away.

We've all got to die sometime, Martha had said. *I'm not gonna waste time complaining about it.* His wife's attitude to mortality had been commendably pragmatic, but—a few seconds away from confronting the intruder—Otto found he didn't share the sentiment. He'd rather die in his sleep and not know anything about it if was all the same with whoever was in charge.

Right. Deep breath. Two steps back. Try to stop the damn gun wobbling like Martha's chest on the trampoline that time in Vegas.

"I know you're in there, you're on my property, you've

broken a perfectly good door, and I don't want to shoot you, but I will if I have to, so come on out."

Otto said it all on one breath to stop his voice trembling, then added, "Schnell, bitte!" in a kind of yelp which probably confused him as much as the intruder, as he hadn't meant to speak in German. He spoke his native language only during monthly calls to his sister. He reverted to English, adding,

"I'll count to three."

A quiet voice replied, and Otto nearly dropped the gun.

"No need. I'm injured. Come in."

———

THE VOICE CAME from the far side of his office, meaning Otto's substantial desk lay between the intruder and the door. This made him feel a little braver.

He stepped inside, pulling the gun hard against his ribs to keep it steady, and drew himself up to his full height. Otto still thought of himself as six feet tall, despite the measurements the doctor reported at his annual check-up. Surely it was physically impossible for him to lose four inches without his knowledge. It suggested a degree of carelessness of which he was not capable.

All the same, Otto was aware he didn't cut a commanding figure; an eighty-five-year-old man in a towelling robe, clutching a shotgun with arthritic fingers.

When he saw the size of the man who had broken in, Otto was very glad of the gun.

There was something quite extraordinary about this huge, bald, green-eyed stranger. He didn't look like a junkie. The intruder had a strange composure that unsettled Otto. It didn't help that the man was covered with blood. His jacket was matted with it, as was the T-shirt beneath. Dried blood on his face and hands, too. And yet his upper body—other than his arm—appeared uninjured, which begged a pertinent question: whose blood was it?

"My arm," the man began. He didn't complete the sentence immediately, and during the pause, an extraordinary thing happened. Otto witnessed it but didn't really understand it. After saying those two words—"my arm,"—the stranger vanished, replaced by someone else. Someone who looked exactly the same, but was utterly different. Otto didn't know how he knew this, but he didn't doubt his senses.

This second man fixed his eyes on Otto. A look of hope, and of trust. Dogs understood Otto would fix them. This man thought the same.

"It's b-b-b-, mm, broken." The green eyes filled with tears and Otto walked around the heavy oak desk to help, his adrenaline and fear dissipating. He left the gun leaning in the corner against the door.

The *Schultz Veterinarian Practice* had officially closed twelve years ago, when Otto retired. He had lost most of his customers to a shiny new practice between Joshua and Reno.

This man wasn't Otto's first human patient. An animal doctor living in a sparsely populated, poor area treated his fair share of people alongside the livestock, horses, and pets. These were folk with no medical insurance, and nowhere else to turn. Otto fixed them up. No money changed hands, but the Schultz's often found pies on the doorstep, and volunteers were always available when work needed doing on the house.

Otto knew how to set a bone, clean and stitch a wound, or treat a child for fever.

The enormous man flinched and pressed himself back in the chair when Otto began his examination.

"Easy, easy, there." Otto, intent on calming his patient, spoke to him as if he were a nervous Labrador. "I will not hurt you, boy. I'm going to fix you up. But I have to examine you. Where does it hurt?"

The stranger pointed at his right arm, then down at his left thigh. Otto clicked on the desk lamp. The arm was taped up. He angled the lamp down. The man's pants were dark with blood.

"What's your name, son?"

The intruder swallowed, looking scared. Otto kept his tone quiet and friendly. "My name's Dr Schultz. You can call me Otto."

"Mm, mm, O- Otto."

"That's right. How about you?"

The stranger answered in the same hesitant, childlike way, his fear and confusion unfeigned. What had happened to the other man, whose voice had been so commanding, his demeanour so controlled?

"I'm T-, mm, mm T-T-Tom."

"I'm glad to make your acquaintance, Tom. I'm going to get something to help with the pain, OK?"

Otto slid his hand behind the corner cupboard and slid the key from its hook.

"Not the best security, but if I keep it anywhere else, I always forget where I put it. Now then."

He put the hypodermic needle and vial of lidocaine in his robe pocket, and popped two oxycodone pills from a blister pack.

"I'll get you a drink," he said, handing the pills to Tom. The big man swallowed the pills dry.

"They take about fifteen minutes to kick in. You hungry?"

Tom nodded.

"How about sausage and eggs?"

"P-p-please."

"Good. I'll be right back."

Otto stepped away, but Tom grabbed his wrist, his giant hand covering the old man's completely. His grip was firm, but not rough.

"N-n-n-no p-p, mm, police."

Otto held his gaze for a second. "We can talk about that later. For now, let's get you better. Starting with food. How does that sound?"

"G-g-good."

Chapter Fifty-Eight

OTTO'S unexpected guest stayed a day and a night.

The bullet wound in Tom's leg needed cleaning up, but the blood loss was more serious than the injury itself.

After wolfing down a plate of eggs and sausages, mopping up the juice with a slab of bread, Tom fell asleep in Otto's office chair, barely stirring even as Otto used a scalpel to cut first the tape, then the jacket beneath. After thoroughly numbing the arm with lidocaine, Otto wheeled Tom—now snoring—into the examination room next door. An X-ray revealed two breaks, which Otto set, splinted, and protected with old school plaster cast. He found a few other bruises and some lacerations, none serious enough for stitches.

Later, Otto squeezed Tom's good shoulder until the man's eyes flickered and opened.

"I have a guest bedroom in the main house, and you need some proper rest. Are you okay to walk?"

Tom slept through the first day. Just after five in the evening, a police cruiser drew up in front of the house. Otto opened his front door and waited on the porch.

Helen Reynolds, one of the area's deputies, raised a hand from the steering wheel before turning off the engine. Helen, the daughter of Peter and Marge Reynolds—Otto and Martha's oldest friends—wasn't smiling.

"Helen. I was about to make some tea. Would you like some?"

"No, thank you. No time. Did you hear the news?"

"News?"

"About Sheriff Critchen. And Desolation Station."

"What did I miss?" Despite Otto's distrust of the Joshua police department, he had tried to like Sheriff Al Critchen, for Helen's sake. But Martha always said there was something rotten about the man. So when Helen told him Critchen was dead, Otto felt no particular sorrow.

"How did it happen?"

"Well, this is between you and me, Otto. It can't go any further."

Helen's choice of career had surprised Otto and Martha, because she never could keep a secret.

Helen lowered her voice, as if they weren't standing on the porch of a house three miles from its nearest neighbour.

"Gonna be a scandal when the truth comes out. They found Al just off the highway, stretched out behind a state trooper's patrol car. The state trooper was dead, too. Looks like they killed each other."

Helen's voice dropped still further. "But that's not the big news."

Other than the stabbing six decades earlier, the local police rarely dealt with anything more serious than live-stock theft and drunken fights. Now a police shooting wasn't the big news?

"A gang attacked Desolation Station. They burned the watchtower down. And a few of the houses. We found four bodies, shot or knifed. No one else. No one at all. Om and his followers had gone. Weirdest day of my life."

Otto frowned. "The bodies you found... If they weren't the townspeople...?"

"We think it's the gang. Maybe they argued amongst themselves."

Otto thought about the young man with a broken arm and the bullet wound sleeping upstairs. He had to ask Helen to repeat her next sentence.

"Did you hear anything, Otto? See anything? Your property is the closest to the Desolation Station turn-off."

Would Otto really protect Tom based on a gut feeling?

It turned out that he would.

"Not a thing. I'm sorry."

"It's fine, Otto. It was a long shot. Thanks for your help."

She paused, one hand on the car door.

"You still...?" She didn't complete her sentence. Otto had drained his and Martha's savings when their medical insurance didn't cover the equipment for her final few months at home. When their money ran out, he re-mortgaged without telling her.

"Moving?" he said. "Yes. I've lived here sixty-one years. And my Martha shared most of them. I'm lucky."

"You decided where you'll go?"

"Not yet. Give my best to your folks, will you?"

When Otto walked back into the house, Tom was standing at the foot of the stairs, watching him.

———

"THERE ARE two dead police officers on the highway north of here. Was that anything to do with you?"

Tom, head down, sitting across the kitchen table,

349

reminded Otto of a shy child. A giant, scarred, heavily muscled shy child with cuts, bruises, a broken arm, and a bullet wound.

"N-, mm, mm, n-n-no." Tom shook his head for emphasis, then added, "O-Otto."

"And the dead folk in Desolation Station?"

"Mm, mm. I th-, I th-think s-so. W-w-, mm, wait."

Tom closed his eyes. His breathing slowed, and his shoulders relaxed. But this wasn't sleep, or anything close to it. Otto's scalp and neck prickled, his own breathing becoming more rapid. Although not superstitious, Otto wondered if this was how people felt when they claimed to sense a spirit. If ghosts existed, Martha would have remained after that last exhausted, drawn-out breath. Instead, he was utterly alone. All he had were memories, and this house, which the bank would take from him in a few months.

Otto took a moment to marvel at his ability to pursue a tangent under such stressful circumstances.

Tom's eyes were open. But the man staring back at him wasn't Tom.

"I won't hurt you, Otto. But I'm too tired to put on a mask. Thank you for looking after Tom."

No hesitation, no stammer. It was the voice who'd called to Otto from the office that morning. He swallowed, his throat suddenly dry.

"You've done a good job on this arm." The man lifted the splinted and tightly bandaged limb from the table. He didn't even wince. "I should be able to use again it in two weeks."

Otto found his voice. "You should not attempt to remove the splint for at least a month. Give your bones time to…"

He trailed off, licked his lips. The man opposite might

have been a statue. There was something incredibly unnerving about a man who held himself so still. Like a lizard on a rock. Which made Otto the bug. For a second, the mental image of Tom's tongue snapping out, wrapping itself around his head, and pulling him in to be consumed, almost made him shriek with laughter.

"I heal fast."

Otto, trying to control his errant mind and body, picked up his water glass with trembling fingers, and drained its contents. When he replaced it, Tom picked up the jug and refilled it.

"I'm vulnerable," said the man. Otto had read an occasional article on dissociative identity disorder, but whatever he was witnessing, he couldn't believe a medical diagnosis would explain it. Not this. Not something this visceral.

"Vulnerable?" echoed Otto, unable to conceal his disbelief.

"Yes. Vulnerable. Injured. Weak."

Otto again fought the urge to laugh or scream. What must this character be like when he *wasn't* vulnerable? When he felt *strong*?

"I need more rest. Then I have to leave. Tom doesn't want me to hurt you."

Another quick review of the sentence, then comprehension of its implications.

"Ah." Otto took another drink.

"Otto, I'm a stranger with a bullet wound. You didn't say anything to your cop friend, but you might reconsider if you believe you're harbouring a murderer."

Otto realised there was a point beyond which it was impossible to be more scared. Now he had reached that point, he experienced a strange, calm clarity. He wondered if the bug felt that way just before the lizard bit it in half.

"I'm eighty-five years old, Mister...?"

"Blue. Jimmy Blue."

"Mister Blue. I'm old. My wife is dead. I wake up every day a little disappointed I haven't joined her. Soon, I will lose the house we shared. I'd be lying if I said you didn't scare me. I am terrified. But not of dying. Not that. So. Tell me. Am I harbouring a murderer?"

Jimmy Blue didn't answer directly. "Your friend was right about the bodies in Desolation Station. They were members of a gang. The Firestarters."

Even Otto had heard of the Firestarters. He'd seen a documentary. A gang that robbed and burned down towns, escaping with tens of millions of dollars, leaving no clues. It made for great TV, but it was terrifying.

"I stopped them."

"You killed all the Firestarters? Alone?"

The intelligent, pitiless, green eyes settled on Otto. "Not all."

Blue sighed. "I—Tom—lived in Pike Point. You know where that is?"

Otto looked blank for a second, then remembered the documentary. "Yes."

"Pike Point was the Firestarters' fifth target. Desolation Station was the sixth. And the last. After killing everyone there and taking the gold, they planned to disappear forever. I stopped all of them except their leader. So, yes, you're harbouring a murderer. Can you live with that?"

Otto remembered a detail from the documentary. The film crew had tried, and failed, to interview the only survivor of a Firestarters' attack. A young woman now, but she'd been a child when the gang killed her mother and father while she hid in a closet.

"Yes, Mister Blue. I can live with that."

Had those green eyes blinked once?

"Good." The eyes finally left his, and Otto was aware of his heart beating like a trapped bird.

"I need to eat, then I need to sleep," said Jimmy Blue. "Chicken, fish, beans. Bread, pasta, rice. Protein and carbs."

"I can prepare something. Which of those would you like?"

"All of them."

After he'd consumed enough food for a hungry family of four, the man who'd killed the Firestarters stood up.

"I'll leave early tomorrow. I'll need your car."

Otto pointed at a hook by the front door. "She's a bit troublesome. Engine won't catch first time. Don't flood the carburettor. Give her a minute, then try again. The gas in the tank will get you to Reno."

He piled dishes in the sink and ran some water, waiting for it to get hot. "Good luck," he said without turning.

"Thank you."

When Otto turned back to the table, the room was empty.

———

OTTO WOKE EARLY AGAIN, surprised he'd slept at all.

This time, he recognised the sound that had woken him: the throaty cough of his old station wagon. He opened his eyes but stayed where he was until, on the second attempt, the engine caught and the car drove away.

Otto pottered downstairs to make tea. It wasn't until he had warmed the pot, and covered a crust with butter and honey, that Otto noticed the note on the table, and what kept it in place.

Having just lived through the most unusual day he could remember, Otto didn't quite know how to react. He

stared at it for a few minutes, then sat down, ate his breakfast, drank his tea, and stared at it some more.

The note contained three words.

Keep your house.

It was held in place by a solid gold bar.

Chapter Fifty-Nine

"IT'S A CAFE, Pops. In a public place. On a Friday evening. With friends. This is how I get gigs. It's not always auditions. Often, it's having a drink together, gossiping. It's— and I know you hate this word—networking. Besides, if I don't go out soon, I'm gonna die of boredom, never mind anything else."

"You can't go out, Han. Not yet."

Patrice Martino gave his daughter his sternest look. He'd never been great at the disciplinary aspects of parenthood, and Hannah had taken advantage of his leniency growing up, but he wasn't shifting on this.

Hannah rolled her eyes.

"Dad, she's gone. Taken off. Escaped. It's been three weeks already. She's on a beach drinking Pornstar Martinis, served by oiled, naked models, because she can afford to buy a private island and do whatever the hell she wants. Or she's had plastic surgery and is running a Fortune five hundred outfit. Maybe she never even made it out of the country, and she's rotting in some cell because a secret government agency picked her up at a Chilean airstrip while she was trying to escape."

"Why Chilean?"

"First country I thought of. Maybe they didn't throw her in a cell at all, just shot the crazy bitch."

"Hey, mind your language, Han."

"You're kinda missing the point, Pops. If she's not dead, Dionne James could be a million different places, but you know one place she won't be? Here, in Brooklyn. Trying to make good on a threat she made before her whole team got themselves killed by—according to you—one dude. A crazy big dude who's supposed to be dead."

Patrice Martino swirled the last of his bourbon in the bottom of a plastic tumbler featuring—as far as he could tell—a pink unicorn farting a rainbow. This was a sixty-dollar bourbon. It didn't seem right.

"I should never have told you that. But I want you to take this seriously. You're in danger, Han. You didn't meet Jesse. I did. This is a woman who planned the cold-blooded murders of one thousand, seven hundred and eighteen innocent people and burned down five small towns. All for money. Her parents thought she was a God-fearing, pious do-gooder. They have no idea what their daughter is capable of."

"How many parents do?" murmured Hannah, but he ignored it.

"You weren't there, Han. When Jesse said she would kill you if I betrayed her, she meant it. So I'm not leaving until she's in jail or dead."

Hannah got up from the couch—currently doubling as Martino's bed, which accounted for the throb in his lower back—and stomped to the kitchen for another soda. Not that the kitchen was a separate room. Only a hamster or realtor would describe this fourth-floor apartment as spacious. The drawn blinds made it feel even smaller, but Martino refused to open them and present Jesse with an easy target for a sniper, despite Hannah's protestations and eyerolls.

Hannah squatted next to Martino, taking his hand.

"Dad," she began, "I love you, and please don't think I'm ungrateful that you're looking out for me. I appreciate it. I really do."

Martino anticipated the *but* and started to speak. Hannah put her finger on his lips.

"No. You need to listen to me now. Really listen. Is it possible Jesse is out there, close by, planning my assassination? I guess so. I'm not denying the possibility. But it's been over a month, Dad. And Dionne James is the most wanted woman in America. Everyone knows who she is, everyone knows what she looks like. If she's still in this country, then she's in hiding. You say she's smart. If you're right, she's long gone, and it's time you accepted it. Go home, Pops. Finish your book. It's gonna be a bestseller, according to Ron."

"You spoke to him?" Martino had been ignoring his agent's voicemail. Before receiving the first draft, Ron Stebbins put out the word to four publishers, and the offers were getting ridiculous. Martino could move back to New York and buy a fancy apartment in Manhattan for the advance they were offering. *If* he finished the Firestarters book. With Jesse's whereabouts still unaccounted for, he'd found it impossible to begin the final chapters, starting with his trip to Los Angeles and ending with the showdown in Desolation Station.

"Yeah, he's taken to calling me, since you won't talk to him. Go home, Dad. Finish the book. I'd like my apartment back. And I want to get back to work. Plus, I need to go to meetings. Recovering drug addict, remember? Also, apart from my stalled career, I'm a single woman with needs. If I bring a nice young man home, having my dad asleep on the couch is gonna be quite the passion killer. But I'm getting desperate, so I might have to risk it."

"OK, OK, I get the message, no need to—no need for —I don't wanna hear about your... just stop, will you?"

Martino sighed, rubbed his face, drained what was left in his unicorn tumbler.

"I hear you, Han. I know I can't stay here forever. If you really wanna go out..."

Hannah hugged him. "I do. Don't take my little speech the wrong way. I love that my father still wants to protect his little girl. I really do."

She kissed his stubbled cheek.

"One condition," he said.

She withdrew, tilted her head.

"Let me follow you."

Hannah gave her father a level gaze. He could guess what she was thinking. He'd seen his face in the mirror every day since the news from Desolation Station broke. Martino looked ten years older, a hunted man whose few hours of sleep were filled with nightmares.

"To protect you," he mumbled.

Within hours of the bodies in Nevada being identified as police officers, the link between the Firestarters had been made, and the media frenzy had reached near-hysterical levels of excitement. Martino had called Sky Pimm, emailed her a statement about his encounter with Dionne 'Jesse' James, naming her as the brains behind the gang.

Hours later, the police named the four dead police officers. Jesse hadn't died in Desolation Station. She was missing.

Martino's information had been enough for a raid on Jesse's Los Angeles home, an arrest warrant being issued, and her face on every front page, every TV channel, and every internet news site in the USA.

When the first twenty-four hours passed without an arrest, Martino demanded FBI protection for his daughter. Sky's response, while sympathetic, was unsatisfactory. She trotted out the same objections Hannah herself raised daily since he'd moved in. Jesse wouldn't risk targeting Hannah. It had been a credible threat, but the circumstances were very different now. Jesse was rich, she was America's most wanted, and she was gone.

Sky had asked a question of her own.

"You think Jesse will blame you for the ambush in Desolation Station?"

"I don't know. I guess she thought I was the only one who knew her plans."

"Were you, Patrice?"

There had been an edge to her voice he didn't appreciate.

"Obviously not, given what happened. If I was going to tell anyone, I would have come to you, Sky."

"We'll discuss that decision later. But you swerved my question. Did you contact someone?"

"Who the hell would I contact?"

"Swerved again. Interesting."

"Not interesting at all." Martino had disassembled and dumped the burner phone after emailing the man who called himself Jimmy Blue. Would that be enough? "Sky. I didn't tell anyone about Jesse's plans, because—if I did—she swore she would kill my daughter. Now the Firestarters are dead, and if she's looking for someone to blame, by her own twisted logic, that's me. Which means Hannah's life is in danger. Which part don't you understand?"

"There's plenty I want clarification over, Patrice, especially the part where you didn't inform us about an attack that might have led to multiple fatalities. According to your statement, you traded one life for hundreds."

"My daughter's life, Sky. What would you have done?"

When Sky continued along the same lines, Martino had hung up. He'd left his cell phone in a Grand Central locker, bought a burner, and headed to Hannah's apartment. The apartment itself was pretty safe: a sublet from one of Hannah's actor friends, with no paperwork. With the FBI busy investigating the Nevadan aftermath, Martino didn't think they would waste resources tracking him down. It wasn't the FBI he was worried about.

Hannah stood up. "You're serious? You wanna follow me? Dad, you're an old man—"

"I'm in my fifties."

"—like I said, old. What are you gonna do if the most dangerous woman in America tries to kill me? Hit her with a strongly worded statement? Throw your hat at her?"

Martino's jacket hung on the back of the chair. He reached into the pocket and pulled out a handgun. Hannah responded with a string of words he'd heard before, but not quite in that order, and not from his daughter.

"I take it you don't approve," he commented.

"You think? What the hell?"

Martino shifted uncomfortably in his seat. Given his anti-gun stance, he had to concede this wasn't a good look. Hannah glared at him.

"I'm," he began.

"A hypocrite. Yes. Yes, you are. Where did you get it?"

An ex-cop, an old friend, loaned Martino the weapon, and talked him through the basics of loading, aiming, and firing. Patrice felt sick even holding the thing, but it only took remembering Jesse's promise to torture Hanna before killing her, to overcome his qualms.

"I borrowed it, Han. I don't like it any more than you do."

"Yeah. Right."

"But who else is gonna protect you from her?"

Hanna shook her head, still looking like a child. "You think you can? You're more likely to shoot yourself."

"You're wrong."

Hannah, surprised, acknowledged the steel in his voice, her outrage fading. "Jesus, Dad."

"Yeah, well, remind me I'm a hypocrite when you have kids of your own. I'm not proud of it, but I'm not changing my mind, either."

"Well, you're full of surprises lately. You look like shit, you're paranoid, and you're carrying a gun. What did you do with my father?"

Martino stood up, put his jacket on, dropped the gun into the pocket.

"Honestly? I don't know right now. I guess he got a little lost. When Dionne James is in prison, or dead, you'll get him back."

Hannah didn't seem convinced. "I hope so."

She turned to the mirror by the front door and started applying mascara. "I'm going to drink virgin cocktails, talk shit with my friends, and remind them I still exist. You do whatever you gotta do."

Martino levered himself out of his chair. "Han, listen. No subways, because she can trap you there. Walk fast. Don't stop for anyone and keep watching for her. I'll—"

She scooped her keys from the table and left.

Martino—his back aching, and his bladder complaining—followed.

———

ON THE CORNER sixty yards away, in a cheap hotel room that didn't insist on ID, a phone screen lit up. A motion sensitive camera watching the door of Hannah Martino's building began streaming its feed.

The building housed thirty-two apartments, so the camera had triggered multiple times per day, and had done so since the hotel room had been occupied. But this was the first time it showed an image of the young woman matching the photographs spread out on the bed—the only relatively clean, flat surface in the room.

Although her exact location had proved impossible to pinpoint, the street Martino's daughter lived in had been easy to find by studying her online posts. Who needed advanced tracking skills when you had social media?

The phone's owner thumped the door to an adjoining room.

"She's on the move. Let's go."

Two figures left via the fire escape, emerging on the street in time to see Hannah Martino step out of the building, turning right towards Brooklyn Bridge, and Manhattan.

Chapter Sixty

MARTINO NEVER THOUGHT he'd regret bringing up his daughter to be an independent thinker, but he was having his doubts now.

He increased his pace, ignoring the ache in his back.

Hannah hesitated at the entrance to Fort Green Park on Dekalb. If he'd had enough breath to spare, Martino would have called out for her to stick to the street. Too many places someone could hide among the trees. But she'd already turned in, taking her usual cut through to Myrtle, then across Flatbush and towards the bridge.

Damn. *Damn.* Martino pushed his body—still not as fit as he'd like, but thank God for those morning runs—harder, breathing through his mouth now, keeping her in sight. As he walked, he scanned his fellow pedestrians, his gaze settling for a few seconds on anyone close to Jesse's height and build. Twice, he half-convinced himself he'd seen the Firestarters' leader, his hand going to the gun in his pocket, only to get closer and find the woman in question looked nothing like her. Hannah said he was paranoid. Maybe she had a point.

The park had its usual complement of families, joggers, cyclists, skaters, necking lovers, and knots of loud teens. A potential murderer could come from almost anywhere. Martino could look forward, even monitor the sides to a certain extent, but what about behind him? He took to swinging around every six to eight steps, checking the faces of anyone behind, but each time he did it, those few seconds when he took his eyes off his daughter induced near-panic.

God, he wished Hannah had given him time to take a piss.

When it happened, there was a kind of inevitability to it, as if, deep down, a committed rationalist like Martino secretly harboured a belief in superstition, fate, or predestination.

It wasn't footsteps, but a quiet rumble of wheels on the smooth paths near the Prison Ship Martyrs' Monument—a concrete column his ex-wife had always referred to as The Fort Greene Prick. The skater, or skateboarder, approached quickly but didn't come alongside, instead skidding to a stop directly behind him. Even as Martino turned, a hand plucked the gun from his pocket, pressed it into the small of his back—ironically, relieving some of the ache there—and a familiar voice spoke quietly and calmly.

"I'll kill you, then her, if you make a sound, so don't. Move over to the bench on the left. Now."

The bench was only five yards away.

"Sit," said Jesse. "Look straight ahead, and don't react."

He sat down, and she did the same, the gun now pressed to his side. Something different about Jesse, but he didn't dare turn to see what it might be.

"Don't react to—agh. What the hell was that?"

At first Martino thought she'd stabbed him, before recognising the sensation of a needle in his upper arm.

"That," said Jesse, "was midazolam. A sedative. It gets used in prison for violent inmates."

Martino didn't need her to tell him. He'd written an essay for the New Yorker on its use in overcrowded private prisons, and had spent the next few months fending off frivolous, but irritating, lawsuits from the corporate owners he'd named.

Jesse leaned in close.

"You'll struggle to lift your head in about thirty seconds with that dose. Within a few minutes, you'll be asleep. By the time you wake up, in a few hours, Hannah will be dead. And that's on you, Martino."

"I didn't—" his tongue was thick and slow.

"You didn't tell anyone? Who are you trying to convince? Right, that should be long enough."

Martino was aware of the woman beside him getting to her feet, but he was stuck like a bug on flypaper. His eyes got heavy, and he fought to keep them open, all the time willing Hannah to notice what was happening behind her, and run.

Jesse's hair had gone. A simple buzz cut, then an application of peroxide. The new colour was bright white. She sported a bright pink jacket and matching hot pants. Round, oversized, purple sunglasses and over-ear headphones pushed down onto her neck. She was on roller skates. She could pass for someone in their late teens.

Jesse bent down. "One side effect noted in some patients is a short-term inability to make new memories. I hope that won't happen to you, Martino. I want you to remember this moment, and what's about to happen to Hannah, for the rest of your shitty life."

With a supreme effort, Martino forced his head—now weighing on his neck like a sack of bricks—to an upright position.

Hannah turned towards him.

Run, he wanted to scream, but no sound would come. *Run.*

The dying sun lit the side of Hannah's face. It could have been a still from a movie. *Run, Hannah, run. Leave me and run.*

She didn't leave, though. Of course not. She saw her dad, then the woman with him. Realised her old man wasn't paranoid after all. That a vicious, cold-blooded murderer had found them.

Hannah made the only decision she could under those circumstances. She started running. Only she ran the wrong way. Straight towards the bench, and Dionne James.

"Guess she's as stupid as her old man." Jesse reached inside her jacket. Martino put every ounce of strength he had into stopping her, but the air had thickened. Instead of moving, his body sank through the bench, and the world hummed and faded.

He saw the knife, though. Jesse made sure of it. With a cold, horrible certainty, he knew she planned to kill Hannah there and then, in front of him.

Everything darkened. Despite his efforts, shapes lost coherence, Jesse becoming ghost-like. Hannah must only be a step or two away now.

Hannah.

His eyelids drooped.

The last thing he saw—and he didn't know if it really happened, or was a by-product of the midazolam—was a dark shape barrelling out of the trees to the left of the bench. A bear? In Brooklyn? Had it escaped from a zoo? Whatever it was, he cursed it for becoming his last coherent thought, then his eyelids closed, and he fell through the bench, passed through the earth below, and continued into a vast cavern, pitch-black and full of echoes, each sound beginning like a half-recognised word, then, over the course of multiple repeats, softening, loosening, and degrading, eventually adding to the constant drone that underscored the space.

As he fell, everything he remembered, everything he knew, everything he cared about, dissolved among the echoes, losing all meaning. Martino's identity similarly broke apart, a page of a book ripped into a thousand pieces and thrown off a cliff.

The last thought that made any sense to him was that he hoped Jesse had got the dose wrong. He hoped he'd never wake up again.

Chapter Sixty-One

WHEN HANNAH LEFT the streets and entered Fort Greene Park, Blue closed the distance between them, staying off the footpaths, sticking to the trees. He kept Hannah and Patrice in sight, but constantly scanned the area ahead and behind them, looking for Jesse.

He'd never believed she'd renege on her threat to Martino. That night in Nevada, when he'd screamed his rage and frustration into the desert night, as his prey eluded him, he had known the truth of it. In Jesse, he had encountered someone with an unbending will and a pin-sharp, laser-focused mind, unhampered by any moral constraints.

Someone like him.

He'd arrived in New York two days after leaving Otto's house in Nevada. A five-minute internet search revealed Hannah Martino lived in Brooklyn. At the airport, Blue cross-referenced the social media posts of Hannah's friends until he found Jay Fischer, a fellow actor subletting his Brooklyn apartment while he toured Europe. Blue compared a photograph of the view from Jay's apartment with Hannah's recent posts, and discovered her favourite cafes, restaurants, and bookstores formed a neat circle around the apartment's location. The photograph gave him the building. Fourth or fifth floor, he estimated.

Blue made a call from the airport. Asked a question. When the answer was yes, he booked two neighbouring rooms in a Brooklyn dive claiming to be a hotel.

Then he'd gone to work.

Jesse had a head start, but she also had a significant disadvantage. Two days after the failed attack on Desolation Station, Jesse's face claimed top billing on every source of news in America. The FBI named her as a person of interest, and an unofficial source leaked the actual story: that Dionne 'Jesse' James was the leader of the Firestarters. A liar, a fraud, a thief, and a mass murderer. The authorities believed Jesse had fled with her stolen hundreds of millions, but if the slightest chance existed that she hadn't, they wanted every American to recognise her face. Twenty-nine years old, dark hair, brown eyes, physically fit. The photograph the newspapers favoured showed her kneeling with her parents at church. A model daughter, a good Christian. Demure, pious, unassuming. A monster. The American public loved it.

Blue visited a security specialist, where he bought tiny webcams and a motion sensor. He also bought brown contact lenses and a theatrical make-up kit. He gave himself an angry scar running diagonally from his left ear to his top lip. Unless he got lucky, there would be witnesses when he caught up with Jesse. It was good practice to give them something memorable for the police description.

Planting the cameras in daylight was a risk, but delaying might mean he missed Jesse's attack. He found a streetlight with stickers for nightclubs and bands stuck all over it. He placed the camera as high as he could reach.

The second cam went on a tree branch. Then he jogged across the street, checking the apartment buzzers for Jay Fischer's name. Finding it, he stuck the motion sensor on the wall beneath. It triggered every time the door opened.

During this time, Blue looked for evidence of Jesse. The fact he didn't find another spycam didn't mean she wasn't here.

The days in the seedy hotel room turned into weeks. As Blue's arm healed—the wound on his leg hardly bothered him—he incorporated it into his exercise regime again. He couldn't afford for his muscles to atrophy. His neighbour was well used to solitude and never complained.

Multiple times per hour during the day, and four or five times an hour during the night, the motion sensor triggered an alarm on Jimmy's phone, and he checked the feed from the cameras on its small screen. The first evening, he recognised Patrice Martino being buzzed in. The next day, the drapes on one fourth-floor apartment were closed, and they stayed closed. Martino expected Jesse to follow through on her threat, too.

Blue patrolled the street, but never at the same time of day or night, and always cautious, his senses open to the slightest movement, sound, or scent.

Jesse didn't show.

Close to dusk, on the twenty-ninth evening since arriving, alerted by the motion sensor, Blue watched Hannah Martino emerge from her apartment building and head towards Manhattan.

Under a minute later, Blue caught up with Hannah and monitored her from the opposite side of the street. Martino hurried along behind his daughter. From the way the writer kept putting his hand on his pocket, Martino was armed, and not comfortable about it.

Blue didn't make Jesse until it was nearly too late,

despite glimpsing her before Hannah entered the park.

Jesse had elected for reverse psychology, dressing like an attention seeker. Bright clothes, close-shaved punky hair, sunglasses, roller skates. She carried a messenger bag and handed flyers to pedestrians as she skated by. Hiding in plain sight was a trick Blue knew well.

Blue signalled his colleague, who gave him a nod of understanding. This was it.

Hannah had stretched out a lead on her old man by the time she ducked into Fort Greene Park, so Blue kept his focus on her as he loped through the trees, which is why he missed the moment Jesse moved on Martino. By the time Jimmy checked, the journalist was sitting on a bench, the peroxide-haired killer leaning in.

Martino's head dropped, and Jesse stood up, her attention elsewhere. Blue looked in the same direction and saw Hannah Martino. Unaware his thoughts echoed those of Martino, Blue willed the young woman to escape, then cursed when she ran back towards her father.

Blue broke from cover, head down in a sprinter's start, propelling his heavy torso at what looked like an impossible angle at first, until he straightened as he hit maximum velocity. His right arm pumped along with his left, but Blue could feel the difference, the freshly mended bones unable to give him one hundred percent.

Jesse, confident in an easy kill, reached inside her jacket. She didn't go for her pocket, which—according to a prompt from Blue's subconscious—now hung heavier, suggesting she'd relieved Martino of his gun. A knife, then. It made sense. This was personal, and what was more intimate than a blade across a throat?

The peroxide head jerked in Blue's direction, but too late. He hit Jesse like a freight train, lifting her off her feet, sending her over the walkway into the bushes beyond.

She was on her feet fast, using her momentum to carry her into a roll. Her left arm hung awkwardly. Dislocated shoulder. The same shoulder he'd shot in Desolation Station. If it hurt as much as he suspected, her face didn't show it.

She scooped up the dropped gun, but Blue was still coming, and he barrelled into her again, his shoulder catching her as she twisted away. The manoeuvre saved her from the brunt of his attack, but the gun spun out of her hand as she fell.

She came up a second time, winded, gasping, ready. Crouching, knife in her hand, eyes on Blue.

In his peripheral vision, Jimmy caught signs of movement. A crowd was gathering, keeping their distance at the sight of the knife. He checked his bandana was still in place. He wanted them to remember the fake scar on his face, not the real ones over his left eye.

Voices called out, scared, but emboldened by the presence of others.

"He attacked her!"

"Leave her alone, man."

"Jesus, look at that fucking knife."

"You wanna walk through a Brooklyn park at night *without* a weapon, sister? I got two cans of mace says you're crazy."

"I've called nine-one-one, people. You might want to calm the fuck down."

Blue watched Jesse make the same calculations he was making. Every passing second brought the cops closer, and the crowd was still growing. She had to move now. If she got a head start on her skates, he doubted he'd catch her. No doubt she had a change of clothes and footwear stashed nearby.

Both of them twitched at the first distant siren.

Stalemate.

Blue tensed for his next attack.

"That's Dionne James. Jesse."

The voice came from Blue's left. His eyes didn't leave his opponent. She stared back, but her stance changed, one foot moving behind the other, ready to go.

"What are you smoking, man?"

"Look."

Someone must have held up a phone with Jesse's photograph, because the mood of the small crowd changed, their hostility focusing on the young woman with the knife.

"Motherfucker. It *is* her."

"That's Jesse James?"

"In the flesh, man."

The sirens came closer. Time to go. Blue saw Jesse reach the same decision, her back foot digging into the grass as she came up from her crouch, knife held ready to intercept anyone foolish enough to get in her way.

The shot came from his right. It hit Jesse in her dislocated shoulder, flinging her backwards. The knife pinwheeled away, flashing in the evening sun.

Someone screamed, then the park fell silent as a young woman stepped forward, the gun Jesse had taken from Martino in her hand.

No one spoke, no one made any move to stop her. The woman—Hispanic, in her teens—stood over Jesse and raised the gun.

Jesse's breaths were rapid. When she looked up at the young woman, and saw the old burns on her neck, she nodded in recognition.

The young woman spoke.

"Mateo and Angélica Garcia." The gun barrel wavered

373

in Lydia Garcia's shaking hands. "My parents. You deserve to die."

Lydia stared at Jesse, oblivious to anything else.

Jesse stared back. She said nothing in her defence. Finally, she smiled.

No one present ever forgot the sound Lydia made as she held eye contact with the woman who had planned her parents' murders and ordered her burned alive. It was a desperate sob, the cry of a child who had lost everything.

She lowered the gun.

"It's OK, Lydia," said Blue. She tilted her head in his direction as he stepped close, but continued to cry.

He put a hand on her shoulder. When Blue had offered her Jesse, Lydia had checked out of the Albuquerque institute and flown to New York. She had barely spoken a word since moving into the Brooklyn hotel.

The sirens were close now.

"You're not like her, Lydia. You're not a killer."

She dropped the gun onto the grass.

Blue picked it up.

"But I am."

Five shots rang out in the otherwise silent park, Jesse twitching as each bullet entered her body.

Blue walked away. No one challenged him.

He stopped at the bench where Hannah Martino cradled her unconscious father.

"He's breathing," she said. "The paramedics are on their way."

She looked at Jimmy. "Thank you. I think you just saved my life."

Blue made sure he had her attention.

"When he wakes up, tell him I want to stay dead. He'll understand."

Chapter Sixty-Two

FOR A FEW WEEKS after the death of Dionne James, Blue stayed in New York. Most days he rode the subway. He had no fixed destination, instead switching lines at random, spending hours crisis-crossing the city, his route covering its underbelly like a child's scribble.

He doubted any investigation would uncover his role in the deaths of the Firestarters. Not without Patrice Martino's involvement, and the writer had emailed promising he would honour Blue's request for anonymity.

The news was still full of the Firestarters, but the story wasn't white-hot anymore, bumped off the front page of the Post this morning by a Ponzi scheme. Blue feigned reading to avoid communication, verbal or otherwise, with his fellow passengers. In reality, he couldn't keep his attention on the newspaper, or anything else.

Martino's upcoming book—already a number one bestseller through pre-orders—would, his email confirmed, conclude the gang turned on each other in Desolation Station.

Jimmy Blue should have felt triumphant, but he didn't.

In as much as anything ever troubled him, this lack of satisfaction did. The unexpected hollowness following Jesse's death kept him here—not just in Manhattan—but in Tom's world. Before Jesse died, he was ready to leave, to sink back into the darkness, the place where he was truly himself, away from the babble and rush. He felt unclean, craving the purity of the deepest shadow, but not quite ready to embrace it.

He let his stubble grow into a beard. Today, he had it trimmed, and moved to the fourth cheap hotel in as many weeks, this time, across the Hudson in Jersey City.

He knew this hanging on, this delay, was down to Jesse. Dionne James was the closest Blue had ever come to meeting another inhabitant of the darkness he called home. The realm from which he drew his strength was, he sensed, vast. Vast enough that its residents could exist there without ever encountering one another.

In the end, he concluded it didn't matter what he thought about Jesse. She was dead. He'd won. And he wanted to be alone again, or as alone as he ever could be. He was tired.

Blue didn't sleep in the new hotel room. He hadn't slept well these past few weeks. Blue didn't dream, but Tom did, and the disconnected, disjointed images that found their way into Jimmy's nights only added to his empty, drained, aimless state of mind.

When he checked in, Jimmy played the part of a cubicle worker thrown out by his girlfriend: crumpled suit, polyester tie, a gargle of vodka to breathe onto the receptionist, a loud phone call in the lobby begging his ex to take him back. One last piece of misdirection, probably unnecessary. Now, he changed into travelling clothes—polo shirt and cargo pants, a decent used pair of hiking boots. A multi-pocketed waterproof jacket, dark green baseball cap, and a pair of cheap sunglasses.

He stuffed his new phone and laptop into a backpack and left the room at four-thirty a.m., exiting by the fire door at the back of the building. He put his old clothes into a laundry bag, which he lobbed into a dumpster four blocks away.

A pale sun found Blue on a bench in Newark Penn Station, looking at the departure boards, not really registering what the words scrolling across them meant.

He was thinking about Tom, and his mind was clearing.

Blue had been here too long. The world had contaminated him, making it harder than usual to disengage. But it was time. He had to go.

Tom's dreams didn't only feature the usual half-remembered childhood scenes. In the moments Blue descended into REM sleep, Tom stood on high summits above the clouds, walked through rain-dappled forests, rested beside clear, icy streams, breathed the fresh, uncomplicated air of the mountains.

On that bench, as the bus station got busier, Tom Lewis swam close to the surface of Blue's consciousness in a way he had never experienced. Briefly, they shared the same space, albeit in a half-conscious state, a hazy, surreal mental landscape.

A new departure blinked onto the electronic board. *Freeport, Maine.*

A good name for a town.

Unaccountably, and for less than a second, Jimmy Blue experienced something close to contentment.

"Your turn, Tom," he said aloud.

Blue stood up, shouldered his rucksack, and went to buy a ticket.

Also by Ian W. Sainsbury

Want a FREE Jimmy Blue novella?

Head to fusebooks.com/insidejob

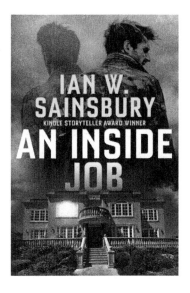

Join our occasional newsletter to receive the free book and be the first to hear about new releases from Ian W. Sainsbury.

Printed in Great Britain
by Amazon

82756670R00222